"I DON
SERIE
DO
PSI-CHANGE
—*All Abou*

Praise for

Kiss of Snow

"I absolutely loved this book! . . . Way to go, Nalini! You truly are a phenomenal storyteller."   —*Night Owl Reviews*

"To die for. Nalini Singh's talent for mixing romance with world building continues to be unmatched . . . There's laughter and tears, hope and fear, love and loss. I loved *Kiss of Snow*, utterly and completely."   —*Joyfully Reviewed*

"If you are anything like me, you too have been breathlessly anticipating *Kiss of Snow* . . . [A] true treasure in this already amazing series."   —*Romance Junkies*

"Definitely worth the wait."   —*Fiction Vixen Book Reviews*

"*Kiss of Snow* delivers . . . Of course, this entire series is great."   —*Smexy Books*

Play of Passion

"I'm chomping at the bit for *Kiss of Snow*."   —*Dear Author*

"Alternately playful and deliciously sexy."
     —*Publishers Weekly*

"Compelling characters and wonderfully dense plotting are two reasons why Singh's books continue to enthrall. There is no finer storyteller around!"
     —*RT Book Reviews* (Top Pick)

continued . . .

continued . . .

Tangle of Need

NALINI SINGH

BERKLEY SENSATION, NEW YORK

THE BERKLEY PUBLISHING GROUP
Published by the Penguin Group
Penguin Group (USA) Inc.
375 Hudson Street, New York, New York 10014, USA

Penguin Group (Canada), 90 Eglinton Avenue East, Suite 700, Toronto, Ontario M4P 2Y3, Canada
(a division of Pearson Penguin Canada Inc.) • Penguin Books Ltd., 80 Strand, London WC2R 0RL,
England • Penguin Group Ireland, 25 St. Stephen's Green, Dublin 2, Ireland (a division of Penguin
Books Ltd.) • Penguin Group (Australia), 250 Camberwell Road, Camberwell, Victoria 3124, Australia
(a division of Pearson Australia Group Pty. Ltd.) • Penguin Books India Pvt. Ltd., 11 Community
Centre, Panchsheel Park, New Delhi—110 017, India • Penguin Group (NZ), 67 Apollo Drive,
Rosedale, Auckland 0632, New Zealand (a division of Pearson New Zealand Ltd.) • Penguin Books
(South Africa) (Pty.) Ltd., 24 Sturdee Avenue, Rosebank, Johannesburg 2196, South Africa

Penguin Books Ltd., Registered Offices: 80 Strand, London WC2R 0RL, England

This is a work of fiction. Names, characters, places, and incidents either are the product of the author's
imagination or are used fictitiously, and any resemblance to actual persons, living or dead, business
establishments, events, or locales is entirely coincidental. The publisher does not have any control over
and does not assume any responsibility for author or third-party websites or their content.

TANGLE OF NEED

A Berkley Sensation Book / published by arrangement with the author

PUBLISHING HISTORY
Berkley Sensation hardcover edition / June 2012
Berkley Sensation mass-market edition / December 2012

ISBN: 978-0-425-25109-6

BERKLEY SENSATION®
Berkley Sensation Books are published by The Berkley Publishing Group,
a division of Penguin Group (USA) Inc.,
375 Hudson Street, New York, New York 10014.
BERKLEY SENSATION® is a registered trademark of Penguin Group (USA) Inc.
The "B" design is a trademark of Penguin Group (USA) Inc.

PRINTED IN THE UNITED STATES OF AMERICA

10 9 8 7 6 5 4 3 2 1

ALWAYS LEARNING   **PEARSON**

CAST OF CHARACTERS

In alphabetical order by first name
Key: SD = SnowDancer Wolves   DR = DarkRiver Leopards

Aden Arrow, Telepath (Tp)

Adria Morgan SD Senior Soldier

Alexei SD Lieutenant

Alice Eldridge Human scientist, in coma after a century in cryonic suspension

Amara Aleine Psy member of DR, former Council scientist, twin of Ashaya, mentally unstable

Anthony Kyriakus Psy Councilor, father of Faith

Ashaya Aleine Psy member of DR, former Council scientist, mated to Dorian, twin of Amara

Ava SD, maternal female, mother of Ben

Bastien DR, brother of Mercy

Bowen Security Chief, Human Alliance

Brenna Kincaid SD, tech, mated to Judd, sister of Andrew and Riley

Cooper SD Lieutenant, mated to Grace

Council (or **Psy Council**) The ruling Council of the Psy race

Dalton SD Librarian

Drew Kincaid (full name: **Andrew**) SD Soldier, mated to Indigo, brother of Riley and Brenna

Elias SD Senior Soldier, mated to Yuki, father of Sakura

Evangeline (Evie) Riviere SD, sister of Indigo, daughter of Tarah and Abel

Faith NightStar Psy member of DR, gift of Foresight (F), mated to Vaughn, daughter of Anthony

Felix SD, horticultural expert, submissive

Garrick Former alpha of SnowDancer, killed when the Psy psychically broke and programmed several of SnowDancer's dominants to attack their own pack

Ghost Psy rebel

Hawke SD Alpha, mated to Sienna

Henry Scott Psy Councilor (presumed dead), leader of Pure Psy, husband of Shoshanna

Indigo Riviere SD Lieutenant, mated to Drew, sister of Evangeline

Jem (real name: **Garnet**) SD Lieutenant

Judd Lauren Psy member of SD, Lieutenant, mated to Brenna, uncle of Sienna, Toby, and Marlee

Kaleb Krychek Psy Councilor

Kenji SD Lieutenant

Kieran Human member of SD, Senior Soldier

Kit DR Novice Soldier

Lara SD Healer, mated to Walker Lauren

Lucas Hunter DR Alpha, mated to Sascha, father of Naya

Lucy SD, nurse, assistant to Lara

Maria SD Novice Soldier

Matthias SD Lieutenant

Max Shannon Human, Security chief for Nikita Duncan

Mercy Smith DR Sentinel, mated to Riley

Ming LeBon Psy Councilor

Nathan (Nate) Ryder DR Senior Sentinel, mated to Tamsyn, father of Roman and Julian

Nell SD, Maternal dominant

Nikita Duncan Psy Councilor, mother of Sascha

Pierce SD Senior Soldier, based in Europe

Riaz Delgado SD Lieutenant

Riley Kincaid SD Lieutenant, mated to Mercy, brother of Drew and Brenna

Sam Human member of SD, Soldier

Sascha Duncan Psy member of DR, cardinal Empath (E), mated to Lucas, mother of Naya, daughter of Nikita

Shawnelle (Shawnie) SD juvenile

Shoshanna Scott Psy Councilor, wife of Henry

Sienna Lauren Psy member of SD, mated to Hawke, sister of Toby, niece of Judd and Walker

Tamsyn (Tammy) Ryder DR Healer, mated to Nathan, mother of Roman and Julian

Tatiana Rika-Smythe Psy Councilor

Tomás SD Lieutenant

Vasic Arrow, Teleporter (Tk-V)

Walker Lauren Psy member of SD, mated to Lara, father of Marlee, uncle of Sienna and Toby

WindHaven Falcons Allied to SnowDancer and DarkRiver

Eclipse

THE PSYNET IS a place of incomparable power and stark beauty, the millions of minds in the psychic network starbursts in the inky black. For the majority of Psy, it is their lifeline, as vital as air.

To disconnect from the Net is to die.

But as autumn whispers on the horizon in the year 2081, it is the Net itself that is dying. Stagnant rivers of rot snake ever deeper into the center, and it is a rot that twists and corrodes, damaging sense and reason to leave only unthinking menace behind.

If the Psy do not find a solution to this cancerous growth, the rot could soon begin to seep into the minds of those uplinked to the Net.

Or perhaps . . . it already has.

Chapter 1

RIAZ CAUGHT A flash of midnight hair and a long-legged stride and called out, "Indigo!" However, he realized his mistake the instant he turned the corner. "Adria."

Eyes of deepest blue-violet met his, the frost in them threatening to give him hypothermia. "Indigo's in her office." The words were helpful, but the tone might as well have been a serrated blade.

That did it. "Did I kill your dog?"

Frown lines marred her smooth forehead. "Excuse me?"

God, that *tone*. "It's the only reason," he said, holding on to his temper by a very thin thread, "I can think of to explain why you're so damn pissy with me." Adria had been pulled into den territory during the hostilities with Councilor Henry Scott and his Pure Psy army a month ago, and had remained behind to take up a permanent position as a senior soldier. She'd fought with focused determination by Riaz's side, followed his orders on the field without hesitation.

However, off the field?

Ice.

Absolute.

Unrelenting.

Glacial enough to bite.

Folding his arms when she didn't reply, he stepped into her personal space, caught the subtle scent of crushed berries and frost. A strangely delicate scent for this hard-ass of a woman, he thought, before his wolf's anger overrode all else. "You haven't answered my question." It came out a growl.

Eyes steely, she stepped closer with a slow deliberation that was pure, calculated provocation. She was a tall woman, but he was taller. That didn't seem to stop her from looking down her nose at him. "I didn't realize," she said in a voice so polite it drew blood, "that fawning over you was part of the job requirement."

"Now I know who Indigo learned her mean face from." But where his fellow lieutenant's heart beat warm and generous beneath that tough exterior, he wasn't sure Adria had any emotions that registered above zero on the thermometer.

Adria's response was scalpel sharp. "I don't know what she ever saw in you, but I suppose every woman has mistakes in her past." The slightest change in her expression, the tiniest fracture, before it was sealed up again, her face an impenetrable mask.

Scowling, Riaz was about to tell her exactly what he thought of her and her judgmental gaze when his cell phone rang. He answered without moving an inch away from the woman who was sandpaper across his temper, rubbing him raw with her mere presence. "Yeah?"

"My office," Hawke said. "Need you to head out, do a pickup."

"Be there in two." Snapping the phone shut, he closed the remaining distance between him and Adria, forcing her to tip back her head. "We will," he said, realizing those striking blue eyes with an edge of purple had streaks of gold running through them, beautiful and exotic, "continue this later."

That was when Adria's cell phone rang. "Yes?" she answered, without breaking eye contact with the big, muscled wolf who thought he could intimidate her.

"In my office," Hawke ordered.

"On my way." Hanging up, she raised an eyebrow at Riaz in a consciously insolent action. "My alpha has requested my presence, so get out of my fucking way," she said with utmost sweetness.

Eyes of beaten gold narrowed. "Guess we'll be walking together."

Not giving an inch until he stepped back and turned to head to Hawke's office, she walked in silence beside him, though her wolf bared its teeth, hungry to draw blood, to bite and claw and mark. Damn him. *Damn him.* She'd been doing fine, coping after her final separation from Martin. That had been a bloody battle, too.

"You'll come crawling back to me. Maybe I'll be waiting. Maybe I won't."

Adria stifled a raw laugh. Martin didn't understand that it was over. *Done.* It had been over the night a year ago when he'd stormed out of their home, not to return for four months. The truly stunning thing was that he'd had the gall to be shocked when she'd told him to find someplace else to sleep and slammed the door in his face.

"Cat got your tongue?" An acerbic comment made in a deep male voice that ruffled her fur the wrong way.

"Go bite yourself," she muttered, in no mood to play games. Her skin felt too sensitive, as if she'd lost a protective layer, her blood too hot.

"Someone should bite you," Riaz responded in a near snarl. "Pull that stick out of your ass at the same time."

Adria growled just as they reached the open door to Hawke's office. The alpha looked up at their entrance, open speculation in blue eyes so pale, they were those of a wolf given human form. However, when he spoke, his words were pragmatic. "You two free to go for a drive?"

Adria nodded, saw Riaz do the same beside her. "What do you need done?" he asked, his tone far calmer than the one he'd leveled at her.

"Mack and one of his trainee techs went up to do a routine service of the hydro station," Hawke told them, shoving back strands of hair the silver-gold of his pelt in wolf form, "but their vehicle's not starting, and they've got components that need to be brought back to the den for repairs."

"No problem," Riaz said. "I'll take one of the SUVs, pick them up."

Even as Adria was thinking the task was a one-person job, Hawke turned to her. "You're now one of the most senior people in the den." His dominance was staggering, demanding her wolf's absolute attention. "I'd like you to get reacquainted with the region, given that you haven't spent an extended period of time here since you turned eighteen."

She nodded. "I'll ask Riley and Eli to work some time into my shift schedule." It was a necessary detour from her normal duties—falling just below the lieutenants in the hierarchy, senior soldiers were often called upon to lead, and as a leader she had to know every inch of this land, not only the section she'd been assigned to during the battle. "It'd be better if I do it on foot." She'd see, scent, so much more.

"You can explore in detail later on. I want you to have a good working knowledge of the area as soon as possible." He handed her a thin plas map. "The trip up to the hydro station will take you through some critical sections—and you have certification in auto mechanics, correct?"

"Yes." It had been an interest she'd turned into the secondary qualification all soldiers were required to possess. Later, it had kept her sane, the ability to fix broken things and make them whole again. "I'll take a look at the vehicle."

"What about the replanting?" Riaz asked, his voice clawing over her skin like nails on one of those old-fashioned chalkboards the pups liked to draw on. "Felix's team have enough security?"

"They're fine." Walking to the territorial map on the stone wall of his office, Hawke tapped the large crosshatched section where the battle with Pure Psy had taken place. "Felix's volunteers and conscripts"—a sharp grin—"are planting the area with fast-growing natives, but for now, it's so open it's easy to monitor, especially with the cats sharing the watch."

Adria thought of what she'd seen on that battlefield filled with the screams of wounded SnowDancers, the cold red and hypnotic gold of a flame so deadly, and wondered at the cost paid by the young Psy woman who held all that power—and their alpha's heart. "What are the chances of another serious Pure Psy attack?" she asked, intrigued on the innermost level by a relationship that appeared so very unbalanced on the outside, and yet one that her wolf sensed was as solid as the stone of the den.

It was Riaz who answered. "According to Judd's sources, close to nil. They've got worse problems."

"Civil war," Hawke said, shaking his head. "If he's right, all hell is going to break loose—so we make sure we're prepared to weather any storms."

"The irritation hits?" Riaz asked, and Adria knew he was referring to the sporadic attempts to lay booby traps in den territory.

"Yeah," Hawke agreed with a scowl. "Scent trails point

to the perpetrators being a number of the Pure Psy survivors who just can't let it go. They're disorganized, and their traps are laughable. Still, I have all the sentries taking care not to accidentally fall into a hole. A hole for crissakes!"

Adria's wolf nodded in disgusted agreement. It really was time to retreat when you had to resort to digging holes and covering them up with leaves in the hope that SnowDancer's people wouldn't sniff them out a mile away. "They'll get tired sooner or later, but it might be an idea to make finding these traps a bit of a joke contest between the sentries."

Riaz angled his head toward her in a very wolfish way, even as Hawke's frustrated expression turned to one of interest.

"From what I've seen," she said, keeping her eyes resolutely away from the man to her right, "the amount of time they have to waste neutralizing the traps is starting to frustrate the soldiers who patrol the borders, and it's the kind of thing that can grow into anger. That's not good for our people, especially coming off the stress of the battle. But if you make it so the sentry with the most sightings gets a prize at the end of each week—"

"It becomes a game," Riaz completed with a thoughtful nod. "That's very good."

Hands behind her back, Adria squeezed the wrist of one hand with the other to keep from snapping back that she didn't need his endorsement. The response was so far from her usual even-tempered nature that she bit down on the inside of her lip to snap herself out of it, her gaze focused straight ahead. Except the stranger who'd taken over her body couldn't simply shut up. "Thank you." Honey sweet. "I'm so glad you approve."

A growl tangled up the air currents.

"Wolves do like a game," Hawke said, his face suspiciously bland. "I think Drew's the best person to organize it—I'll get that in motion." He glanced at the time projected on the wall. "You two better head out so you can get back before dinner."

Walking out of the office with the man whose very scent—dark, of the forest, with an edgy undertone of citrus and a brush of woodsmoke—made her skin itch, she said, "We should get some food." The drive wouldn't be quick, plus Mack and his tech hadn't planned to be up there this long and would be hungry.

"Should be something in here," Riaz said, entering the senior soldiers' break room.

They worked with honed efficiency to slap together some sandwiches, and were ready to go ten minutes later. Clenching her abdominal muscles as she got into the vehicle with Riaz, Adria told herself to concentrate on the route, the geography, anything but the potent masculine scent of the man in the driver's seat . . . because she knew full well why he incited such violence in her.

RIAZ drove them out of the garage and into the mountains, very aware of the arctic silence from the passenger seat. The more time he spent with Adria, the more he realized how unlike Indigo she was, in spite of the superficial similarity of their looks. One of the reasons he'd always enjoyed the other woman's company was her up-front nature—Adria, by comparison, was a closed box, with *Do Not Enter* signs pasted on every surface.

He understood that. Hell, he had his own "no go" zones, but with Adria, it was armor of broken glass that drew blood. "This track," he said, doing his job because, personality clash or not, he knew his responsibilities, "is the most direct route to the hydro station."

"Not according to the map Hawke gave me." A quick, penetrating glance. "So what's wrong with the other road?"

Reining in his wolf when it bared its teeth at what it read as a challenge, though the rational part of him knew he was just revved up for a fight after her earlier provocation, he said, "Sheer cliff face right in the middle." As a lieutenant who'd had her under his command on the field, he appreciated her intelligence and determination to learn—regardless of how often she used that sharp mind to slice into him with verbal claws.

Making two tight turns, he continued onward through the mountains that seemed to touch the sky. "Meant to delay any aggressors if they ever get that far."

Adria didn't say anything for several long minutes, studying the map and their passage into the mountains. "I'll need to request another senior soldier go with me on some of my exploratory trips"—her naturally husky voice low in thought—"so I don't miss things like that. I didn't have reason to memorize or even know all this as a teenager, and I'm sure security details have been changed in the meantime anyway."

"I'll take you," Riaz said, because damn it, he was a lieutenant, even when it came to a prickly piece of cactus like Adria. "Indigo made sure I was familiar with the details after I came back from my posting in Europe." He'd been away long enough for many of the subtle security precautions to have been altered. "It'll be good for me to review the knowledge."

Adria blinked, fingertips tightening on the sides of the plas map. "I appreciate it." It was the only thing she could say without giving everything away.

Riaz snorted, his hands strong and competent on the manual steering wheel as he navigated a particularly steep embankment, his bronzed arms dusted with a sprinkling of fine black hair. "About as much as you appreciate a root canal," he said, thrusting the vehicle into hover drive, "but whatever your problem with me, we have to work together."

Setting her jaw, she focused on the view beyond the window—of the most magnificent scenery on this earth. Summer had faded, fall a crisp promise in the air, but here the land was swathed in dark green, the peaks in the distance touched with white. She'd grown up on this land, and even now, after she'd been away for so long, it sang to her wolf, as it did to every SnowDancer. Den territory had a way of being home to all of them, no matter if they'd given the name to another place.

I can heal here.

It was a thought deep in her heart, one that almost managed to unknot the tension wi— "Who's that?" She jerked forward as a big tan-colored wolf raced across a verdant meadow to their left, chasing a sleek silver wolf she immediately recognized. "He's being rough with Evie." Fury boiled in her blood. "Stop the car."

Riaz's chuckle held pure male amusement, fuel to her temper. "That's Tai, and Evie won't appreciate the interruption, Aunt Adria."

Biting back her harsh response, Adria glanced at the two wolves again, saw what she'd missed at first glance. They were playing, all teeth and claws, but with no real aggression to it. Just as Riaz turned a corner, cutting off the view, the two wolves nuzzled one another and Adria realized Tai and Evie weren't playing, they were courting.

"She's too young." While Indigo was very close to Adria in age, Tarah had borne Evie later in life. The little girl had toddled around after her older sister and Adria when they'd been in their teens, sweet natured and stubborn and beloved. Adria couldn't imagine her submissive niece was in any way ready to handle a dominant—and having met Tai, she knew he was a hell of a lot stronger and more dangerous than Evie.

"She's still a wolf," Riaz said, his deep voice a rumble that vibrated uncomfortably against her achingly tight nipples, "an adult female wolf. You might have forgotten, Ms. Frost, but touch is necessary for most of our kind."

Her hand fisted, that nerve far too close to the surface.

A year.

It had been a year since she'd shared intimate skin privileges, a rawly painful kind of isolation for a predatory changeling in the prime of her life. Even before then, things had been fragmenting for a long time, her wolf starved of affection. But she'd been handling it, handling the broken pieces inside of her, until Riaz and the raging storm of a sudden, visceral sexual attraction that gripped her in its claws and shook, until she could barely think.

"If we're throwing stones," she said, protecting herself by going on the offensive, "I'm not the only one who prefers a cold bed." Riaz was a highly eligible male—the fact he'd taken no lovers was a point of irritation with the SnowDancer women who wanted nothing better than to tussle with him. "Maybe that's why you're such a prick."

Riaz's snarl was low, rolling over her skin with the power of his dominance. Wrenching the wheel, he brought the SUV to a stop on the side of the road. "I've had it." He pinned her with his gaze. "What the *hell* is your problem with me?"

Chapter 2

"DRIVE," SHE SAID, almost ready to crawl out of her skin with the need to rip off his T-shirt and use her teeth on all that hot, firm muscle. "Mack is waiting for us."

"He can wait a few more minutes." Eyes that were no longer in any way human slammed into hers. "You've had a hard-on for me since you transferred to the den. I want to know why."

Gut twisting, she snapped off her safety belt and pushed open her door to step out into the cold mountain air, summer a distant memory this far up. The chill did nothing to cool the fever in her blood, the need ravaging her body, a need that threatened to make her a slave when she'd finally found freedom.

Desperate, she focused on the majesty of her surroundings in an effort to fight the tumult within, her wolf clawing at the inside of her skin in violent repudiation of her choice to back off. In front of her lay tumbled glacial rocks, huge and imposing, beyond them the rich, deep green of the firs that dominated this area. Above it all was a sky so blue it hurt.

Home.

The slam of a door, followed by the thud of boots on the earth shattered her fragile attempt at control, and then Riaz was standing in front of her. Suddenly her view was hard muscle and implacable strength, the wild, dark scent of him in her every inhalation.

"We are not leaving," he said, his skin caressed by the sunlight that gilded his hair a gleaming blue-black, "until we work this out."

Feeling trapped, suffocated, she shoved at his chest and slipped out to stand beside the car rather than with her back to it. "Don't you put all the blame on me." Fighting back was instinct, her internal composure shattered. "You've been picking at me since the day I was pulled into the den."

He growled, and the rough sound rasped over her skin, wrapped around her throat. "Self-fucking-defense. You took one look at me and decided you hated my guts. I want to know why."

Jesus, Adria thought, how had she gotten herself into this? She wasn't this woman who couldn't control her words, her thoughts. She was calm, stable, sensible, had been the level-headed pivot for her friends when they'd all been hormone-fueled teenagers. *She* was the one who'd talked them down from the adrenaline-induced ledge she was now riding.

"Look," she said, making the conscious decision to wrench herself back before her frustrated wolf took control and she found herself feasting on male lips currently thin with anger, "it's nothing personal. I'm generally a bitch." According to Martin, she was one with a stone heart.

Riaz snorted. "Nice try, but I've seen you with others in the pack." He took another step toward her, invading her space and her senses, the scent of the forest serrated with a sharper edge that was pure furious wolf. "I've even seen you smile. How about you crack open one for me?" Eyes of dark gold drilled into hers.

Hell if she was going to allow him to walk all over her. "Get out of my face."

"You sure you want me to?" he asked, a dangerous angle to his jaw. "Maybe the reason you react like a hissing cat around me is because you want me even closer."

She sucked in a breath.

Riaz's eyes widened.

"Damn." It was a wondering statement.

A fraction of an instant later, strong, rough-skinned hands cupped her face, a voracious mouth slamming down on her own, the potent scent of aroused male and the exotic, luscious taste of citrus and bitter chocolate flooding her senses.

Adria froze for a second before her touch-starved body took over, her wolf clawing to the surface. Grabbing at his shoulders, she devoured that sensual, demanding mouth, tangling her tongue with his, licking and sucking. When he hitched her up with a single powerful move, she wrapped her legs around his waist and let him slam her against the door of the rugged all-terrain vehicle. He tasted as sexy and dangerous and infuriating as he looked, one big hand thrusting into her hair, the other gripping her hip.

Parts of her body that had been in cold storage for a lot longer than a year sparked to wakefulness, hungry and wild and more than a little feral. Riaz growled when she drew blood with her claws on his nape, only to deepen the kiss, shoving the hand on her hip under her shirt to close over her breast and squeeze.

The shock of the proprietary hold almost snapped her out of the madness, but then he pushed up her bra and the rough warmth of his palm on her bare flesh was a jolt to the system that splintered rational thought. Unable to get enough of his mouth, she sucked on his tongue, his lips, before kissing her way down the stubble of his jaw to grip at the tendons of his neck with her teeth.

Growling deep in his chest, he pulled her head back to take her mouth again. He wasn't the least bit gentle, but she didn't want gentle, her claws digging into his shoulders as her body moved with raw impatience against him. Taking his hand off her breast, he tore the button off her jeans, tugged down the zipper. It was as she broke the kiss to gasp in a breath that he shoved his hand into her panties and through the damp curls between her thighs—to spear two blunt-tipped fingers into her in a hard thrust that made her scream and break apart in a powerful clenching of muscles.

The orgasm was a naked blade, one that cut her in half with the primal viciousness of it and left her bereft at the same time. Opening her eyes when he withdrew his fingers, she saw a glittering expression she understood all too well. *Fury.* At her. At himself. "Put me down," she said, shaken to the core by the violent depth of her response.

Never, *never* had she orgasmed that hard . . . and felt so lost, a block of ice in her gut.

Not saying a word, he did so, putting his hands on her waist to help stabilize her when her legs wobbled. "Get your hands off me." She'd be damned if he'd touch her with that look in his eyes, his anger a brutal heat that slapped her with every breath.

LETTING go of the stiff woman in his arms, Riaz turned on his heel. "Fuck." What the hell had just happened? He didn't even *like* Adria, and yet he'd betrayed his mate with her, would've had his cock balls-deep in her by now if she hadn't stopped things. That cock pulsed, so rigid it was painful. *No.*

"Here."

He turned in time to catch a bottle of water.

"Wash your fingers," she said, red streaking the defined arch of her cheekbones. He knew the color had nothing to do with embarrassment, even before she bit out, "I don't particularly want to advertise my lapse in judgment," through gritted teeth.

A second later, she was inside the car, a sculpture in ice, no hint remaining of the demanding female wolf who'd been wet and hot and tight around his fingers not two minutes ago.

Chapter 3

COUNCILOR KALEB KRYCHEK examined the consciousness of the individual he'd first been alerted to by the NetMind, the neosentience that was the librarian and guardian of the Net. The consciousness in front of him was moderately powerful—that of a Gradient 5.7 telepath employed by a major corporation. The male's Silence was flawed, minor fractures visible to the careful eye. But that was an ordinary enough situation, and not what interested Kaleb.

This male had the bad luck to be uniquely susceptible to the unnamed and largely unnoticed disease that was carving silent, deadly runnels through the PsyNet. Others had been infected earlier, and were all now dead or insane. The mass outbreak at Sunshine Station had claimed one hundred and forty-one victims, eleven of whom had originally been put into involuntary comas in the belief they could be saved.

They couldn't.

Subject 8-91, however, continued to function in spite of his advanced infection, leaving Kaleb to conclude that something had altered in the sickness within the Net, making it able to survive longer within its host. Contracted via direct contact with one of the "diseased" sections of the Net—though Kaleb was apparently immune to the effect, likely as a result of his connection to the twisted twin of the NetMind—the infection didn't yet spread from person to person, but there was a high chance it would mutate further, becoming even more noxious.

Subject 8-91 was the first host the NetMind had found of the new variant, and as such, he'd become Kaleb's barometer, his "canary in a coal mine." The old saying was apropos. If 8-91 continued to react as he'd done to date, he would show the catastrophic effects of the quietly spreading rot before anyone else in the Net.

No, Kaleb corrected himself, *8-91 is already showing the effects.* The male had had a violent outburst in his sleep two days ago, so violent that he'd broken several bones in his hand when he punched it into a wall. What made the violence interesting was that it had no connection to the male's Silence—though he didn't know that. It had been initiated by the changes the infection had caused in his brain.

Subject 8-91 had been smart enough to create a cover story before he went to see one of the M-Psy about his hand, but the NetMind watched him constantly, knew his every move. And since the NetMind and its twin, the DarkMind, both spoke to Kaleb, he was never unaware of the status of the subject.

Continue to watch, he told the NetMind, his order given less in words than via an intuitive psychic connection he could explain to no one, not even another Psy. *Protect him from exposure.* Kaleb needed 8-91 to remain an active part of the Net. Any interference would shadow the picture, dull the clear view of the progress of the male's impairment and Kaleb's understanding of it.

A stream of consciousness from the NetMind, a question.

No, Kaleb said in response. *You can't save him. He's too damaged.* The rot had invaded 8-91's physical brain, was eating away at parts of his frontal lobe—a change so subtle the M-Psy would likely have missed it, even if he had been a neural specialist as opposed to orthopedic. As the infected from Sunshine Station had proved, there was no cure, and this new variant was more complex than the one that had resulted in the outbreak. Even if there had been a cure, Kaleb would've given the same answer—8-91's death was inevitable.

Someone had to be the canary.

Dismissing the man from his thoughts after taking note of the development of the infection, he returned to his physical body, stopping only long enough to ask the NetMind and DarkMind both a question. *Do you know the location of this individual?* He sent through an image, along with a psychic profile built from his memories and the data files he'd hacked over the years.

???

The puzzlement was the same response he'd received each and every time he'd asked after his personal quarry ever since he'd first made contact with the twin neosentience. It was as if his target no longer existed in the Net, but Kaleb knew differently. And nothing, not even the inexplicable failure of the NetMind and DarkMind to sense the truth, would stop him from hunting down that target.

Chapter 4

HAWKE SNAGGED SIENNA'S hand as they passed in the corridor, dragging her into a corner hidden from the eyes of curious packmates. "Where are you going in such a rush?" His wolf was delighted to see her, rolling around in the autumn and spice of her scent like a pup. It made him remember how he'd awakened her this morning, how he'd licked up that delectable scent in a much more intimate fashion.

Sienna's voice was low and caressing when she replied, the fingers of her free hand spread over his heart. "I'm meeting some of the leopards for lunch."

"Kit?" A feral growl.

"Yes." Her scowl matched the straight line of her mouth. "He's my friend."

The boy had also kissed her, dared to put his hands and his scent on her. "No." It was an order from the wolf, a wolf used to obedience.

But Sienna Lauren Snow had never once bowed down to him. Tugging her hand from his hold, she rose on tiptoe to thrust both into his hair. "Yes."

His stare was met by her own, his dominance countered by the steely will of a cardinal X. "I think it's time I bit you again," he muttered, rubbing his finger over the curve where her neck met her shoulder, his favorite spot to mark her.

The threat made Sienna pull playfully at his hair. "You did that this morning. It's my turn." A quick nip of his lower lip. "Do you want to join us?"

Hell, yes—because while he might not be able to intimidate his smart, sexy, dangerous mate, he damn well could and would warn off the baby cat alpha she called friend. But—"I have to meet with the maternal females." Wincing at the reminder, he bent his head so she could pet him more effectively. "They're on the warpath about some of the juveniles."

Laughing, Sienna ran her nails over his scalp, the caress making his wolf arch its neck in wild pleasure. "You sound scared."

"Any man not scared of a bunch of maternals ganging up on him needs his head examined." Hackles still raised by the thought of her lunch date, he straightened to his full height, his mate's hands sliding to his shoulders. "If that cub puts his hands anywhere near you, I don't care if he is your friend, I'll rip his arms off." He wasn't joking—this soon after mating, the wolf was possessive beyond belief, the mating bond raw.

Sienna's smile faded. "You know I would never—"

"Of course I know that," he snapped, annoyed that she'd even contemplate he didn't trust her. "That's not the point."

A raised eyebrow, tiny nails digging into his shoulders. "What *is* the point then, Your Alphaness?"

He snapped his teeth at her for that smart-ass remark. "The point is you're mine. End of story. No touching by any other male." He paused, considered. "Special family-affection dispensation for those related to you."

When she didn't respond, he leaned in close and whispered, "I did warn you," his lips brushing her ear. He'd told her *exactly* what it would mean to be his, how hard he'd be to handle, how totally he'd claim her. And still she'd come to him, but he wondered if she was only now understanding the true depth of what he'd demand from her. The thought that he might be distressing his mate by being who he was made both parts of him go motionless, watchful.

Shivering in response to his touch, she pushed him back until she could meet his gaze. Her glare was dark . . . but then she laughed, the sound of it wild lightning along his fur. "I guess," she said, the stars vibrant in her eyes, "that serves me right for mating with an alpha."

His wolf relaxed. His mate had no fear in her scent, in her teasing smile, the bond between them vivid with the red and gold fire that was her brand. Running his hands down the sleek curve of her back, he nuzzled at her. "I may get a little more . . . flexible after we've been mated for a while."

"No, you won't." Sienna pressed a hot, wet kiss to his jaw, her fingers stroking the heat of his nape. "But I love you exactly as you are—and I know how to stand my ground. So do your worst, beautiful man."

He was alternately proud of her strength and aggravated by her intransigence. A familiar occurrence when it came to this woman. Sienna might be younger and physically smaller, but she'd go toe-to-toe with him without a blink. The thought made him grin, every part of him aware they'd likely be butting heads for the next century. He couldn't wait.

"So," she said, tracing his smile with a fingertip, "what are the maternals mad about?"

He was used to talking to his lieutenants and senior pack-mates about pack business, but it felt utterly different talking with Sienna about the same thing. Because she was someone of his own, someone who listened not because it was Snow-Dancer business, but simply because she liked being with him, liked knowing things that mattered to him.

"The word 'hormones' was used," he told her, already feeling the dull pulse of a throbbing headache. "Some of the older juveniles are apparently getting too frisky. I'll probably end up dragging the boys off to remind them to keep their paws to themselves." Groaning, he bent so his forehead touched hers. "And then I'll have to do the same thing with the girls." Normally, Indigo and Riley would take care of the situation, but sometimes only an alpha's voice would get the message across.

"But skin privileges are an accepted part of pack life." Sienna's breath kissed his lips. "I know my friends had relationships when they were younger."

"There are still boundaries," Hawke said, restraining the urge to undo her braid, to knot his hands in that pretty ruby red hair. "Sometimes the wolf has to be reminded that it needs to wait for the human half to catch up."

Sienna's gaze turned thoughtful. "Yes, I understand. That's why you let your wolf be in charge when you were younger—you said it was more mature."

He played the end of her braid over his fingertips. "Controlling the wolf is something we learn as children and have to maintain as we grow older. Without that control, there'd be a lot more rogues." Changeling wolves who gave in to their animals turned into vicious killers—and they most often targeted those who had been their own.

"Do you think the juveniles are responding to the stress of being evacuated out of the den?"

"Yes, but if it's unsettled them to that degree, we'll have to organize supervision and retraining for a whole lot of young ones."

Sienna stroked his nape. "I know it's a headache for you, but what I feel for you only grows deeper every time I see how you care for each member of the pack, young and old, strong and weak."

He'd never needed verbal petting—but when Sienna said things like that, yeah, it mattered. Raising his head, he released her braid and ran his knuckles down her cheek. "Go, have your lunch." It cost him to say that, to know that he was sending her out with a man who had once shown an interest in her. "You're not leaving den territory?" It was too dangerous to chance yet.

The Council now knew she was alive. Ming LeBon, the man who had attempted to turn her into a weapon when she'd been barely more than a child, knew she was alive. And Sienna's abilities were of unrivaled potential—no one understood or could predict how her power would develop as she grew older . . . because there had never been another cardinal X-Psy who'd survived to adulthood.

His gut twisted at the thought of Sienna broken and dead at the hands of the enemy, and he had to clench his fists to keep from grabbing her and stashing her in their quarters, where she'd be safe. He fought the urge because the one thing he would never, *ever* do to Sienna, was cage her. She'd already spent far too much of her life behind bars, the psychic prison designed to contain her power turning into a place of mental torture.

"No," she assured him. "I wouldn't risk that when things are so unstable. Kit and the others are going to meet us in the White Zone, and we'll go down to the waterfall."

"Us?"

"Riordan, Evie, and Lake are also coming."

His wolf settled. The boys would make sure no one

attempted to poach on his territory—and he'd just keep that thought to himself, he decided with a somewhat feral internal grin. "You want to have dinner with the kids?" he asked, knowing they had only a couple more minutes.

That smile again, the one she hadn't given him before, when they'd been circling each other . . . and that she gave him every day now. It was a kick to his heart every single time. "Yes," she said. "You don't mind how much time we're spending with them?"

"Of course not." Toby was her brother, Marlee her cousin. They were Pack, pups to love and protect. "Since Walker's stopped giving me the death stare, it's actually become comfortable." The eldest Lauren was very protective of those under his care, considered Sienna his daughter. Hawke had no doubt the other man would quietly, methodically gut him at the smallest sign that he was causing Sienna distress. His wolf approved.

Laughter wrapping him in silken ropes, the crimson fire of his mate's touch flickering through his blood. "Lara will protect you." Stealing another little kiss, she stepped away, paused, her next words vibrant with emotion. "I love you."

He knew what it meant to her that she could say those words and know no one would hurt her for daring to feel, for daring to love with all the power of her strong, loyal heart. Closing the short distance between them, he answered with a kiss as tender as he knew how to give, his fingers closing possessively around her throat.

"Are you sure you have to go to that meeting?" she whispered when he lifted his head, her lips wet and luscious, her body arching toward his own.

His wolf was tempted. Sorely. "Nell and her crew will hunt us down and interrupt." Maternal females were not to be messed with. "Then they'll make us feel like shamed five-year-olds." He took another kiss, rubbing his thumb over the flutter of her pulse and reining in the urge to bite. *Later*, he promised his wolf. "I'll see you tonight."

He watched after her until she disappeared around the corner, the possessiveness inside him a primal craving that made him want to haul her over his shoulder and drag her to his bed. Maybe tie her to it for good measure.

"Don't even think about it," Riley said as he walked over to join Hawke for the Meeting of Doom.

Hawke met his senior lieutenant's brown eyes, always so calm and stable. "The only way you could know what I was thinking was if you'd had similar thoughts yourself."

"Mercy forgives me . . . most of the time." A slow smile. "Come on, enough procrastinating."

As they walked, Hawke said, "Adria and Riaz. Problems?"

"Personality clash, I think. They seem to work well enough together despite it." The lieutenant glanced at him. "Why? You want me to split their shifts?"

"No, better they work it out." He'd picked up something more violent and intense than a simple personality clash, but his wolf knew when to be discreet, so he didn't mention it. Instead, he turned the conversation to the juveniles, and the remainder of their walk passed in shoptalk.

While meetings such as this one promised to be weren't ever on his favorite-things-to-do list, it felt good to be doing something as normal as worrying about the juveniles. Not discussing Psy surveillance or planning to defend against an attack. Not stockpiling weapons or checking medical supplies as they waited to evacuate their vulnerable. Not even meeting with the DarkRiver leopards to assess a suspected threat.

It had been months since his wolves had had a chance to just be Pack.

However, Hawke knew the fact SnowDancer and its allies had won the battle didn't mean their enemies wouldn't regroup and return. But he was a wolf. He also knew how to live in the moment—a time in which he was mated to a woman who challenged, loved, and teased him; his pack was safe; and the den was filled with the vibrant sounds of children's voices once more. "How's the planning going for the mating ceremony?" Sienna was indelibly his, but his pack needed to have a chance to celebrate their alpha's mating, and they'd get that chance four days from now.

"Drew suggested dancing girls."

Hawke grinned. "How many?"

Riley shot him an unamused look. "Don't encourage him, or I swear to God I will hire a troop of strippers, complete with spangled pasties, and watch cheerfully while Sienna barbecues you."

Wondering what else Drew had been suggesting, Hawke stifled his laugh. "Seriously, how's it going?" Riley and Nell were sharing the overall organizational load, in charge of ensuring all the pieces came together into a cohesive whole.

"Good. My brother, when he isn't e-mailing me brochures about Brazilian samba dancers and Vegas showgirls, has found a job for every single person who wants to be involved in the preparation."

That was why, Hawke thought, Drew was so perfect for the position he occupied. Not quite part of the hierarchy, he was Hawke's eyes and ears in the pack, accessible to even the weakest of their number, those who might feel intimidated approaching one of the other dominants. No one was intimidated by Drew, and that was an incredible achievement, given that the other man was SnowDancer's tracker, charged with finding and executing rogues if the need arose. "It'll be a good night."

"The best," Riley said quietly, then took a deep breath. "We're here."

Hawke folded his arms and stared at the door with a sour expression. "I hate these meetings."

"We should make Drew attend instead. Teach him a lesson."

They both stared at each other and grinned. Yeah, he thought, pushing through the door, it was nice to be doing something as ordinary as grousing about a meeting with the maternals.

ALICE

FROM: Lara<lara@snowdancer.org>
TO: Ashaya<ashaya@darkriver.net>;
Sascha<sascha@darkriver.net>;
Tammy<tamsyn@darkriver.net>;
Amara<amara@sierratech.com>
DATE: Aug 26, 2081 at 11.00 a.m.
SUBJECT: Patient A

I thought you'd all appreciate a quick update on Patient A. She
remains unresponsive, in a comalike state. I say coma*like*, because
frankly, she confuses the instruments. However, I can say with
certainty that she isn't brain-dead, so that remains a positive
indicator.

I'd almost think J had imagined his conversation with her, except
he's not the imagining type.

I'm making sure her limbs are exercised and that she's getting
the nutrients she needs. Otherwise, I'm at a loss.

Let me know if any of you have had a breakthrough.

FROM: Ashaya<ashaya@darkriver.net>
TO: Lara<lara@snowdancer.org>
CC: Sascha<sascha@darkriver.net>;
Tammy<tamsyn@darkriver.net>;
Amara<amara@sierratech.com>
DATE: Aug 26, 2081 at 1.00 p.m.
SUBJECT: re: Patient A

Amara and I are continuing to work on the chemical traces
discovered in her blood. We hope to find clues as to an antidote
that'll work better than our emergency formulation, but some of
the chemicals appear to be unknown.

FROM: Amara<amara@sierratech.com>
TO: Ashaya<ashaya@darkriver.net>
DATE: Aug 26, 2081 at 1.02 p.m.
SUBJECT: re: re: Patient A

Not unknown. Simply uncategorized. You and I both now know
about them.

FROM: Sascha<sascha@darkriver.net>
TO: Lara<lara@snowdancer.org>
CC: Tammy<tamsyn@darkriver.net>;
Amara<amara@sierratech.com>;
Ashaya<ashaya@darkriver.net>
DATE: Aug 26, 2081 at 4.45 p.m.
SUBJECT: re: re: Patient A

I'd like to see her. My empathic senses have been in a heightened
state since the birth, and there's a higher chance I may sense
something, especially since she did wake up once. One thing I know
for certain: there *is* someone within her body. We just have to find
a way to set her free.

Chapter 5

ADRIA DIDN'T KNOW how she'd survived the rest of the trip up to the hydro station; the silence in the SUV had been excruciating. The journey down, the mountains bathed in the gentle afternoon sunlight, was better—she chose to ride in Mack's vehicle, having been able to fix the problem that had stalled it. Her excuse about needing to be with him in case the truck broke down again was accepted without question. Mack's trainee rode with Riaz, and Mack, with his silver-threaded curls and skin of warm brown marked by quiet laugh lines, was a man comfortable with silences.

Back in the den, she didn't stop until she was in her quarters with the door safely shut. Only then did she collapse on the bed. "Christ, Adria." Shaking from the impact of a day that had spiraled out of control from the instant she'd run into Riaz, she just sat there, trying to get a grip on her emotions.

The knock on the door was familiar, but she ignored it. Her visitor persisted, having obviously scented her presence, until she muttered, "It's open."

Indigo, dressed in jeans paired with a plain white tee that flattered the curves of her tall body, closed the door and leaned back on it. "Hurts me to say this, Ri, but you look worse than you did after you caught the plague when you were seventeen."

The "plague" had been a nasty case of food poisoning. "Thanks for the pick-me-up." She scowled at the woman who had been her friend most of her life. "Now go away."

Rolling her eyes, Indigo strode across the room to sit beside her instead. "Martin's not been hassling you, has he?"

"No. I made it clear we were done." He hadn't taken the

news with any grace, all traces of the funny, gentle man she'd fallen for corroded to nothingness by years of slow bitterness. But Martin wasn't the male on her mind right then. "You had a thing with Riaz, right?"

Indigo blinked at the blunt question. "Yes, but years ago, well before he left for Europe. We were friends."

It wasn't such a strange thing to hear from a changeling. Sharing intimate skin privileges was an integral part of their nature, and there was nothing wrong with being with a friend who cared enough about you to ensure your pleasure. It didn't matter if the lovers knew their friendship would never lead to a relationship—friendship was a precious thing to a wolf, to be cherished on its own merits.

Indigo nudged at Adria when she didn't continue, her namesake eyes perceptive. "Riaz?"

"Yeah." Knowing no further explanation was needed, she shoved her hands through her hair, messing up her braid. "It's weird. You're my niece."

Indigo made a distinctly inelegant sound. "Please. We grew up as sisters."

"Even worse."

"Would you cut that out?" A sharp elbow to the ribs. "Everything else aside, we happen to be two dominant women in one pack with a bare few years between us—the only surprise is that we didn't cross paths with the same man before now."

In spite of the fact she was the one who'd brought it up, Adria's wolf was sanguine about a past long gone. The human part of her, too, knew that Indigo and Riaz's old relationship had no bearing on the present situation, not given the time that had passed and their complete lack of interest in one another now. It would've just made it easier to hide from the turbulence of her own emotions if it had been an issue.

"I don't know what I'm doing, Indigo." No man had ever incited her to behave as she had today. "I almost attacked him." She'd wanted to rip his clothes off, shove him to the ground, taste every inch of his bronzed skin with her lips. "I *drew blood*." The taste of iron, metallic and distinctive, had been hot, strong . . . exhilarating.

Indigo's laugh was affectionate. "That's fairly normal

when a female wolf is as on edge as you've been." A playful waggle of her eyebrows. "Long time?"

"A year," she said and knew exactly when Indigo understood the ramifications of her statement, because she seemed to stop breathing for a second.

"So, when you and Martin came to the dinner to meet Drew . . ."

"I'd ended it months earlier." The flash of hurt in Indigo's eyes had Adria nudging the other woman's shoulder in a silent apology. "I wasn't ready to talk to anyone—needed to get my head on straight." When Indigo squeezed her hand, she continued. "I'm not proud to admit it, but I used him when I 'gave in' to his persistent efforts to win me back and asked him to come along that night."

It hadn't taken Martin long to realize the invitation didn't equal one to her bed or to her life, and he'd been in an ugly temper by the time they'd arrived. Feeling guilty for having consciously misled the man who had once walked by her side, she'd tried to reach out, pacify him.

His response had, for a single painful second, returned her to the ruins of their relationship, before it hardened her resolve. "I thought you were making a horrible mistake." The realization that Indigo was seeing a man whose dominance didn't match Indigo's own had chilled Adria's blood.

"And you wanted me confronted with the results."

"I'm so sorry." It had to be said, because Drew was nothing, *nothing* like Martin, his adoration of his "Indy's" strength open.

"I understand." Indigo's response was fierce. "You won't have any of those problems with Riaz. He's strong enough not to be scared of your hunger, and"—a smile that lit up her eyes—"he's got enough wildness in him to lead you astray."

Most lone wolves did. As a young woman, Adria had always steered clear of them, aware that while such a male might make love to her with primal intensity, he was as likely to disappear into the mountains come morning. She'd always known she needed someone more stable, more rooted. But things had changed. *She* had changed. "You're not saying something." Adria knew Indigo too well not to have caught the subtle hesitation.

The other woman took a long time to reply, her expression troubled. "He told me something in confidence, and I can't break that promise," she said at last. "But Adria, you need to know . . . any relationship with him, even more than with another lone wolf, is unlikely to ever turn permanent."

The fact that Indigo hadn't flat out warned Adria off told her it wasn't a case of Riaz already being involved with someone else. Which either meant he played the field—and nothing she'd heard indicated that—or he wanted someone he couldn't have. Though Indigo couldn't know it, that realization eased the cold knot inside Adria, allowed her to breathe, come to a decision.

"I need to talk to him." Wolf and woman in agreement, she rose to her feet. "We left things in a bad place." No matter what happened, she didn't want this to affect their working relationship, and by extension, the pack.

Waiting until she'd redone her braid, Indigo walked out with her. "Are you enjoying being back in the den?" she asked, reaching back to tighten her own ponytail.

"So much." Adria narrowed her eyes at Tai when the young soldier with uptilted green eyes and wide shoulders walked down the corridor.

"God hates me," she heard him mutter. "Now there are *two* of them."

Neither she nor Indigo said anything until he was out of earshot. Then Indigo's lips twitched. "Poor baby." Affection laced the words.

"He's solid?"

"Loves Evie." Wolfish amusement danced in her eyes. "Doesn't mean we don't get to mess with him."

Since Evie was gentle and in no way dominant or aggressive, Adria agreed. "Don't get me wrong," she said, returning to their earlier topic of conversation, "Matthias is a great lieutenant to work under." Darkly beautiful and with those eyes that had talked many a woman into bed, Matthias had been a friend as well as her lieutenant.

He'd called to check up on her a couple of times since

she'd relocated to the den, and it was a measure of her trust in, and respect for him that she hadn't bristled. "But that region's got too many bad memories for me, you know? Den's a fresh start." One she'd allow nothing, not even the hot burn of a shocking need, to steal from her.

"Here's my stop." Indigo halted in front of one of the break rooms. "Having an informal chat with some of my novices and newer soldiers." She raised an eyebrow at the young woman who was all but crawling down the hall. "What happened to you?"

"Riaz the Sadist's new configuration of the training run is an excuse for heinous and unparalleled torture," Sienna muttered before nodding hello at Adria and limping inside—to a chorus of sympathetic groans from others who'd obviously been subjected to the same torture.

Indigo hung back, her eyes returning to Adria. "Remember what I said." Open concern on her face . . . tempered by a glint of wickedness. "But don't be too sensible. Claws and teeth are part of the fun."

Adria's grin faded as soon as Indigo walked in to join her soldiers. Martin had been the biggest chance she'd taken in her life, overriding the concerns of those who didn't think the dominant female/less dominant male pairing had a hope of working. The spectacular failure of that risk had savaged her confidence, until sometimes she felt as if the core of her was a patchwork quilt, the stitches barely holding.

It would be easy, so easy, to stay "safe," to never again stick out her neck, but Adria was a dominant, a SnowDancer. She was *not* a coward and would never shame her wolf by allowing herself to become one. Even if that meant she had to go claw to claw against a lone wolf who was nothing she'd ever wanted in a man—and who compelled her beyond reason.

Chapter 6

JUDD LAUREN WAS still alive.

Ming looked down at the unexpected report. He'd ordered the Arrows to eliminate Judd soon after the continued existence of the rogue Tk-Cell became known. It had been meant to be a first, debilitating strike before the much more important elimination of Sienna Lauren, the X a far bigger threat. Though the Arrows were no longer his, he hadn't expected Aden or his men to have a problem with taking care of the rebel Arrow.

Since the Tk-Cell had abandoned the squad when he defected, it was clear the Arrows had disregarded Ming's order not out of any loyalty to their former comrade, but to make it clear to Ming that they would no longer support him in any form. A critical loss, but not crippling. Looking up to meet the eyes of the man who'd brought him the report, he said, "Do we have anyone with the training to take on Lauren?"

"No. Only an Arrow can successfully contain another Arrow."

Ming had to agree. The Arrows were too highly trained to be easy prey. He'd been one of their number in his youth, but he'd been out of active service for two decades, no longer had the same level of skill when it came to covert assassinations. Add to that the fact Judd Lauren could teleport, and it made no rational sense to go after the rebel Arrow himself.

However, Sienna Lauren was neither an Arrow nor a telekinetic. *He'd* trained her, and so he knew her exact skill set. There were murmurs in the Net that she'd further honed those skills during her time with the wolves, but that didn't alter his conclusions. If it came down to it, the battle would be a psychic one—and he'd trapped her with his mind once. He would do it again.

"Keep monitoring the situation," he ordered. "Unobtrusive surveillance. No contact." Sienna hadn't appeared in public since the lethal wave of her X-fire had consumed a significant percentage of Henry's Pure Psy army. No one was yet certain that she hadn't perished in the aftermath. If she had, it would've been because she'd been physically executed by one of her own—because unless his power release theory had borne out, the psychic implosion of a cardinal X would've taken out the Sierras themselves. "Your goal is to discover if Sienna Lauren survived the battle."

If she was alive, she could not be allowed to exist off the leash of Ming's psychic control.

Chapter 7

TEMPER STILL SIMMERING—and that wasn't the only thing—Riaz got dressed in plain black athletic pants made of a light material that didn't overheat, his upper body bare, and walked out to the training run just in time to see a group of the more experienced soldiers cross the finish line. "How did it go?" he asked Judd, who'd been overseeing the session.

"Curses were cast on your name." Judd's expression remained unchanged, his sense of humor a subtle thing. "The course is a tough one, but wolves enjoy challenge."

"So do Psy." He knew that as a Tk, Judd was brutal competition. "Me and you." The painful fury of energy in his body needed somewhere to go.

But Judd shook his head, dark hair catching the deep orange rays of the slowly setting sun. "I have dinner with Walker and the kids. Tomorrow?"

"Sure." Riaz opted to remain behind after the other lieutenant left with the rest of the group, deciding to run the course on his own. That was when he caught an unexpected scent on the breeze.

Crushed ice over berries . . . licked with an unexpected undertone of lingering warmth.

His jaw tightened when Adria emerged from the trees, his wolf reacting with a snarl even as his cock hardened. The response was so hot, so fast, and so beyond his conscious control that it infuriated him.

Not saying a word, Adria kicked off her boots and socks.

"You're not dressed right." It came out a near growl.

A fluid shrug that revealed the lithe muscle on that tall frame. "Jeans are worn in."

His wolf heard the unspoken challenge, flashed its canines. "Then let's go." With that, he ran up the smooth wooden log that had been the downfall of more than one SnowDancer, conscious of Adria making the climb with an almost feline grace.

Instead of a wall at the top of the slope, there was now a specially designed rope climbing frame that required rigid muscle control to navigate. It favored those of lighter weight, and Adria beat him to the top—and to the ring ladder that tested upper-body strength. He was much stronger than her by any measure, and they were neck and neck again by the time they reached the final set of rings.

Dropping to the firm ground, he made his way through the dark and narrow tunnel built to provide no purchase for claws and nails, its walls seeping a slick gel that frustrated forward movement. He'd created the obstacle, but he was swearing by the time he got to the end—beside an Adria who had tendrils of jet black hair stuck to her temples and cheeks, and then they were wiping off the gel and scrambling across the jungle gym.

Focusing only on navigating the complex structure, he shut out the presence of the woman he could still taste, still feel clenching so tight and liquid on his fingers. He'd always known he would one day take a lover. Lisette—a near-blinding stab of pain—was happily married, would never belong to him. It was a truth nothing could change, and he understood he'd have to accept that before it destroyed him.

But *he wasn't ready yet.*

Even if he had been, he'd always assumed the woman with whom he ended his celibate existence would be warm, affectionate, someone who understood the wound that was his heart.

Not a near stranger who might as well have been a razor blade.

His arms aching, he came down on his feet after successfully reaching the end of the jungle gym and looked back to see Adria hanging on to a section that had fallen in, courtesy of the random algorithm that had almost dumped him on his ass halfway through. There was no way she'd catch up to him now, but teeth gritted, she pulled herself back and onto the top of the structure.

Impressed despite himself, he didn't do her the insult of not putting his all into the rest of the course, the ground hard beneath his bare feet. He was cooling down when she crossed the finish line and collapsed to her knees. "Sienna was right," she gasped, her braid falling over one shoulder to lie against her breast. "You are a sadist."

"An easy course teaches them nothing." Leaving her to recover, he ran to the den to grab two bottles of water from a cooler kept close to the nearest exit and jogged back.

Stretch completed, she took the bottle he held out. "Thank you."

No sound, except that of water being drunk.

Twisting closed the lid of her bottle, Adria pushed back the sweat-damp strands of her hair and said, "Look, what happened—"

"It's over with." The memory of his betrayal brought bile into his throat—regardless of the raw pulse of his body, he wasn't yet willing to accept the inevitable and forget the woman meant to be *his.* "Doesn't need a postmortem."

Flawless creamy skin with the barest touch of sun gold pulled taut over Adria's cheekbones. "Burying your head in the sand won't make it go away." Her tone made it clear she hadn't missed the rigid evidence of his arousal.

Forcing himself not to pulverize the bottle he held in hand, he took his time replying. "What exactly would you like to discuss?" he asked in a tone that told her to back off if she knew what was good for her.

Adria didn't take the hint. "We're sexually attracted to one another," she said, feet slightly spread and hands by her sides. "Maybe you didn't realize it consciously until today, but now you do."

"I'm also a lieutenant," he said, furious he hadn't understood his own antagonistic response to Adria in time to strangle it, "and that means I can control my urges." Neither part of him had any intention of giving in to this unwanted desire, the wolf's rage as primal as the man's.

"So can I." A hidden tone in that husky voice that rubbed against his skin, a near tactile caress. "But I'm saying we don't necessarily have to." She held the brutal dominance of his gaze for a long moment before her wolf forced her to look away, her hands fisted so tight, bones pushed white against skin. "I don't want a permanent relationship, and Indigo told me you wouldn't be interested in one either."

"Did she?"

At the silken question, Adria once again met his gaze, though her chest rose and fell in jagged breaths, her wolf undoubtedly fighting her because it knew he was the stronger, more dangerous one in the clearing. "She didn't breach your confidence."

He respected that she'd stood up for Indigo at once, but that didn't excuse what she'd dared to suggest. His anger turned quiet, deadly, cold. "You just want to sleep together, is that it?"

Slender fingers flexing, clenching again. "I'm talking about sharing intimate skin privileges"—red painted her cheekbones—"nothing forbidden or taboo among packmates. I don't see why you're reacting like I'm suggesting something awful."

"Because I don't like you," he said, saw her flinch.

Ruthless though he could be, he wasn't usually such a bastard, but Adria had torn open the greatest wound on his heart, then rubbed salt on the injury with her casual approach to something that savaged him. He could barely see straight, much less think, but he knew one thing. "You're not a woman I'll ever want in my bed."

Adria could feel her face burning, the heat blistering, but she didn't run off, tail between her legs. "Can't get much clearer than that."

Riaz didn't respond, just watched her with those lethal eyes of beaten gold.

"We have to work together," she said, refusing to allow him to intimidate her, though his dominance shoved at her own until it was an almost physical force. It took everything she had to hold her ground. In truth, her wolf should have already backed down in front of a bigger, deadlier predator, but her little "secret" about her exact place in the hierarchy gave her just enough latitude to withstand the unleashed power of him for a few more moments.

"I don't want the . . . issues between us"—raging sexual arousal fused with the red haze of the anger that licked the air—"to bleed over into our working relationship. Let's agree to stay out of each other's way as much as possible, and be polite when it's not."

"Fine." No blink. No change in his stance.

Sweat broke out along her spine, and it took teeth-gritting control to respond with only a curt nod before she left, her hand squeezing the water bottle so hard she crushed the plas in a jarring crackle. It humiliated her that even now, when he'd made it cuttingly evident what he thought of her, the tug she felt toward Riaz was a dark twist of need in her gut. But she hadn't made senior soldier at twenty-five because she was weak.

Claws slicing out of her hands, she felt her eyes turn the amber of her wolf.

Riaz Delgado wouldn't ever get another invitation from her.

Chapter 8

ADEN WALKED AWAY from the back steps of the house of worship where he'd met Judd Lauren for the second time since the city's showdown with Pure Psy, coming to a halt beside the teleporter who'd brought him to the location.

Vasic's eyes remained trained on the former Arrow until Judd disappeared around the corner and into the streets of San Francisco, a shadow among shadows. "He still moves like one of us."

"In all the ways that matter, he still is one of us."

Vasic said nothing more, but a second later they were no longer in the trees behind the church, but on an isolated mountain plateau draped in the silken veil of night. The night sky was crystal clear, dotted with stars so bright, they cut like glass.

Many termed the PsyNet, the vast network that connected all Psy to one another, a starscape, but Aden had come to realize the PsyNet was missing something fundamental. Its essence, its *life* was devoid of that which drew even an Arrow's eye to the night sky. "I expected the desert."

"Both locations allow us to talk without being overheard." Vasic's eyes, a cool gray that never gave away anything, stared out past the edge of the plateau to the gnarled trees that sprawled out into the sumptuous black of a moonless night.

Aden knew what Vasic sought in the darkness, but they would not talk of it this night. Instead, he said, "Do you think Henry Scott is dead?" The Councilor had been hit by the cold fire of an X, but no one had seen him burn to ash—and he'd been surrounded by teleport-capable Tks.

Vasic's hair lifted in the wind, the strands having grown in the past months, until they were now past the unspoken

regulation length for Arrows. "Unconfirmed, but he had his
best men around him. The probability is high they pulled him
out in time."

Aden had come to the same conclusion. "If he is alive,
he's learned some new tricks, or someone is helping him
conceal his presence in the Net." The changes in Henry had
become apparent prior to the battle. Before the sudden emer-
gence of an unexpected and impossible military expertise,
the Councilor had been the beta member of the Henry-
Shoshanna pairing.

"Ming." Vasic continued to stare outward even as he
spoke, and Aden wondered how much of him remained here,
on this cold, windswept plateau.

"Yes."

"He may have advised and used Henry to his own ends,
but Ming wouldn't protect him once he was weakened and
no longer of any strategic use."

Aden's thoughts meshed so perfectly with Vasic's, he
didn't waste time voicing his agreement. "The surviving
members of Pure Psy remain fanatically devoted to him."
Silence was meant to have eliminated all emotion from their
race, but cracks had begun to appear in the chill fabric of
the conditioning each and every one of them underwent as
children. Pure Psy might decry those cracks and style itself
as the proponent of "Purity," but the depth of their commitment to Henry brought their own conditioning into question.
"There might well be a strong telepath amongst them." One
skilled enough to block the visible presence of Henry's mind
in the Net.

"Have you begun a trace?"

"Yes." Chosen for Arrow training only because his parents
had both been Arrows, Aden was officially a field medic, his
telepathic touch so subtle, he'd always been classified in the
wrong—much lower—Gradient. Walker Lauren was the first
person who had understood the dangerous power of Aden's
mind . . . and he had kept Aden's secret, taught him skills
Aden used to this day. "If Henry is alive, I'll find him."

Checking an incoming message on the computronic gauntlet on his left arm, a gauntlet that Aden had watched become
a living part of his body after the experimental fusion took

final hold this past year, Vasic said, "Did you speak to Abbott again?"

"Yes. He stays with us." The Tk had been on the verge of defecting from the squad to join Pure Psy.

"What did you say to convince him?"

"That Pure Psy wants to maintain the current power structure when that power structure has proven irreparably defective." Arrows were not stupid, had never simply been brawn—until Jax. Long-term use of the drug turned them into mindless weapons, but unbeknownst to those who would leash them, Jax was no longer administered to a single Arrow. "What Abbott wants," Aden continued, "is something else altogether."

"An Arrow cannot want anything if he is to remain an Arrow."

There was nothing in Vasic's voice to betray the memory, but Aden knew his fellow Arrow had learned that lesson after having his leg broken multiple times as a six-year-old who'd expressed a desire to return home. "I'll make sure he understands not to expose himself to outsiders." Loyalty within the squad was unspoken and absolute.

Stepping up to the very edge of the plateau, Aden felt more than saw Vasic come to stand beside him. The mountain fell away steeply in front of them, and it was a stark reminder of the plunge the Net was on the verge of taking.

The only question was how many would die in the fall.

Chapter 9

SIENNA ADORED BEING mated to Hawke. Living with him, however, she thought as the hands of her antique clock flicked over to seven a.m., was taking some adjustment. It wasn't that she wasn't used to cohabiting with others—since her defection from the ice of the PsyNet, she'd lived primarily with Walker and the kids. It was the fact that Hawke was so dominant, he tended to take over all available space simply by breathing.

"This is mine," she said, staking a claim on seventy-five percent of the closet. It had been only last week that they'd had the chance to transfer the majority of her things to Hawke's quarters, they'd both been so busy with other duties in the aftermath of the battle with Pure Psy. "You can have this section."

He shrugged those glorious shoulders and put down his mug on top of the small set of shelves that had once stood beside the door to her single-occupancy room, the scent of his coffee rich and evocative. "Okay."

Fine, she admitted in a grumpy internal mutter, that hadn't exactly been a big battle. Her gorgeous, maddening mate lived in T-shirts and jeans—though when he did put on a suit . . . the word was "delectable." "Also," she said, refusing to be derailed from her bad mood, "stop stealing my coffee." It was a special blend Drew always brought back for her from a very specific shop in San Diego.

Hawke grinned and took another sip before returning the mug—gifted to him by Marlee, after her cousin had painted a somewhat wolflike creature on the ceramic—to its resting spot. "It's good coffee." Stripping off the sweatpants he'd put on after his shower, he pulled on some jeans, his lips curving in a smile that made her breath catch. "You look good in my T-shirt."

Groaning, she sat down on the bed, resisting the temptation to walk over and rub her cheek against the soft pelt of hair that covered his chest, her need for him a gut-deep pulse. "I sound demented." Shrewish and spoiled. "Of course you can have the coffee." She'd made enough for two, was utterly delighted by the fact he enjoyed the way she brewed it.

He waited for her to make it every morning, always kissed the curve of her neck in thanks. The same way she waited for him to slice the bread he picked up a couple of times a week from a bakery just outside den territory, when she could as easily do the task herself. Little rituals. Little pieces of their lives. The idea that they were laying the foundations of their shared history . . . it made her so happy it hurt. Which was why she was bewildered by her fit of temper. "I don't know what's *wrong* with me."

"Hey." Expression suddenly solemn, he came down on his haunches in front of her, his jeans only partly buttoned and all distracting. "I know what's happening."

She raised her eyes from his chest—and lower—to his face. "You do?"

"Yeah, baby, I do." A sheepish look. "I'm crowding you, pushing you, even in our quarters, but I swear I'm not doing it on purpose."

She had zero resistance against him when he got like this, when she could see both man and wolf watching her with a tenderness that, quite simply, undid her. Closing her hands over the warm silk of his shoulders, she stroked and petted until a lazy growl rumbled in his chest. "I'm glad," she said. "I'd hate it if you were holding back with me."

"Impossible." He angled his neck in a silent request, and she gently massaged a spot that would've made him purr had he been a cat.

Mine.

The possessive thought was familiar—Hawke brought out her most primitive instincts. "Just so you know, when I get really mad, I might singe your eyebrows," she murmured, because she knew if she gave an inch, he'd take not a mile, but the entire road.

"Fine." Lashes lifting, he curved his hand around her neck to tug her down. "Then we can kiss and make up. Twice."

She laughed into the slow, deep seduction of his kiss, her breasts tightening against the soft cotton of the T-shirt she'd grabbed when she woke—the whole idea of a nightgown or pajamas was ridiculous with an alpha wolf in bed with her. Nothing ever stayed on. Half the time, the nightclothes ended up shredded. So now she just stole his T-shirts when she woke. He, of course, was pure changeling, had no problem with nudity.

Not that she minded the view.

Breaking the kiss to take a breath, she brushed back the damp thickness of his hair, her thighs spread on either side of his body, his hands warm and possessive below the hem of the T-shirt. "What do you have planned today?" she asked, her heart wrenching at the perfection of this moment where she had the right to touch him, to care for him, to call him her own.

He nipped at her fingers before answering, the wolf playing with her. "I think I'll spend most of the day with Felix and his team."

She couldn't help her instinctive flinch at the memory of exactly how the area being replanted had become so barren, every tiny blade of grass turned to ash.

Hawke's response was to bite sharply at her lower lip. "I told you not to do that."

Scowling, she rubbed at the sting. "I'm allowed to think about what I did."

"What you did was save the lives of your packmates." Tugging her close, he suckled the spot he'd bitten, soothing the momentary hurt. "That's what counts."

"I'm not sorry I did what I did." It had been a choice made in battle, against an enemy that wouldn't stop. No matter how many years she lived, she would never forget the crunching, ugly sound of a hundred guns smashing into the skulls of dazed and wounded SnowDancers. Her act had been the right one at that time, in that place. "It's just . . ." She'd annihilated the Pure Psy army, killed so many men and women who'd had the misfortune to pick the wrong side.

Her wolf held her gaze. "Talk to me."

So she did. And he listened. He understood. Until she could breathe again, her chest expanding with each inhale. It wasn't the first time they'd spoken of that terrible day, neither would it be the last—but knowing that he'd be there anytime she needed him, it was everything.

"Any other plans for the day?" she asked afterward, fixing his hair because she loved playing with it . . . and because touching Hawke calmed her on the deepest level, until sometimes, when the memories hit too hard, he simply shifted and allowed her to pet the huge silver-gold wolf that was the other half of his nature, as long as she needed.

"I'll take Harley down with me," he said, arching his neck

when she ran her nails over his scalp the way he liked. "It'll give me an opportunity to see how he's developing." Another pleasured growl, his hands flexing against her skin.

Her mate made her so damn glad she was a woman. "Has he stabilized?" The young male was shaping up to be a powerful dominant.

"He's getting there. Boy's got a strong will." He squeezed her thighs with those hands she'd felt on every inch of her body. "Like someone else I know."

"Remember that."

"That's why the wolf pushes you," he said, pressing a kiss to the inside of her knee that made her shiver. "Wolf and man both know you'll push back. It'd be no fun if you were a weakling."

Seduced, she was being utterly seduced by a wolf who knew her far too well. "The thing with the maternal females?" They hadn't had a chance to talk much the previous night, the dinner going later than expected. Given the people around the table, it was unsurprising the talk had turned to the increasing instability of the PsyNet.

Judd had disappeared around ten, heading for a meeting with his contacts, so it was likely he'd have more data to share with Hawke today. After he did, Sienna knew Hawke would make it a point to talk the information over with her—a true alpha pair needed to forge a trust that ran deeper than sensuality, than the mating bond. It had to encompass the very heart of what it took to keep SnowDancer strong. "You survived the meeting at least."

Hawke's groan was eloquent. "I have a headache just thinking about it. Ask me again after sex, and I might have the will to talk about it."

She laughed. "Nice to know I'm not the only one scared by Nell."

"Nothing scares me, least of all a woman who is maybe all of a hundred-and-ten pounds and happens to be three years my junior."

"Keep telling yourself that."

Narrowed wolf eyes. "Smart-asses get their comeuppance." Stroking his hands up under the edge of the T-shirt, he ran his thumbs over the sensitive crease of her thighs, smiled a very wolfish smile at the tremor that shook her. "You were quiet when we were discussing the mating ceremony last night."

Playing with the hair at his nape, she bit the inside of her lip. "I wish we'd done it earlier." They'd decided to wait until things calmed a little and all the evacuated children had settled back into the den, but the delay had caused her nerves to fray. "It'll be the first pack event since . . ." Since everyone had discovered what she could do, what she *was*. "Maybe we should do it together with Walker and Lara's ceremony," she said, though she knew it was too late, the celebration only days away.

"Each ceremony is unique and suited to the couple." Hawke bracketed her face in his hands, and she knew he understood what she didn't say. "They want a quieter affair."

And he was alpha, the ceremony celebrating his mating one of the biggest events to be held in the den in recent memory. Every packmate, young and old, wanted to contribute, to be part of the festivities, and Sienna wasn't going to cheat them of that—not even if she wanted to hide in a corner and hope no one would notice her.

Hawke pressed a finger to her lips before she could speak. "I told you, baby, we're wolves." Wild affection, the endearment one he used with her alone. "We respect strength."

"I'm only a soldier." Hierarchy was a critical component of the pack's stability—and their relationship fell outside of it. Never would she give it up, but the impact of it on the pack still worried her at times. "Young and inexperienced."

"It isn't always about age or experience," Hawke said, eyes of husky blue holding her captive. "Maybe you'll have to earn your stripes when it comes to your personal dominance, but you've already got their loyalty—because you gave the pack your own, laid your life on the line to protect. That's what matters."

Curling her arms around his shoulders, she leaned into his embrace. He hugged her close, stroking a big hand down her back. No one in the pack had said or done anything to make her feel unwelcome after the battle, it was true. There had been more than a few smiles thrown her way, and the teasing they received as a newly mated couple was merciless, but—"Some people are scared of me," she whispered.

Hawke chuckled. "Baby, *most* people are scared of me." He nuzzled a kiss into her neck. "It goes with the territory."

RIAZ ducked his head into Hawke's office the morning after his confrontation with Adria but found the alpha missing. "Riley," he called out, running to catch up to the lieutenant. "You seen Hawke?"

"He's gone to join Felix's team." Riley glanced at the small datapad in his hand. "No set time for returning to the den— try him on his sat phone."

"No, I think I'll run down and pitch in." Hard, manual labor would be good for him. He was strung tight from the primal fury that had raged through his body in the midnight hours. And it wasn't Lisette's face that had haunted him. Not last night.

"Felix says the ground is perfect for planting, as if it had been fertilized." Riley's eyes were intent. "He's never seen anything like it. I guess none of us have."

No, nothing had ever come close to the deadly beauty of Sienna's cold fire. "I know she's young," Riaz said, remembering not just the red-gold glow of that voracious flame but also the screams that had come before, the sickening crunches of bone as SnowDancer after SnowDancer fell, bloody and broken. "But anyone who can control that much power has my respect."

Riley's response was unexpected. "Make sure you share that view with packmates when the opportunity rises."

"Trouble?" He hadn't sensed anything, but he wasn't as connected to the heartbeat of the den as Riley. Based here his entire life, the senior lieutenant was not only an anchor for his packmates, Hawke included, he was also a man trusted by everyone from hard-eyed soldiers and busy maternals, to rebellious juveniles and elders.

"No," the other male now said. "But the battle was the first time most of the pack became aware of what Judd and Sienna can do. Right now, everyone's high from the success, but once the adrenaline fades and they start to think about it—"

"People will begin to realize exactly how dangerous those two are." Riaz nodded, seeing where Riley was headed. "We need to bolster that good feeling now, so even when the high wears off, everyone will continue to see them as strong packmates who'll use their strength to protect the weak, not Psy they need to be wary of." Wolves might be predators, but the majority weren't dominants. SnowDancer's most vulnerable members would be all but helpless against the kind of power wielded by Judd and Sienna, and, though most people didn't realize the strength of his telepathy, Walker.

"Yes." Riley kept his voice low as they spoke. "I'm probably being overcautious, but"—a rueful smile—"that's why they pay me the big bucks."

"No, you're right. Better to subtly reassure everyone now, when they're already predisposed to love the Laurens, rather than later, after fear's crept into the fold." He made a note to have some quiet, casual conversations with certain people. "You need me for anything today? If not, I'll head down to join the planting team now." He needed to do *something* physical—his skin felt stretched too tight, too thin over the raging need of his body.

It had never been this bad. As a lone wolf, he was predisposed to periods of solitude that would drive his packmates crazy, and he could last even longer without touch. He hadn't been with anyone for roughly four months when he'd met Lisette six months ago and felt that stunning, indescribable kick to the gut that was the instinctive knowledge of his mate.

Intellectually, he'd understood that while it wasn't common, it could happen in such a way—that a wolf could turn around and just *know* a woman was meant to be his own, without ever having spoken to her, but nothing could've prepared him for the impact of that moment. Every cell in his body had sung at the nearness of Lisette's presence, his senses utterly attuned to her, his body vibrating with the realization that it was *her*. More than a lover, more than a friend, a mate was meant to be a changeling wolf's other half, and he'd found his.

The soul-savaging fact that she belonged to another . . . it might've stopped the mate bond coming into being, but it did nothing to quiet the mating urge that had gripped him in sharp teeth and held on tight. Deeply intertwined with that urge was a promise so primal, he'd never before given it any thought . . . a promise of fidelity: A wolf who found his mate only ever shared intimate skin privileges with her.

That promise came from so deep in his wolf's heart that regardless of the fact Lisette would never be his, he'd been unable to bear the thought of any other woman's touch, his gut roiling. As a result, it had been close to a year since he'd shared intimate skin privileges—a long time for even a lone wolf, especially a dominant, but he'd had a grip on it. The lack of contact had hurt at times, but it hadn't been all-encompassing, threatening to blind him.

Then had come Adria and the constant prickle across his skin, the irritation he hadn't understood until she'd pushed him to ignition point. His cock hardened at the memory of her coming so wild and hot around his fingers, the ice and crushed berries of her scent intermingled with a dark feminine musk that had acted like a drug on his senses. She'd been right in the clearing. Now that he'd come face-to-face with the vicious lust that had driven his response to her from the start, he couldn't undo it, couldn't go back to a time when he didn't want her, the echo of their explosive encounter taunting him in his dreams.

"Go for it." Riley's voice broke into his thoughts. "Felix needs as many warm bodies as he can get." He pulled up a file on his datapad. "Grab some juveniles on your way down." A pause. "The males. It'll keep the maternals happy *and* make the boys too tired to get into trouble."

A sudden memory made Riaz grin. "Remember that time Hawke, Coop, you, and I got caught with *those* films?"

Chapter 10

"THOSE FILMS WERE worth scrubbing the toilets for a month." Riley's expression was solemn, in direct opposition to the amusement dancing in his eyes. "I learned a whole lot of things. Still trying to track down a copy of that third film."

Wolf huffing in laughter, his tension momentarily eased, Riaz went off to grab the misbehaving boys. They groaned at being conscripted but didn't protest. Instead, falling in beside Riaz as they ran down at an easy pace, they peppered him with questions about training, the battle, and how best to court girls without it crossing over into forbidden territory.

It was the last thing Riaz wanted to think about, much less discuss, but he didn't snarl at the lanky young teens—from the way a number of them had been moping around yesterday, they'd obviously already gotten an earful from either the maternals or Hawke, more than likely both.

Pulling on the resources that made him a lieutenant, he answered their questions with blunt truths—there was no use coddling wolf males at this age. Their laughter and friendly ribbing of one another, especially at the occasional embarrassed blush, further calmed the feral wolf inside him, until he was nearly sane by the time he arrived at what had been a wasteland directly after the battle, but was now a hive of activity, hundreds of saplings already set out, ready to be snugged into the earth.

"Shovels." He passed them out from the stockpile in one corner, then led his group over to Felix, who set them all to digging, the actual planting being done by those the horticultural specialist had trained in how to handle the roots of the saplings. When Joshua showed an interest in the task, Felix paired the juvenile with Lucy, so he could learn to do it correctly.

Surrounded by the scents and voices of his pack, Riaz's shoulders relaxed that final inch.

The time passed in a burn of muscles, and the moist, rich smell of the earth and of budding, growing things, and he was quietly contented by the time darkness whispered on the horizon. Having sent the younger kids back much earlier, with most of the other helpers following an hour ago, he assisted Felix and the small group that remained in tidying the empty pots, forgotten shovels, and discarded gloves.

"It's a massive project," he said, leaning the last shovel inside the temporary storage shed before stepping back so Felix could secure the door.

"It'll be done faster than you know it." Door shut, Felix turned to wave off the final truck but for the one he intended to drive up, his features as refined as an aristocrat's. That classically handsome face, combined with his muscled six-feet-three frame, had made him a successful model while in college. Even now, luxury-goods companies chased him to front campaigns, but Felix's true love was the earth and its flora, his thickly lashed brown eyes bright with satisfaction as he looked out at what they'd already achieved. "Hawke's going to conscript me helpers on a constant rotation. Six weeks max and we'll be done."

Their alpha walked over at that moment, clapping Felix on the shoulder. "Six weeks? Bloody hell, Felix, you're a drill sergeant in disguise."

Felix grinned, glancing up to meet Hawke's eyes for a fleeting second before his gaze skated away, his submissive nature uncomfortable with the eye contact. However, his position in the hierarchy made no difference on this playing field—here, they all took orders from him, because here, Felix was the one who knew what he was doing.

Now, the other man shoved his hands into the front pockets of his jeans. "I'm pumped to see it coming together after all the planning. It'll take a while for the area to regenerate, but a few years from now, no one will be able to tell this patch from any other in the territory."

Hawke looked up at the sky streaked with the final fading

embers of sunset, lines of tension bracketing his mouth. "I hate that we've got this massive gap where the satellites can spy on us."

"It's on the edge of the territory," Riaz pointed out. "Unless you plan to put on a ballet performance while covered in nothing but chicken feathers, they aren't going to see anything interesting."

"Damn," Hawke said with a straight face. "And here I'd already plucked the chickens."

Laughing, the three of them headed for the truck. The alpha jumped into the flatbed at the back, alongside Riaz. As they were the final three to leave, it was a peaceful if yet barren view that drew away from them when Felix started the engine and began the journey home.

Back propped against the cab of the truck, Riaz let the wind rifle through his hair, grunting when the ride turned bumpy. "Doesn't this thing have hover facility?"

"I'd answer but I think I just lost a tooth."

The hydraulics sounded on the heels of Hawke's words, creaking and groaning before they successfully lifted the truck off the ground.

"It's well past time we replaced this," the alpha said, patting the side of the truck. "But Eli was the one who originally bought it for the pack, and he's attached to the rust bucket. I think he calls it Sheila."

"Sheila?" Riaz grinned. *This* was why he'd come home, heart-bruised and licking his wounds, wary of the solitude that had always been so integral to his nature. No one could fix the hurt, but his pack . . . they gave him the gift of laughter, wrapped him in warmth, and kept him busy. Until he could almost forget the jagged hole that was his heart, its edges bleeding and raw.

A wild tangle of a kiss. A lithe female body twisting against his own, her legs locking around his waist. His fingers slick with her need. His cock pulsing with the urge to thrust deep.

Hissing out a silent breath, he strangled the roar of sensory memory. He'd damn well forgotten his mate then, hadn't he? Not only forgotten, but betrayed in the basest of fashions. The worst of it was that the memory of his hotly erotic encounter with Adria aroused him every single time, his gut clenching not in repudiation, but in claw-raking desire.

"My father," Hawke said as they passed under the shadow of a towering pine, its thick trunk scarred with the marks from a hundred claws, "was a lone wolf."

Folding his arms on his knees, Riaz continued to keep his eyes on the forest path retreating behind them, the failing light turning the trees into distant smudges. "I know." A year older than Hawke, he'd been a gangly boy about to head into his teens when Hawke's father was killed, the pack drenched in blood.

Even so young, Hawke had already begun showing his inclination to be at the center of pack life, while Riaz had preferred to prowl alone through the mountains. Yet in spite of their differences, they'd gotten along. Some part of him had seen in the boy Hawke had been, the man he would one day become. And when the pack almost broke under a hail of pain and violence, he'd made the decision to follow that boy rather than striking out on his own as so many lone wolves did.

"That's why," Hawke continued, "I understand lone wolves better than most."

"Your father was mated." It was the single thing that changed a lone wolf's soul-deep need for long stretches of solitude—transforming it into a devotion so intense, they became more possessive and protective than any of their brethren. Some people said a lone wolf spent his life searching for that one person who could become his lodestar.

"He had friends who weren't." Hawke propped his arms loosely over his knees in a mirror of Riaz's position. "That means I know lone wolves have friends. Who are you talking to, Riaz?" It was a blunt question. "Not Coop, or he'd be down here kicking your ass so I wouldn't have to."

Riaz gripped the wrist of one hand with the other, squeezed. Cooper and he had grown up together, gotten into trouble together, and made lieutenant together. The other man knew him better than almost anyone else on this earth—which was why Riaz couldn't afford to show his face in Cooper's sector. The only reason Coop hadn't picked up on the fact that something was wrong when Riaz first returned home, was that he'd been distracted by his pursuit of Grace, the woman who was now his mate.

Instead of admitting the fact he'd been avoiding Coop, Riaz said, "Since when are we girls who have to have heart-to-hearts?"

His flippant answer didn't faze Hawke. "You think I'll let you get away with bullshit, you don't know me." A hard stare. "Have you even been to visit your folks?"

His parents were currently based in San Diego. They'd wanted to be closer to their only grandchild, three-year-old Marisol, the child of his younger brother, Gage. "Are you seriously asking me that?" It was a snarl of disbelief. "Of course I went. Right after I came back into the country." If he hadn't, his mother would've been knocking on his door, and there would've been hell to pay. No one messed with Abigail Delgado

Hawke's shoulder brushed Riaz's as Felix tilted the vehicle to get around an overgrown elderberry bush. "I think you need to go visit them again."

Riaz's wolf bristled. Maybe Hawke was alpha, but Riaz was a lieutenant—that meant he had the strength and the dominance to bloody the other man in a fight. "What delusion makes you think you have the right to give me orders about my personal life?"

Hawke's response was a harsh bark of laughter. "Fuck, you remind me of what I was like a few months back. Don't be a stupid ass like I was."

Riaz released his wrist. Blood began to flow again in a hot rush, causing painful pinpricks of sensation. Hawke, he thought, was perhaps the one person in the pack who wouldn't just understand, but would *know* what it had done to him to lose Lisette without ever having had her. Still . . . "I can't talk about it yet," he said, the words rocks scraping his throat.

"Fine," Hawke replied, the wolf in his voice. "But, Riaz? You're home now. The pack is only going to give you so much rope—and we certainly won't let you hang yourself with it."

He should leave, Riaz thought, get the hell away from den territory, from an alpha who saw too much, and most of all, from a woman who incited a raw sexual hunger that made him so angry it was a white-hot flash through his bloodstream. But the painful fact was, he wasn't ready to walk alone again, a hard thing for a lone wolf to accept.

Maybe Hawke was right. Maybe he needed to go see his family. He'd eat his mother's divine cooking, tease his pretty little sister-in-law, play with his dimpled hellion of a niece, drink a beer with Gage and his father, and get his head screwed on straight. The one thing he did not need to do was to give in to the gnawing compulsion to track the subtle scent of wild berries crushed in ice until he had Adria's nude, sweat-slicked body pinned under the hard demand of his own.

ADRIA came around a cedar, its distinctive red-orange bark gray in the dark, to see Sienna waving at her. "Are you taking over my shift?" the younger woman asked.

"Yes." Again, Adria was struck by Sienna's youth, her instincts as protective toward the novice soldier as they were toward Evie. But she had to accept that those cardinal eyes . . . they were of someone far older and wiser. "Anything I need to know?"

"See that tree over there?" Sienna pointed out the huge black oak, its canopy a sprawling shadow. "Pair of nesting eagles. Steer clear—they're being very territorial." She tugged on her braid. "I almost lost this when I ventured too close."

Having fallen foul of a nesting eagle herself once, Adria knew Sienna had had a lucky escape. "Before I forget—Evie asked me to remind you that you two have a dinner date." Again, it was a surprise that her gentle niece was best friends with this tough young woman who'd been forged in deadly fire.

"I've been looking forward to it all day." A guarded but not unfriendly smile. "Evie said you're an expert in martial arts."

"A particular discipline," Adria corrected. "It's one of the more aggressive forms." She'd had to utilize it in the battle in a bid to protect fallen SnowDancers from the enemy. Her own ears had been bleeding heavily after the sonic blast, her balance shot, but she'd still been able to function on some level, and so she'd fought.

Right beside Riaz.

His arm all but flayed to the bone by a laser burn, his eardrums shattered, he'd nonetheless refused to go down.

And when she'd been too slow and taken a fracturing kick to the shoulder, he'd acted as a living shield until she could punch in a localized painkiller and rise to fight again. The man might be a bastard personally, Adria thought, her jaw tight, but he was blood-loyal with unflinching courage under fire. "I was thinking of talking to Indigo about offering a class to her novices," she said, strangling her body's unwanted response to thoughts of the dark-haired lone wolf. "Are you interested?"

An immediate nod. "The reason I was asking is because Evie told me it can be modified to suit a physically smaller individual."

Smart girl—aware not only of her strengths, but also her weaknesses. Then again, no alpha wolf, much less Hawke, would've been attracted to anyone who didn't have a brain. "Yes, absolutely. This might be one of the times we split classes according to height and weight." She glanced at her watch. "You'd better head back, or I'll hear all about it from Evie tomorrow."

Sienna laughed, more comfortable with Adria than she usually was with people she didn't know well. And it wasn't because the senior soldier shared a strong family resemblance with the Riviere women, all of whom Sienna trusted. The truth was, Adria reminded Sienna most of Riley.

They both had the same quiet, unflashy confidence intertwined with an earthy warmth, the same sense of being a rock in the storm. Sienna didn't know the pack as well as Hawke did, but she had the gut-deep feeling Adria would soon become one of the unspoken anchors in the den, a woman people went to for levelheaded advice given without judgment or pity.

As she said, "Have a nice night," and headed off, she saw Adria's smile fade, to be replaced by a much more stark expression, her eyes going the amber of her wolf. And it struck her that perhaps, the protective armor of someone like Adria was the hardest of all to penetrate—because she gave the appearance of being an open book . . . until no one was even aware of the tangled emotions that might lie beneath.

Chapter 11

VASQUEZ'S GREATEST SKILL was in going unnoticed. It was part of why Councilor Henry Scott had handpicked him to lead the Pure Psy army before the confrontation with the changelings. The fact Vasquez had survived that annihilation spoke both to his intelligence and his ability to come out on top in any given situation.

And the fact he continued to support Pure Psy even as civil war loomed in the PsyNet spoke to his belief that Silence was their race's only hope for survival. His dedication to the cause had nothing to do with something as useless and debilitating as emotion, for his conditioning was flawless, and everything to do with history: Who had the Psy been before Silence?

A broken race on the verge of extinction, murderous and insane.

Now, they ruled the world . . . or had done until the changelings gained a clawhold on power. Even the humans were stirring. All as a result of a weak Council, its members ineffectual in holding back the tide of the lesser races. That Council was no longer an issue, and Vasquez had a new set of orders.

Repeating them back to ensure he'd understood correctly, he nodded to the person who had given him those orders. "I believe we have three operatives capable of undertaking the task, but I want to watch each carefully, do another deep background check before I consider which one to approach. We must be certain of the operative's commitment."

Good. No mistakes this time.

Responding verbally to the telepathic statement, he said, "No. This time, even an X will be powerless to stop us."

Chapter 12

"NEXT TIME YOU decide to stay in the city to attend a lecture series," Sienna told Evie when she arrived at the den to find the youngest Riviere woman waiting for her, "take your cell phone."

Evie wrinkled her nose. "Tai already growled at me for forgetting when he picked me up yesterday."

"I doubt it—Tai lets you get away with murder."

"He *did*." Evie folded her arms, but her lips were twitching. "Thank God. I was beginning to wonder if he planned to treat me like porcelain forever."

Sienna snorted. "Poor Tai's going to get a rude awakening the first time he realizes you have a spine of steel." Evie had an internal strength that'd take her through any storm.

"He knows," Evie said, unhidden tenderness in her deep gray eyes. "He's also a dominant male, so he thinks he'll always be able to get his own way if he pushes hard enough."

"I know *all* about that."

Evie's laughter wrapped around them before she linked her arm through her best friend's. "How about—" Evie bit off her words. "I was going to say how about we grab some food from the kitchen and go to your quarters, but you have a mate now." A look of pure delight.

"Hawke's not in the den." He was in a meeting with Lucas, Nikita, Anthony, and Nikita's security chief, Max. Sienna knew that because he'd detoured on his way out of den territory to kiss her, their bodies pressing chest to toe in that affectionate changeling way she'd once envied in other couples. It was utterly as wonderful as she'd thought it would be.

"Meeting was meant to be tomorrow," he'd told her, his

breath a hot caress against her lips. "But Nikita"—a growling tone—"has to head urgently out of the city to sort out a business situation, so it's been brought forward. Normally, I wouldn't care if she lost some of her billions, but it might affect a workforce of a thousand-plus."

"Are you getting together to do a security review?" Everyone in the region had worked together to repel Pure Psy, and that cooperation continued in the aftermath.

"Yes. The present calm's no excuse to let down our guard. Especially with what's apparently happening in the PsyNet."

Putting aside—for tonight at least—the solemn knowledge that what was coming would likely be far worse than what had already gone, Sienna glanced at Evie. "Come on, there's food in the galley in our quarters."

"Tell me you have snacks," Evie said after they'd entered. "We'll be healthy and have vegetables later."

"I'm Psy. I don't eat snacks." It was something she'd once said to Evie, bewildered by the other woman's overtures of friendship. Evie hadn't backed off, her stubbornness sweet, gentle—and relentless.

Now, the two of them laughed as she grabbed a bag of potato chips for Evie, as well as a toffee apple for herself. Her additions to the galley had made Hawke shake his head . . . then bring her a sugar-laden treat every Friday. Biting into the apple with a smile, she dropped onto the sofa beside Evie and toed off her boots and socks, propping her feet on the coffee table.

"That'll rot your teeth," Evie said, crunching on a potato chip, the lustrous ebony of her hair curling over the shoulders of her white cashmere cardigan.

"Pot. Kettle. Black."

"God I love salt." Another crunch. "Since I have no shame, I'm going to ask you what's it like being mated."

"Wonderful." Breathtaking enough that it scared her at times. "It's the other things that shake me up now and then."

"Such as?"

Sienna had to finagle toffee from her teeth before she could speak. "Such as knowing I've become part of the center of

the pack when my natural inclination is to be on the periphery."
She was an X, a cardinal, had been trained to be a covert
operative. "I feel so exposed sometimes." As if everyone was
watching her.

Evie got up to grab them bottles of fruit juice. "That's
normal, Sin. Any woman who mates an alpha—forget about
mating the alpha of the biggest changeling pack in the
country—is going to stress a little at the sudden change in
status and responsibility. If you didn't, you'd be a robot."

Sienna knew that tone. "You think I need to cut myself
some slack."

"I knew constant sex with Hawke hadn't rotted your
brains."

Sienna almost choked on the bite of apple in her mouth.
Gulping the juice to wash it down, she pointed a finger at
Evie. "I should be used to the things that come out of your
mouth by now."

Evie smiled, beatific.

Shaking her head, Sienna said, "Thanks for the advice."
Evie had a way of cutting right to the heart of a matter, and
doing so with a kindness that was innate.

"You're welcome, Ms. Type A Personality." A gentle
nudge followed by a glimpse of open vulnerability. "To be
honest, I was a little worried our relationship would change
with you being mated. It's nice to know you still want to talk
like we used to."

"I'll always need to talk to you, Evie." Friendship was a
cherished gift to Sienna, the one she shared with Evie her
first and deepest. "I was scared, too," she confessed, "that
maybe you wouldn't feel comfortable with me anymore,
would censor yourself."

Evie rolled her eyes. "Idiot."

A knot Sienna hadn't even been aware of unraveled in her
chest. "Talking of mating—you and Tai?"

"There's no bond," Evie said, following Sienna to the galley as she hunted out the ingredients for a salad. "That's not
unusual at our age. But he's mine." She began to wash the
lettuce. "I'm going to make him get an 'I belong to Evie'
tattoo."

Sienna laughed. "Possessive much?"

"Tai's oblivious"—a satisfied smile—"but some of the older women have been giving him the eye since he filled out." Evie's own eyes shifted from gray to a vivid yellow-gold. "Just because I'm submissive doesn't mean I won't find creative and nasty ways to make them sorry if they dare come on to my man."

"I'll help you."

"Of course you will. It's in the best friend code."

Such an ordinary byplay, but one Sienna couldn't have imagined having five years ago. Her life had shifted on its axis more than once during that time, but she'd found her footing before and she'd do it again in this most exciting new chapter in her life.

A pulse along the mating bond, a "kiss" from her wolf, a reminder that no matter where the journey took her, she would never again be alone in the dark.

RIAZ hadn't warned his mother of his intention to visit, so when he walked into the house midmorning the next day, she not only dropped the plate of cookies she was holding . . . but burst into tears.

Riaz would've been alarmed except that she was cupping his face in her soft hands and kissing his cheeks, speaking two thousand miles an hour in a rapid-fire mix of English and Spanish as she berated him for staying away so long.

Dropping his overnight bag on the otherwise spotlessly clean floor, he enfolded her diminutive form in his arms, the softness she insisted on calling her "padding" and his father called "sexy as hell," familiar and comforting.

Her arms wrapped around him in return, strong as steel. Chin resting on her hair, he breathed in fragrant spring flowers, sugar, and warmth. It was the scent of kisses on skinned knees, hugs after school, proud touches when he made soldier, a million fragments of memory.

"You're staying," she said, drawing back and lifting the edge of her apron to wipe away the remnants of her tears.

He knew an order when he heard it. "Yes, ma'am."

That got him a pat on the cheek and a "Sit, I'll bring you cookies."

He picked up the broom instead to sweep up the detritus from the broken plate and its contents, got a look of approval. Riaz hid a grin. He was well trained. "Where's Dad?" His father, Jorge, had retired from his job as a teacher but still spent most days handling issues to do with the pups and juveniles in the San Diego area—it kept him content, *and* out of his mate's hair.

"We're bringing a group of the young ones to the mating ceremony. Jorge is organizing the final details today."

Riaz knew Hawke would be delighted. "It'll be good to see you there."

Taking off her apron after putting out a fresh plate of cookies for him, his mother said, "I have to go to the grocery store in a bit—do you want to track down your brother? I'm sure you can talk Gage into taking an early day."

Shaking his head, Riaz said, "I'll drive you."

His mother laughed and dragged him down so she could ruffle his hair. "My precious boy. You're going to make some woman very happy one day."

It took effort to keep the smile on his face, to not let his mother see what her words did to him. Wrapping an arm around her, he tucked her against his side and tempted her into a cookie, determined to enjoy his time in San Diego . . . but he couldn't escape the jaw-clenching realization that all thoughts of Lisette were now linked to Adria and the desire that had scorched them both.

ADRIA ran into Hawke on her way to a meeting that afternoon. When he mentioned that Riaz was in San Diego, shock turned her breathless. Not because Riaz had left the den for what appeared to be a short visit to his family, but because of her own response to the knowledge.

A tremor of relief rippled over her skin, her spine no longer tight with a fine ever-present tension. She wasn't so naive as to believe the attraction had run its course—nothing that gut-wrenchingly deep could be so easily conquered. Even now, embers of darkest need flickered in her blood. No, the only reason for her relief was because with him gone, there was no longer any chance she'd forget her vow to keep her distance from a man who had made it crystal clear he'd rather sleep on a bed of nails than with her.

"How are you doing with the territorial exploration?"

Hawke's question snapped her head back into the game—she knew her alpha had to be evaluating her performance as a transfer. "I'm doing a new section each day. I discuss it with Eli or Riley before and after to make sure I don't miss anything."

The light caught on the distinctive silver-gold of Hawke's hair as he cocked his head a fraction to the right—the wolf, listening to her. "Good," he said, his easy expression doing nothing to tone down the sense of naked power that clung to him like a second skin. "Another thing, Adria"—a moment of searing eye contact—"if there are any issues I need to be aware of, you let me know."

"Of course." Leaving the alpha, her senses prickling with the knowledge that Hawke saw far more than either part of her wanted him to see, she made her way to the weekly senior soldiers meeting. Elias, the man in charge of the group, ribbed her gently for being late, before calling the meeting to order from his leaning stance against a scarred wooden desk so sturdy it would take four men to shift.

It was a perfect fit for a break room that was happily shabby with its worn-in furniture and massive notice board hung with party invites, take-out menus, printouts of the roster, and an eclectic collection of photos. Word was, the maternal females had been politely but implacably rebuffed when they'd made noises about refurbishing it to match the bright new community areas in the den.

Adria was glad—this room had its own identity, its steady, comfortable look reflecting the pragmatic men and women who most often used it. Unlike the lieutenants, who had to deal not only with political issues, but also with matters that crossed sectors, senior soldiers had charge of the day-to-day security and running of their particular sector of the territory. Riley took care of overall assignments, making certain the dominants in the den functioned as a smooth unit, but Elias was the one who handled issues specific to the senior soldiers. And it was his advice Riley asked when the lieutenant wanted to know how best to utilize those men and women.

"Right," Elias now said, "first thing we have to do is hash out assignments during the mating ceremony."

Adria knew everyone would want a chance to attend the celebration, but the pack's territory couldn't be left undefended. "One-hour rotating shifts?" she suggested from her seat on a sofa beside dark-eyed Simran. "We have enough people even without the lieutenants." Indigo, Riaz, Judd, and Riley would need to remain at the Pack Circle.

Kieran linked his hands behind his head and leaned back, balancing his chair precariously on two legs. "Works for me." The smooth brown of his skin gleamed with health. "But anyone on the inner perimeter will have to do a two-hour block—have to allow travel time. Outer perimeter's going to be a problem. It's too far."

"Cats have agreed to cover it." Elias shook his head. "Don't know when we stopped trying to skin them for their pelts and started to trust them."

"Shame, I could've used a new rug," some wit commented from the back.

Adria grinned. Like the others, her own wolf was still getting used to an alliance that had gone beyond blood and to the heart. For a pack like SnowDancer to trust its borders to anyone, much less a leopard pack strong enough to be a threat, spoke of ties so deep, nothing would fracture them.

The change hadn't happened overnight. It had taken years . . . years while she'd been trapped in amber, driven by a painful hope that had died a slow, cruel death. But, she thought, never would she have to look back and wonder if she'd given up too soon. No, she'd *tried*. Until her heart broke.

"Back to the shifts," Eli said, deep brown hair the shade of burnt toffee sliding across his forehead. "Anyone who takes the inner perimeter only has to do a single shift for the night, so if you want one of those, let me know."

There were a few raised hands, mostly from those who wanted to have the early part of the evening off so they could attend the ceremony with their children. "And," one of them pointed out, "it's not like the party's going to stop."

A round of laughter followed, deepening when Drew quipped something in his usual sly way. Adria had been surprised to see him at the first meeting she'd attended, his place in the hierarchy was so mutable, but she supposed he was technically closest to the senior soldiers. Of course, Riley's brother and Indigo's mate had a way of being welcome anywhere he went—she'd spotted him with the mechanics the other day.

"Okay, now that that's sorted," Elias said, glancing once again at the board on which he'd scribbled his notes. "We need to talk about—"

"Hey, Eli," Kieran interrupted, gray-green eyes wicked with mischief. "Is that one of those scratch-and-write boards they use at elementary school?"

"What?" Unfazed, Elias continued to write on the pink slate. "You just noticed?"

Adria laughed, wondering if Sakura had given the board to her father. From beside her, Simran said, "I think it's great."

"You're a girl," Kieran pointed out. "It's pink. Manly men spit on pink."

Roundly booed by the females in the room, Kieran threw out his arms. "Hey, hey, I like girls." Pure charm. "A lot."

"Quiet," Elias said in his no-nonsense way, "or we'll be here all day. Next thing we need to sort out are some new training modules. We now have a climber with Level 4 certification in the group, so she'll be doing a lesson tomorrow for those of you who climb like bears after hibernation."

It took Adria a second—and Elias's amused look—to realize she'd been volunteered.

Chapter 13

"WORKS FOR ME." Climbing had always been a huge joy for her—to the point that Martin had once joked she must've been a cat in a former life. It was in fact the one thing they'd enjoyed doing together almost to the end. As if in facing the challenge of a mountain or a sheer cliff face, they'd become partners once more rather than adversaries. "I can handle the lesson on my own," she said, gently closing the lid on memories that had no place in her new life, "but I hear Drew's a good climber, too."

"Yes, he is. Which is why he'll be running things with you."

Drew saluted her from across the room. She couldn't help but smile—how could she do anything but love the man who adored the woman who was, in every way that mattered, her sister. "Level?" she asked Elias.

"Beginner to intermediate. We can't keep letting the cats show us up when it comes to climbing."

Several "Hell yeahs" sounded from around the room.

Adria shook her head. "Don't get any ideas about scrambling around in the trees like they do"—their bodies were just built differently—"but I can get you to a competent level if we do the lessons once a week for, say, two months."

"Done." Elias glanced around. "You know if you need the course—stick your name down so I can make sure you're not on shift at the time."

A lazy voice—Brody—drawled a question from the back. "I'd like to get in some advanced sniper training while things are quiet. Can you rope in Judd or Dorian?"

Nodding, Elias made another note, then the group took care of a couple of other matters before breaking up. Drew walked over to discuss their joint task as the others ambled out. "You got time now to scout a location and talk about how we want to run the first session?"

"Yes." Walking out beside him, she grabbed an apple from the bowl by the door.

Drew'd already taken a bite of his by the time she polished it on her shirt and bit in. The crunch was satisfying, the sweetness refreshing, the air outside the den a cool caress. As a partner, Drew was flexible and intelligent, and they had no problems mapping out a strategy for the lesson.

That lesson, when it rolled around the next afternoon, went down like a house on fire. Surrounded by her peers, dirty and dusty and sweaty, she felt a sense of absolute rightness. This was home.

Nothing and *no one* was going to push her out.

. . .

SIENNA went to avoid Riordan's kick but knew she'd moved a fraction of an instant too late. She winced at the whack she was undoubtedly about to get to the ribs except . . . nothing happened. Blinking, she realized he'd pulled the kick. Nothing wrong with that—she did it herself all the time in training, because the aim wasn't to beat your fellow combatants bloody, but to teach and test one another. The only problem was, Riordan should've still tapped her hard enough that she'd remember her error.

Something hot and dark and infuriated boiled in her blood. "What was that?" she demanded, halting the session.

"What?" He shoved a hand through his chocolate-dark curls.

"That excuse for a kick."

"You stopped us to critique me?" He scowled. "You can do that after—let's get back to it before I go gray."

Already stressed over the mating ceremony the following day, Sienna was not in the mood for male-wolf bullshit. "How about I incinerate your hair so you don't have to worry about that?" It just slipped out.

She waited for fear to fill eyes that had always looked at her with friendly affection, stomach curdling at her error— she'd playfully threatened Hawke with singed eyebrows but had been so careful not to remind the rest of the pack of what she was. But instead of fear, all she got was an "aw shucks" grin and a shrug. "I figured you wouldn't want to be bruised for your big day tomorrow." Charming eyes, big and brown and guileless.

It almost made sense. Except now that she thought about it, she realized he'd done the same thing during their last training session—only he'd been a bit more cunning about it, grazing her so she knew she'd been "hit." However, in spite of his boyish charm, Riordan was a dominant. The more she pushed him to admit what he'd been up to, the more intractable he'd get. "Okay," she said with a smile she hoped didn't betray her bloodthirsty mood. "Thanks. Ready?"

He dropped back into the correct stance.

Not giving any warning, she went at him full tilt—her foot

connected hard with his ribs, her elbow with his jaw, her fist with his stomach. She did keep her blows away from his pretty face, since he had a date for the ceremony. However, when he blocked her moves but made no aggressive ones of his own, she narrowed her eyes and went to kick him upside the head, which, if it connected, would surely create a nice big black-and-blue bruise down one side of his face.

"Fuck!" Slamming up a hand, he gripped her ankle the instant before she would've made contact with his skull and flung her away and to the ground, coming down on top of her an instant later, his much heavier body pinning hers facedown on the mat. "You trying to kill me?" It was a growl.

Instead of replying and though he'd knocked all the air out of her, she went to slam her head back into his face. He jerked out of the way with another brutal word, setting her free. Pressing up to take a seated position on the mat, she raised an eyebrow at Riordan when he gave her a distinctly wary look from where he sat on the other side. "Oh, sorry," she said with sweetness that would've done a candy bar proud, "were we only *pretending* to train?"

Another growl, this one harsh and from the chest. "You're my alpha's mate," he snapped out with a raw anger she'd never before witnessed in him. "My wolf can't hurt you."

It knocked the air out of her all over again. She'd been so focused on how packmates would feel about her now that they knew of the cold fire, she hadn't really considered the more direct effect of her relationship with Hawke—especially since her closest friend, Evie, had been so easy about it. But the fact was, she wasn't just Sienna Lauren, novice soldier and Riordan's friend anymore. She was Sienna Lauren *Snow*, mate to the SnowDancer alpha.

Stunned by the far-reaching implications of Riordan's statement, it took her several long seconds to formulate her reply. "An alpha can be challenged," she said slowly, "so lower-ranked soldiers *can* get aggressive toward him, and by extension, his mate."

Sighing, Riordan fell backward, until he lay flat on his back. "Do you know what Hawke would do to me if I hurt you?"

"Not if the injury happened in this context." No matter his protectiveness, Hawke would never get in the way of her development and growth as a soldier. He'd taken her to the mat more than once when he thought she was getting lazy with her physical training—not to mention, he was the one who'd thrown her into that physical training in the first place.

"If you can't or aren't able to grasp that," she said, "I'll ask Indigo to make sure we're not partnered up again." It wasn't a threat, but the offer of a friend who understood his wolf's nature. "No harm, no foul."

Riordan snapped up into a sitting position. "You're flicking me off because I don't want to hit you hard enough to bruise?" Simmering fury.

"I'm saying I can't get better if my partner treats me like fine china." Her enemies certainly wouldn't worry about hurting her when they came after her, and not all of them would use solely psychic methods. "I need to be lethal in every way if I'm going to survive Ming and the rest of the Council."

Riordan blew out a harsh breath. "It makes me so angry that you have to think about shit like that."

She was the one who shrugged this time. "It's part of life." The good things more than made up for the bad.

Getting to his feet, Riordan held out his hand, tugging her up when she accepted the offer. "Okay," he said quietly. "I'll stop holding back. But Sin . . . I'm a wolf. It might get sketchy at times." A mock punch to her jaw. "Just thump me around the head to set me straight."

Her smile was in her heart. "Deal."

Later that night, when Hawke got into bed after a long comm meeting, she snuggled into the wild heat of him and told him of her confrontation with Riordan. "He was much better after, even pulled me up on a couple of mistakes."

Hawke folded one arm under his head, the other around her, his fingers tracing curving patterns on her lower back. "I was expecting some of that—you're the only one who can deal with it."

Because the instant he stepped in, he negated her power. "Thank you," she said, running her foot over his shin, "for loving me enough to let me fight my own battles."

He fisted his hand in her hair. "No—some I'm claiming as my right."

"Okay. As long as you don't get greedy and try to handle

them all." Sensing his surprise, she braced herself on one elbow and looked down into the incredible beauty of his night-glow eyes, the translucent blue lit with white fire. "Gorgeous wolf."

"I like the way you pet me."

"Before," she said, stroking her fingers down his chest in a caress that pleasured them both, "I used to fight you all the time because it felt as if you didn't trust me to do anything, as if I had to force you to *see* me." She pressed her fingers to his lips when he scowled, went to speak. "Doesn't matter if it was true or not—that's how I felt.

"Now I know different . . . so I can give in sometimes." Such conscious surrender wouldn't change his wolf's respect for her, wouldn't make him think her any less. It would simply let that wolf know she trusted him with her vulnerability—and that was as important as her own pride.

Hawke moved with quicksilver grace to press her to her back, his muscled thigh pushing between her own, his hand still clenched in her hair. His kiss, when it came, was a hotly tender thing. "So strong, my Sienna, so beautiful." His mouth, wet and possessive down the line of her throat, making her body arch toward him. "Thank you," he said in a rumbling echo of her own words, "for loving me enough to understand my need to take care of you."

"Hawke."

"Shh . . . Lie back and think of England."

Laughter reawakened inside of her, bubbling its way past the raw burn of emotion. "I'd rather think of you."

She felt his smile against the curve of her abdomen, his jaw rough with stubble that made her shiver as he kissed his way oh-so-slowly down her body.

Chapter 14

THE DAY OF Hawke and Sienna's mating ceremony dawned bright and clear. Though Adria had done an evening shift, she was up and awake by ten, ready to pitch in with the final preparations. Nell, the maternal female in charge, assigned her to grunt work in the kitchens. Adria was perfectly happy with that—she liked working with her hands, even if it was only to peel two thousand potatoes.

"Hey." A broad-shouldered man with dark hair and tanned skin pulled up a stool across from her, his smile wide, the dimple in his left cheek giving him a roguish air. "I've been sent to join the foot soldiers." He held up a peeler. "Name's Sam. You're Adria, right?"

It was impossible not to smile back. "Yes."

"I didn't know Indigo had another sister."

The mistake was an easy one to make if you didn't know the family well. "Tarah's my sister," she said. "So I'm technically Indigo's aunt."

"Bullshit." Lines between his eyebrows.

Her wolf was at once amused and delighted. "Scout's honor." Her parents had been—according to her mother—"deliriously ecstatic" at their surprise pregnancy soon after they'd celebrated the mating of their eldest child.

Indigo had been born a mere four years later.

"Huh." A long pause as they peeled. "So, you have a date for the mating ceremony?"

It felt good to be flirted with, to exercise her own rusty flirtation skills. "Are you telling me you're not taken?"

A shrug. "I didn't want to make anyone jealous, so I was going to go stag, but now . . ." A look so charming it could've come from a feline. Impressive, given that Sam was human.

She almost said yes—he was adorable and sexy and frank about his attraction to her. But . . . he was so innocent. In his late twenties and clearly both tough and courageous from what she'd seen of his actions on the battlefield, but not even a little hard. Though the actual age gap between them was likely to be five or six years, she felt ancient in comparison. "I'm not good for you, Sam."

His smile faded at her quiet words, his brown eyes velvet soft and intent. "Maybe I'm good for you, hmm?" He peeled another potato, as if waiting for her to say something else. When she didn't, he issued a dramatic sigh. "Fine, I'll accept defeat—on one condition."

God, but she liked him. "Doesn't sound much like accepting defeat."

"I'm a SnowDancer." A sinful grin. "Promise you'll dance as many dances with me as I want."

"Just dancing," she said, pinning him with a grim stare. It wouldn't be fair to Sam to permit him to think it might progress any further—not when her wolf remained fixated on another man. The painful, unwanted desire was something she'd conquer, but she would not hurt anyone else along the way.

"Okay." Sam's suspiciously meek agreement was followed by a smug smile.

Adorable, she thought again, knowing he'd definitely try to sneak a kiss if nothing else. *"Sam."* Laughter canceled out her attempt to be stern. All at once, she felt light and young and carefree, something she'd never again expected to feel.

Dimple appearing to dangerous effect, he touched her boot with his, playful as a pup. "We'll have fun."

"Yes," she said, her wolf padding happily inside her skin, "I think we will."

RESTED and calmed by the time he'd spent in San Diego before returning to the den on an early morning flight, with his parents and their charges to follow that afternoon, Riaz helped set up the sound system for the ceremony—well, mostly he hefted things while the techs told him what to do.

"I think they're enjoying this a little too much," he said to Elias when he and the senior soldier paused for a water break.

"How often do they get to give orders to a lieutenant?" Elias grinned . . . and almost tumbled forward when a small whirlwind attacked him from behind, wrapping her arms around his legs.

"Daddy!"

Throwing his bottle of water toward Riaz, Elias reached back to grab Sakura, hauling her up into his arms. "You almost made me do a face-plant, baby girl."

Sakura giggled, her fine features painted with the well-known markings of a fictional warrior princess. "Neal was chasing me." She peered over his shoulder. "There he comes!" Wriggling out of her father's hold, she took off around the corner, arms and legs pumping with a strength that belied her thin frame.

A boy her age streaked by a moment later, a fluorescent green water bomb held in hand.

Wolf stretching in amusement, Riaz returned Elias's water bottle. "Looks like the kids have started the party early."

Instead of replying in kind, the senior soldier stared after where the children had disappeared, his expression pensive.

"Don't worry," Riaz said, thinking Eli was worried the boy would hurt Sakura. "Drew checked the water bombs. They don't hit with any kind of impact—it's just about getting the other person wet."

"What? Oh." Elias shook his head, shoving a hand through his sweat-damp hair. "No, it's not that." A pause as he drank. "Thing is . . . I haven't seen that smile on her face since before the burns."

Hit by laser fire in an unprovoked Pure Psy attack, Elias had suffered injuries so severe, he'd been in shock by the time they got him to the infirmary. Little Sakura had been disconsolate—she was the apple of her daddy's eye, her sadness all the more poignant for being so silent. She'd been this big-eyed, shocked waif it had broken the pack's heart to see.

Riaz knew both Eli and his mate, Yuki, continued to worry about the long-term impact of the trauma on their child. "It'll take time," he said, his mind on another child, another father, "but she'll get over it. Kids are tougher than adults think."

Elias met his gaze. "You sound certain."

"My dad was badly hurt in the fighting when Garrick died." His teacher father had known he had no chance against the dominants who had turned, but he'd stood firm in defense of the innocent. "It really shook me." He didn't like thinking about it, even now. "Because dads aren't supposed to get hurt, you know? Best thing my parents did was to not baby or coddle me or my brother afterward—the normalcy helped us settle down." And even as a boy, he'd known that he was lucky, so lucky.

Riley had lost his parents.

Hawke had lost his father . . . and not long afterward, his mother.

So many other friends had been made orphans or been left with only one parent.

"Just love her," he said. "That's all she needs."

"I'll never forget what the den was like back then, after everything was over." Chill shadows whispered into the warmth of Eli's eyes. "How eerie, how quiet. So many of the strong were dead. I was a novice at the time, and terrified the pack was going to shatter around us."

But SnowDancer hadn't broken. It had grown stronger. Until tonight they celebrated the mating of the boy who had given up his childhood to lead the pack out of the darkness. Nothing and no one, Riaz thought, his own wolf fierce in its loyalty, would ever sway the pack's devotion to Hawke. "Come on," he said to Eli, "the megalomaniacs called the techs are gesturing for us to hurry up."

It was two hours later that the other man said, "Done! Don't know about you, but I could do with a beer."

Picking up the T-shirt he'd stripped off earlier, Riaz used it to wipe his face as he nodded. He draped the T-shirt around his neck as they left the Pack Circle, and wasn't really paying attention when a group of female packmates walked past, carrying small boxes loaded up with decorations.

Until a wolf whistle pierced the quiet.

Glancing back, he found himself being observed by a sexy dark-eyed beauty with curly blonde hair to the middle of her back. She cocked the box on her hip, her full breasts pushing against the cotton of her navy blue tee, her smile an invitation. Most hot-blooded males would've closed the distance between them to accept it, but Riaz shook his head with a gentle smile to soften the rejection, and continued on his way.

Elias didn't say anything until they'd passed out of the heavily forested area immediately around the Pack Circle, and to an otherwise empty section of track. "You already have a date?"

"Not interested." His wolf peeled back its lips in a snarl that exposed razor-sharp canines—because the words were a lie. There was one woman who interested him a whole damn lot.

A short pause. "Do you . . . er . . . swing the other way?"

Riaz halted, stared. "What the hell, Eli?"

Elias shrugged, unabashed. "Word is, the women are starting to wonder why you keep turning them down when it's obvious you need to share skin privileges. And don't shoot me, but Lara's apparently been asked a few pointed questions, too."

"Great." Riaz gripped the ends of his T-shirt, twisted. "My cock is fixated on a woman who makes my blood boil"—a fixation that kept shoving Lisette into the background—"and the pack thinks I'm either gay or incapable." He didn't know whether to roar his aggravation or break something.

"The one you want"—unhidden curiosity—"she in the den?"

"Doesn't matter." He wouldn't allow it to, regardless of the fact that he'd woken up with a hard-on as rigid as stone this morning, his mind filled with the husky voice and erotic taste of the woman he'd almost fucked against the cold metal of a car door.

"Fair enough." Elias's genial words broke into the teeth-clenched intensity of his thoughts. "Though you should know—I have a feeling a number of the single women are planning to ambush you tonight and get an answer once and for all."

"I should've seen that coming." He was a strong, eligible male without a partner. It would've been more surprising if he *hadn't* been playfully stalked. He was also dominant enough to scare them all away, but just because he was in a shit of a mood didn't mean he wanted to ruin the night for women who were only behaving as their natures dictated. "Why the hell did I come back to the den?" It was a snarl.

Elias slapped him on the back. "You know you love us."

Yeah, he did. So he'd swallow his irritation and frustration, and dance every dance if it came down to it—each with a different partner, so no one would get ideas about staking a claim.

The one woman he would not be dancing with was Adria.

It shamed him to the core, destroying everything he thought he knew about himself, but he wasn't sure he could touch her without shoving her to the earth and ripping off her panties to thrust himself into the scalding tightness of her body.

Chapter 15

HAWKE CAUGHT AN unexpected scent on the breeze when he stepped outside with Judd, wanting to get some fresh air after the comm-conference they'd just had with Lucas, Sascha, Nikita, Max, and Anthony. It was the second time in a week they'd all connected, unusual for their strange alliance, but necessary given the growing volatility of the PsyNet.

It had become dangerous enough that both Nikita and Anthony had made contingency plans in case of their own assassinations. For the first time, he'd found himself feeling a reluctant respect for the former Councilors—the two had considered the impact of their deaths not only on their business empires, but also on the people who counted on them for stability. He wasn't ever going to trust or like either, not when he knew how much blood they had on their hands, but he'd accepted the need to work with this particular enemy to protect SnowDancer and the region.

Not a scenario he'd have anticipated even a year ago, but he wasn't going to think further on it today. This night, it was about his mate and his pack. About wolves and play. Laughter and affection.

That scent again.

"Is Alexei here?" His youngest lieutenant had wanted to attend the ceremony, but Hawke had nixed the request. While none of the sectors outside den territory had as yet been targeted, SnowDancer couldn't risk reducing security in those regions—and it wasn't only the Psy they had to worry about. Alexei's sector was on the very edge, near the border with Oregon, close to the lands of a much smaller but aggressive wolf pack.

Judd gave him an inscrutable look. "He's not scheduled to arrive for at least another month. We discussed it at the last lieutenant meeting."

"I know, but I could swear . . ." Shaking his head, he shoved a hand through his hair. "Where'd Riley say he'd meet us?"

Judd nodded at the water glinting through the trees, the sun fracturing it in bright splashes of silver and cobalt. "In the clearing on the other side of the lake. Said he wanted some time out from the insanity inside."

Wolf not happy with its mistake about the scent, but willing to let it go, he continued to walk beside his lieutenant— a man who, as a result of his incredible feats during the battle in San Francisco, now had a fan club. Complete with "I ♥ Judd" and "Judd Is My Boyfriend" memorabilia.

In the normal course of events, civilians wouldn't have gotten anywhere near the former Arrow, but it had been impossible to evacuate the entire city prior to the Pure Psy attack. His name, at least, should have remained under wraps, but a number of intrepid journalists had risked life and limb to cover the battle—and one of them had overheard the other fighters calling out to Judd, revealed it in the ensuing article. "Did Brenna show you the website?"

"Yes." A dark mutter.

Hawke's wolf huffed in laughter, thinking of the secret stash of "I ♥ Judd" T-shirts and buttons Drew had purchased for everyone to wear at the next lieutenant meeting. "I'm thinking of making you my new PR person."

"I'd hate to turn my niece into a widow so soon," was the cool answer.

"I hear women are posting their phone numbers on the site for you." Accompanied by sexy videos and photos.

Judd's eyes gleamed. "Not after Brenna hacked the site and plastered a message on their homepage pointing out that I'm very happily mated to a wolf with sharp teeth, razored claws, and a wild case of insane jealousy." A small smile that was, nonetheless, quietly satisfied. "She also uploaded several gruesome photos of feral wolf kills."

Hawke grinned in pride—he'd expected nothing less. "That's my girl." Catching another scent, he halted. "Damn it, that was, Matthias."

Judd watched him without blinking, the perfect expressionless Arrow. "Did you get enough sleep?"

"Funny." Growling low in his throat, he picked up his speed. "Jem. Kenji. Cooper—" And suddenly, he was in a clearing filled with his lieutenants, male and female, from the youngest to the most experienced, from every sector across SnowDancer's massive territory.

A "whoop" went up at his entrance, and then he was being hugged and slapped on the back and even kissed. "I'd have hit that beautiful mouth," a grinning Jem said, touching the cheek to which she'd pressed her lips, "but I hear your mate is a possessive woman."

He was not in the mood to laugh. "What the *hell* are you all doing here?" Never had his men and women so blatantly disobeyed his orders.

"Relax, boss," Tomás said with his usual irreverence. "We came down using our best sneaking skills to duck under the radar—no one's going to miss us for one night. Every one of us has people we trust holding the fort and"—he held up a sat phone—"we're in constant contact with our sectors."

"With," Riaz added, holding up his own sat phone, "Judd, Riley, Indigo, and me acting as double backups in case of an emergency."

Hawke glanced at Riley. "I assume WindHaven is flying patrols over the territory?" His lieutenants were too smart not to use every resource available to them.

"I told you he'd figure it out." Alexei smiled that "supermodel" smile of his—as once described by Tomás . . . right before Alexei gave him a black eye. "We had to be here. You can yell at us and kick us out, but we'll just shrug and turn right back around."

Kenji, his hair dyed a deep purple and sprayed with tiny gold stars, nodded. "We're like termites—you can't get rid of us."

He was alpha, his word law. He also knew when he was beaten.

Wrapping an arm around Jem's petite form, he squeezed her to his side, his wolf nuzzling at her own in welcome. To have the loyalty of men and women of such strength and heart was a gift—even if it meant he had to face the occasional challenge to his authority. And this particular challenge . . . it showed a depth of love any alpha would be hard-pressed to repudiate. "I guess we'd better find somewhere for you lot to sleep."

Cooper snorted, the smooth mahogany of his skin bisected by a jagged scar on the left-hand side of his face. "Who plans to sleep?"

"Not me." Tomás's grin was infectious. "I intend to dance till dawn, hopefully with the sexy little wolf I spied earlier, then sneak home before anyone knows I was even gone."

"I think the single women are wise to you, mi amigo," Matthias drawled with a grin, one arm around Indigo where she leaned against his muscular bulk. "But don't worry. I'm sure the grandmothers will appreciate the company."

Turning toward the big lieutenant, Tomás shook his head, his expression mock solicitous. "I'd be careful if I were you— Drew might deck you again if he hears you've been touching his Indy here. Didn't he whip your sorry ass the last time?"

Indigo patted Matthias's arm. "They've made up."

"Was there kissing?" Tomás asked, clapping his hands to his chest. "I can't believe you didn't invite—"

Having strolled over, Jem grabbed his face between her hands and laid one on him. "There you go, Tommy."

It was the first time Hawke had seen Tomás speechless. Everyone else cracked up.

Hawke's wolf bared its teeth in a happy grin—it had been years since alpha and lieutenants had all been in one place at one time, and damn but it felt good. He knew it would be good for the pack as well, a quiet declaration that SnowDancer wasn't scared or cowed by its enemies into running and hiding.

They were wolf. And they were strong.

Chapter 16

COUNCILOR KALEB KRYCHEK dropped out of the PsyNet and back into his physical body where he stood on the edge of the balcony of his home on the outskirts of Moscow. That balcony had no railing, and the gorge below, swathed in the dark veil of night on this side of the world, was sheer, signaling death for anything that couldn't fly . . . or teleport.

His lashes came down, swept back up.

His ability to teleport to individuals meant nothing, not in this particular situation. For some reason, he could not teleport to the one person he'd spent years learning to know, to understand. Opening his psychic eye again, he considered the pathways he'd already traversed. He was getting closer, that much was inarguable. The only question was whether he'd be fast enough to—

Councilor.

Shifting his focus at the telepathic hail, he slipped back into his mind and out again onto the PsyNet, this time devoid of the shields that made him invisible. "Silver."

His aide's mind was crystal clear, with none of the hairline cracks that signaled broken or compromised conditioning. "Sir," she said. "My family did not lose its contact inside Pure Psy in the fight against the changelings, and his most recent communiqué makes it clear the group is stirring again."

"I assumed as much." Pure Psy had been heavily damaged

but not destroyed by the cold violence of Sienna Lauren's X-fire combined with a fierce fighting force of changelings, humans, and Psy.

An unusual mix.

Kaleb had watched from a distance, weighing up what the group effort meant for the future not simply of his own race but of the world.

"Their new goal?" he asked.

"Unidentified. Information is being communicated to a select number of individuals on a need-to-know basis. The only fact our contact was able to confirm is that they've shifted their attention from the changelings to the Net."

Kaleb considered the radical change. After the decisive defeat Pure Psy had suffered, it made sense for the group to rethink its objectives, but it had to be more than that. Fanatics did not think in a logical fashion, and Pure Psy was a construction of absolute fanaticism, no matter what its adherents told themselves about the "Purity" of their Silence.

More than likely, the Pure Psy membership had decided that anyone who had not supported the group's attack on the changelings was to be treated as the enemy, including those of their own race. "Thank you, Silver."

"Sir." Her roaming presence streaked away, a shooting star.

Kaleb stared out at the gorge on the physical plane, but on the psychic, he was reaching for the DarkMind. *What do you hear? What do you see?*

The broken, twisted neosentience, created of all the emotions the Psy refused to acknowledge, much less feel, twined around him, a pet seeking affection. Except it was no pet but a nightmare, and Kaleb didn't understand the concept of affection. Still, he could mimic it enough to calm the DarkMind.

The neosentience showed him minds disrupted, areas of the Net disturbed, but Kaleb had seen that for himself, monitored Subject 8-91 on a continuous basis. *Pure Psy*, he said, narrowing the search parameters.

The DarkMind had nothing new to show him on the topic.

So, Silver was righter than she knew—Pure Psy was keeping all information about its new plans under a mental and psychic lockdown. That meant its members had to be limiting their communications to telepathy or in-person meetings. Slow . . . but an excellent safeguard to ensure no one would uncover their objective until it was too late.

Chapter 17

SIENNA LOOKED IN the mirror, startled by the woman who looked back at her.

Everything else new she'd purchased over the past couple of years, she'd acquired on shopping expeditions with friends. But not the dress she wore today. Hauntingly aware that this night when she made a public claim on her wolf, was claimed in turn, would resonate in her soul for the rest of her life, she'd needed it to be a private thing.

She'd picked the design on her own, sourced the emerald green fabric, cut out the pattern using the template, then asked Tarah to sew it for her. The result was breathtaking. Made of a silky material that caressed rather than clung, it had straps that crossed her upper chest before curving around her neck in a halter, and a graceful, flowing skirt that kissed her ankles. Supremely elegant—but for the hidden slit on one side that hit mid-thigh and appeared only if she moved a certain way.

It made her feel young and sexy, beautiful and graceful, at the same time.

For her feet, she'd chosen not respectable heels, but the very unrespectable thigh-high boots she'd worn the night Hawke had carried her out of *Wild*. That was the night they'd danced their first dance, a dance she would never forget.

Her hair she'd left down, because her wolf preferred it that way.

That wolf now growled. "Come here so I can take a bite."

Her thighs clenched. "Behave." He looked gorgeous in a

formal black shirt and pants, his hair and eyes thrown into startling relief, but she had another outfit in mind. "I bought you a present."

A slow wolfish smile. "I have one for you, too." Closing the small distance between them, he made her hold out her hand, palm open.

"Oh," she said in delight, "which one did you get?" The intricate toys he'd given her during their courtship were some of her most cherished keepsakes.

When he put the old-fashioned mechanical toy on her palm, she stopped breathing. It was a tiny representation of an atom, complete with colored ball bearings standing in for neutrons, protons, and on the outside, arranged on arcs of fine wire, electrons. Turning the key on the side made the electrons move, what she'd thought were ball bearings actually finely crafted spheres of glass that sparked with color.

A brilliant, thoughtful, wonderful gift for a physics major.

Eyes burning, she swallowed. "It's perfect." It still shook her at times, how he remembered things that mattered to her—even when she didn't think he was paying attention. The other day, a book had appeared on her reader that she'd only mentioned wanting in passing.

He rubbed his knuckles over her cheek, as if he understood exactly what his care meant to her . . . then she realized he did. The mating bond connected them on a level that was as primal as the heart of the wolf.

"Why magnesium?" she asked, identifying the atomic number of the light metal.

His hand on her jaw, his mouth on her own. "Because it's beautifully explosive, just like my X."

Her heart skipped a beat. "I like the way you pet me, too." The way he made her feel as if her cold fire was a gift, not a curse.

Placing the toy on the vanity when the clockwork mechanism wound down, she reached for the box she'd laid on the seat in front of it. "This is for you." Nerves knotted her stomach. "If you don't like it, it's okay," she said as he pulled off the ribbon with male impatience and opened the lid to reveal the contents.

Silence.

"I can send it back, reorder another—" His kiss stole her breath, stole her words, would've stolen her heart if it hadn't already belonged to him.

Touching her fingers to her passion-swollen lips, her breasts straining against the bodice of her dress, she watched him put the box back on the seat and strip off his shirt, exposing the beautiful chest she'd licked and sucked in the shower not long ago—her mate could be patient now that "the edge was off," though patience was a relative thing.

She'd ended up pinned to the wet tile, her legs wrapped around lean hips. Petting her with lazy possessiveness, he'd stroked into her slow and deep until she came in a rain of pleasure. Yet her body pulsed for him all over again, the sensory memory of rubbing against his chest sensitizing her nipples to aching points.

Hawke's nostrils flared, but he didn't stop what he was doing.

Dropping his shirt onto the bed, he lifted out and shrugged into the one she'd spent hours upon hours searching for online. When he raised his hands to the buttons, she stepped into his space. "I'll do that." She couldn't resist kissing each hard, muscled inch before she covered it up.

"*Sienna.*"

A shiver rippled over her skin at the sound of that deep growly voice. "We can't be late to our own ceremony."

Tugging back her head, he nipped at her lower lip, his eyes wolf blue. "I'll put it on your tab."

"Or maybe I'll put it on yours," she said, giving him a little bite with her "claws."

"I promise to pay up." His free hand, proprietary and warm, on the curve of her hip. "With interest."

Slotting in the final button, she resisted the urge to undo her work and stepped back to watch him tuck the shirt into his pants and do up his belt. There was something intensely erotic about seeing her man getting dressed, and Sienna had the feeling that would never change. Not with Hawke.

"So?" he said afterward.

She straightened the collar. "Take it off, you're too handsome."

"No, it's already my favorite shirt." Hawke remembered

seeing Lucas in a T-shirt that exactly matched his eyes not long ago, and feeling the hard stab of envy at knowing the leopard alpha's mate had purchased it for him. He'd thought the wild beauty of such a bond forever out of his reach.

Now, he was being petted by a woman who had somehow managed to find a shirt that matched the unusual shade of his own eyes, the ice blue threads so fine, it felt like wearing a kiss against his skin. Sienna's kiss. "What are you getting me for my birthday?" Both parts of him admired his reflection, his hair almost glittering against the foil of the blue.

"It wouldn't be a surprise if I told you," was the arch response.

Delighted with her, he stole another kiss before tangling his fingers with her own. "Ready?"

"Yes." The slightest hitch to her breath. "I know these events follow their own rhythm, but do you have any idea of what we should expect?"

"Good chance the lieutenants are going to kick it off with a speech." Hawke glanced down, glimpsed the black leather-synth of her boot through the slit, and remembered that hushed night when he'd first allowed himself to hold her, though it had been torture to do only that and nothing more. "Then we'll dance and celebrate." Normally, Hawke would be the one who spoke first at any mating or bonding ceremony, letting the new couple know their pairing was accepted and welcome. The impact of that moment was luminous, an inexplicable but powerful something passing between an alpha and his people.

"Dance all night with me?" Sienna asked as they left the den for the walk to the Pack Circle.

He enjoyed the feel of the wind flicking her dress against his legs, the supple warmth of her a familiar caress under the hand he'd placed on her lower back. "I know Tomás is planning to steal a dance, and Drew's claimed one already."

"You're rescinding the no-touching rule for tonight?" It was a laughing tease.

"Since there are no baby cats around, yes." His wolf snarled at the reminder of her friendship with Kit. "But, on that note—" Not giving her any warning, he bit her on the bared skin of her right shoulder.

"Hawke!" She thrust a hand into his hair, found that instead of pushing him away, she was holding him to her while he licked over the mark with a molten sensuality that made her toes curl.

"There," he murmured, slits of ice blue visible between lowered lids. "Now everyone knows you're mine." Another proprietary lick.

Pulse thudding against her skin, she laughed. "As if people were in any doubt."

Satisfied—and very alpha—smile on his face, he placed his hand on her lower back again, and they continued down the path. "I'll allow the pack to monopolize you until midnight"—a low murmur that was a rough stroke over her skin—"then I'll dance with you until the stars fade and the sun rises."

Heart shattering at the beauty of her mate's promise, she entered the Pack Circle with him.

The cheer that split the air was deafening. Grinning, Hawke led her to where his lieutenants waited in front of a crowd that included every member of the den's population, except for the few on security rotation.

Matthias raised his arms to get the pack to quiet down, but gave up the floor to Riley once he had the crowd's attention. Hawke's most senior lieutenant stepped forward and, cupping Sienna's face in his hands, said a single simple word, "Welcome."

The howl that went up in the clearing was multiharmonic and piercingly joyful, a song that was a gift. Linked as he was to Sienna, Hawke felt her stunned wonder and knew she didn't realize the significance of the act.

"They're welcoming you," he whispered, his chest vibrating with the need to add his voice to the song, "not as my mate, but as their alpha's mate." The distinction was important, and when untrammeled sunshine lit up her face, he knew she understood.

A rustle of giggling and whispering sounded on the last echo of the harmony, and suddenly, they were faced with the pups. Tarah stood unobtrusively to the side, where the youngest ones could see her. A graceful wave of her hand and the children began to sing, their voices high and sweet and full of innocence fragile as glass.

He saw from the surprise on Riley's face that the kids had managed to keep this a secret. His wolf's heart burst in pride. Tucking Sienna's hand to his side, he glanced down to see an iridescent shimmer over the night-sky of her gaze. Her cousin, Marlee, was among the singers, as was her brother, Toby— still young enough to not mind joining the children, but old and lanky enough that he'd had to find a space right at the back. He held a chubby two-year-old in his arms, her singing enthusiastic if not altogether coherent.

It was on the final chorus that his mate surprised him, adding her voice with a playful grace that delighted the children. Afterward, hands linked, the pups took multiple giggling bows while thunderous applause filled the clearing. When a little girl escaped on sturdy legs to make a beeline for Hawke, he scooped her up and received a bright-eyed and somewhat sloppy kiss for his trouble.

Grinning, he passed her to her laughing father, her baby pink dress frothing over the man's sun-browned arm. "This one's going to give you trouble."

"She's the nursery flirt," the other man said, tapping at the pup's nose in loving reproof.

It was a far more elegant female who came forward next, her petite body sheathed in an ankle-length cheongsam of deep yellow silk, her glossy black hair in a neat twist. Nell represented not simply the maternals, but everyone in Snow-Dancer who didn't identify as a dominant. In her arms she held a beautiful handmade quilt, the craftsmanship exquisite. "Each family in the den contributed a piece to this, thus each block is unique." She handed the precious gift to Sienna.

Reaching behind her to another one of the maternal females, Nell accepted what appeared to be an old-fashioned tapestry. "We created this from threads sent in by families across the territory." This, she put into Hawke's arms, pressing her lips to his cheek before turning to do the same to Sienna, the evocative brown of her uptilted eyes shimmering with affection. "You are loved, and you are ours."

Handling the gifts with the care they deserved, Hawke

and Sienna gave them into the gentle keeping of two of the elders who stood with them. A moment later, quiet, often reserved Alexei stepped forward and leaned in to kiss Sienna's cheek, one strong hand cupping her left shoulder. "Welcome." The young lieutenant's hair glinted gold in the colored lights strung across the Pack Circle as he turned to Hawke and began swearing his fealty.

It was an unexpected development, but Hawke responded automatically, slicing his palm with the knife Tomás threw him, so that a single drop of his blood splashed onto Alexei's open hand.

Sienna watched, calm as a mountain lake, but he could feel her tension along the mating bond. He'd forgotten to explain to her—because it had slipped his own mind—that when an alpha mated, or bonded to a permanent partner, his lieutenants had to reaffirm their allegiance. It was a directive meant to protect the pack if an alpha chose a woman the pack couldn't trust or respect—because even the most powerful wolf couldn't rule without the loyalty of his strongest pack-mates. In such a situation, the pack inevitably split, the old alpha leaving with his supporters.

It was a measure of Hawke's bond with his men and women that he hadn't even *thought* of the possibility of that outcome.

Alexei fisted his hand over the drop of blood and stepped back, the moment solemn . . . until he winked at Sienna. Hawke felt her tension ease at once, right before she was picked up off her feet and kissed on the mouth by Matthias, her startled hands flying up to land on the arms of the lieutenant who was built like a tank.

Hawke growled. "Careful."

An unrepentant grin creasing the smooth dark of a face that had beguiled many a woman, Matthias put Sienna on her feet. "He ever chase you down a corridor again, sweetheart, you know who to call."

Sienna held her own. "I think I rather enjoy being caught."

Then Matthias was in front of him, swearing his allegiance. And so it continued until all ten of his lieutenants had completed the task. Each oath was different, because there were no set words for this. It was only the meaning that mattered.

The loyalty. A sigh of happiness rippled around the Pack Circle as Riley closed his hand over the drop of Hawke's blood.

It was done.

His pack had accepted both his mate and his mating. Not simply accepted, he thought when another multiharmonic howl went up, but celebrated. This time, he didn't resist, and drawing Sienna's back against his chest, he threw back his own head to sing, his cut hand fisted tight to still the blood flow. Against him, he could feel his mate's body vibrating with the beauty of the music, the wildfire of her blinding along their bond.

When Tomás grabbed her for a dance, Hawke didn't protest. Possessive though it was, his wolf understood that Sienna belonged to the pack, too, and that they'd lay down their lives for her. It didn't mean she'd have an easy road when it came to making her place in SnowDancer, but tonight, his wolves told her they knew she was the right mate for their alpha, regardless of her age and inexperience. They would stand by her as she grew into her strength.

It was a gift to Hawke's heart.

Chapter 18

RILEY'S SHOULDER NUDGED Hawke's, as in front of them, other couples joined in the dancing and Sienna was passed from Tomás to Kenji. "You do realize you'll have to fight to get near her tonight?"

Hawke glanced at his senior lieutenant to see Riley's eyes lingering on his own mate. Dressed in a graceful azure dress that hit a few inches above the knee and flared out when she spun, shiny black ankle boots on her feet, her red hair pulled off her face by two small combs, Mercy was currently dancing—and laughing—with Drew. She was the only leopard in attendance, because this was a private moment for the pack—and as far as SnowDancer was concerned, Mercy was theirs. No matter how much Lucas might disagree.

Lips curving at the thought, he said, "I promised my mate I'd dance with her from midnight to dawn, and I don't break my promises." He'd be patient until then, his wolf content with keeping an eye on her while she was claimed by Snow-Dancer on the deepest level.

"I'm scared. What I did . . . I'm afraid no one will look at me the same again."

Words she'd spoken after the violence of her ability had devoured the pack's enemies, and in one way, she was right. No one would ever again look at Sienna the same—because now, each and every SnowDancer understood the lethal power that ran in her veins. Yet there was no fear in the air tonight, only the cold-eyed approbation of the predator that lived within their hearts.

Well aware how much the man at his side had done to ensure that, to make certain respect didn't turn to fear, he caught Riley's gaze. "Thank you."

"No need between us. Never has been." A pause, quiet humor in his next words. "I seem to recall you allowing me to beat up on you once upon a time when I was courting Mercy."

"I don't remember you winning."

"You have selective memory."

Wolf and man both laughed, happy to be here in this moment with his friend, his pack, and most of all, with the woman who sent him a secret smile from the far side of the clearing.

ADRIA smiled as she felt muscular arms slip around her waist from behind. "I was wondering where you were," she said, her throat raw with emotion from the haunting simplicity and beauty of the mating ceremony.

Nuzzling at her, Sam kissed her jaw. "Come, dance with me."

She slid into the play of bodies, his hand clasped around her own, and danced until her pulse was a drum, her blood running hot through her veins. Sam did try to steal a kiss, and bubbling with the wild joy of the night, she let him, but pressed her fingers over his lips when he tried again. "No."

Undaunted, he spoke against her fingertips, dimple denting his cheek. "We'd have fun. I have no hang-ups about your dominance if you're worried about that. I'll even let you bite." A rub, nose to nose. "In fact, I'd like it if you did."

Playful and gorgeous and intelligent, he was a lover who'd make her feel good, both physically and in the soul. There was only one problem—her body hummed with a near-painful awareness of another man, a man who aroused far more violent, dark emotions. And who was currently twirling a tiny, curvy woman whose eyes were a golden echo of his, shouting their relationship, his cheeks creased in a true smile.

It infuriated her that she couldn't strangle that unwanted awareness, but she wouldn't use beautiful, sexy Sam in an effort to do so. "I'm not ready." One day, she thought, spine steely with determination, she *would be* ready to gather up her courage and take another chance, having conquered this unhealthy compulsion toward the wrong man. Sam, innocent and never broken, wasn't the right one, her heart too scarred for him, but that didn't mean she didn't cherish him. "I wish I was, because you're rather wonderful."

Stroking his hands down her back, he took the rebuff with good grace. "In that case, be my friend. I like you."

The direct opposite of the knife-edged words Riaz had flung at her, his statement made her miss a step before she cuddled a little closer into him. "I like you, too." She turned her face deliberately away from the part of the Circle where Riaz stood with his arm around his recent dance partner and an older man Adria couldn't see well. Deep inside her, her wolf snarled, but that wolf, too, remembered how brutally it had been rejected.

It didn't fight Adria's decision.

RIAZ'S eyes had locked on Adria the instant he'd spotted her, the strange, unique complexity of her scent in his every breath, though it should've been impossible to pick it up, given the number of people in the Circle. Especially when she was pasted up against Sam, the younger male's lips by her ear as he said something that made her laugh, the sound soft and intimate.

His claws pricked at his palms.

Excusing himself from his parents after handing his mom back to his dad, he hauled Jem into a dance.

"Thanks for asking," she said in an acerbic tone, but slid her arms around his neck. "Stop scowling. Your mother is going to think I'm torturing you."

"Sorry." Forcing himself to keep his attention away from Adria and Sam, he looked down at the blonde lieutenant . . . and had the sudden realization that she didn't fit right in his arms. She was too small, her head reaching midway up his chest.

Jaw clenching at a thought that had its origins in his primal attraction toward a long-legged female whose voice was rough silk across his skin, he said, "Did you dance with Kenji yet?" The two had something going—no one was quite sure what.

"Bite me."

"Temper, temper." He tucked her closer when she narrowed her eyes. "I'll behave, promise."

"Do I look like I have 'sucker' written all over me?" She went rigid a minute later.

Riaz understood why as soon as he saw Kenji appear out of the dancers.

"Can I steal her away?" The challenge in the other man's tone wasn't directed at Riaz.

All but able to touch the electricity in the air, Riaz stepped back, saw Kenji's arm slide around Jem's waist, and thought, *Yeah, they fit.*

"You look beautiful, Garnet," Kenji said in a low tone, using Jem's real name, the purple and gold of his hair sliding forward to shadow his expression as he pulled her stiff body close.

"Kenji—"

"Just a dance."

It was all Riaz heard before he found himself making his way to where Adria leaned against a tree on the other side of the clearing. The shadows of the forest concealed her from the crowd, until it was almost a private alcove . . . but for the vivid tug of her scent.

Crushed berries in ice tangled with a hotter, deeper musk.

He didn't know why he halted only a foot from her, whatever he'd wanted to say wiped from his mind by the jolt that rocked him at the single cool glance she deigned to throw his way. Conscious his eyes had fixated on the pulse in her neck, so delicate and bitable beneath creamy skin kissed with sunshine, he forced his attention back to the dancers.

Hawke's hair changed colors as he danced with Brenna under the multihued bulbs the juveniles had strung through the trees, until the entire area was a wonderland. Several of those juveniles sat in pairs or in small groups in the thick branches, watching the festivities and flirting. A kiss was sneaked here and there, but nobody made any move to leave. Perhaps because they were under notice from the maternals, but more likely because right now, it was about being with Pack.

His hand snapped out to grip Adria's arm almost before he was conscious of her getting ready to move. "Dance with me." It came out harsh, crushed rocks in his throat.

Adria wrenched away her arm, shuddering at the contact. "I don't think that'd be a good idea." Riaz was a drug her body craved—and like all addictive substances, he was not good for her.

"Scared?" Eyes gone night-glow.

"No," she said, her own wolf rising to the fore. "I just happen to have some self-respect."

Stepping out of the shadows, she saw Matthias walking toward her. Her mood shifted immediately. "It's so good to see you."

The big lieutenant lifted her up and kissed her on the lips as he'd done Sienna. "Come dance with me, pretty girl."

Her wolf could feel the dark burn of another male's eyes between her shoulder blades, but she didn't hesitate to accept Matthias's offer. "How is everyone back in your sector?" she asked once they'd begun to sway to the music.

Mathias's chest rumbled as he spoke, his hand moving gently on her back. "Ticking along. We miss you—do you plan to visit?"

"I can't." Not yet. "Maybe in a few more months . . ."

Matthias's jaw brushed her hair. "No pressure, darling."

They danced in warm silence until Adria caught a scent that made her spine lock—right before Matthias said, "I think someone's about to steal you away."

Not wanting to make a scene and mar the celebration, she didn't protest when Matthias stepped back. "Take care of my girl," he warned.

Riaz muttered something pithy in Spanish that made Matthias laugh, but all Adria could hear as he took her into his arms was the frantic beat of her pulse, thudding in time to his own. Too fast, both of them, their skin too hot. "Why are you doing this?" she whispered, her voice stripped bare.

Riaz's answer sounded torn out of him. "I can't stop myself." He shifted her closer, the move so unexpected, she didn't resist—and found herself plastered to the hard strength of him. His arousal pushed into her abdomen, the hot male scent of him seeping into her veins until she could taste the dark forests and biting citrus of him against her tongue.

Breath coming in small pants, she shook her head, but the words she wanted to say wouldn't come, her brain hazed by need, such vicious *need*. When Riaz backed off, only to take her hand and tug her deep into the thick black of the trees, she knew she shouldn't go, but her feet kept moving forward, following him into the concealing shadows. The music continued to play behind them, but here, it was hushed and quiet.

Private.

Shoving her against a tree, he kicked her legs apart and suddenly his mouth was on her own, ravaging and taking and demanding. The civilized, rational part of her brain just stopped working. She gripped at his shoulders, her nails digging into heavy muscle as his tongue licked at her mouth, tangled with her own, the kiss an open, wet, voracious fury of contact.

Their gasped breaths were loud in the silence, their heartbeats thunder, and his hand, when it closed over her breast, a shocking brand. Her cry swallowed by the rough demand of his mouth, she found herself rubbing up against him, trying to rise on tiptoe to create the perfect fit. Her frustration when she couldn't was shattered when his fingers squeezed her nipple through the silky material of her top, rolling and tugging. His hand dropped all too soon . . . to slide under her top and spread on her abdomen, his fingers brushing the waist-band of her sleekly tailored black pants.

His hand had touched her there once before.

A thread of reason broke through the blinding haze of passion, but his mouth was on her own again before it could penetrate, his free hand around her throat, and she was drowning. He was so big and strong, and he wanted her so desperately. It stroked the wolf's battered ego, made her claws prick out and dig into his flesh through the fine black cotton of his shirt.

He hissed out a breath, but it wasn't a sound that told her to stop. Instead, he kissed her harder, his fingers tugging open her fly to cup her possessively over the lace of her panties. Jerking, she felt herself grow even wetter, and from the growl that poured into her mouth, vibrating against her nipples, he felt it, too.

Then his fingers pushed aside the gusset of her panties and the thread of reason became a scream.

"I don't like you."

Shoving him back with every ounce of her strength, she wrenched herself away from the tree. "Oh God, *God.*" Her shaken gaze landed on his passion-fevered face, his cheek-bones slicing against the dusky brown of his skin, his eyes a dangerous, brilliant gold.

Her wolf lunged toward him.

But she was human, too. Reining in the wolf with an iron grip, she somehow managed to do up her pants and tug down her pretty, silky black top hand-painted with a single stunning butterfly on the back. The material was thankfully immune to wrinkles, and her hair, it was still in place—Riaz had been so focused on her mouth . . . and lower.

Her lips felt swollen, but the apparent result of a few stolen kisses would catch no one's attention. As for the fact that she was covered in his scent—she'd just been dancing with him. All that went through her mind in a single split second as her sense of reason, of *self*, reawakened with a violent howl, her entire body quivering from the shock of halting an erotic dance that would've had her pinned against the tree in another couple of minutes, her bare legs wrapped around his waist as he fucked her.

And that, she thought with grim honesty, was all it

would've been. Because whatever the cause of the rage she sensed in his kiss, Riaz, tall and strong and blood-loyal to SnowDancer, wasn't capable of anything else. Not with her. "I'm worth more," she told him, wiping the back of her hand across her mouth. "Affection, respect, tenderness, I'm worth all of that, so don't you dare come near me again until you're ready to offer it."

Chapter 19

RIAZ SHOVED SHAKING hands through his hair as Adria turned and walked away, her hips swaying in unintended provocation beneath the exquisite fit of her pants, the insubstantial silk of her top alternately floating and caressing her body. His hand flexed, the sensory echo of her so warm and responsive a mocking taunt.

Gritting his teeth against the urge to drag her back, he punched his fist into the tree where he'd almost had her. He knew he could find another lover tonight. It wasn't simply that people were in a celebratory mood. As Eli had pointed out earlier, he'd been offered a number of invitations since his return from Europe, and not all of those women wanted anything from him other than a good, hot tussle in bed.

There was just one problem—he didn't want any other woman. He wanted the violet-eyed soldier who had, completely justifiably, told him to fuck off.

HIDDEN in the midnight shadows on the periphery of the large clearing, the Ghost watched the SnowDancers talk and laugh and play. Not ten feet from him, a giggling woman pressed her lover to a tree and suckled a kiss to the base of his neck before darting out of reach and back into the crowd.

Groaning, the obviously disappointed male adjusted his jeans and followed.

The Ghost didn't know why he watched. He'd kept an eye on this region since before the battle with Pure Psy for reasons of his own, had dropped by tonight as part of a routine sweep, and caught the faint sound of music twining through the trees. It had taken him a significant investment of time to find this exact location—he'd never before ventured this deep into the heart of SnowDancer territory, conscious the wolves would go on red alert at the first sign of an intruder.

Now, taking extreme care *not* to touch any surface that'd hold a scent, he came close enough to see, but not be seen. Sienna Lauren's hair, he thought, glimpsing her in the arms of a tall man—not the SnowDancer alpha—had darkened considerably. Her height, however, remained much as it had been at fifteen.

A single scan and he found Judd. Garbed in black, his fellow rebel was standing on the edge of the dance circle, but he wasn't alone. A small blonde woman, a slice of cake on the plate she held in hand, leaned her back against his chest. One of Judd's arms was wrapped with familiar ease around her waist as he spoke to a man the Ghost recognized as a SnowDancer lieutenant.

Kenji Tanaka.

Forking up a bite of cake, the blonde woman twisted and offered it to Judd. He leaned down to accept, the curve of his lips set in an unmistakable smile. The Ghost had only ever seen Judd in another context, and though intellectually he'd understood the former Arrow had a life beyond the rebellion, seeing it in reality made him take a risk, remain longer. For this, too, he could offer no rational reason. This was not a life he would ever have. It may as well have been an alien wilderness.

Yet . . . he continued to watch.

NOT far in front of Sienna, Mercy hauled Riley into a wild kiss. The senior lieutenant's surprise lasted a bare instant before he snapped his hands around the leopard sentinel's waist and dragged her close.

Turning to Hawke, Sienna said, "This is just so . . ." No words seemed enough.

"I think someone's about to steal you from me again."

Opening her mouth to protest that she'd hardly spent any time with him all night, she sensed the psychic energy of the person behind her. Her heart burst with love. "Sorry," she murmured, touching her fingertips to Hawke's jaw. "I'm going to ditch you."

"Remember"—he rubbed his thumb over her lower lip before putting her hand into her new partner's—"the midnight dance is mine."

Always. It was a whisper along the mating bond. Out loud, she said, "Where have you been?" and fixed her brother's hair.

He scowled. To her shock, she realized he'd gained several inches of height when she hadn't been looking. No wonder he looked like a beanpole, if this was how fast he was growing.

"Jeez, Sienna. Don't do that *here.*"

"Oops. Sorry." Sometimes, she forgot he was heading toward thirteen, and then the incipient teenager in him would make an appearance. "You look very handsome."

His smile was shy and sweet, and she had the thought that her empathic baby brother was going to grow up into an incredible man. "Thanks. I went online shopping with Lara." Spinning her around in a slick circle, he grinned at her startlement. "Drew taught me that."

"Why am I not surprised?"

Toby's smile shimmered into a deeper, more poignant expression. "It hurts my heart in the best way that you're so happy."

"Oh, Toby." Always, she had loved the brother she hadn't been permitted to know as a child, but never had she been able to protect him from the psychic price demanded by her gift. "You're the best kid brother a girl could have."

I love you, Sienna. He spun her out again, sending her skirts flying.

When he finally relinquished her, it was to another member of her family. Walker's hold was as calm as Toby's had been exuberant, his pale green eyes intent. "He's your mate,"

Walker said, the warning clear for all that it was made in a tempered voice, "but if he ever does anything to hurt you, you come to me."

"Are all men so bloodthirsty?"

"Lara's father showed me his tools—then we had an illuminating conversation about how easy it would be to cut a person in half using one of the lasers. It was very civilized."

Sienna stifled a laugh at the idea of gentle Mack threatening Walker, and tipping back her head, looked into a face she'd never seen violent either in anger or in love. That meant nothing. She knew Walker would die for her without blinking, that he loved her so fiercely, some part of her had sensed it even in the darkest part of her Silence.

"Thank you," she whispered. "For being my father." In every way that mattered.

Walker's expression altered only the minutest fraction, but she saw the storm of naked emotion crash across the green before he stroked his hand over her hair and kissed her gently on the forehead. "You make me proud each and every day."

Tears stung. Swallowing, she hid her face against the wide chest of the man who had always found a way to tell her that she mattered, that she wasn't just an X but family.

COOPER waited until the dancing had gentled, and he and Riaz were sitting having a couple of quiet beers, before saying, "She's gone."

"What?"

"You're looking for the tall senior soldier with those amazing eyes. Adria, I think." Cooper shifted the upturned wooden crate he was using as a seat, settling it more securely. "She slipped away with Sam a few minutes ago."

Riaz's hand clenched on the bottle. He wanted to deny his raw compulsion toward Adria, but Coop knew him too well, would call him on it. "Enjoying the night?"

"Not even a question." Dark eyes watched him with relentless patience. "You going to talk about it, or do I have to remind you I'm bigger and stronger?"

"In your dreams."

Coop tipped back the bottle he held, his throat muscles

moving. When he lowered it, he shook his head. "Something's wrong with you, man. I should've picked it up earlier, but Grace scrambled my brains."

Riaz looked out at where a lushly curved woman with ebony curls and skin like cream was dancing with Alexei, her smile shy. Big, bad Cooper's mate was a sweet submissive, but she was managing to handle the male lieutenants—all of whom considered it their right to dance with her. "I can see how," Riaz said, having claimed a dance earlier. "She's something else, Coop."

"I know." The other man's expression shifted from brutally tender to hard-ass the instant he returned his attention to Riaz. "Adria, she messing with your head?"

"Fuck, man," Riaz said, finishing off his beer and dangling the bottle between his fingers, "let it go. It's a night to enjoy yourself."

Cooper raised an eyebrow. "Who screwed my head on straight when I was courting Grace? I woke you up at two thirty in the fricking morning *twice* and you didn't tell me to shut the hell up. So talk—or we'll be here all night."

Riaz knew he could stonewall the other lieutenant. He also knew Coop wouldn't stop battering at that wall until it gave. But he refused to taint the happiness of his friend's mating with the bitter taste of his pain. "It's a mess, and it's a mess I might not ever be ready to talk about." He held the near black of the other man's eyes, let him see his resolve. "So I'm asking you to drop it."

A long silence before Coop got up and grabbed them two more beers, moving with a predatory grace that was unusual given his size—and that made him a hunter no one ever heard coming. "You're a stubborn asshole."

"You surprised?"

Snorting, Cooper leaned forward with his forearms braced on his thighs. "Fine. I won't push—for now." Open warning. "I see you going downhill, I will come down on you like a ton of bricks. I will not let you go it alone, lone-wolf style."

"I came home," Riaz growled. "Not exactly lone-wolfing it."

"I call bullshit." Cooper held his gaze, his wolf apparent in the ring of yellow that now encircled his irises. "You fuck-

ing pick up the phone when things get too dark, or I swear to
God, I will tie you up and ship you to my territory."

Riaz's claws slid out. "I'm not a juvenile, so back off."

"No, you're my hardheaded idiot of a friend." He glanced
up. "Grace is coming over, so let me just say this—the pack
needs you whole and stable. Keep that in mind before you let
whatever it is that's messing with your head swallow you up."

SLIDING her fingers around the cup of coffee Inés handed
her, Adria took a seat around the laz-fire one of the other
senior soldiers had set up far enough away from the main
party that no one would stumble upon them by accident. It
was a few minutes after midnight, and not a single Snow-
Dancer was even close to ready for the celebration to end.
Even the pups were trying valiantly to keep their eyes open—
no one had the heart to send them off to bed, so they'd been
snuggled into sleeping bags around the Pack Circle, watched
over by elders who preferred to rest their bones.

"I didn't realize you were doing this," she said to Inés, not
wanting to step on any toes since she hadn't officially been
invited. Sam was the one who'd brought her along.

Inés shook her head. "It wasn't planned. Elias has some
good news to give, decided tonight was the right night for it.
He mentioned it to Simran, who mentioned it to me, I mentioned it to Sam, told him to grab you—"

"And presto." Adria grinned. This kind of thing had happened in Matthias's sector, too, different parts of the pack
breaking off to have their own informal gatherings during
the course of a larger event. "Good idea to ask everyone to
bring along some food from the Circle."

Several purloined plates of cookies, cakes, and sandwiches, along with a bowl of corn chips with a side of gua-
camole, were being passed around, as was the thermos of
coffee. Someone had also brought in beers and champagne
for those who had already finished their assigned shifts on
watch. Adria had one coming up, so she'd stick to coffee.

"That was Eli," Inés said, stretching out her legs as they
sat side by side on a fallen log. "He thinks of everything."

"And the good news?" Adria asked.

Inés had just opened her mouth to reply when Sam, who'd gone to grab a sandwich, reappeared at Adria's side without food, a concerned look on his face. "Inés, am I crashing a party for the senior soldiers?"

"Would it worry you if you were?" A dry response.

"I thought you might have a secret ritual you were about to do or something."

"Like dance naked around the fire?" Inés raised an eyebrow. "I bet."

Dimple flashing, Sam leaned his back against the log, one arm hooked companionably over Adria's knee. "Fine, I'm staying until someone kicks me out."

Now that he'd pointed it out, Adria realized Sam was the only soldier of lower rank here. And since Inés had specifically invited him . . . *Hmm.* She glanced at the other woman in silent question. Inés winked. Adria bit back a smile, the contentment inside her nothing she'd expected to feel after that brutal encounter with Riaz.

Her hand tightened on the coffee cup, her skin tingling from the heat. *No*, she said silently when her mind tried to claw her back to a carnal madness that had come perilously close to stripping her of her self-respect. Taking a deep breath, she narrowed her attention to the gentle warmth inside of her, and to the people responsible for her emotional equilibrium.

These were her peers, the packmates she'd be working most closely with over the coming months and years, and though they were relative strangers yet, she liked their energy as a group. Temperate and stable for the most part, senior soldiers were the workhorses of the pack, people you could count on to get a task done.

Inés, she thought, had the potential to become a close friend—the fleet-of-foot woman had a snarky sense of humor that made Adria's own wolf chuckle.

Right on the heels of that thought, Inés said, "Me and Simran"—she nodded at where the more reticent soldier sat talking to Brody about something—"have a bad movie night once a month. You should come."

Her wolf stretched out, back bowed. "Thanks."

"Am I invited to this movie night," Sam interrupted to say, "or were you planning to ignore me sitting *right here*?"

"The ignore one," Inés answered, quick as a shot.

"My heart is broken."

"I bleed for you."

"Cruel."

"It wasn't my best effort."

Elias stood and clapped his hands, cutting off the pithy dialogue. Once he had everyone's attention, he said, "It's time for the secret ceremony," with a straight face.

Chapter 20

SAM SNICKERED . . . AND sobered when he realized everyone was staring at him, not a giggle to be heard. "Um, sorry."

Adria was trying so hard not to burst out laughing, she had to fake a coughing fit. Several people seemed to have been struck with the same affliction—though Inés managed to keep it together, slapping Adria helpfully on the back. "Must be the pollen in the air," she murmured in faux concern.

Adria would've kicked the other woman if Sam hadn't been sitting in front of her.

"As I was saying," Elias continued, a rare strand of silver glinting in the rich brown of his hair, "it's time for the ceremony. But since we appear to have an intruder, we'll have to deal with him first."

Sam rose to his feet, dusting off his jeans. "Look, hey, I can book if you guys—"

Elias raised a hand for silence, moving to stand in front of Sam.

"Sam Baker," he said, his face solemn, "according to those witnesses who weren't unconscious at the time, you ran onto the field of battle time and time again to rescue injured pack-mates, though you'd been hit with a bullet yourself."

"It was what any one of us would've done." Sam's words were quiet, the playful soldier replaced by the courageous man who'd fought with all his heart, even when surrounded by blood and agony and an enemy devoid of mercy.

"Yes," Elias said, reaching out to pin something on Sam's stone gray shirt, "and we're proud to call you one of our own."

Adria saw the instant it hit Sam. His fingers trembled as he touched the regal form of the small silver wolf on his shirt collar. None of the senior soldiers wore the pins in daily life, but each one did so tonight—her top too light to hold it, Adria had attached hers to a thin silver bracelet on her left wrist. That tiny badge was a source of enormous pride, not being simply an indication of promotion from soldier to senior, but of acceptance within the rank.

Slapping a still-stunned Sam on the back, Elias raised his glass, "To Sam!"

"To Sam!" Adria cried with the rest of the group, and right then, she knew she'd make it. Maybe her unhealthy and unten-able attraction to Riaz showed no signs of abating, the clawing need tearing at her gut, but she was more than the primal urges of her body. She was part of this strong, loyal group, a woman who had built a new life, new friendships from the cold ashes of the old.

No man was ever again going to drive her to question her own worth.

Her wolf's body thrummed with defiant, determined pride. And when the newest senior soldier in the den threw back his head and celebrated with wild abandon, she lent her voice to his song alongside those of her packmates.

THE bristles on Hawke's jaw caught on Sienna's hair. She'd watched him shave before the ceremony, but it was now on the edge of dawn and they were finally in bed, his arm holding her to his chest. Enjoying the intimacy of talking with him as much as she'd enjoyed dancing in his arms until the sky shimmered with the first pearly kiss of morning, she glanced up when he shifted to fold one of his arms behind his head.

Eyes of wolf blue met her own. "Your friends snuck off to do some mischief." An alpha's amusement. "I expected you to join them since you're the head troublemaker."

"I warned them they'd be on their own tonight . . . last night now." The friends she'd made were friends she intended to keep for life—but the night had been hers and Hawke's. "I waited so long for this moment," she whispered, touching her fingers to his jaw, the stubble rough against her fingertips. "Sometimes, I think I'm dreaming, and I'm so scared I'll wake up."

Hawke didn't try to talk away her fears—he understood the life she'd lived, this wolf who had never known the PsyNet, and yet who *knew* her. He understood that some nightmares couldn't be overcome by logic or reason. Only time had that power. Her fear of losing him, as she'd lost her kind, gifted mother, as she'd lost her brother and the rest of her family for so long, was a darkling thought that had made her gasp awake more than once, her heart pounding as if she'd been racing desperately toward him.

Then she'd feel her wolf strong and warm beside her, or open her psychic eye to the wild silver-blue and flame-hued passion of their bond, and the terror would abate. One day, she thought, it would no longer return, but until then, her wolf would walk beside her into the darklands. "I wanted my mother at our ceremony," she confessed, eyes burning.

Indigo and Tarah had done their best, been there for her every step of the way, but it wasn't the same. "I don't even have anything of hers to hold on to." It had all been destroyed after her mother's suicide, while Sienna had been trapped in a psychic prison with a monster named Ming LeBon.

"This beautiful hair," Hawke said, his chest rumbling under her palm. "Judd once told me it reminded him of his sister." He played his fingers along the strands. "*You* are a piece of her, you and Toby."

"That's nice," she said, hiding the wonderful thought away in the secret place inside her mind where she'd kept everything that mattered to her for so long.

Judd, having learned the skill from Walker, had shown

her how to build the impregnable telepathic vault when he'd grown old and experienced enough to teleport to her without alerting Ming. Though she no longer needed the vault, she liked having her most precious memories in one place.

"Toby has her hair, too," she said. "He doesn't otherwise look like her"—as he grew, her brother's features had begun to lean more toward the harder angles of Walker's face—"but sometimes I see her in his smile."

"That's a gift."

"Yes." Stroking his chest, she said, "You missed your parents, too, didn't you?"

"My father would've been so proud to see how the pack reacted to us," he said in answer, a poignant smile on his lips, "and my mother, she'd have been sitting in a corner, sketching as fast as her hand could move."

Images formed in Sienna's mind, created from the photos Hawke had shared with her. Of a tall man with golden hair, eyes of blue a shade darker than his son's, and a white-blonde woman, her bones fine, her skin porcelain. The snapshots of his mother, Aren, were lit with laughter, while her mate, Tristan, had been more guarded, his gaze piercing . . . except in the few precious photos Hawke had of the two of them together. There, it was clear who held Tristan's heart, nothing guarded or remote about the intensity of his love.

"Psy don't give credence to the idea of an afterlife," she said, trailing her fingers over the hard ridges of his abdomen, "but I'd like to believe that last night, all the people we miss were there dancing alongside us."

Hawke's hand stroked under her hair to settle on her nape. "Yes."

They were quiet for a long time, happy to simply be together. Breathing in the hot, wild scent that was Hawke, she felt a sense of wonder bloom deep within.

"What's got you smiling?" her mate asked in a slumberous voice, though she lay with her cheek on his chest, her face hidden from view.

"No one who saw us interacting before we mated," she said, pushing up so she could look down into curious wolf eyes, her hair pooling on his chest, "would ever believe we could be so peaceful together." She'd been half afraid they *would* clash the entire time, because that was all they'd done for years. What she hadn't understood until afterward was that the passionate need she and Hawke had fought for so long would become a molten river. Connecting them. Making them whole.

Even in this peace, the embers glowed. Always would.

Hawke chuckled. "*I* would've recommended a good shrink if someone had suggested it to me six months ago."

Laughing, she braced herself on one arm and began to play with his hair, petting him until his eyes closed. He was still awake, his fingers brushing lightly against her back, but he was a lazy wolf now, contented and sleepy. Yawning, she snuggled down against his body and let the rhythm of his heartbeat lull her into a sleep devoid of fear . . . and filled with dreams of an alpha wolf who ran beside her as she explored the mysteries of a night-dark forest.

RIAZ watched the cold dawn from his position seated against a large ponderosa pine on the edge of a mountain lake rippling with gossamer whispers of wind. The mating celebration had finally wound down about forty-five minutes ago, every one of the lieutenants remaining till the very end.

The out-of-towners had slipped away as stealthily as they'd arrived, while those who called den territory home had broken off to head to bed, or to otherwise relax after the night's festivities. The most interesting departure had been Jem and Kenji's—they'd left together, and Kenji had a bruise on his cheek he refused to explain.

It had been instinct for Riaz to come up into the mountains. Man and wolf, they were both used to aloneness, often needed solitude, especially after a social event, but over the past minutes, he'd realized this aloneness was of a different kind.

It hurt.

A dull, throbbing ache, the pain was centered in the place where the mating bond should've been, as if he had an open wound deep inside him. The joy and warmth of his packmates had muted the ache over the night, but surrounded by nothing but the chill air of the Sierras, the sky a crimson-orange cauldron, he could no longer avoid the truth. He'd come home to heal . . . but the wound, it bled darkest red.

The echo of a male voice.

Catching the unexpected sound on the wind, he looked across the lake to glimpse a small, sleek wolf padding beside a tall male dressed in black. The wolf's body brushed the man's as they walked along the misty earth, the man's fingers trailing through the animal's fur when he bent as if to speak to her.

Riaz's hand fisted, a corrosive bitterness flooding his senses.

The ugliness of it was a cold slap.

Breathless, chest pounding in shock, he looked up in time to see Brenna and Judd disappear into the mist. However, his mind was no longer on the other couple, but on the staggering insight into who he was becoming, who he was *allowing* himself to become: a bitter, angry man filled with the acid of envy.

That wasn't who he wanted to be, wasn't who he'd ever been. Just like he hadn't ever been a man who liked to hurt women on any level.

An image of Adria's stunning eyes, the icy whip of her anger, the sway of her hips as she walked away from him.

God, he'd been a shit to her. Shame was leaden in his gut. Nothing excused the way he'd treated her, the way he'd tried to use her. Adria was right. She deserved more than a man who had permitted his anger at fate to eat away at him until he almost didn't recognize who he was anymore. His wolf, always so proud, lowered its head, its tail limp, but both parts of him knew this silent penance wasn't enough. The man he wanted to be, the man he'd been before Lisette, blamed no one else for his own faults and faced up to his mistakes.

The sun touched him with golden fingers but did nothing to ease the ice in his soul.

Chapter 21

MING EXAMINED THE satellite images captured when Sienna Lauren had allowed her cold fire to feed. Though taken in the night-darkness of the battle, there was no absence of light, the red and yellow of the deadly fire an inferno.

Setting those images aside, he looked at the ones taken directly after the battle. The carnage was absolute, the forest a wasteland. No sign remained of the Pure Psy army.

An incredible weapon.

One Ming had been certain he wanted destroyed if she *had* survived, because she could not be controlled. Except . . . His eye went to the small steel box on his desk. It held within it a single chip, the last remaining prototype from Ashaya Aleine's aborted project to instigate Silence on a biological level.

That chip could also be utilized as a leash.

The problem with using it in such a fashion had always been twofold. One, the chip was unstable. Two, Ming would need to have a controller chip implanted to interface with Sienna's, and even had he considered the risk acceptable, this was the single surviving chip of which he had personal knowledge. He'd had it excised from one of the victims the Scotts had implanted, after the male's suicide. Neither Henry nor Shoshanna had ever realized he knew of their unauthorized experimentation. Ming's scientists hadn't been able to reverse engineer the chip; however, one had just informed him that there was a very slight chance it could be altered to allow control via a remote device.

"Do it," he said into the intercom.

If the device worked, he would own an X. If it failed, Sienna Lauren would die in an implosion of brain cells.

A perfect solution.

Chapter 22

HAVING HAD A message that the senior lieutenant wanted to see her, Adria knocked on the door to Riley's office three days after the mating ceremony, found herself being waved in though he held a phone to his ear. "Grab a seat," he said. "This'll only take a sec."

As she waited, she took in his office. It was—and wasn't—what she would've expected. Ordered and clean, it was free of clutter. That fit the lieutenant's rock-solid, calm nature. What didn't fit was the framed poster behind his desk—of the kaleidoscope of color, flesh, feathers, sequins, and more that was Rio de Janeiro's Carnaval.

Or perhaps it did fit, she thought with an inward smile. After all, pragmatic, sensible Riley had crossed dangerous pack lines to claim a leopard sentinel as his mate. No one, she reminded herself, was one-dimensional . . . not even the angry man who'd had his hands so hot and rough on her skin. "Have you been?" she asked Riley when he hung up the phone, shoving the raw memories away before they could derail her all over again.

Following her gaze to the poster, he nodded. "Survived it, too." A smile that had a story behind it. "How was the outer-perimeter shift? You got back this morning?"

"Yes, it was good. Peaceful." She'd left the afternoon after the mating ceremony, taking over from one of the leopards. "I'm happy to do extra shifts up there."

Instead of accepting the offer, Riley leaned back in his chair, dark eyes intent. "You're a highly experienced senior soldier, Adria—running patrol will frustrate you if you don't have other outlets for your skill. Matthias tells me you were in charge of training the novices in his region."

It had been incredibly hard to walk away from "her" kids, but she'd been worried her emotional troubles would spill over into her teaching. So she'd trained up a replacement and made sure her novices were comfortable with the other soldier before she left. Things had changed in the interim, and she missed working with their young, but would not do so at the expense of another packmate, especially one she loved.

"Indigo's brilliant at what she does." Though she tried to keep her tone even, her wolf bristled.

"No argument," Riley said at once. "I have something else in mind for you." He waited, as if giving her the opportunity to interrupt. When she didn't, he continued. "According to Matthias, you're very good with the submissives. Which doesn't surprise me, given the true status of your rank."

Of course Riley would know. "A trainer working with submissives," she said with a smile, "has to realize that while they're never going to be soldiers, they have unique strengths of their own." The most vulnerable in the hierarchy didn't respond well to the necessarily ruthless teaching style utilized to train the dominants.

Riley gave a small nod. "I'd like you to take over the self-defense training of twenty-five submissive kids, ages fourteen to eighteen. They've had the normal course, but Hawke wants them to get as much advanced training as they're able to handle."

"The continuing hostilities," Adria said, knowing the alpha had to be thinking about a situation where the dominants were killed in large numbers. A hard thing to contemplate, but it had to be done.

"You should talk to Walker." Riley passed across a datapad loaded with a list of names and photos. "Your group's skewed toward the younger age group. He gave most of those kids their basic training. The older ones, Eli handled."

"I'll touch base with them both." Adria knew how important it was that the three of them work as a unit. "Who's training the maternal kids?" A second later, she clicked her fingers, her wolf nudging at her. "I bet you it's Drew."

Riley laughed. "My brother knows how to walk that fine line between making sure they never forget he's more dominant, and not pissing them off. He's got forty in his group, been working with them for months."

Adria whistled. "Those are big numbers."

"Turns out we had more than the usual number of births fourteen to eighteen years ago. A statistically significant percentage of those pups are turning out to be dominants—soldier and maternal, but it's affected every level of the hierarchy."

Adria's wolf lifted its muzzle in a silent, mournful howl as understanding whispered through her veins. Changelings were the least fertile of the three races, but it had been observed over and over that when a pack lost a brutal number of its own within a short time frame, birth rates spiked in the years following. And SnowDancer had suffered heartbreaking losses two decades ago.

Riley had the same solemn knowledge in his eyes when he said, "Questions?"

"Anything I need to know about the kids that might not be immediately apparent?"

"Walker's probably the best person to answer that," Riley said, picking up his phone. "I'll see if he's available."

Walker wasn't in the den, but they were able to catch him on his cell. "Call me at any stage," he said after they'd finished going through the list, his insight into the pups she'd be taking on displaying a sensitivity to the needs of the young that resonated deeply with her. "They know they can come to me no matter what, and might do so until they begin to trust you— I'll let you know if any issues crop up."

"Thanks."

Ending the call soon afterward, Riley said, "Half your group's on a field trip, but they'll be back by seven. Unless you have another commitment, we'll meet at eight."

"Eight works. See you then." She headed out of the office, deciding to use her free time to further explore the territory as Hawke had requested.

She'd only been walking for a minute when she saw the most amazing sight.

Two small leopard cubs scrabbled around the corner, obviously racing each other . . . to come to a dead stop, claws scraping on stone, when they saw her. Two heads lifted. Two pairs of beautiful green-gold eyes held her own.

Glancing around, Adria saw the corridor was otherwise deserted. "I don't think," she whispered, crouching down to run her hand over the fur of the one closest to her, "you're supposed to be here." DarkRiver and SnowDancer were blood-allies, but leaving a child to roam the den alone was a huge step beyond that. So either these two adorable troublemakers—both of whom were now demanding to be petted—had escaped their frantic mother, or they'd somehow snuck in. Adria would've said they were too small to navigate the distance from DarkRiver land, but she'd known too many children.

The sound of more claws against stone, right before a tiny wolf pup attacked the cubs from behind. Stunned, she was about to pull them apart when she realized the growling and snarling and clawing was all for show. She rose to her feet, her wolf too amused to think about spoiling their fun.

"That's a sight."

The hairs on her nape rose at the low, deep timbre of that male voice, but she didn't startle, having scented the exotic dark pine and biting edge of citrus that was Riaz's scent. "Yes," she said, proud of herself for keeping her cool.

Another scent. Unfamiliar. Feminine.

The cubs and pup jumped apart as if they'd been doused with cold water, and suddenly, they were sitting quiet and lovable, three of the most well-behaved little ones Adria had ever seen. "Little fakers," she said, attempting to hide her laugh.

Beside her, Riaz coughed just as a tall brunette turned the corner.

"What," the woman said to the cubs, "did we discuss before we left home?" Folding her arms, she tapped an impatient tattoo on the floor with her booted foot.

The wolf pup barked.

"Hush, Ben. These two were supposed to wait for me to finish talking with Lara."

Dropping their heads, the cubs made piteous mewling sounds. Adria caught the amusement in the eyes of the woman who had to be their mother, but her voice, when it came, was stern. "You have a choice of punishments: either no playtime with Ben and the other pups, or no chocolate cake for dessert tonight."

All three children looked at the woman in unmitigated shock.

Who didn't budge.

The leopard cubs nodded at their friend—who was apparently more attractive than chocolate cake. Bending down, the brunette grabbed and kissed each sweet face in turn, including Ben's. "Now go wait for me over there"—she waved to a spot a couple of meters down the corridor, where they'd remain in her line of sight—"unless you want playtime permanently canceled."

Only when the boys had padded away to take meek seated positions, did the woman rise and meet Adria's and Riaz's gazes. "They give me three new gray hairs hourly." Exasperated affection.

"Tamsyn," Riaz said, the heat of his body too close, too aggressive, "this is Adria."

Adria forced herself to think past her gut-clawing awareness of the male next to her. "The DarkRiver healer." All senior personnel had been briefed about DarkRiver long ago.

"If you say you're not related to Indigo," Tamsyn said in response, "I'll eat my boot . . . if the twins haven't already."

Laughing at the dry codicil, Adria admitted to the familial relationship. "Social visit?"

"Ashaya's here, too," Tamsyn said, referring to the M-Psy mated to a DarkRiver sentinel. "We want to discuss Alice, go over some new scans."

"Alice" was Alice Eldridge, a human scientist who had been put into cryonic suspension over a hundred years ago and now slept in a coma no one could break. Adria couldn't imagine what Alice's life would be like if she did wake—the world had shifted dramatically since the beginning of her forced sleep. Her friends, her family, each and every one was dust. And yet Alice endured.

"I better get back and organize an escort for the hooligans," Tammy said, looking over her shoulder at the children with an affectionate smile. "It was nice to meet you, Adria."

The silence that fell after Tamsyn and the boys left was awkward. However, when Adria would have continued on her way, Riaz shifted to block her. Lines of strain marked his face, a heavy shadow over the beaten gold of his eyes, but his words were unexpectedly generous. "I have some time free— why don't I show you some of the more hidden parts of den territory?"

Unsettled, Adria glanced up, found herself unable to read his expression. She'd spent far too much time with another man whose face she couldn't read, so she was blunt in her disbelief. "What possible reason could you have for inviting me to spend time with you when we both know how you feel about me?"

Riaz had expected the claws, his wolf taking the hit without flinching. "Because," he said, carrying through the decision he'd made that cold, lonely dawn after Hawke and Sienna's mating ceremony, "it's not your fault you're not my mate." It felt as if he'd stripped off his skin with the admission, but he owed Adria the truth. "And I'm sorry I punished you for that."

Adria had frozen after his first sentence, horror dawning black and violent over her clean, beautiful features. "You found your mate? How could you kiss me?"

He didn't want to talk about it, wanted to pretend he'd never set sight on Lisette, but the time for hiding behind anger and an obstinate refusal to admit the truth was over. "She's married." In love with another man. Coop was right—he could allow that to destroy him, or he could rebuild a new life from the broken shards of the old.

He was a wolf, a dominant, a protector. To give up and leave his pack without his strength was simply not in his nature. So he'd find a way to survive, and to once again become a man he could face in the mirror with pride.

In front of him, Adria's eyes turned the pale, haunting amber of her wolf in painful sympathy. His jaw set. He didn't want pity, had told her only because she'd borne the brunt of his rage when she'd never been at fault. But there was no hint of pity in her response, simply a warm generosity of spirit that rocked him. "If your wolf isn't troubled by my presence," she said, "then I'd appreciate your help."

Troubled?

Riaz swallowed a harsh laugh. "We'll drive out of the

section you already know well," he said, determined to treat her with the courtesy he should've shown her from the start, regardless of the touch-hunger that continued to claw at him, "and explore a less accessible part of the remaining area on foot."

Adria stayed silent until they'd driven for at least ten minutes, but it was a silence heavy with things unsaid. When she did speak, he flinched.

"Did you . . . have a chance?"

His hands flexed on the wheel. "She loves her husband. I just found her too late." He regretted saying as much as he had as soon as he'd spoken, his wolf uncomfortable with the sudden, stark vulnerability. "Indigo knows the bare facts"— and he wished she didn't—"but no one else does, so if you could—"

"I won't say a word," she promised in that slightly husky voice that was an unintended provocation. "You can talk to me about it, you know." A hesitation. "It can't be good for you to hold everything inside."

Shifting the vehicle into hover mode, he took them over a rocky patch. "There's not much to talk about." He wasn't being obdurate—what else was there to say? Lisette belonged to another man, and Riaz had to figure out a way to live with that.

"No, I suppose there isn't." Not speaking again till they stepped out of the vehicle in a relatively isolated section of den territory, she said, "Let's stay in human form. It'll be easier to talk."

He nodded—a few sections would be tricky to navigate on two feet, but they could always reconsider shifting at that stage.

As they walked, he saw Adria take in everything with those stunning eyes of blue-violet. It was the first time he'd *really* looked at her, not blinded by the caustic mix of anger and desire that had colored their earlier interactions. There was a steely strength to her gaze—as if she'd been tempered in pain and come out of it harder, less breakable.

His fascination with her shifted a fraction, became more subtle, more complex . . . more disturbing, as he realized he wanted to know of the crucible that had honed her. "There's something you should see here," he said, caught between the competing needs of a fidelity that would destroy him, and a silken betrayal that might tear him apart.

Chapter 23

"DO YOU SEE your parents often?" he asked almost two hours later, unable to resist the urge to solve the mystery of her.

A pregnant pause filled only with the sound of the wind rustling through the trees. "Not as much as I should."

Reading the tension in the line of her spine, he knew she wanted him to drop it, but regardless of all else, he'd never been a man who took orders when he didn't want to take them. "Odd for a wolf."

No response as they walked through the spring green meadow. Just when he was beginning to believe she'd simply ignore the question, she said, "I was in a relationship. It made my parents unhappy." Plain words that told him nothing.

"Did they make you choose?"

"No, but we ended up arguing about it every time I went to see Mom and Dad." She blew out a breath. "Tarah, Indigo, neither of them approved, but they let me be for the most part."

Riaz wondered what the hell had been wrong with the male Adria had chosen that her entire family hadn't liked the guy. However, the shuttered expression on her face told him the discussion was over; he could push, but this time, he decided for patience. Dominant female wolves didn't react well to pressure beyond a certain point.

As she walked ahead a few steps, his eyes lingered on the soft skin exposed at her nape, beneath the silken rope of her braid. The golden warmth of it glowed in the harsh mountain sunlight, and he wanted only to push that braid aside and run his fingers over the spot.

Adria jerked out and to the side, her hair brushing the back of his hand.

And he realized his fingers had done exactly as he'd imagined. "Shit, I'm sorry."

Brilliant blue-violet eyes streaked with precious gold watched him with too much knowledge. "You need to do something about your hunger, Riaz."

The idea of being with any woman but Lisette made his entire body revolt, but even then, the scent of Adria, the remembered feel of her, it was a drug, an addiction that gripped him in powerful teeth and shook. "Can you get back on your own?" The words were harsh, his wolf too close to the surface.

Adria gave a simple, "Yes," before turning and walking away from him a second time, a tall, strong woman with hair as dark as onyx and a pride that he knew would never again allow her to invite him into her bed.

ADRIA bent over with a shudder, hands on her knees, after Riaz disappeared in the opposite direction. Her body felt as if it wanted to burst out of her skin, torn by a chaos of competing needs and desires. When Riaz had touched her, she'd almost melted into the rough heat of his fingers in spite of her every vow to the contrary, her body already conditioned to expect primal pleasure.

Inhaling another shaky breath, she took a detour on her way down to the den, following an overgrown path that, if memory served her right, led to a small hidden waterfall. She'd found it as a young girl, and it had become her secret place, where she came to think over important decisions or to indulge in frustration and temper.

A smile tugged her lips. God, she'd been such a serious, temperamental child. As she'd grown, that wildness of emotion had matured into a quiet intensity of passion, restrained and tempered.

"You're magnificent and I can't wait to learn all of you."

Words Martin had spoken to her during their first year as a couple.

Her smile faded, into a sadness so deep, it lodged in her chest, a heavy lump. Even the sight of "her" waterfall, small and secretive and effervescent, didn't lift her spirits. Her mind was with the woman she'd been, so very ready to start what she'd thought would be the next phase of her life, with a man she'd believed would walk beside her as they both changed and grew. And for the first time since she'd made the decision to end their broken relationship, her anger was washed away by grief.

The Martin she'd known hadn't been the standoffish man he so often was with strangers, a man secretly uncomfortable in social situations. He'd been so sweet in private, with a wicked sense of humor and a way of looking at her as if she were the most alluring woman in the world. Not only that, but he'd celebrated her achievements as she'd celebrated his.

She'd taken him to dinner in a posh restaurant when he was awarded his doctorate, and stranger to the kitchen though he had been, he'd once put on an apron and baked her a cake when she'd completed a particularly grueling training course. It had collapsed in the middle and been uncooked around the sides and it had been wonderful. They'd giggled and gotten drunk on cheap pink champagne, eating so much cake that they'd solemnly sworn, "Never, ever again."

That was what she'd tried to save for so long, unable and unwilling to believe that something so innocent and bright could sour into such hostility. She'd thought if she tried hard enough, she'd be able to fix it. It was how her brain worked—even as a child who had found martial arts didn't suit her blunt style of movement, but who knew the skill would come in useful as a soldier, she'd just gritted her teeth and practiced over and over until her body moved with flawless grace.

Only after she'd been broken on the ruins of their relationship had she understood that no matter how hard she tried, it wouldn't have mattered. Because somewhere along the way, a poison had infiltrated their relationship. Quiet and stealthy, it had eaten into the fabric of emotion that bound them until that fabric was threadbare . . . and her wolf had withdrawn totally from the relationship.

Martin had known. It had only deepened his resentment.

Moisture on her cheek, a trail leading down to her mouth. *Salt.* It was the taste of the first tear she'd shed since shutting the door in Martin's face over a year ago, knowing she'd never again open it. So fragile, the single iridescent droplet nonetheless shattered her defenses. Dropping to her knees, she allowed the sorrow to pour out of her, her shoulders shaking with the force of her sobs.

RIAZ caught Adria's scent as he ran, and snarled, frustrated that her phantom presence continued to haunt him. When it grew stronger instead of fading, he realized she hadn't returned to the vehicle, but had instead continued on foot. He would've carried on, except that he caught the barest whisper of a sound that made his wolf snap to attention. Frowning, he moved close enough to ensure that she wasn't in trouble . . . and heard the raw, painful sound of a woman whose heart was breaking.

His chest knotted, protective instincts roaring to the surface, but he didn't approach. Adria was a proud, strong woman, wouldn't appreciate anyone finding her at such a vulnerable moment, her defenses shattered. But even as he told himself to leave, the ragged sound of her tears ripped him apart.

She jerked up her head the instant he came into view, her face ravaged by tears. "Go!"

Wanting to hunt down whatever had so devastated her, but aware it wasn't a physical foe he could defeat, he went down on his haunches and took her into his arms. She began to struggle, all sharp elbows and tightly fisted hands. "Let me help, damn you." It wasn't the smoothest or most charming of things to say, but it came from the gut and the heart, his voice rough with the wolf's frustration at being unable to *do* anything.

Another heartrending sob, and then she was melted wax in his arms, as if she couldn't deal with the agonizing depth of her pain and hold him off at the same time. Cuddling her as close as he could, his knees spread to tuck her in between, he cupped the back of her head with one hand, wrapped an arm around her waist . . . and simply held her as she cried.

He'd seen strong women cry before, but never like this. Until it felt as if she were being torn apart from the inside out. Hand clenched in her hair, tangling in her braid, he pressed his cheek to the inky black and let her fingernails dig into his back as she wrapped her arms around him in a fierce embrace.

A minute, a lifetime, later, those hands turned into fists again, and she punched at him. The blows had no impact because of her position, but the agony in them was excruciating. His wolf raged at its helplessness, but even then, it pressed against Riaz's skin, wanting to soothe, to reassure. But all they could do was hold her, the scent of crushed berries in ice drowning in salt.

The wind was quiet, the sun lower in the sky when she went silent, lying against him in a way that said all the fight had been taken out of her. He'd known her a fragment of time, but he hated seeing her so defeated. Adria was pride and spirit and strength. Not a woman who gave up. "Did you lose someone?" Death was the only thing he could think of to explain the depth of her despair.

"It's been long dead." Rasped out words. "I just wasn't ready to mourn until now."

He rubbed his cheek against her hair, one wolf attempting to comfort another. "Do you feel better?"

"I feel like I got run over." And that quickly, she was Adria again.

Shoving away and to her feet, she walked to the pool at the bottom of a tiny waterfall he could just make out, cupping her hands in the cold water and using it to splash her face. At any other time, with any other woman, he would've waited, but he could tell from the stiff curve of her spine that she hated the fact he'd seen her like this, so he turned and walked away.

His wolf snarled but didn't resist. Because it, too, understood that Adria was no helpless maiden in distress. Riaz had seen her fight beside him with unwavering courage, witnessed her steely-eyed determination as she crawled into the line of fire to drag an injured packmate out of the danger zone, trusted her to watch his back when the enemy threatened to surround them.

A woman like that would not want any man—much less one with whom she had only the most fragile of cease-fires—to see her defenseless and fractured by grief. He wondered if this would create another barrier between them, as she sought to distance herself from the memory. The idea pricked at his insides, a sharp, unexpected discomfort.

ALICE

FROM: Sascha<sascha@darkriver.net>
TO: Lara<lara@snowdancer.org>
CC: Tammy<tamsyn@darkriver.net>;
Ashaya<ashaya@darkriver.net>;
Amara<amara@sierratech.com>
DATE: Sep 3, 2081 at 11.14 a.m.
SUBJECT: Patient A

Lara—I spoke to Tammy and Ashaya, got the latest update on our patient. Though my last attempt didn't work, I've been going through my book (yes, *again*), and reading between the lines, it seems I have a distinct empathic skill that may help our patient.

I can't prove it, as there's no way to test the theory except on someone in her condition, but if you don't think it'll interfere with anything else we're attempting, I'd like to try it.

FROM: Ashaya<ashaya@darkriver.net>
TO: Sascha<sascha@darkriver.net>
CC: Tammy<tamsyn@darkriver.net>;
Lara<lara@snowdancer.org>;
Amara<amara@sierratech.com>
DATE: Sep 3, 2081 at 11.17 a.m.
SUBJECT: re: Patient A

As you all know, earlier today, Lara injected Patient A with a chemical agent Amara and I suggested. It *may* lead to a rise in the patient's level of consciousness. I think it's reasonable to assume that will only make her more receptive to Sascha's empathy. I can't see any harm in it, in any case. Amara agrees.

FROM: Lara<lara@snowdancer.org>
TO: Sascha<sascha@darkriver.net>
CC: Tammy<tamsyn@darkriver.net>;
Ashaya<ashaya@darkriver.net>;
Amara<amara@sierratech.com>
DATE: Sep 3, 2081 at 11.58 a.m.
SUBJECT: re: re: Patient A

I'm open to anything that might help her. Sascha—I'll give you a call and we'll arrange a time for you to drive up. It might be better to wait till we can see if Ashaya and Amara's formula is having any effect.

One of the senior techs has been in this week and recalibrated the equipment we're using to monitor the patient, so we'll see even the slightest blip of consciousness.

FROM: Tammy<tamsyn@darkriver.net>
TO: Lara<lara@snowdancer.org>
DATE: Sep 3, 2081 at 2.02 p.m.
SUBJECT: Life

I didn't get a chance to talk to you about this while I was at the den, but I hope you're not letting the situation with Patient A consume you, Lara. I know how hard it is not to get emotionally invested—most of the time pack healers have no choice—but we both know that's not healthy, especially with this patient, given her prognosis.

I'm worried about you. Call me.

FROM: Lara<lara@snowdancer.org>
TO: Tammy<tamsyn@darkriver.net>
DATE: Sep 3, 2081 at 3.15 p.m.
SUBJECT: re: Life

I just tried to call, but your phone went to voice mail. I think you must be at the boys' hockey practice. (Lord, how adorable do they look in those miniature uniforms?! I don't know how you bear it.)

I'm okay, really. Walker and the kids keep me grounded, and Walker's so protective, he literally carries me out of the infirmary if I'm being stubborn about resting. I'm not joking—he threw me over his shoulder the other night! Said I'd already gotten my warning.

I have to admit I might have snarled (okay, yes, I did), but I figure that's healthy when my rational Psy mate suddenly turns into a caveman. And here I thought I'd have it easier than all of you mated to dominant changelings. Shows what I know.

Lara
p.s. The snarling didn't last long. I have no willpower when he goes all strong, silent, and possessive. Just call me Woman of Goo.

FROM: Tammy<tamsyn@darkriver.net>
TO: Lara<lara@snowdancer.org>
DATE: Sep 3, 2081 at 3.27 p.m.
SUBJECT: re: re: Life

You are so crazy for your Psy, I can see the silly smile on your face right now. :-)

Nate mentioned to me the other day how he and Walker agree completely when it comes to "taking care of" their healers, even if we're "totally unreasonable" about it, and—when I got over the urge to smack him—I decided to kiss him instead. We lucked out, babe.

Apparently they're bonding. Nate dropped by the practice to see the boys, and I've been informed we're all having dinner tomorrow night. I'm not sure if we should be scared about this development, but I can't wait to see you so we can talk properly.

Here's hoping Patient A responds to Sascha's attempt.

Tammy
p.s. Attaching photos of my gorgeous little troublemakers from their game this weekend. Jules only got sent to the penalty box once, and Rome actually stayed in the game rather than coming off in solidarity. I'm happy to say that tightly knit as they are, they're also turning into fierce little independent men.

<sent via mobile datacomm>

Chapter 24

HAWKE LOOKED AT the document BlackSea had sent through a few minutes ago and tapped Riaz for a consult, since the lieutenant had had multiple face-to-face contacts with members of the unusual "pack" while he'd been in Europe. He caught Riaz on his way down from the higher elevations, had to wait forty-five minutes for him to arrive.

"Had lunch?" he asked when the other man walked into his office. It was half past three, but he hadn't had a chance to eat.

Riaz sprawled into the chair in front of Hawke's desk. "No, but I won't fade away."

"I might." Putting through a call to the main kitchen, he asked one of the kids on after-school kitchen duty to bring over two plates. "Pasta okay with you?"

At Riaz's nod, he added in a request for dessert and grinned at the pert response of the head cook, Aisha, when the juvenile on the phone conveyed the request. Hanging up, he handed Riaz a copy of the BlackSea docs. "What do you think about this?"

Unlike most changeling groups, BlackSea wasn't composed of one particular species of changeling, but was a conglomerate of all water-based changelings. Several worked on Alaris, the deep-sea station located in the Pacific Ocean, not far from the Mariana Trench, though the station personnel were by no means solely changeling.

A large number of BlackSea's people had normal occupations—in cities located by the sea or near large bodies of fresh water, depending on their individual species. There weren't, however, any water-based changelings in the greater Bay Area, or along the California coastline. Given Snow-Dancer and DarkRiver's heavy dominance in the region,

BlackSea's people had given it a wide berth, not wanting to inadvertently cause a territorial skirmish.

Now they wanted not only permission to move freely in the waters in and around the territory, as well as leave to work in the region, but also an alliance with SnowDancer. However, their vision of the alliance process was very different from Hawke's. Hence the consult. "Wait," he said when Riaz began to speak. "Let me comm Kenji in since he's the point person with BlackSea."

Toby knocked on the open door right then, using his foot, his hands occupied by a loaded tray. A tug of pride in his gut at the sight of the boy who was now family, Hawke waved him in. "I hear you volunteered to do extra shifts in the kitchen." According to Sienna, her baby brother was turning into an excellent cook.

Toby nodded, dark red hair sliding over his forehead as he placed heaping plates of chicken and mushroom fettuccine on Hawke's desk, followed by a large bowl of salad, big hunks of warm garlic bread, two bottles of water, and two enormous slices of baked cheesecake. Last was the cutlery.

Beaming at having completed the entire operation without spilling anything, Toby leaned the tray carefully against the wall. "Aisha said to call if you need more."

"Thanks, Toby. Give Aisha a kiss from us." Hawke winked.

Toby left the office with a grin, closing the door behind himself at Hawke's nod.

"I think she's trying to fatten us up." Riaz groaned as he dug into the fettuccine.

"Sorry, too busy dying of gastronomic bliss to talk."

There wasn't even a crumb left when they finished. Deeply satisfied, Hawke brought Kenji into their discussion via the big comm screen on the wall to the right of his desk.

"To what do I owe this honor?" Kenji asked, putting down a half-eaten burger, the mysterious bruise on his cheek from the night of the mating ceremony no longer in evidence, though his hair remained a sleek purple sans the gold stars.

Riaz held up the document in silent explanation.

Kenji grimaced. "Yeah, what's that about? I didn't say anything to their negotiator, but it's not exactly how we do things."

Face-to-face, changeling-to-changeling, that was how SnowDancer began a relationship that had the potential to turn into an alliance.

"BlackSea isn't usual in any way, shape, or form," Riaz said, stretching out his legs in front of him after changing position so he could look directly at the screen. "Because they're scattered worldwide, they've had to develop other ways to connect. It doesn't help that the majority of their membership is secretive and reticent to the extreme."

Hawke rubbed his jaw. "Yeah, no one's ever confirmed if some of the changeling species that are officially part of BlackSea even exist." Water-based changelings didn't advertise their species, and many chose to live on the small floating cities in international waters that had been permitted them under the accord signed after the Territorial Wars.

The cities were open to anyone—*if* you could find transport to the location: BlackSea had uniformly chosen dangerous stretches of water to anchor its cities, waters a fish alone would be able to navigate. And since they made sure there were no appropriate surfaces on which to land flying craft, the only visitors to their cities were invited ones.

Even the Psy left BlackSea alone, most probably because the water changelings did everything they could to stay out of the spotlight. Which brought up another question, but Hawke shelved it for now, because Kenji was speaking.

"So, what," he said, gulping down his soda, "they function like the Psy?"

"In a sense," Riaz said, furrows between his eyebrows. "Don't make the mistake of thinking they're not ferociously loyal to one another just like in any changeling pack, but everything's recorded and verified so it can be shared with members across the world."

Kenji tapped a laser pen against his cheek. "Honestly, I love the idea of being allied with BlackSea. Their information network alone is invaluable. The question is, can SnowDancer adapt enough to work with a group that functions so differently?"

It was an astute question.

Shoving the pen behind his ear, Kenji continued. "We can't treat them as we do our Psy business contacts, because as Riaz says, they are changelings and it would piss them off. But, it doesn't look like we can have the kind of relationship with BlackSea that we do with DarkRiver and are building with WindHaven."

Hawke nodded. He trusted the alphas of the leopard and falcon packs on a gut level. Neither Lucas nor Adam would ever knife him in the back, of that both parts of him were dead certain. "According to the official line," he said, "they don't have an alpha, but a 'Conclave' that represents all the major and minor species groups in BlackSea."

Riaz shook his head. "That's a load of PR bull. Her name is Miane Levèque, and she knows everything that happens in BlackSea."

"That's what I thought." Miane was someone Hawke had kept a quiet eye on, as he did the alphas of most major packs. "Whatever else happens, a face-to-face meeting is nonnegotiable." His wolf would accept nothing less.

Riaz tapped the rolled-up papers against his knee. "My advice: we treat this request seriously, go over the contract, and ask for changes as needed. I think they're feeling us out, seeing if we *are* able—or at least willing to try—to adapt to their unique way of doing things."

"Could be a power play," Kenji pointed out. "The minnow trying to get the whale to do as it wishes."

Hawke grinned. "Excellent marine analogy, rock star."

Kenji played some outstanding air guitar. "I've been saving it up."

"It's definitely a little of that, too," Riaz said, clearly in no doubt about BlackSea's predatory instincts. "So we make sure they realize that while we'll work with them, we won't budge on the critical meet between Miane and Hawke."

"And," Hawke added, "guaranteed transport in and out of their cities." Movement had to go both ways for an alliance to work. "If they plan to stonewall us there, the deal is off the table. And warn them if it happens after we agree to an alliance, we'll consider it a fatal violation and a declaration of aggression." SnowDancer had plenty of teeth, and he didn't want BlackSea in any doubt that they would use those teeth the instant the other group tried to manipulate the situation.

Riaz's eyes glinted in agreement, his wolf prowling close

to the surface. "We also need to stipulate a permanent comm link. No dodging our calls and blaming it on nautical interference—before or after. Make sure they know Snow-Dancer doesn't give second chances."

"That's a very good point," Kenji said, swallowing a bite of what looked like cherry pie. "I hear BlackSea's great at delaying things until it's too late."

"I'll follow your lead—between you, you have more experience with BlackSea than anyone else in the pack." Hawke was very aware that he either respected the strength and skills of his men and women, or he lost them to boredom and frustration. "The two of you have full authority to negotiate. Just keep me in the loop."

"There's one other thing." Riaz's expression was thoughtful. "Aren't you guys wondering why they're sticking their necks out now?"

It was the question Hawke had earlier shelved. "Yeah, when they've seen the consequences of allying with us in stark detail." As an ally, BlackSea would be expected to provide support in any future conflicts.

"Last few times I met a changeling from BlackSea," Riaz said, "I had the feeling something was up. Like this subtle tension under the surface."

"I'm getting the same feeling." Kenji took another bite of pie, chasing it down with more soda. "They're in some kind of trouble, and whatever it is, it's making us look attractive."

Both his lieutenants glanced at Hawke, an unasked question in their eyes.

"We continue the process." The advantages of having BlackSea as an ally were vast. "No point bringing it up now." The aquatic changelings didn't trust SnowDancer enough to tell them the truth. "Once the other pieces are in place, that's when we pin them down—if they refuse to cooperate, it ends there." He wouldn't ally his people with a group that might lead them into unknown harm.

"You know, everything else aside, they're bloody fascinating." Riaz's tone held intense interest. "A changeling group even other changelings don't get."

"Creepy as hell at times, too," Kenji muttered. "Those

black eyes some of them have—it's like looking into the face
of a mako shark."

"You might be," Riaz replied with a grin. "And damn,
Kenji, do you live on a diet of junk food?"

"My sushi's in my other bento box." Unrepentant, he bit
into a piece of cake.

Hawke listened to the two men discuss a couple of preliminary matters before Kenji signed off and Riaz stood.
Hawke remained concerned about the lieutenant, but as he'd
told Riaz, he knew lone wolves. He'd give the other man a
little more time. The one positive in the situation was that
Riaz had come home, and he'd stayed.

"I'll have a look at the contract tonight," the other male
now said, glancing at his watch. "I'm due to call Pierce in a
few minutes—he said he'd be up late."

Pierce was the lone wolf who had taken over Riaz's duties
in Europe. "Tell him to keep his nose clean or I'm putting him
on rotation to Siberia." Unlike Riaz, Pierce was a flirt—his
face had been introduced to more than one jealous male fist.

"Then we'd have WhiteSteppe to deal with," Riaz said
with a grin, naming the sole wolf pack in Siberia. "They'd
probably declare war on us after he seduced away some lieutenant's girlfriend."

Laughing as the other man left, Hawke nodded at the teenager who'd just come to the doorway. "Here to grab the dishes,
Silvia?"

A shy smile. "Yes." She quickly gathered them up, no sign
remaining of the injuries she'd suffered in a severe fall.

"How are your sessions with Ava going?" he asked, knowing the maternal female had taken Silvia under her wing.

"Everything she teaches me," the teenager said, "it fits.
Like I already kind of knew it. I wanted to ask if I could
maybe have more time with her?"

Shyness or not, there was strength there, Hawke thought,
warm and strong. "Mention it to Nell," he said. "She'll work
something out."

As Silvia left with another small smile, Hawke recalled the
note Nell had sent him this morning. Picking it up from his
desk, he considered how to deal with that particular situation.

He should make Riley handle it—it was his damn fault for putting ideas in the juveniles' hormone-drenched heads. The thought cheered him up for a second, but he knew this was a task for an alpha, so he sucked it up and made the call. "You at the cabin?"

"Yes," Lucas answered. "Bring some of Aisha's chocolate pie for Sascha if you're heading this way. As far as my chocoholic is concerned, it's ambrosia."

"Anything for Sascha darling."

"That doesn't work now that you're mated."

"Damn." Hawke hung up, then called Aisha to arrange the pie—the cook adored how Sascha craved her baking, so it was a mutual love affair. Poking his head into Riley's office after picking the pie up, he told the lieutenant where he'd be if needed. "Do you know where Sienna is?" He could sense her through the mating bond, track her if need be, but he'd made a promise to himself that he would only ever do that in an emergency. Never did he want his mate to resent the bond between them, to see it as a leash or a cage.

Riley brought up the roster. "She's got study time, so I'm guessing the library."

"Thanks." Even with a couple of interruptions by packmates wanting to talk, it didn't take long for Hawke to walk over to the den library, where he found his mate with her head downbent over a piece of paper on which she was writing formulas that made his brain ache. Physics and math texts lay open on several large datapads around her, and the small computer she'd signed out was running what appeared to be a complex equation.

Putting his hands on either side of her desk from behind her, he nuzzled a kiss to the sensitive spot below her ear, the autumn and spice of her calming and invigorating his wolf at the same time. "Ms. Sienna Lauren Snow," he teased, "what're you doing working on something as archaic as paper?"

Chapter 25

A HINT OF color on her cheekbones. "It helps me think."

Chuckling, he made a mental note to buy her a ream he'd seen at the little stationery store next to the shop that made the mechanical toys he collected—if he recalled right, the paper was specially formatted for the type of calculations she was doing. "How much do you have left to do today?" He knew she was working on an extra-credit project to gain early entry into an advanced course on thermodynamics—the behavior of energy.

Sienna wasn't certain the information would help her understand the cold fire that lived within her, but it couldn't do any harm. Knowledge, he thought, gave her a control that had so often been stolen from her life.

"A couple of hours," she now said, tipping up her head, her hair catching on his shirt, "but I can do that tonight. I could do with a break."

He tapped her nose with his finger. "Come on then. I'm going to see Lucas—you can visit with Sascha."

"Oh, great! I haven't cuddled Naya since several days before the mating ceremony." She quickly stacked the data-pads neatly in her cubicle, then gathered up and put her computer and notes away in the attached locker. "I'm ready."

They were halfway to the garage when Toby ran up to them, a small backpack slung over one lanky shoulder. "Are you going out? Can I come?" he asked, pushing back hair that wasn't anywhere close to the cardinal night-sky of his eyes. Habit, Hawke thought, wolf grinning at the memory of the haircut he'd given the boy.

Sienna reached out to straighten his collar. "You complete your kitchen chores?"

"He did," Hawke answered to Toby's grin. "Brought me some food not long ago."

"I even finished my homework," the boy added, and got the permission he'd requested to join them. Smiling, he fell in beside them. "We got out of school early today, and we don't have to start till after ten tomorrow because we have a night class." Toby all but vibrated with excitement. "Elias and Sam are going to teach us how to track in the dark. It's going to be real late, when everything's quiet."

Hawke remembered those classes from his own youth, the memories poignant . . . because his lieutenant father had been one of the teachers. Looking at Toby's eager face, it seemed impossible that he'd ever been that young, but his wolf vividly recalled stalking through the nocturnal whispering of the forest, trying to be quiet, so quiet. It made him proud that in spite of everything that had happened, SnowDancer's young continued to have the chance to be children, to learn and play and grow.

"Where are we going?" Toby asked once he'd finished regaling them about Eli and Sam's plans.

"To see Sascha."

"Great!" Toby scrambled excitedly into the backseat of the SUV when they reached the garage. Though he was a great kid, Hawke's wolf worried about his good behavior. The boy had never *once* been in trouble—and that was completely unheard of for a pup his age. Hawke was concerned Toby was afraid of acting out, for fear the people he loved would leave him—as his mother had when she suicided.

He'd spoken about it to Judd and Walker, as well as Sienna, and they were all keeping a quiet eye on the boy. However, Sascha—who spent regular time with Toby, teaching him how to handle his empathic abilities—had told Hawke not to worry. "He's very centered and happy. If I'm a normal case as far as empaths are concerned, you'll have more trouble with him around fourteen to sixteen.

"I didn't consciously understand it then of course, but my abilities went hypersensitive about that time. I used to swing from anger to joy to frustration within the space of a few minutes." The cardinal had given him a wry smile. "If I hadn't been so afraid of being rehabilitated, I'd have been hell to handle."

Toby, Hawke thought, didn't have to fear that he'd be punished for having emotions by being sentenced to the psychic brainwipe, didn't have to worry that his personality would be erased in an act of brutality. And when adolescent angst hit, whether or not it was exacerbated by his empathic abilities, he'd have the necessary support, love, and discipline to come out of it stronger on the other side.

Now, listening to the boy chatter to Sienna, Hawke's wolf stretched in contentment. He had a family of his own again, he thought, the realization still so new that it was a kick to the gut each time. As alpha, everyone in SnowDancer was part of his family, but it wasn't the same as having people who were *his*.

"Toby," he said during a lull in the conversation, "are you dating yet?"

Toby's face went bright red in the rearview mirror. "Um, er, no."

Hawke had guessed as much from what he'd seen at the mating ceremony, but the kid was heading toward thirteen. He'd obviously noticed the opposite sex, even if he wasn't ready to take the next step. "But you know some of the older kids who are, right?"

"Uh-huh." Toby leaned forward, stretching his safety belt. "On my soccer team mostly."

"Any of them talk about the leopard girls?"

Sienna laughed. "Oh no."

"Oh yes." He glanced at Toby in the rearview mirror again. "Toby?"

"Um, yeah." A quiet hesitation. "I don't want to get anyone in trouble."

"Don't worry, you won't." He'd had a chat with the over-eighteens about inter-pack flirting, so they knew what was expected of them as far as acceptable behavior. However, if the younger age groups were starting to socialize, both packs needed a more concrete policy. "I think definite rules would help everyone."

Toby's nod was hard enough that Hawke caught it in his peripheral vision. "No one's dating or anything," the boy said, "but I think some of them want to—except they're kind of scared."

"Go on," Hawke said.

"They think that maybe they'll do something wrong and the leopards will get mad and it'll hurt the alliance. It's not just the boys."

No more dodging the bullet, Hawke realized, they had to formulate inter-pack guidelines and quickly—because while DarkRiver and SnowDancer were both predatory packs, there were subtle differences between them that adults appreciated, but that could land the young from both sides in hot water unless they knew to follow a few basic rules. "Thanks, Toby." He'd suggest a working group made up of maternal females from both SnowDancer and DarkRiver when he brought up the subject with Lucas.

A tug along the mating bond.

Wolf pricking its ears, he glanced at Sienna. "You called?"

"There's at least one seriously developing relationship in the over-eighteens."

"Names?"

"I wouldn't be able to show my face to my friends if I told you."

"Sienna."

Another message along the mating bond, this one with a nuanced depth of emotion. His wolf, unused to defiance, blinked, shook his head. And he realized his mate was reminding him that he wasn't her alpha, never would be. Gritting his teeth, he snarled. "I hate that rule." Not the truth, but at times like this, it sure as heck irritated him.

"That's why we need it." Sienna leaned across to nip affectionately at his jaw.

From behind them, Toby said, "I like being around you guys. You're happy deep inside even when you fight."

Wolf and man in satisfied agreement with Toby, Hawke tangled his hand with Sienna's, lifting it to his lips and snapping his teeth. Her startled yelp made Toby laugh.

My family.

SEVERAL hours after her breakdown by the waterfall, with the sky turning a post-sunset smoky gray, Adria finally walked into the den. Her throat was so raw her voice sounded akin to a croak when she entered the infirmary. "I need to look and sound human for a meeting at eight."

Lara's perceptive gaze saw too much, but the healer didn't ask prying questions. "Open." A cool spray hit the back of Adria's throat. "That'll take care of the voice."

Adria stroked her fingers over her neck. "Already feels better."

"As for your eyes—" Lara pointed to a patient room. "Lie down and I'll put a gel pack on your face. You have two hours before the meeting. I'll wake you when it's time."

"I'd like to shower first." Her bones, her skin, everything hurt.

Lara found her a change of clothing from the supplies kept in the infirmary. "Through there."

Stripping off inside the small shower, she allowed the hot spray to pummel her body until Lara knocked on the door. "I have the gel pack."

Adria got out of the shower, dried off, and dressed before she lay down on one of the beds, needing the armor of clothing after the nakedness caused by her emotional breakdown. Lara's wild corkscrew curls and fox brown eyes were the last things Adria saw before the coolness of the gel pack covered her puffy eyelids and cheeks.

The dreams took her under soon afterward.

Strong arms, a heavy male body, eyes of a brown so pale they shimmered gold, the night filled with the sounds of harsh breaths and hands sliding over sweat-slicked skin. When he flipped her onto her front, she waited in quivering anticipation.

Hot breath against her cheek, a big hand sliding under her body to close over one of her breasts with blatant possessiveness, the hard ridge of his erection insistent against her lower back. She attempted to arch upward, demand more, but was pinned down by his body.

A shift, his fingers brushing her unbound hair off her neck. His weight lifting.

She rose toward him in silent invitation.

His cock and his teeth sank into her at the same instant.

Jerking awake, she pulled off the gel pack to see that Lara had closed the door to her room, leaving her in blessed privacy. It was seven fifteen according to her watch, so she had a little more time.

Allowing herself a shudder of bone-deep pleasure, she stretched, her arms above her head, her feet pointed. But her mind replayed not the erotic dream, but her conversation with Riaz after they'd spoken to Tamsyn—and, though it made her wolf stiffen, the way he'd held her beside the waterfall. The man she'd glimpsed that morning, and the one who'd cared enough to put his arms around a packmate who was hurting, he was dangerous, someone who spoke to her soul beyond the primitive tug of sex.

The way he'd rubbed his cheek against her hair, attempting to give comfort though she'd taken none . . . she'd never have expected such rough tenderness from the abrasive, angry man she'd first encountered. And he was *loyal*, so much so that he was destroying himself in his fight not to betray a mate who was forever lost to him.

No woman, Adria thought with a prickling sense of unease, would be immune to such a man.

Chapter 26

KALEB TOOK THE printed documents Silver held out, relating to a business arrangement between him and the BlackEdge wolves. "Any issues?"

"No. They've agreed to the changes you requested." She glanced at her datapad, looked up. Hesitated.

Such hesitation was unusual for the ice-blonde who had been his aide since before he became a Councilor, but Kaleb had an excellent idea of the reason behind it. "You're wonder-

ing why I would subcontract any type of security to the
wolves."

"Yes. You have the Arrows, and your own men. You don't
need BlackEdge."

"They have certain unique skills," he said, scanning the
first page of the contract as he did so, his mind taking in the
data at a speed that, when Silver first started working for him,
had caused her to believe he wasn't actually reading. He was.
His mind processed each word as he swept his eye over it,
embedded it in his memory.

Flipping the page, he continued. "Even Psy can be tracked
by scent."

"True," Silver said, "but changelings can't evade a telepathic
sweep."

Kaleb glanced up. "A weakness only if the Psy in question
is aware he or she is being stalked. Many of our race ignore
any skill or ability beyond their own."

A longer pause, and he could almost hear her mind working methodically through his words. It was what made her
such a good aide. He didn't trust her—he didn't trust anyone, and Silver's first loyalty was to the powerful Mercant
family—but he knew she wouldn't betray him so long as he
had her respect.

For the majority of the time since he'd become aware of
them, he'd believed the Mercants were swayed solely by
power and wealth—of which Kaleb had amassed a great deal.
However, after monitoring them for years, he'd seen multiple
Mercant family members remain with failing companies until
there was no chance of salvage. He'd also seen them betray
wealthier employers if the price was right. It had led him to
revise his earlier conclusions.

Power and money might purchase a Mercant's skills, but
earn their cold-eyed respect and they would not only become
mute when it came to your secrets, they would also stand fast
in the face of trouble. In the past year, Kaleb knew he'd moved
onto the very exclusive list of people the Mercants would not
sell out.

Their connections and abilities, added to that of the Arrows,
brought him another step closer to taking total control of the

Net. Of course, there had always been a second option when it came to the Net, one he hadn't yet discarded. It all depended on the outcome of his search.

"You are correct, Councilor," Silver said at last, her voice cool, clear, flawless. "Do you need me to collate data on the individual you're tracking?"

"No." He had long ago discovered and memorized every shred of available data on the one person he searched for with remorseless persistence.

Scanning the penultimate page of the contract, he indicated for Silver to wait. Thirty seconds later, he was done. Picking up a pen, he signed the document in triplicate and passed it across the desk. "Tell BlackEdge I have no need of their services at present." The wolves would serve their purpose after he'd located his target—because that target was highly likely to refuse his hospitality. And in this case, a psychic leash was not a viable option.

Of course, Selenka Durev, the BlackEdge alpha, wouldn't agree to hunt just anyone, but after years of meticulous research, Kaleb understood the finest details of how the pack functioned. If and when the time came, he'd get what he wanted. No one would be permitted to stand in his way.

"Sir," Silver said after double-checking he'd signed and initialed all the required places in the contract, "about Henry Scott."

He'd asked her to keep her ears open for any information on the Councilor who hadn't been seen since Sienna Lauren's X-fire decimated the Pure Psy army. "Is he alive?"

"Only according to unsubstantiated rumors—those could be a strategic attempt by Pure Psy to bolster their membership. Without Henry's backing, the group has negligible power."

Hmm . . . "There's a man named Andrea Vasquez. Thirty years of age." It was the DarkMind that had brought him the name of Henry's general. "What do you have on him?" he asked, though he'd already done his own research. However, the Mercants had a way of knowing things no one else did.

"If you'll excuse me a moment."

He gave a curt nod. Having finished finalizing a memo in the interim, he put it aside for Silver to deal with, and turned in his chair. The crystal clear floor-to-ceiling wall looked out over the busy square below, black-garbed commuters scurrying to work, their heads downbent, breaths frosting the morning air.

His mind catalogued the visual intake, but it was an automatic act, his concentration on the psychic search he'd been running continuously in the back of his mind for years. Except now, he utilized every spare minute to run it in the foreground—because he was close. Very, very close. Enough that he might make a mistake if he didn't move with utmost stealth.

Alerted by the psychic reminder, he paused, reworked his search algorithm to halt at the first sign of a trip wire or sensor. By the time Silver walked back into his office, he was facing his desk once more, even as his mind hummed with a task that would've taken the full attention of most normal cardinals.

Kaleb had never been normal. Not in any way.

"Vasquez," Silver began, after taking a seat opposite his desk, "is a Gradient 8.3 telepath who was placed into Arrow training as a child. However, he was deemed unfit for the squad at age fourteen and reassigned to a regular black ops unit where he served with distinction until his apparent death."

All of which correlated with Kaleb's own findings. "Wet work?"

"Not on file, but given the nature of his psychological evaluation, it's a reasonable assumption that he was used for close-contact assassinations."

Kaleb had no doubts about Vasquez's status as a trained killer—Henry had never liked getting his hands dirty. "When did he fall off the grid?"

"Eight years ago. Death verified."

"Of course." It was the only way to vanish outright from the Net. "Let me guess—an accident that left no remains but for a fragment large enough to provide DNA."

"The crushed and partially burned remnants of the smallest finger from his left hand. Easy enough to replace with a prosthetic."

And speaking of a man dedicated enough to mutilate himself.

"He hasn't been seen, or DNA typed, since then." His aide tapped the screen of her organizer to bring up several images she turned toward him. "However, since you brought up his name in relation to Henry Scott, I took the liberty of going through the surveillance images of Henry taken during the six months before his disappearance. Vasquez isn't present in any of them."

That, Kaleb knew, meant nothing. The man was a trained ghost. "It's unlikely he looks anything like he did eight years ago."

"I agree, but," Silver continued, earning her paycheck with the next words she spoke, "it appears that, prior to his disappearance, Henry was making regular six-figure-sum deposits into an account in the Caymans. While the account itself is untraceable, Henry tagged the payments with the initials 'A. V.' at his end."

Kaleb was almost expecting it, that it would be such a simple thing that would destroy the wall of secrecy Vasquez had built around himself. Henry had never been good with details. "You have something further," he said, watching her bring up another file.

A slight nod, not a single strand out of place in the neat twist that was her hair. "The payments stopped after Henry's encounter with Sienna Lauren. However, it now looks as if someone is reorganizing his financial assets." Her eyes, an unusual color between blue and gray, met his. "Our banking contacts were able to confirm it isn't Shoshanna."

Shoshanna was Henry's wife, the relationship a fiction to placate the human and changeling population. "That's excellent work, Silver." He didn't ask her to forward him the files—Silver was his aide because she did things like that without being asked.

Rising, she held the organizer to her side. "At present, this 'A. V.' is a phantom the same as Vasquez, but I've alerted my family that he has become an individual in whom you have an interest." She left without further words, the click of her heels muffled by the carpet.

Kaleb considered the possibilities. The first was that Vasquez had taken over after Henry's death and was setting himself up as the new leader of Pure Psy. However, from everything Kaleb had discovered about Vasquez, the male was not a leader. While training to be an Arrow, he'd followed orders with dogged fidelity. The sole reason he'd been excised from the squad was because of a psychological imbalance that made him a risk in the field, given the sensitive nature of many Arrow operations.

It must've been a difficult decision for those in charge of the squad, as according to the classified training file Silver had just sent Kaleb, quite aside from his lethal combat abilities, Vasquez possessed a critical skill: being able to organize at the minute level. If he now had control over Henry's finances, that meant he'd foreseen the need for it, had ensured he'd have the necessary access.

Silver, he said after a quick telepathic knock, *the reorganization of Henry's finances. Where is the money going?*

Unknown. Even our best people haven't been able to track the funds. We can, however, confirm that the money isn't going to the Caymans.

No, Kaleb thought, Vasquez was no rogue.

He was simply following orders to hide the existence of his master.

Chapter 27

RIAZ HADN'T SEEN Adria since the waterfall, so when he ran into her on the outskirts of the Pack Circle a week later, they both froze. Her wariness was writ large across the clean lines of her face before she blinked and wiped it away.

Edgy about his inability to control his touch-hunger when it came to her, he'd done his best to stay the hell away. But now she stood in front of him, and though her presence was nothing simple, nothing easy, he found he couldn't simply let her pass. "Are you helping with the preparations?" Lara and

Walker's mating ceremony wasn't for another week, but everyone was already gearing up for it.

"Yes—my trainees volunteered to do the setup." She twisted what looked like a piece of twine around her index finger, offered him a guarded smile. "Walker and Lara's ceremony coming so soon after Hawke and Sienna's is going to be great for the pack."

She was, he realized, trying to make conversation— distant conversation. And he knew this proud, strong woman wanted to erase the fragile tie created between them by those heartrending moments by the waterfall. Reining back the dominance within him, a part of his nature that fought to crash against her cool facade until it cracked, he glanced around. "Looks like you need a hand with the tables."

An intent look, the scent of her a lingering caress. "Are you volunteering?"

"I'm yours to command." Even though it would've been far more sensible to walk away.

A hint of true warmth in the luminous blue-violet. "Come on then." Picking up a hand-drawn plan, she said, "Lara wants the picnic tables positioned on the edges of the dance area, except for this section where the band's planning to set up."

"Got it." About to conscript three of the bigger boys from her crew, he wrenched himself back just before he would've spoken. These kids were Adria's. As a lieutenant, he had to support, not undermine, her authority. "Who can I have?"

An inscrutable look before she put two fingers to her mouth and whistled. "Israel, Charlie, Vincent. You're with Riaz."

After he'd given the boys a quick tutorial, Riaz's team began to snap and screw together the tables and benches. Since except for the occasional event, most wolves preferred to sit or sprawl on the ground, the pack put up and broke down their outdoor furniture as needed. It ensured the forest remained as uncluttered and as untouched as possible, and with the separate components taking up very little room when stacked, storage space wasn't an issue.

From what he'd glimpsed of the plan, Walker and Lara— or if Riaz had to guess, Lara—had decided on a night picnic, followed by a jazz dance. Soft glowing lights in all the shades of the rainbow would ring the area, the festivities kicking off soon after sunset. The early start made sense, since Walker had a young daughter and was basically Toby's dad as well.

"It'll be beautiful," Adria said to him as he wiped his forearm across his perspiration-damp forehead a couple of hours later. "Suit who Walker and Lara are as a couple."

Riaz had sent the boys off a few minutes earlier, when Adria dismissed the rest of her crew, and was now completing the final table with her holding the boards in place. "The check marks on the plan," he said, twisting a rivet into place. "I couldn't figure out what they were."

Adria's sudden laugh was husky and uninhibited. "Giant butterflies—Marlee's contribution to the decorations. Sienna and Brenna have been conscripted into the task force."

Man and wolf both chuckled. "Walker Lauren is not exactly the butterfly type." The lone wolf in Riaz had recognized the other man as dangerous from the first.

"He's a good dad." Adria consulted the plan, made him move the table a few feet to the left. "That's it. Thanks."

Glancing up at the orange glow of the early evening sky, he said, "I might jog down to the stream, take a dip." He needed to chill the embers in his gut, a dark, hot flame.

Adria frowned. "I didn't know there was one nearby."

"It's about a ten-minute jog." He described the sector, but the lines between her eyebrows didn't disappear. "Come with me," he said, clenching his abdomen against the continuing impact of her presence. "It won't take long."

Her reawakened wariness betrayed itself in the finest flicker of tension across her lashes, but Adria was a Snow-Dancer soldier. She gave a small nod. "Let's pack up everything here first."

That done, Riaz led her into the trees and toward the secluded area where the hidden stream widened into a cold, clear pool half hidden by the gnarled roots of two ancient trees before snaking away and underground again. Though his wolf knew Adria wasn't his mate and the craving confused it, it clawed at him, wanting to lick up the taste of her. As a result, his jaw was a painful line by the time they reached their destination.

"No wonder I missed it," Adria said, stepping in front of him and to the water's edge. "It's literally tucked between . . ."

He didn't hear the rest of what she said, his eyes locked
on the bare skin of her nape, her braid having slid over her
shoulder. His hand curved around that nape before he was
aware of moving. She wrenched away, her eyes slamming
into him, bright cobalt touched with purple. For an instant,
he froze, but then his wolf roared to the surface and he knew
he'd been fooling himself about his ability to resist her.

THE electric charge in those eyes gone a vivid wolf gold
raised every hair on Adria's body. "No." Not even if the rough
heat of contact had rocked a lightning bolt through her. "I told
myself I'd never again invite you into my bed, and I meant it."

Riaz flinched. "I'm doing the inviting."

Bruised pride made her want to repudiate him as he'd
repudiated her, but if being with Martin had taught her one
thing, it was that her pride could be a terrible weakness.
"You'll just hate me for it." And she'd had enough of a man's
hatred.

Shuddering, Riaz stalked forward to cup her cheeks in his
hands. Startled at the tender hold, she didn't jerk away when
he bent to press his forehead to her own. "No." A hot breath
on her lips, his hands warm and callused on her face. "It's on
me." Raw, his soul stripped bare. "I can't carry on as I have
been doing."

"So I'm the bitter pill?" Even as she said that, part of her
resonated with the tumult of need and pain tearing him apart.

"Adria—"

"No." A finger pressed to the firm curves of his lips.
"You're right. You need to make a clean break . . . and so do
I." She gave him that piece of herself so this wounded wolf
would know he wasn't the only one going into this with the
most painful of motivations. It wasn't simply about the sex
any longer, wasn't simply about assuaging the skin hunger
that haunted them both. It was about saying good-bye to a
dream that had never had a chance. "But," she whispered,
forcing herself to hold the potent dominance of a gaze that
was pure wolf, "you have to be sure."

"I am." No hesitation, even if the words were jagged as
broken stone. "There's nothing for me in the past."

Yes, she thought, the past was forever gone, for both of them. "All right."

His eyes glowed wild and beautiful in her vision as he dipped his head, stole her breath. She let her lids flutter shut, knowing that regardless of what happened after this, whether they remained lovers or walked away, one thing she would never, ever be able to change—that she was the first woman to lead him into betrayal.

A dull ache, an accepted pain.

Then her wolf came to life inside her body, and the thought fractured under a chaos of sensation. Wrapping her arms around his neck, she met the fever of his kiss, her bones molten with passion. Yet . . . there was a hesitancy to them that hadn't been present before, and Adria wondered if their time had passed. A twisting in her chest. A hurt that was deeper. More dangerous. But when she made as if to pull back, the growl that rumbled out of Riaz's throat was a primal thing.

His hand closed over her breast, his mouth sucking on the pulse in her neck almost before she'd processed the fact he'd taken her to the grass, the earth still holding the sun's warmth. Any thought of retreating fragmented, the hunger inside her a wild craving. Clawing at his T-shirt, she heard something tear. He snarled against her, thrusting one hand under her own tee to push up her bra and spread his fingers over the bare flesh of her breast, cupping and shaping.

"Oh God!" Arching into the firm, confident touch, she tore at his T-shirt until it was in pieces around them, his big, muscled body rising over her own, his mouth busy on her lips, her jaw, her neck.

His skin was a shade of burnished brown, warm and beautiful, her pleasure at touching him—*at last*—almost painful. When he shoved up her T-shirt and lowered his head to her breast, her womb clenched in anticipation. His breath on her skin . . . the hot suction of his mouth. Twisting wildly, she fisted her hand in his hair, attempting to pull him off. The pleasure, oh God, the vicious pleasure was too much, her body too sensitive.

He used his teeth.

Crying out, she was bewildered at the sudden cold on her

damp flesh. "What—" An instant later, he was unzipping her jeans, pulling them off, along with her boots. She felt something rip, knew her panties were gone. When he unzipped and moved between her thighs, she spread them against the heavy intrusion, ready until her skin ached.

A single hard thrust and he was seated deep inside her, the thickness of him a pulsing brand.

She froze for a minute, her body stunned at the almost violent possession. Long unused muscles ached, but below all that was *need*. Such naked, raw need. Rising toward him, she met eyes glowing against the dusk. She wasn't the least surprised by the warning growl, or by the hand he fisted in her hair to arch her neck. The bite along the sensitive slope where her neck flowed into her shoulder was hard enough to sting, hard enough to push her over.

Even as she came with a scream, he pounded into her with such wild fury, the feel of him reverberated through her very bones. A brutal word in a masculine voice so harsh, it was almost unrecognizable. Her internal muscles spasming in erotic response. His hand clenching on her breast. The primal heat of him spilling into her.

RIAZ lay on the grass, so angry with himself that he couldn't look at Adria. But he could sense her pushing her bra and T-shirt back down into place. She didn't rise to find her jeans, and he wondered if they were even in one piece. "I'm sorry." His voice was coated with gravel.

A pause. "Why?"

"I've never hurt a woman like that." He knew damn well she had bruises, and that bite on the smooth curve of her shoulder wasn't going to disappear anytime soon.

Adria sighed, stretching out under the twilight colors of the sky. "I wasn't complaining, Riaz, and I'm strong enough to have gutted you if you'd been doing anything I didn't want you to do."

"Damn it, Adria." He lifted himself up on one elbow to glare at her, his body still pumped with adrenaline. "You deserve more than a fuck in the grass."

Her eyes widened.

He went to say something else, lost the thought when his eyes fell on half-parted lips. Kiss-bruised and lush, her mouth was the most erotic temptation, the need inside him nowhere near sated by their frantic coupling. Breath coming in harsh gasps, he managed to get out a single word, the only question that mattered, "Adria?"

"Yes." Permission.

Promising himself he would give her tenderness this time, even if it killed him, he sucked on her lower lip, played his tongue across the part, but didn't push for entry. Instead, he licked and tasted and teased as he should have done earlier . . . until her hands landed on his shoulders, her claws releasing just enough to prick his skin in silent female demand.

Smiling, he thrust one jean-clad thigh between her own and pushed up. She hissed. Breaking the kiss at once, he reached down to stroke one hand over her calf, her leg raised and bent at the knee. "Sore?" Hardly surprising since he'd shoved into her with all the finesse of the average eighteen-year-old.

She nodded, lifting her fingers to his mouth. He held position and let her explore. When she tugged him back down, he claimed a kiss that was all tongue, deep and wet and an unashamed taste of the things he wanted to do to her, before removing his thigh and shifting so that he was on the bottom. "I think," he said, holding her steady with his hands on her waist as she pushed herself up to straddle him, "it's my turn to take the pounding."

ADRIA was caught by the playful smile tugging at Riaz's lips, the harsh angles of his face relaxed to reveal an intoxicatingly attractive male—one who was playing with her just a little . . . but coming from a lone wolf . . .

"No?" Riaz said when she didn't move, his head angled in a way that told her his wolf remained very much near the surface.

Leaning forward, she brushed his hair off his forehead. She knew it was a tender move, one that went beyond sex, but she needed to do it. The truth was, no matter what she'd said

to him that day at the training run, no matter what she'd tried
to convince herself because it hurt too much to do otherwise,
she wasn't a woman who could ever have sex for sex's sake.
It wasn't in her.

Home and hearth and family, that's what you're built for.

Words spoken by Tarah long ago, so long ago that her
sister had probably forgotten. Adria hadn't. That woman continued to exist inside of her, and in spite of the cracks in her
heart, she still wanted a family of her own, a home filled with
love, a man who adored her and who she could adore in
return. This lieutenant who held her with warm, strong hands,
his heart already given to another, wasn't the one with whom
she would ever fulfill that dream, but that didn't mean their
joining had to be a cold, hard thing.

Riaz didn't pull away from the gentle touch, and one of
the cracks deep within her healed a tiny fraction. "Let's be
friends," she whispered to the golden-eyed man who watched
her with such predatory focus, the wolf in his eyes.

His hands flexed on her hips. "I can't be platonic friends
with you, Adria." Not a rejection, just a blunt truth from male
to female, wolf to wolf.

"I know." Now that they'd touched, the need in her had
only grown stronger.

Thumbs stroking gently over the curve of her hip. "Friends
who share intimate skin privileges then?" A quiet clarifica-
tion. "Do you think we can be?"

"Yes." But she understood why Riaz hesitated, though it
was clear to her he needed a friend as well as a lover. "I'll
take you as you are," she promised, wanting him to understand that she wouldn't demand what he didn't have to give,
wouldn't hurt him by reminding him of what he'd lost. "No
expectations. No ties. No promises." Just a friendship that
might help them both heal.

Riaz caressed his hands down to her bare thighs, back up
to slide under her T-shirt, the calluses on his palms scraping
over her skin with a rough seduction that made her shiver.
"You almost sound as if you prefer that."

"I do." No lies, she thought, not here, in this beautiful
moment with the world so hushed and private around them.

"I've been . . . lost for a long time. I'm wolf enough to want the contact with a man I'm not only physically attracted to, but who I'm beginning to like," she said with deep honesty, thinking of the tenderness of his kiss, of the way he'd handled her trainees with both affection and discipline this afternoon, "but I need my freedom."

Despite the dreams of family she nurtured in a secret part of her soul, she knew she was damaged. Until she fixed herself, if that was even possible, she couldn't, wouldn't, steal a commitment from anyone, least of all a man who belonged to another in a way that could never be erased.

He reached up to tug the tie loose from her braid, unravel her hair. "Friends." It was a promise, the wolf gold of his eyes glowing. "Tell me about him."

And because she understood how hard it was for a dominant male like Riaz to be vulnerable, to have her keep his secrets, she did. "To understand how it happened, you have to know the beginning." She shared how she and Martin had been apart for long periods for the first five years after they met, while Martin did a postgrad degree in England and she focused on intensive soldier training.

"My family tends to lump all those years together, but they only saw me sporadically," she told him, thinking back to that demanding, exciting time. "My parents were posted to the other end of the territory, Tarah was busy with Evie,"—it made her heart clench painfully tight even now to remember how weak Evie had been as a child—"and Indigo was still in school in den territory, while I was in the Cascades."

Riaz nodded. "They would've had no idea of your day-to-day life."

"Or how insane it was. As well as the soldier training, Hawke had me taking certain college courses online." Things that had given her a grounding in basic business principles, so she could act as a sounding board for a lieutenant should it ever become necessary. "I barely had time to breathe, much less start a committed relationship."

"It was like that for me when I first became a lieutenant," Riaz said, his fingers moving on her skin, the slight roughness of his fingertips an exquisite caress. "Steep learning curve."

"I guess that was part of why I was drawn to Martin when he came home for visits, why I said yes when he asked me out on dates. He was warm, intelligent, funny—he made me relax." Tainted by the darkness that had come later, everyone else seemed to remember only the bad times, but it wasn't the angry man he'd become that she'd fallen for.

"He'd talk me into watching silly movies, tell jokes in this deadpan voice that would have me in stitches." But he'd only shared that part of himself with those he knew well. "One thing most people don't realize is that Martin is shy, always has been. It sometimes comes across as arrogance or conceit and means he doesn't make the best first impression—he didn't on my parents."

However, she'd seen and liked the man behind the mask, sincerely believed her family would, too, once they got to know him. "We didn't have explosive chemistry," she admitted, "but I never expected that kind of passion." Had thought her wolf too sensible for the wildfire she'd seen burn so many others in the pack. "I didn't go around accosting brooding lone wolves then."

Riaz's eyes warmed with quiet amusement, but he didn't interrupt.

"We were compatible in so many other ways, from our outlook on life, to our belief that loyalty was the core of a relationship, to the things that made us laugh that when he suggested we take our relationship to the next level, I said yes." Her wolf had liked Martin well enough not to interfere with the human's decision, but it had never demanded more, never hungered to tangle with Martin's own wolf . . . never *chosen* him.

"You didn't worry about the dominance issue?"

"Initially, yes." It had been too important a question to blow off. "But you have to realize—by the time we moved in together, we'd known and casually dated each other for years." Regardless of the impression others, including Tarah and Indigo, might've formed as a result of his remoteness around strangers, not once had Martin done or said anything to make her believe he couldn't handle the fact of her dominance.

"When I made senior soldier while we were dating, he gave me a beautiful ceremonial knife," she said, wanting Riaz to understand how she could've made such a terrible mistake and how it might not have been a mistake at all—not then. "He'd bought it months ago, because he was so certain I'd get the promotion. He was *proud* of me."

Stroking hands on her thighs, the calm watchfulness of the predator that prowled behind the captivating shade of his eyes. "When did it start to go wrong?"

"I can never quite pinpoint it." The only thing she knew was that the change had bewildered her. "Maybe it was the reality of living day to day with a woman whose wolf was dominant to his own, the realization that if it came down to it, I didn't need him to protect me." All she had were guesses, because the death of their relationship had been a slow, insidious thing, hard to see until it was too late.

"From what you've said, it sounds like he was the one who pursued you—could be he felt more for you than you did for him," Riaz said quietly. "We both know you didn't love him, not as a strong female wolf should love her man."

Stricken, Adria said, "While I was in that relationship, I gave him everything I had to give." Hadn't realized she had the capacity for wild passion, that the dark intensity she'd witnessed in packmates was a part of her nature, too. "If he was unhappy, why didn't he say anything?"

"Because he was a weak prick," was the cold summation. "I can see why he might've reacted badly, but that doesn't mean I have any sympathy for him."

Yes . . . Martin had made his own choices, held the responsibility for them. "I should've walked away when I first began to realize he'd started to resent me for my strength, but I couldn't bear to give up and prove to those who'd warned me off a less-dominant man that they'd been right." God, she'd been so stubborn, so proud.

"You're a dominant female—being bloody-minded is part of the package."

She laughed, leaned down to play her fingers through his hair once more. "Yes, I've forgiven myself for that." Because underneath the pride had been the honest desire to salvage a relationship that had started out with such promise. "And I think I would've accepted defeat sooner and walked away, but then . . . Martin saved my life."

She'd been out in a bad storm, searching for a pup everyone thought was lost when a tree had fallen on her. It had broken her leg and dislocated her shoulder as it knocked her into a stream that had been bloated to dangerous levels, where she'd hit her head on an exposed rock. Dizzied and disoriented, she'd begun to gasp in water instead of air.

Having described the accident to Riaz, she said, "Martin has a bone-shaking fear of the water after almost drowning as a child, but he came out into the storm because he was worried about me, and then he dove into a raging torrent to save my life." However, that wasn't the most important part of the jagged jigsaw that had been their relationship. "He got me out, but as he was pulling himself out, a huge rock smashed into him, crushing most of his ribs and doing serious damage to his organs. He was in the infirmary longer than I was."

Riaz sat up, stroking his hands along her spine. "He used it, didn't he, to hold you?"

The top of the tattoo on Riaz's left shoulder just visible to her in this position, she traced the curved lines of it. "I don't know if it was conscious, but yes." The pressure had been so subtle, she hadn't realized what was happening for a long time. "I always had this sickening bubble of guilt inside me whenever I thought of ending it with a man who'd risked everything to save me."

After the relationship did end, she'd found herself unable to understand *why* Martin had fought to hold her even when it had become agonizingly clear they'd be happier apart. But if Riaz was right, if Martin had loved her in a way she hadn't been able to reciprocate . . . it explained so much, even as it didn't excuse the hurt he'd caused her.

"Loyalty's nothing to be ashamed of." Riaz's breath warm against her skin.

"No . . . but taken too far, it can become a flaw." Sliding her hands over his shoulders when his gaze darkened in knowledge, she gave a rueful smile. "Hindsight is always twenty-twenty, isn't it?"

He rubbed his cheek against hers. "That's why it's a bitch."

Again, she laughed, startled at the vein of humor within the solemn wolf with the golden eyes. "Well, I'm done with looking back," she said, tasting the salt and citrus bite of his skin, the hint of bitter chocolate in his kiss exotic and intriguing. "I'm ready to live in today."

This time, their loving was an intimate dance.

Long, drugging kisses, lingering strokes of her hands over a firm chest lightly covered by a sprinkling of hair that was an erotic caress against her breasts, and a ride so deep, so slow. His body arched under her own, his tendons straining white under the dusky hue of his skin as his hands clenched on her hips.

She'd never felt as beautiful, as powerfully female.

Chapter 28

KALEB LOOKED DOWN at the body laid out on the cold metal slab, lit by the frigid white of the morgue lights. The corpse had been discovered four hours ago, been prioritized at the highest level of importance. "Your conclusions?" he said to Aden. The Arrow medic—trained to perform autopsies on fallen Arrows—had done the task himself.

"Cause of death was a broken neck," Aden responded. "From the on-scene examination, it appears he tripped and fell down the stairs."

Not an unbelievable occurrence, and nothing that would've drawn Arrow attention, except for the fact the victim was an anchor. All anchor deaths were investigated by Arrows, even when old age was an evident factor—born with the ability to merge totally into the Net, those of Designation A were too integral to its psychic fabric to risk any mistakes.

Anchors had many functions, but their most important one was to stabilize and "hold" the PsyNet in place. They were the reason Psy could cross the world on the psychic plane without mental stress. The death of the one who lay on the slab had caused some minor ripples, but the temporary fail-safes had come into play the instant he disappeared from the Net, ensuring no major damage. Those in the affected zone would've experienced a faint headache at most before the network of anchors in the region realigned their spheres of influence to cover the gap.

A single death would in no way stretch the network thin, but the loss of any anchor was a cause for concern. However, only a telekinetic at the scene could've prevented an accident that appeared to have been caused by a split-second physical error.

"Do you believe the on-scene report?" he asked Aden.

"Vasic and I both did a sweep of the premises, found nothing out of order. The footage from his private security system also proved to be clean. Theoretically, a teleport-capable Tk could've 'ported in and 'assisted' in the fall, but why kill an anchor?" It was the most crucial question. "They have no political power, and their deaths do nothing except weaken the Net."

And regardless of political affiliation, every single Psy in the Net needed the biofeedback provided by the vast mental network. Sever their Net link and those of his race died an excruciating death in minutes.

"Non-Psy?" Kaleb proposed.

"If there was an intruder, it would've had to be a Tk. No other designation could've evaded the security system."

He met Aden's gaze. "Judd Lauren is a Tk outside the Net." It was a statement he made for many reasons.

"Judd also has an emotional attachment to the members of his family," Aden pointed out. "It's reasonable to extrapolate that he wouldn't want to cause harm to the young in the Net, and there is no way to control the widespread effect of an anchor's death."

Weighing all the factors, Kaleb gave a small nod. "Even the most important aren't immune to accidents," he said, taking in the bruises on the body of the middle-aged man. "However, I want no unanswered questions. Do a secondary scan of the premises, ensure your first impression was correct."

Aden said nothing, but Kaleb knew it would be done. He and the Arrows had come to an understanding—but he didn't make the mistake of thinking he had their total support. The most lethal fighting force in the Net was still making up its mind about him. What the Arrows didn't realize was that Kaleb was evaluating them, too, the purpose of that evaluation nothing Aden and his men would ever guess.

Chapter 29

RIAZ PRESSED HIS forehead to the wall of the shower and let the water pound over him, washing away the sweat and grass stains, but doing nothing to erase the memories of the passion that had swept over him not long ago . . . and of the wild, sensual woman whose lush mouth was quickly becoming a private addiction.

Shame, anger, desire, they all vied for prime position within the rigid tension that was his body. The idea of being with anyone else once he'd found the woman meant to be his mate was so anathema to everything he had ever believed that both man and wolf were bewildered, lost. But that wasn't the only thing that had him feeling like shit—regardless of what Adria had said about being with him every step of the way during their first primal coupling, he wasn't a man who mistreated women. It continued to shame him that he'd been so inconsiderate with her.

A snapshot of memory, Adria's hair tumbling around him in a silken waterfall as she leaned down to suck his lower lip into her mouth, releasing it in a delicious tease of a bite. *No more guilt, Riaz.* A husky order. *I needed that as much as you did. We can go slow this time.*

Wrenching the water to ice-cold when his cock surged at the mental replay of exactly how slow they'd taken it, he grit his teeth until his wolf cried foul. Since he was about to turn blue, he got out, dried off, and pulled on a faded pair of jeans, the threads barely holding together above the left knee. A white T-shirt, socks, and boots, and he was done. He ran a comb through his hair, rubbed his jaw. It scraped, the bristles hard. Since it was far too late for Adria's delicate skin, he shrugged and left it.

Heading to the small office he'd been assigned, he began to go through some paperwork Pierce had asked him to look over, figuring he'd grab dinner from the kitchen later, as it was only seven thirty.

However, Riley popped in his head a minute later. "Dinner at my place tonight."

Riaz had returned to the den because he'd known he needed his pack. But after what had just happened, the painful decision he'd made to forget Lisette and continue his strange, sensual friendship with Adria, his wolf raised its hackles, wanting to be left alone. "Thanks, but I have a lot of work." It wasn't a lie—he was the lieutenant in charge of SnowDancer's international business interests, Pierce and the others under his direct command.

Riley leaned against the doorjamb, arms folded. "If you wanted to isolate yourself," he said, "you wouldn't have come home."

"Don't push me, Riley." He could feel his claws pricking the insides of his skin.

"It's what friends do. We're running down in ten minutes."

Realizing he'd only end up brooding if he remained behind, Riaz gave in and joined Riley, Drew, and Indigo outside the den, the sky a soft dark not yet dotted with stars. "We waiting on someone?"

Riley glanced over his shoulder. "Here they come."

Riaz didn't need to turn to know that Adria was part of the group. But he did so anyway, saw that Hawke walked beside her. The alpha was laughing at something Adria had said, her face turned toward his, her damp hair caught in a loose braid.

That laughter faded when her eyes fell on him, but her smile didn't.

Something hard and jagged in him eased a fraction, his wolf settling.

And then they were moving, the pace comfortable, conversation being exchanged as they flowed through the trees. Adria and Indigo ran ahead, following Riley and Hawke, while Drew had ended up beside Riaz. It would've been an unexpected pairing a few months ago, but he and Drew had made their peace, the other man so settled in his mating with Indigo that nothing could shake him.

A burst of feminine laughter, husky and generous.

Compelled by a woman who was becoming important to him in a way that threatened to undermine the foundations of his world, he wondered what Adria and Indigo were talking about that had them so amused, decided it was probably one of those things a man didn't want to know.

"Sienna's missing," he said to Drew. "Unusual." Newly mated men liked to be near their women as a rule—and Hawke was alpha, with the concurrent primal drives. His mate had also been in brutal danger not long ago. Continued to be, in many ways.

"She's training with Judd." Drew must've done something via the mating bond, because Indigo gave him an arch look over her shoulder before returning to her conversation with Adria. Grinning, Drew added, "They'll come down together after."

It wasn't, Riaz knew, because Judd was a lieutenant that Hawke trusted the other man with his mate when the possessive urges of mating had to be running rampant through his body. "She's so young." It worried him at times that Sienna Lauren wouldn't be able to bear the weight placed on her shoulders.

"You saw what she did." A solemn response. "That kind of power ages a person."

"Yes." Sienna showed no overt signs of it, but he knew she had to have paid a price for the cold fire that had saved so many SnowDancers. "Doesn't matter, though—part of me still wants to protect her." She had his respect, but that didn't mean his normal instincts were dead.

"Me, too," Drew admitted. "Don't think that worries her— the girl's tough enough to handle an alpha."

Just like the woman in front of him, Riaz thought, was more than tough enough to handle anything he threw at her, the delicacy of her scent belying a steely core that had begun to fascinate his wolf.

"You two are as slow as old ladies," Hawke said, having dropped back to join them.

Drew whistled. "Sounds like a challenge to me."

"That it does." Catching Drew's eye, Riaz slammed into Hawke without warning, taking the alpha to the ground.

"What the—"

Drew had already pulled off Hawke's boots, stripped the laces, and thrown everything in four different directions by the time the alpha managed to get past Riaz and to his feet. "Those are my favorite boots!"

Drew rubbed his hands. "Better find them then. Meanwhile, we'll beat your ass to Riley's."

Hawke bared his teeth—and the race was on, the women and Riley joining in. Riaz's wolf grinned as it ran, happy in the most uncomplicated sense. The trees whipped by at lightning speed, and they spilled into the clearing that fronted Riley's home, a graceful stone-and-wood chalet set halfway between DarkRiver and SnowDancer territory, less than ten minutes later . . . to find Hawke and his boots waiting for them on the steps.

"Damn it." Drew scowled, hands on his knees. "We need to cheat better next time!"

Hawke's eyes went night-glow. "Touch my boots again and I'll have Aisha broil you for lunch."

Chest heaving, Riaz shook his head. "We should make him run one-legged." The alpha had been fast as a boy, but now he was *fast*. "Maybe weigh him down with rocks."

Hawke leaned back on the steps, resting on his elbows. "You'd still be eating my dust."

"Oooh." Drew shook his head. "That's a declaration of war."

"Boys!" Mercy stepped out of the house. "Be nice." Her amused expression changed when it landed on Riley—who raced up the steps to claim a kiss, his hand large and gentle against her cheek.

Dorian and Ashaya arrived at almost the same instant, pulling up in a hover vehicle they parked at the edge of the clearing. Riaz knew the man was one of Mercy's closest friends, as well as Judd's training partner on occasion. It seemed a strange combination—the former Arrow and a man who'd fit right in on a surf beach—but among other things, Dorian was deadly accurate with a sniper rifle.

"Come on in." Riley waved everyone into the house.

They entered en mass to find the air rife with mouthwatering smells.

"Yes." Mercy fell back against Riley's wide chest with a dramatic sigh, the back of her hand pressed to her forehead. "I slaved and slaved for you. I hope you appreciate it."

That was when a male head sporting the same distinctive red hair as Mercy's popped out of the kitchen. "I see someone's pants are on fire."

"Shut up, Bas." Mercy shooed away the tall man—who walked over to wrap his arm around her neck and tug her to his side in a scowling grip, as if she wasn't a sentinel with her lieutenant mate standing right there.

"Say sorry."

"Never." Elbowing the man to free herself, Mercy made the introductions. "Everyone, this is my brother, Bastien, otherwise known as a pain in the neck, and an excellent cook. Bas, these are wolves who will fall upon you and devour you if you so much as blink wrong."

"I have wolf-defurring tools, too," Bastien muttered before jerking his head toward the kitchen. "Food's ready. Me and my serving wench will bring it out." He dragged Mercy off with a brotherly lack of concern for her insulted expression.

Riaz's gaze connected with Adria's laughing eyes, his own lips curving.

SENSING his mate's approach half an hour after the rest of them had arrived at Riley's, Hawke headed into the trees, squeezing Brenna into a hug when she appeared first. "Judd sprung you from your late shift, I see." His wolf had a soft spot for this small woman who'd survived a monster and come out of it sane.

"Mariska said she'd cover." An unexpected frown. "I wish she'd get out more. Next time, I'm bringing her."

Aware the gifted senior tech was both extremely shy and a submissive, Hawke nodded. Submissives weren't uniformly shy, not by a long shot, but when such a strong combination—as in Mariska's case—happened, it tended to make them timid and introverted. The pack had to be careful those wolves didn't get lost in the shuffle of their stronger, more dominant packmates. "Tell her we don't bite."

"I don't lie to my friends."

Hawke tugged on her ponytail for that smart-ass remark, just as Judd and Sienna appeared behind her. "How did you beat them down?"

Brenna gave him a look of pure, haughty affront. "I'm a wolf." Walking over to her mate, she held out a hand. "I won. Pay up."

"Tell me the shortcut," Judd demanded.

Innocence in the fractured blue-brown eyes that spoke of Brenna's unwavering strength. "What shortcut?" She batted her lashes . . . and shrieked as she was lifted into the air without warning. Shriek turning into delighted laughter after a second, she did a backward flip.

Beside Judd, Sienna, her hands on her hips, said, "Judd, this is an inefficient use of your—" A startled cry as she found herself floating, too.

Grinning, Hawke walked over to rescue her, grabbing her around the hips to pull her back down to earth. "That'll teach you to sass a Tk."

"I'm an X. Why does no one have any respect?" she said, rubbing her nose against his as Judd and Brenna—back on her feet and with her hand linked to her mate's—disappeared toward the house.

He tucked her deeper into his body, his legs splayed. "You're late." A warning nip on her lower lip.

Sienna nipped back. "You knew I was on my way."

Yes, he had, having allowed himself the rare luxury of keeping an eye on her through the mating bond. She'd known, had understood. "So?" He'd permitted everyone to believe Sienna and Judd were undertaking a normal session of psychic combat, had even forced himself to remain in the den rather than going with them, so as not to raise suspicions.

In truth, Judd and Sienna, as well as Walker, had been attempting to gauge her psychic stability. The psychic "valve" in Walker's mind was an external control on the X-fire, but

Sienna's power remained an unknown for the most part. It was impossible to predict how it might develop and grow. None of them were just going to sit back and hope it would all work out for the best.

"It went really well," she said with a relieved smile. "I'm emitting energy at a constant rate, but the level's so low it's being absorbed into the SnowDancer Web without having a discernible impact on any one individual."

"I'm more interested in you, baby." It infuriated him that he couldn't protect her on the psychic plane, but he had rock-solid faith in Sienna's capacity to master her incredible abilities.

"My shields are airtight, and Judd says the energy transference between me and Walker is becoming smoother as our brains adapt to the process." A tender kiss, her fingers playing with the hair at his nape.

He bent his head so she could reach him more easily. "Any problems?"

"I don't want to jinx it, but . . . so far, so good."

He understood why she couldn't give him a concrete answer—because no one had any neat solutions for an X, much less a cardinal. But his wolf didn't panic, able to see the crimson and gold flame of her through the mating bond. Though always dangerous, it was stable. Yet in spite of that, he continued to sense a deep vulnerability and quiet fear within his mate. He hated that such fear lived in her even now, but Sienna was glad of it.

"I *should* be afraid of my strength," she'd said fiercely. "It stops me from ever becoming lazy in my control."

Hawke could follow her reasoning, accepted that she'd never be able to be as carefree as other women her age, but that didn't alter his instincts when it came to her. Now, his wolf rubbed against his skin, nuzzling at her. "Since when are you superstitious?" he teased in an attempt to subdue the vestiges of fear and worry that lingered in her eyes.

"Since Evie made me watch three horror movies in a row the other night while you were on mountain patrol." Her look of faux terror made him chuckle. "I missed you when you were gone. I'd like to come next time if I'm not on shift."

He didn't like being away from her overnight, but that

particular patrol section was difficult, even for SnowDancers in wolf form. As a result, the duty was rotated between him, Riley, three of the more experienced senior soldiers, Riaz, Indigo, and a surprisingly nimble Tai. Judd could've done it, too, but Hawke had made an alpha decision to conserve the lieutenant's telekinetic strength where possible, in case of unexpected attack or emergency. "It's too dangerous," he said now. "If you fall, you'll shatter your bones." Sienna's psychic power might be immense, but physically she was far more breakable than a changeling.

Stubborn intransigence. "And you won't?"

He growled. "You're meant to be Psy. Be rational."

"I can wait at base camp while you do the sweep. See, a compromise? It's that shiny new word we're trying to learn."

Chapter 30

"BRAT." FRUSTRATED THOUGH he was, man and wolf both laughed, delighted with the woman who was his own. "I'll talk it over with Riley," he said, placing a finger on the lush fullness of her lips when they parted. "Rules."

Biting lightly at his finger, Sienna tugged on his hair. "I hate that stupid rule."

"Serves you right."

"Riley's so fair," Sienna muttered, "I can't ever argue when he decides something in your favor."

"And vice versa." It was integral to his and Sienna's relationship that Hawke not be able to use the fact he was alpha to overrule her. However, Sienna's place in the hierarchy meant the pack wouldn't accept her as a free agent. Neither would such sudden lack of discipline be good for her—she'd made that point herself.

"Just like a wolf, I need the structure provided by the hierarchy," she'd explained. "It suits the military way my mind was trained, helps me manage the X-fire."

It had been decided that Riley, the most senior person in SnowDancer after Hawke, would be the one who gave Sienna her orders as a novice soldier, and who okayed or vetoed things Hawke would normally handle for anyone else in SnowDancer. In effect, Riley acted as her alpha.

So far, it was working.

"Hungry?" he asked as she continued to pet him with those little touches that had become integral to his existence.

"Yes, but I'm not ready to go in yet." When she asked about his day, he told her, listened with ears pricked when she reciprocated.

"Evie wants to go on a double date." An almost wolfish amusement in her grin.

"What does Tai say?" The difference in his and Sienna's ages had worried him before they mated, but he no longer felt any guilt over claiming her, not after she'd almost executed herself on the field of battle. The memory always made him incandescent with rage—and certain he'd made the right decision. Who else would be able to handle his smart, headstrong troublemaker?

Now, she laughed in unholy glee. "Tai looks appalled every time she brings it up."

Hawke was unsurprised at the young soldier's reaction, but he also understood that sweet Evie, who saw far more than most people realized and who loved Sienna like a sister, was sending *him* a message with the joking idea.

The people at Riley's cabin right now were all high-ranking individuals, an utterly disparate group from Sienna's circle of friends. That didn't mean she'd be uncomfortable—his mate wasn't ever intimidated—but this wouldn't, he realized, be the same relaxed event for her as it was for him. "Double date's never going to happen."

"And I was so looking forward to it."

He tapped her lightly on the butt, making her dig her nails into his nape. "Careful," she warned. "I bite, too."

"I have the marks to prove it." Pressing his lips to her

cheekbone, he lifted his head. "I can't ever be anything but their alpha, baby." Those lines could not be blurred.

"I know." No distress, her voice gentle, affectionate. "I was teasing."

He considered Evie's silent message once more. Thought of how many changes Sienna was having to learn to handle in adapting to life as the SnowDancer alpha's mate. "But," he said, decision made, "there's no reason they can't join us tonight." They were her friends, her support structure—a structure she'd need more than ever as her responsibilities grew.

No matter what, Hawke had to remain alpha, but with Indigo and Adria here, as well as Sienna, Evie would feel no discomfort. As for Tai, the boy was Judd's protégé and sometimes trained with Dorian. He'd be fine.

Sienna stilled, looking up at him with eyes gone pure ebony. "Sometimes, you do things that make me fall in love with you all over again."

His wolf preened. "Yeah? Come show me."

RIAZ was enjoying himself far more than he would've believed possible. Having ended up on the verandah along with everyone else, a beer in hand, he grabbed another one of the little pie things Bastien had brought out.

A female groan sounded just as he was thinking that Mercy's brother, a financial whiz in real life, could make a serious go of it as a professional chef. "Bas, if I wasn't already mated, I'd drag you into the woods right now." Indigo popped the remainder of her samosa into her mouth, leaning into her sister as they sat on the chair swing.

Bastien, perched on the verandah railing beside Drew, Dorian, and Tai, legs hooked around the wooden bars, grinned and took a sip of his own beer.

"Since all of you have the bad luck to be mated or otherwise engaged"—Adria tucked up those long, long legs in the ragged but comfortable armchair she'd claimed—"I guess he's all mine."

Several "boos" sounded, with Bastien assuring the women there was more than enough of him to go around. Riaz looked up at Mercy when she perched herself on the arm of his chair. "Your brother always flirt with death?"

"He likes to live on the edge." Placing her glass of fresh lemonade on a small card table that already held a tray of food, she braced her forearm against his shoulder. "And he knows *precisely* how far he can push things. Believe it or not, he's the most well behaved of my brothers."

"Your poor mother."

"Uh-huh."

Riley crooked a finger from where he sat in another arm-chair. Smiling, Mercy rose in a sinuous movement and saun-tered over. "You called?"

Riaz had never seen that teasing look on Riley's face before. It made him feel . . . not an intruder, but . . . family. Pack. As for the woman with the gold-streaked eyes of intense blue-violet whose husky laughter made his wolf prick its ears, he didn't know who she was to him, but he knew that their molten intimacy in the grass had only temporarily assuaged the flame that burned between them.

MERCY watched the lights of Dorian's car fade into the trees, just as Riaz disappeared into the forest, Drew and Tai by his side, Indigo, Evie, and Adria up ahead. Judd and Brenna had left a little earlier, as they both had an early start the next day, and Bas had hitched a ride with her middle brother, Sage, who'd turned up an hour ago. The final two, Hawke and Sienna, intended to take a different route to the den from Riaz's group.

"Hey, Sienna," Mercy called out, and when the young woman turned to look over her shoulder, said, "You know the whole 'let me show you a beautiful spot' line? It's the change-ling version of 'let me show you my etchings.' "

Hawke slung an arm around his grinning mate and dragged her close. "Riley, show your mate your own etchings so she doesn't worry about mine."

Mercy laughed at the bad-tempered snarl, leaning back into Riley's embrace. "You showed me quite a few etchings after Sienna did her nuclear battery thing," she murmured as the other couple walked into the star-dusted night.

"First time I wore you out." Riley's lips brushed her neck, his voice a teensy bit smug.

Leopard and woman both had to admit he was entitled. "Too bad the energy wave didn't cross over to me." It had proven that the connection between the SnowDancer and DarkRiver webs formed by their mating was very much *only* a mating bond. Nothing else came through. As a result, after Sienna's abilities went supernova, Riley had been bursting out of his skin with energy—all of it focused oh-so-sexily on Mercy—while she'd alternately moaned in breathless pleasure and begged for sleep.

The memory made her toes curl. "Got any new etchings to show me?" She closed her hands over his arms, loving the warm, solid feel of him. *My Riley.*

"As a matter of fact . . ." Riley nuzzled at Mercy. "Want to go for a walk first?" The night was stunning as only a Sierra night could be, lit by a full moon and a million stars.

Mercy did a feline stretch in his arms. "I feel too lazy after Bas's concoctions. Can I sit in your lap instead?"

"Come here, kitty cat." Tugging her back, he took a seat in one of the large cushioned wicker chairs her parents had gifted them on their mating. Mercy immediately curled into him, her legs hanging over the arm of the chair, her head against his shoulder. Fiery curls of hair cascaded down his arm where he braced her back, the lithe muscle of her thigh warm under his other hand.

Content in a way he'd rarely been before Mercy, he simply stroked her until she purred. It delighted him as it always did. "I made you purr."

A lazy yawn. "I'm faking it."

Lips curving, he dipped his head to kiss her. It was a familiar exchange, a little private game they could play because they were utterly besotted with one another. The word "besotted" had first been used by a disgusted Sage, but Riley didn't mind being besotted with Mercy. "Fake it some more," he said, his hand on her abdomen.

However, when she tilted back her head, a smile tugging at her lips, he froze, caught by a delicate softness to her features that struck him out of nowhere. Mercy wasn't a vulnerable woman—and yet at that instant, his wolf roared to the surface, wanting to protect, to shelter, to *take care of her*. The urge was so violent that he fisted a hand in her hair, the one on her abdomen flexing until all his tendons stood out in stark relief.

"Riley? What's wrong?" Sitting up from her languorous position, Mercy ran her hands through his hair, over his nape, down his chest.

Petting him. She was petting him in an effort to comfort.

"Talk to me, tough guy." Open concern, her eyes night-glow.

Riley tried to fight the primitive impulse, only to feel it shoving back with so much urgency he stood no chance. Shocked, he shuddered as the wolf took over, but instead of using that control to initiate the shift, it retreated . . . leaving him with a luminous piece of knowledge, a brilliant faceted jewel that almost blinded.

"Oh," he whispered, looking down. "I didn't understand." It was an apology to his wolf. "It's my first time."

Mercy tugged on his hair. Hard. "You're scaring me."

He looked up, wonder in every heartbeat. "Guess what?"

Mercy's gaze dropped to where he'd spread his hand. She went motionless, eyes huge. "Riley, are we— Do you— How—"

"Yes," he answered. "We are, and I know because a changeling male always knows before anyone else when it comes to his mate." He'd heard the healers hypothesize that the realization was caused by a minute change in a woman's scent, a change so subtle no one else would sense anything, but that the wolf in Riley had scented at once.

Mercy's eyes held equal parts shock, and delight. *"Riley."*

He felt his lips stretch even wider. "I think we need to celebrate with some brand-new etchings."

His cat's laugh was surprised and warm and the sound of home. "It's your etchings that got us into this position." Stealing a kiss when he bent his head, she wrapped her arms around his neck. "I'm so happy." It was a conspiratorial whisper.

Cuddling her tight, he said, "Can I tell everyone?"

• • •

AFTER Drew tugged Indigo away somewhere a small distance from the den, Tai and Evie decided to stop at the waterfall, leaving Riaz and Adria to make the rest of the journey alone. Neither of them spoke, and it wasn't quite a comfortable silence, but it wasn't the edgy anger that had existed between them for so long either.

The night air a cool kiss against their skin, they passed into the White Zone not long afterward, and then they were at the den. Instead of splitting with her, he walked her to her room. Reaching the door to her quarters, he waited for her to unlock it, but made no move to cross the threshold. She, in turn, made no move to invite him in, her eyes dark with a dawning awareness that something had changed, the bonds they'd forged that afternoon deeper than they should be. "Good night."

"Good night." Waiting until she closed her door, he walked back out of the den, his wolf needing the quiet freedom of the night. Stripping in a secluded area, he put his clothes carefully in the hollow created between two pines that had grown into each other, and shifted.

Agony and ecstasy, pleasure and pain.

The black wolf that lived within him took form in sparks of color, its nose picking up a thousand unique tendrils of scent. Shaking its head to clear it after the shift, the wolf began to run, disturbed by its own confusion. All its life, the wolf had been the one who felt nothing but certainty, been alternately amused and frustrated by the man's way of complicating things.

Not now. Now it asked the man for clarity . . . and together they ran, the wind ruffling through the pitch-black of the wolf's fur, the forest a familiar playground, the trees watchful sentinels. The freedom of it was intoxicating, until the wolf could almost forget the strange turmoil within. But when the sky grew lighter, and its steps slower, it knew the time had come to return home. The wild called to both parts of Riaz, yet something drew man and wolf to the den, the tug so deep that he rubbed a fisted hand over his heart after shifting.

Time to get some sleep, he thought, and having dressed,

began to walk toward his quarters . . . then suddenly, he was tracking another scent. Delicate and strong. Fragile and steely. A puzzle that suited the enigma of a woman for whom the need in him burned hot and intense. He caught up to her just as she reached her door.

A pregnant pause, last night repeated.

Not turning, she pushed through.

Entering behind her, he shut the door, turned the lock.

Chapter 31

HIS CRAVING FOR her, a craving that hadn't abated even a fraction, roared to the surface when she reached down and pulled off the T-shirt she'd been wearing, baring the long, toned sweep of her back, broken only by the lines of a black sports bra. He used a claw to shred the bra off her body, his hands sliding around her torso to close over her breasts.

Her breath hitched, her nipples tight points against his palms. When she tilted her neck to the side, the invitation was clear. Taking it, he sucked a dark red mark on the lower slope, making her twist against him. So, she was exquisitely sensitive there. Something to remember.

An acid stab of guilt, a reminder that this was not the lover he should be learning how to please, how to adore. He strangled the voice, determined to hold to his decision to move forward . . . but it wouldn't quieten, the black tendrils of betrayal wrapping around his mind and twining through his blood.

Slender, warm fingers on his own. "We aren't the only people in this room right now, are we, Riaz?"

Backing off, he shoved his hands through his hair, beyond angry at himself. "I'm sorry. I didn't mean for it to go like this." He'd come to her in honest need, but now that need was tangled with the caustic taste of infidelity, the chill rain of grief. The fact that he knew he had no rational reason to feel disloyal meant nothing when the primal heart of him was fighting itself, tooth and claw.

Instead of turning on him in fury, a reaction he would've understood from a predatory changeling female of her dominance, Adria toed off her boots and crawled into bed, still dressed in her jeans. Giving him her back, she said, "Come here. Lie with me."

Every muscle in his body locked, torn between two fiercely opposed desires. "I don't know if I can." The admission was ripped out of him.

"No expectations, just two wolves taking comfort from one another." A pause heavy with things unsaid. "I need the touch, too."

The hidden pain of her, it smashed through the tumult inside him to touch the protective core. Kicking off his own shoes, he stripped off his T-shirt and stretched out behind her. He'd left enough space between their bodies that he could see the graceful curve of her spine, the creamy gold of her skin flawless. It was instinct to run his hand over her back, to accept the skin privileges she'd offered him, even as he petted the pain out of her for a fragment of time.

Sighing, she swept her braid off her back and over her shoulder, saying nothing as he continued to touch. Though she was the one who was ostensibly receiving pleasure, he gained as much from the contact. He'd come to her broken and lost, and with her vulnerability, she'd given him the tools he needed to reclaim the reins—to help him, this strong woman had had the courage to rip open her own scars. Driven by protective instinct, he curved his bigger, heavier body around hers, his chest pressed to her back, his hand stroking down her arm, slow and easy.

Her eyes, he saw, were closed, but he knew she was awake. So when she spoke, he wasn't startled—but neither was he ready for her question. "Will you tell me about her?"

His answer was automatic. "There's nothing to say."

Her lashes remained soft shadows on her cheeks. "Of course there is, and you can't speak to anyone else. I won't make any judgments or offer any advice. I'm just here to listen."

His hand clenched on her arm before he forced himself to relax his grip. The only reason he'd said anything to Indigo when he first arrived home was because he hadn't wanted to see her mess up what he'd sensed was the right relationship for her. He didn't regret that choice, made as it had been out of friendship, but he still sometimes wished she didn't know—because it was his greatest weakness.

And Indigo knew the barest facts. Adria already saw too much of him . . . and was a woman strong enough, honest enough, to admit to her own wounds. "Her name," he said, knowing that honesty deserved his own, "is Lisette."

Speaking of her caused a sweet, dark pain inside of him, but there was wild joy, too. At last, he could say her name, share her with someone. "She's French but works in Venice." He'd seen her at an elegant ball held in one of the oldest buildings in the sunken city, its stately lower half submerged, its upper half a masterpiece of ornate architecture.

"The Human Alliance is based in Venice."

"Lisette's husband, Emil, is a computronic specialist with the Alliance." He was a successful, smart man who loved his wife. Riaz had wanted to kill him on sight, been stopped only by the realization that that love was reflected in Lisette's blue eyes—to harm Emil would be to harm Lisette, and Riaz would never do anything to cause her pain. "On the surface," he continued, "Lisette is a business manager for an unrelated company, but I'm pretty certain it's a cover for an Alliance communications operation."

Adria opened her eyes. "You didn't ask?"

"No." His task had been to watch, to learn, to make contacts. While SnowDancer's relationship with the Alliance had thawed enough that the pack was willing to do some business with the group that represented a vast network of human enterprises, neither party was anywhere close to ready to share secrets.

"If she runs their comm team, she must be intelligent."

"No doubt," he said, mind filling with echoes of the conversations they'd had while he fought his most primal instincts to steal what time he could with her. "But the first thing I noticed about her was her laugh." Gentle and warm and so alive. "My wolf wanted to roll around in it."

He'd never forget walking into the ball in Venice, the sight of her a punch to the solar plexus, the thick mass of her shoulder-length hair shining in the light, such a pure gold it hurt. "She's tiny, five feet one maybe, but you don't notice that when you first meet her." All he'd noticed was the feminine strength of her.

"I met with her a number of times—the company she heads produces certain comm technology that could be useful to SnowDancer." Alone in an office with her, he'd wanted to lunge across the desk separating them, nuzzle his face into her neck, bite her, mark her. "She felt something, too. I could sense it. It rattled her." Because Lisette was a faithful, loving wife. "I knew she'd hate herself if she ever betrayed Emil."

"She sounds like someone I'd like."

Thinking of the strong, compassionate woman Adria called sister, he said, "Yes, I think you would." Lisette and Tarah had the same gentle steel to them, the same inviting openness of spirit.

Realizing he was completely curled around her, the arm he'd placed under her head bent to wrap over her upper chest, he played her braid through his fingers. "Do you have to go anywhere this morning?" It was seven thirty, the den's corridors certain to be filled with packmates starting their day.

"No." Her lashes closed, throwing charcoal shadows onto her cheekbones.

Exhaling quietly, he closed his own eyes and slept with her, skin to skin, his wolf finding unexpected peace in the nearness of a packmate who didn't judge, didn't ask things from him he couldn't give, and who shared her body with a rare kindness of spirit. Adria Morgan was a woman he would never forget, no matter if their liaison lasted a week or a year.

HAWKE glanced at Sienna. She'd been pensive since they'd left the home of Mercy's parents ten minutes earlier—where Mercy and Riley had broken the news of Mercy's pregnancy to their respective alphas, though both Hawke and Lucas had known the instant they got within ten feet of the redhead. It was funny how that worked—the previous night, they'd had no clue, but now that Riley knew, it was as if Mercy's leopard had decided it was okay to allow others in on the secret.

Hawke's and Lucas's unhidden glee at this most primal seal on the DarkRiver-SnowDancer alliance had garnered them a snarl, though everyone was too goofy with happiness to work up any kind of a good mad. However, right that second, his mind wasn't on the news that had delighted his wolf enough to put it in harmony with the leopard alpha.

"Hey," he said, switching the car into hover mode to ensure he didn't crush any of the tiny forest plants in this area. "Are you pining for your country music?" She'd forgotten her portable music player, which she usually connected to the onboard stereo. "Cruel and unusual punishment, that stuff."

"You liked the one we slow danced to last night."

"I tolerated it." The truth was, when they danced, he didn't hear anything but the whisper of her breath, the beat of her heart, the low murmur of her voice. "Talk to me, baby." It sounded like an order, and yeah, it kind of was.

A narrow-eyed glance aimed his way. "I should refuse on principle."

"What if I say please?"

Sienna's laugh was soft, intimate, that of a woman who knew him, accepted him. She never let it slide when she thought he was pulling shit, but she didn't bust his ass for acting who he was—an alpha wolf. "I was thinking," she said, her laughter fading, "about children. We've never talked about it."

It was the last thing he'd expected her to say. "You want babies?"

Out of the corner of his eye, he saw Sienna sink her teeth into her lower lip. "I didn't really consider it before. Because . . ."

"I know." His hands tightened on the manual steering wheel at the reminder that she'd lived her life believing she'd die before she ever had a chance to live.

"I'm still scared." A quiet confession.

Wolf sensing her need, he found a clearing and pulled into it, setting the car down so he could turn, brace his arm along the back of her seat. It wasn't enough, not for either part of him. Shoving back his seat, he slid her across and into his lap. She came without the least protest, a silent indication of just how troubled she was feeling.

"We have years," he said. "There's no rush."

She sat up so she could look into his face. "It's not that."

"Talk to me."

"It's a genetic mutation, the X-marker, appearing randomly in the population," she said, a quiet urgency in her every word, "but there is a very high probability I'll pass it on to any child I conceive, and I won't do that, Hawke. I *won't*."

"Hey." Cradling her face in his hands, he rubbed his nose affectionately against her own. "Changelings don't like the way Psy constantly mess with the DNA of their offspring, but even we make an exception for diseases that could harm a child's welfare." He continued before she could interrupt, his voice fierce. "As far as I'm concerned, your X-fire isn't a disease. It's a gift." It had saved the pack, saved so many lives. "B—"

"Walker's helix," Sienna broke in, her skin flushed with the intensity of her emotions. "I know it keeps me stable, but there's no predicting the result when the X-marker first goes active." Tears glittered in the midnight of her eyes. "Our baby could burn up, and we wouldn't be able to stop it."

He cupped the back of her neck, squeezed gently. "Which is why I was going to say that in spite of the fact I see your ability as a gift, if you want to see a genetic specialist before we try for a child, I'll be right there beside you."

"Really?" Slender fingers on his jaw.

"Always," he said, tucking her hair behind her ear, his Psy with her capacity to love with a passion as wild as the crimson and gold of her X-fire. "But I'm not budging on the hair." He rubbed the ruby red strands between his fingertips.

No smile, fear lingering in the ebony shimmer of her eyes. "The other thing is," she whispered, "I don't know how pregnancy will impact my abilities. I know of no case where an X has even been pregnant, much less carried a child to term." Her throat moved as she swallowed painfully. "The changes caused by pregnancy could destabilize me, kill our child, hurt the pack."

"Ah, baby." Stroking his hand around to cup her cheek, he ran his thumb over the delicate arch of her cheekbone, warmth cascading through his veins when she turned her face into the touch. "I won't say that's not a real worry, but what I will say is that you're becoming stronger with each day that passes. Fuck, I'm proud of who you are, who you're becoming." His wolf strutted around the den with its chest puffed out. "I *know* when the time comes to make that choice, we'll be ready."

"I know the other mated couples don't use anything to prevent conception because the birth rate for changelings is so low, but—"

He kissed the words off her lips, laving affection on her until the tension left her body. "Anything that eases your mind, I'm good with." Changeling pairs rarely had more than one or two children, and it was highly unlikely Sienna would fall pregnant so soon after mating—but there was no reason to chance it with his mate's life at stake. "I'm sure Lara will know the best option for Psy physiology." The healer had been gathering medical knowledge about Psy since the family's defection to SnowDancer.

"I *know* that," Sienna said, a pert look to her that made him chuckle.

"Was I taking over?"

"Just a little bit." Fingers weaving through his hair.

His wolf rubbed up against his skin, wanting that touch. Later, he promised.

"I spoke to Lara and got what I needed when I first became an adult," Sienna told him, "I was so afraid about passing on the X mutation." The mate bond vibrated with quiet passion. "I didn't purposefully keep it a secret—it just never came up before."

"I know." Sienna's honesty was an integral aspect of her nature. "It's a good thing you took care of that or we'd probably be wrangling a litter in a year or two, rabble-rouser that you are."

A playful thump against his chest. "I think that maybe, I might not be a bad mother," she said with a shaky smile, "but I'm not ready yet."

"Hey, I'm not sure I am either." He might be wolf, might

be alpha, but he was also a man who'd just found his mate after believing he'd never have that bond. "I want this time with you." Curving his hand around her rib cage, he slanted his mouth over hers in a slow, petting kind of a kiss, licking out at her lower lip, nipping at her upper one.

"Hawke." His name a caress, Sienna wrapped her arms around his neck and melted into the kiss. A far more pleasurable kind of tension rippled through her body, her eyes devoid of stars for a reason that had nothing to do with fear or worry when she broke the kiss to run her lips along his jaw.

He groaned, went to slide his hand under her shirt . . . but Sienna shifted without warning. Tumbling out of the car after shoving the door open, she shot him a look of pure challenge. "Twenty-minute head start. I get to our grotto before you. Winner does what she wants with the loser."

His wolf jerked to attention. "Go." There was nothing he liked better than playing with Sienna, especially when he had more than one new trick up his sleeve. Baring his teeth in a feral grin, he waited exactly twenty minutes before taking off after her.

Chapter 32

ADRIA WAKENED TO find herself wrapped in hot, muscled male flesh. Not for an instant did she wonder who it was that held her, the dark woodsmoke and fresh bite of Riaz's scent intimately familiar. Sensing he hadn't yet awakened, she remained motionless, the crispness of his chest hair against her palm an exquisite temptation, the thickness of his thigh shoved between her own—pressed against the part of her that was going damp with a slow, inexorable arousal though she tried to fight the response.

She hadn't invited him into bed to demand sex, but there was no way he'd fail to sense her body's response. His erection rubbed against her almost the instant the thought passed through her head, and then he was rolling her over onto her back, still sleepy-eyed, his hair tousled and unbearably sexy.

"Riaz," she said, thrusting a hand into the jet black strands to keep him in place when he would've gone for her breasts.

Except there really was no way to stop a dominant changeling male who outweighed her by a good eighty pounds from going after what he wanted in bed, not unless she wanted to say an unequivocal "no." Because that would get through. The thing was, she didn't want to say no. She just wanted to make sure he was fully conscious.

"Oh God!" Her back arched up off the bed as he took one of her nipples into his mouth and sucked. Hard.

He fondled her neglected breast with his free hand, a little rough, and so perfect it made her ache. Wanting to rub up against the thickness she could feel hot and rigid against her thigh through the jeans neither of them had taken off, she forced herself to concentrate—and pulled at his hair hard enough that it had to hurt.

Growling against her skin, he let her feel his teeth. "Damn it," she demanded, "are you awake?"

He bit down on her nipple . . . very, very carefully. She was still attempting to gasp in a breath when he lifted his head and sleepy gold eyes blazed at her. The wolf was in charge, she thought, and its wildness called to her own. Twisting beneath him, she hissed out a breath when he clamped his hand on her hip, his claws pricking at her skin just enough to tell her he was running the show.

Awake. Very much so.

"Get your claws off my skin." It was the snarl of a female wolf who knew her own strength.

"I think you like my claws." A feral smile, but he did retract the sharp tips.

His response unbalanced her wolf—men of his dominance weren't so easily commanded.

"I also think," he said in a dark whisper that made the tiny hairs on her body quiver in warning, "you'll like this even more." Sliding his hand over her navel—the skin so exquisitely sensitive her toes curled—he thrust it under the waistband of her jeans and into her panties in a single unpredictable move.

It shattered her to look down and see his muscled forearm, a sprinkling of fine black hair on the dusky brown of his skin, disappearing into her jeans . . . where he cupped her with stark intimacy within the tight confines of her clothing. Chest jerking, she rose up against him in a vain effort to find relief.

"Undo your jeans." His voice edgy in her ear, the scrape of his unshaven jaw an erotic temptation.

Her fingers brushed his arm as she obeyed the order that promised to give her what she wanted. Removing his hand to rip off her jeans the second she unzipped the fly, he kicked her legs apart to settle himself in between, his jean-covered cock pushing up against the white lace and blue satin of her panties in blatant demand. "Tell me," he said, the hairs on his chest rubbing over her already sensitized nipples, threatening to steal what sense of reason remained, "something you've always wanted to do in bed but never dared."

"Why?" she asked, her skin stretched taut over a body it couldn't contain.

"Because I want to play." It wasn't until the words were out that Riaz realized what he'd said. Playing with a bedmate . . . for a lone wolf, it was beyond friendship, beyond need, a step into an altogether different kind of a relationship.

No, he contradicted himself the second after the thought passed through his head. Neither one of them wanted a relationship, least of all Adria. They were in this to give each other a little surcease. And there was nothing wrong with playing with a friend, even if his wolf rarely played with anyone. "No?" he said when she remained silent.

Her eyes a pale, haunting amber—the wolf looking out at him—she said, "If you promise to reciprocate."

Wolfish curiosity rose to the fore. He nodded at once.

She went to speak, halted, hot red painting her cheeks. Her sudden, unexpected shyness only deepened his curiosity— until he glimpsed the darkness that shadowed her eyes without warning. And he knew she was no longer fully with him, the past tangling with the present.

Gripping her jaw, he growled, "Me and you. No one else comes into this bed. Got it?" It was a vow as much as it was a demand.

"Yes." Amber clashing into his. "For both of us."

"Yes." He closed their deal with a hot, openmouthed kiss, grazing the bottom of her left breast with his thumb as he did so.

Adria jerked away from the kiss with a gasp. "I've heard some women can orgasm just by having their breasts caressed," she said, her husky voice breathless. "I've always wondered if I could." Her cheeks were blazing by the time she finished.

"Somehow, I didn't think you'd be shy." It did something to him to know she trusted him enough to drop her guard. "Anything else you want to share about this fantasy?"

Adria shook her head, feeling naked in a way that had nothing to do with exposing skin. Allowing more of his weight onto her body, Riaz took her mouth in another kiss. A raunchy, wet, demanding one that had her digging her nails into his shoulder as she ground her body against the rigid intrusion of his cock.

"Hmm," he said, lifting his body off the aching need of her own, "this experiment won't work if you can do that." He moved to lie beside her, but when she turned to face him, he said, "On your back."

Everything in her wanted to push him to *his* back, ride him to erotic bliss.

"Giving up so soon?"

Eyes narrowed at the low-voiced challenge, she turned onto her back. When he picked up her arms and told her to wrap her hands around the bars in the headboard, she gripped the cold iron. The position left her breasts blatantly exposed, but for her braid, which had fallen over her shoulder.

Taking that braid, Riaz undid it with leisurely motions, fanning her hair out over one side of her chest. The long strands covered her breast, but for the taut peak of her nipple. "Look at that," he murmured in that deep voice rough with an earthy sensuality that spoke to her own, "so pretty and pink."

Her throat went dry. There was something about seeing

her body through his eyes that changed everything. Each breath she took lifted her breasts, as if in invitation, her nipples begging for his mouth, shameless and plump.

"Hmm." Riaz captured one sensitive nub between thumb and forefinger, the lightness of his touch an exquisite tease.

The instant she arched her spine in an attempt to intensify the caress, he shook his head, his fingers turning featherlight. Understanding the unspoken order, she forced herself to lie back.

The slightly rough pads of his fingers squeezed her nipple tight. "Good girl."

She growled low in her throat. "Don't push it."

He chuckled, eyes gleaming. Then he dipped his head and flicked his tongue over the nipple he'd been teasing. It shot an electric current through her body, but the sensation disappeared almost before she'd sensed it, the air cold on the wet slickness of the tightly furled nub. Chest rising and falling in jerking breaths, she clenched her fingers around the metal that had warmed under her touch, and opened eyes she hadn't been aware of closing to see Riaz pushing her hair aside to reveal her bare breast.

A kiss of air followed, his lips torturously close, his hand sliding to her rib cage. "Do you like this?" He rubbed his thumb across the bottom of the taut curve.

She shuddered, her claws pricking the insides of her skin. "More."

The forearm of his free hand braced by her head, Riaz initiated a languid seduction of a kiss, his tongue licking lazily against her own, his thumb continuing to move slow and maddening across the agonizingly sensitive lower curve of her breast. "Mmm." The low male murmur made her womb clench as he broke the kiss with a suckling taste of her upper lip.

Her skin shimmering with sensation, she held the wild gold of his gaze, hissing out a breath when he moved his fingers to her nipple again, rubbing and tugging with much more force.

It tore a groan out of her, her eyes fluttering shut.

A single hot breath was the only warning she had before he took part of her neglected breast into his mouth, scraping up with his teeth until he caught her nipple. A flick of his tongue and she arched up off the bed, thrusting her hands into his hair. "Forget about the experiment," she snarled, and twisted, taking him to his back.

He'd let her do it, she knew that. Because while she was a strong dominant, he was a lieutenant, far stronger and with faster reflexes. It didn't matter, not in bed, not with lovers who cared about one another's pleasure. And they did. Her wolf felt happy, playful for the first time in years. It was a giddy sensation, champagne in her bloodstream.

Reaching forward, she pinned his wrists above his head, his bones solid and powerful under her hold. "It's time for you to behave."

A heavy-lidded look, slits of bright gold. "What's my incentive?"

She shifted down his body until the satin of her panties, her most delicate flesh slick with desire beyond the fine barrier, rubbed over the heated steel of his cock. "How's that?"

HE'D seen her angry, seen her heartbroken, seen her pleasured, but this was the first time Riaz had seen Adria with sensual mischief in her eyes. His wolf responded, lunging with playful intent. Jerking up even as she began to shape and pet his chest, he flipped her onto her back again, ending up braced on his hands and knees above her. "Pretty good, but I've never been one to give up on a challenge." Bending his head to her breasts, he used his teeth, nipping and biting.

She dug her claws into his shoulder. "Stings."

Raising his head, he said, "No?"

"I didn't say that."

"Good, I like the taste of you." He returned to what he'd been doing, sucking on her nipples until they were ripe little berries before licking the lower curve of her breasts and taking another bite. Her legs rose up to hook around his hips, a sweet, tight prison. Not fighting, he settled heavily against her, enjoying the tensile strength of her married with the lush tang of her femininity, her breasts filling his hands.

Her fingers wove into his hair again, fisted.

Releasing her breast, he rubbed his unshaven jaw against the soft curve. She uttered a stark sound of pleasure and attempted to slide her delicate heat against the painful rigidity of his cock, but wise to her tricks, he pinned her to the bed with his greater weight. She made her frustration clear in the claws he felt biting into his skin.

Slicing out his own claws, he squeezed her hip in warning.

A snarl.

Kissing his way up the center of her chest, he sucked a mark on her throat. It made her moan, the snarl transforming into a husky sound of pleasure. He squeezed one breast, dipped back down to rub his jaw over the other, the creamy flesh marked by his attentions.

A jolt shook her frame. "Riaz."

Hearing the fracture in her voice, he bit down just a little too hard on one nipple as he rolled the other between his fingertips. She shattered with a sudden, shocked cry, her thighs clenching around his hips, one hand fisted in his hair, the nails of the other digging into his shoulder. A hint of blood scented the air and his wolf bared its teeth, not in anger but in primitive satisfaction.

Breaking her hold, he pulled down her panties, got rid of his own remaining clothing and slid into her in a single, deep thrust. She welcomed him with a wild tangle of a kiss, her body continuing to ripple with aftershocks of pleasure that squeezed his pulsing cock, the pressure dragging him to the edge.

He broke the kiss, gasped in a jagged breath. Two long, hard thrusts and he felt his spine lock. Gritting his teeth, he tilted her so that his pubic bone would press against her clitoris, and then he thrust again.

Tiny muscles spasming anew around his cock, a molten fist.

His mind went black.

Chapter 33

THOUGH VASIC TELEPORTED directly into Anthony Kyriakus's office, the Councilor's patrician face didn't display any hint of surprise. Leaning back in his chair, the silver threads in his hair glimmering in the sunlight pouring through the window behind him, he met Vasic's eyes. "It's been a while."

"Yes." His goals had once aligned with Anthony's, but Vasic's loyalty would always be to the Arrows. "The Council is fractured."

"It's not yet common knowledge," Anthony said, putting down the laser pen he'd been using to make notes on a datapad.

"No—but rumors are beginning to spread." He studied the comm screen on the wall to his right, currently displaying the logos of a number of companies, some well known, others discreet powerhouses. "Satisfied clients?" Anthony controlled the largest network of foreseers in the world. Corporations paid millions to get predictions from a NightStar F-Psy before making decisions on everything from investments to product development.

"Very." Anthony didn't rise. "Do the Arrows require a prediction?"

Vasic had always wondered if Anthony had a touch of the F ability, though he was listed in the official records as a high-Gradient telepath with a minor illusion ability. An ability he'd apparently passed on to his daughter, Faith. "Pure Psy has moved on from licking its wounds—indications are it has an operation in progress."

"I see." Rising from his chair, Anthony turned to walk to the window.

Vasic joined him, his eyes on the landscaped park below, the grass jewel green, the trees lush with foliage. "An unusual view." Psy corporations preferred to be in city centers, in high-rises created from glass and steel. The internal NightStar compound, by contrast, was all low, earth-toned buildings designed to flow into the environment.

"Events have led NightStar to question the need for isolation in order to guard the mental health of even our most powerful F-Psy, but foreseers do have unique requirements in comparison to the other designations." Anthony nodded at a sturdy-looking man who'd walked out of the opposite building to take a seat beneath the spreading branches of a large oak. "He's obviously had a strong prediction, and it's drained him. I find my Fs function better—thus increasing our profits— if they have not merely soothing surroundings, but the freedom and space to recover."

Vasic could understand that need better than Anthony would ever know. He often teleported to deserts cloaked in moonlight, because it was only there, surrounded by an endless nothingness that was strangely alive, that he could truly think. "Some would say such a need is an emotional response and should be conditioned out of your foreseers."

"No," Anthony said without looking away from the recovering F-Psy. "Nobody would dare—my people are too necessary to the continuing success of the businesses run by the most powerful. Something I make certain no one ever forgets."

And that was why Vasic had first agreed to work with Anthony—the man was ruthless, but he had the same kind of loyalty to his foreseers that Vasic had to the Arrows. "Do your F-Psy know anything about the Pure Psy situation?"

"A number have foreseen what they call a cataclysmic change in the Net," Anthony replied. "The visions are so violent the medics have had to intervene in three cases to bring the foreseers safely out. If they hadn't been under supervision"—the slightest pause—"we'd have lost them."

Vasic wondered if the pause had been an unconscious reference to Anthony's daughter. Faith NightStar was the most powerful F-Psy in or out of the Net, the reason the squad had kept a covert eye on her since her defection to DarkRiver. Her Silence broken, there was a strong likelihood she'd been one of the foreseers Anthony had referenced. While Faith was no longer under M-Psy supervision, she was connected to her jaguar-changeling mate by a type of psychic bond Vasic didn't understand. Perhaps that bond protected her in some way. "No details?"

Anthony shook his head. "But it's worse than anything they saw prior to the battle with the changelings. The scale of the deaths will be catastrophic."

Chapter 34

FEELING MORE HIMSELF than he had in months, Riaz was out looking for a wind-fallen tree he could mine for a hunk of wood when something caught the sunlight—and his eye. He bent down, picked up a twisted piece of metal. Seeing the scorched and broken tree trunks around him, he realized he was at the spot where one of Henry Scott's stealth craft had crashed prior to the final confrontation. It wasn't surprising the small piece had been missed, the debris had been spread over such a large area.

Placing it into one of the pockets in his cargo pants, he decided to do a quick grid search to see if there were any other fragments. It didn't take long under the bright Sierra sunshine. The techs and novices had done an excellent job— but for the damage to the environment, the area was pristine. That damage, too, would heal. SnowDancer would make sure of it.

Satisfied, he took a quick glance at his watch, saw it was four. Since he'd already found a small chunk of the type of wood he needed, he was about to head back to the den to complete his review of SnowDancer's international business plan, when he caught a vague hint of a scent that shouldn't have been there.

Metallic. Cold. A Psy drenched in Silence.

It could be nothing, a remnant attached to another piece of debris, though the probability was low, taking into account the time that had passed. And all the penny-ante annoyance hits to date had taken place on the edges of den territory. Why would any Psy want to seriously antagonize SnowDancer now, after the pack's decisive defeat of Henry's army?

Tracking the scent on silent feet, he came to the top of a small rise. Here, the lingering scent was as thick as soup to his changeling senses. He frowned. The position offered the watcher no strategic viewpoint in terms of figuring out Snow-Dancer's weaknesses. All he or she would see was a small, naturally open field surrounded by scrubby bush that merged into a stand of lodgepole pines.

A curvy young female with lush black curls—Maria—jogged across the clearing at that very second, accompanied by a dark gray wolf who spotted Riaz a second before Maria did. The soldier waved, while the wolf howled a greeting before they both disappeared into the pines.

Hmm . . .

Psy had been known to use SnowDancer land for meetings, which wasn't as stupid a move as it sounded, not given the spread of den territory, and how simple it was to teleport into isolated sections. This spot might qualify, *except* as Maria and Lake had just proven, anyone on this hill would be silhouetted against the sky, openly visible to a passing sentry.

Gut-certain he was missing something, he kicked off his boots and stripped. His sense of smell was acute even as a human, but nothing beat the wolf's nose. Circling the area after shifting, he checked twice to make sure he had it right, then changed back into human form and quickly got dressed.

Racing to the den, he pushed into Hawke's office without waiting for an invitation. "We need to talk."

The alpha turned from the comm screen where he was talking to a man who wore a neat three-piece suit, his graying hair combed sternly back to reveal a defined widow's peak. "We'll have to continue this another time, Mr. Woo."

Pursing his lips in disapproval, the man on the other side nonetheless made no demur as Hawke signed off. "What is it?" His eyes flicked over Riaz's shoulder, sharpened.

Riaz had already turned to greet Riley, pushing the door closed behind the senior lieutenant. "Do you have what I asked for?" He'd called Riley during his run to the den.

Nodding, the other man input a data crystal into the comm panel. "These are the watch routes I've assigned the soldiers and novices over the past two weeks." A longer period than warranted by the intensity of the scent, but Riaz hadn't wanted to risk missing a pattern because of too tight a date range.

"I've color-coded the individual soldiers," Riley continued, "so you can see who was where when at a glance."

Riaz pinpointed the rise where he'd caught the scent, inserted an asterisk to mark the spot on the map, then checked which packmates had passed within sight of it. Fury ignited in his blood. "The shape of the scent on the earth," he said, after filling Hawke and Riley in on his discovery, "says the intruder was lying down." It was the only way he or she could have escaped detection.

"Sniper?" Riley asked in a grim tone.

"Or surveillance." Ice in Hawke's voice, the wolf stalking behind pale eyes fixed on the assignment map. "No reason for the Psy to watch Maria, Tai, Riordan, or Ebony."

That left one name.

"We knew this would happen," Riaz said, tracking the deep aqua color Riley had allocated Sienna, his anger transforming into a cold determination to keep safe the young woman who'd walked into battle willing to die for Snow-Dancer. "Everyone in the Net now knows what she can do."

"I hoped they'd leave her alone a few fucking months at least." The words were gritted out between the alpha's clenched teeth.

"How'd they know she'd pass through that field?" Riaz thrust a hand through his hair. "Riley mixes up assignments." SnowDancer had had one traitor in their midst—another one would kill them; but the question had to be asked. "You think they have an informant?"

"No." Hawke's response held utmost confidence. "I'm betting they've been using spy satellites to scan our territory— the canopy makes it difficult in most cases, but there are open areas."

Riaz gave a slow nod. "All they'd have needed was a single glimpse of Sienna"—her hair that distinctive ruby red—"and then they just had to be patient." He considered the other implications if Hawke was right. "No normal person would have access to that kind of satellite data. Or to a teleporter." Flying or driving any unauthorized vehicle into the territory without being caught was so difficult as to be impossible.

"Pure Psy," Riley said, his eyes on the map, "lost the majority of their Tks in the fight. If Judd's right about the rumblings in the Net, the group's probably got other priorities at this point."

"Ming is the most obvious suspect." Riaz was aware the man had been the military mastermind of the Council. "But we don't have enough information to rule anyone out. Kaleb Krychek for one." The lethal telekinetic could see Sienna as a threat to his own power.

"Shoshanna's gone suspiciously quiet, but she was the force behind Henry for most of their sham of a marriage," Hawke said, and Riaz knew the alpha's brain was working with cold efficiency in spite of his rage. "And Tatiana's always been very good at hiding her involvement in any number of ops."

"I'll talk to Judd." Shutting down the map, Riley retrieved the data crystal. "He might be able to get us more concrete data."

"I'll tap my contacts in Europe," Riaz added, knowing Ming used an estate in the Champagne region of France as his home base. "See what I can dig up." Glimpsing the look in his alpha's eyes, he said, "No one will get near her, Hawke. We won't let them."

Hawke knew his people would bleed to protect his mate, but he didn't want Sienna to need that protection, to be forced to live in another cage. "We make sure she's safe on our land," he said, his anger an icy blade. "This needs to be her home, where she can walk without fear."

Riaz's phone beeped a sharp alarm into the silence. "Damn," the lieutenant said, glancing at the screen after switching it off. "I have the comm-conference with Kenji and the BlackSea rep."

"Go," Hawke said, thinking past the fury that clawed

through his veins. "That's your priority." BlackSea brought far too much to the table to disregard. "I need to talk to Sienna anyway." Any defensive response SnowDancer formulated would need her input—she knew the strengths and weaknesses of her enemies better than anyone.

Riley shot him an openly concerned look after Riaz left. "It might go better coming from me."

Hawke didn't take it wrong—Riley wasn't only his senior lieutenant, he was also Hawke's friend, knew exactly how this might make him behave. "No, I've got it."

HAVING tracked Sienna to the nursery where she was doing a volunteer shift, Hawke watched his mate talking with a two-year-old. Thank God she was inside today—he didn't know if he'd have been able to handle his primal response if she'd been out in the thick green of the forests.

He knew she'd sensed his presence, but she didn't break off what appeared to be a serious discussion. Nodding solemnly at something the little boy said, she helped him finish building his wooden-block masterpiece before rising to her feet and walking over to Tarah.

A short conversation later, she headed toward him. "I asked to leave early," she said, and he knew he'd failed in his attempt to shield the raw emotions that had his wolf pacing, claws out.

"Walk with me."

Not asking questions, she accompanied him down the corridors and to an exit from the den that led into a less utilized section of the White Zone. Where he leaned against the moss-covered wall of the den and gathered her into his arms, just held her for a long, long time.

Sienna was intensity and fire and energy, but today, she stood quiet, letting him take what he needed, his mate who knew him better than he knew himself.

When he drew back at last and told her what Riaz had discovered, the cardinal starlight of her gaze turned to endless midnight. "It was predictable," she said, no shock in her, just an anger as deep as his own. "No one likes a rogue X."

A growl rumbled up from his chest. "I will not allow anyone

to hunt you." It was a vow from the heart of the wolf. "Brenna and Mariska are already working on further fine-tuning our surveillance systems, so we have a better chance of detecting these incursions." The fact that it was near impossible to stop teleport-capable Tks from going anywhere they wanted meant nothing—no one in SnowDancer was planning to make it easy for those stalking Sienna.

His mate placed her right hand against his chest. "I'll speak with them," she said, "let them know a few elements they can factor into their calculations. Judd will probably be able to provide more guidance."

At times, he forgot how Sienna had been brought up, the inhumanity of her childhood. Then she showed this depth of strength, keeping a steely calm through an ugliness that would've shoved many back into the darkness, and he remembered that his young mate had lived a lifetime in nineteen years. "Good," he said, his pride in her a blinding fire. "You also need to talk to Riley about your watch rotations."

A guarded alertness. "Why?"

"So he can make sure your shifts never fall into any kind of a pattern, timing or location wise. We don't want those watching being able to guess with any hope of accuracy where you'll be."

Her shoulders lost the fine tension that had flowed into her with his earlier words. "Yes, that's an excellent precaution."

Cradling her face with one hand, he said, "I won't ever clip your wings, baby." Regardless of how much he hated the fact that she was in danger—because to do so would be to put her back in that cage, and his mate had spent more than enough time locked in the dark.

"I know you want to protect me," she whispered, long, slender fingers spreading over his heart. "I can feel your need in every pulse of your blood."

"I can't promise that I won't check up on you every so often during your shifts," Hawke admitted, because it would've been a lie of monumental proportions to do otherwise, "but every part of me understands who you are." Not simply his mate, but a dangerous, beautiful woman with her own dreams and desires.

It would've been easier if she'd been someone else, a

woman who followed his every dictate and who never put herself in harm's way. But he didn't want easier, didn't want anyone else. He wanted Sienna. Only Sienna.

She turned her face into his hand. "All right." A simple acceptance that said she knew, understood . . . followed by an unexpected smile full of mischief. "Scuttlebutt is, Riley's been running into Mercy 'accidentally' during her shifts since they found out about the pregnancy."

Hawke's wolf was startled out of its anger into a chuckle. "I hope Mercy lives up to her name."

Sienna laughed, no fear in her, only a strength that made his wolf want to throw back its head and sing in joy that she was his.

Chapter 35

RIAZ LINKED IN with Kenji in the conference room usually used for SnowDancer lieutenant meetings. The other man's hair was now a shocking pink with vivid blue streaks. It was a welcome distraction. "You look like fucking Japanese cotton candy."

"How the hell can cotton candy look Japanese?" Kenji shot back before picking up a datapad. "Any new thoughts on the outline agreement since our last call?"

Knowing they were short on time, Riaz decided to update Kenji on the situation with Sienna later, and brought up the contract on a split screen that would be visible on Kenji's end, too. "Yeah, one." He quickly set it out. "You see any problems?"

Kenji shook his head. "No, that's a good amendment." He highlighted a section in the agreement they'd discussed earlier. "I'm still not sure about this."

"They won't consent to a complete strikeout, and it's not

a deal breaker for us," Riaz said, "but let's bring it up and see what concessions we can squeeze out of them."

"Works for me."

One of the other comm screens in the room chimed a five-second countdown as Kenji finished speaking. Clearing away the contract, Riaz was ready when the third screen filled with Emani Berg's elegant face. Born in a small village along one of Norway's remote fjords, Emani had skin of a deep, silken shade of brown and eyes of midnight. Her black hair had been in curls the last time Riaz had seen her—in Venice— but fell sleek and straight around her face today . . . complete with a single streak of shocking pink.

Amused, Riaz said, "Good call."

Emani's nod was regal. "Mr. Tanaka does keep things interesting."

Kenji looked disgruntled. "How did you guess?"

"I have someone in your region." Not even a hint of a smile, though Riaz knew her well enough to know she was tweaking Kenji's nose. The woman was a killer poker player.

"Fleeced any innocents lately?" Riaz asked, recalling the soccer tickets she'd won off him and Pierce, the same serene expression on her face the entire game.

"I'm planning to do so in the next few minutes," was the smooth response.

Laughing, he lifted the printout of the outline. "This," he said, "is fine as far as the basics go, but we'd like to make some changes with regard to the details."

Her surprise was concealed with such flawless ease, Riaz would've missed it if he hadn't been watching for just such a reaction. "I'm listening," she said in that calm, temperate voice.

Riaz nodded at Kenji, who began to go through Snow-Dancer's list of requested amendments. Emani frowned at some of their stipulations but didn't voice outright disagreement. Once Kenji had completed the run-through, she looked up from the copy on which she'd been making notes. "I'll need to run this past our Conclave, but while we'll certainly be coming back to you with our own changes, I don't foresee any major problems."

"Good." Riaz folded his arms. "BlackSea realizes we're already in alliance with DarkRiver and WindHaven?"

"Of course. We understand that should we agree to a full alliance, BlackSea would be expected to come to their aid when necessary."

"And vice versa," Kenji pointed out.

Emani gave a graceful nod. "As DarkRiver and Wind-Haven would effectively become our allies should Snow-Dancer and BlackSea come to an understanding, our Conclave would like to have a comm conversation with both Lucas Hunter and Adam Garrett of the WindHaven falcons before we take the final step into an alliance."

"I don't see a problem with that," Riaz said. "We also have a request: a face-to-face meeting between Hawke and Miane." He didn't mention the fact the request was nonnegotiable, wanting to gauge how well BlackSea was willing to play with SnowDancer.

"I see." A small pause.

He raised an eyebrow. "Is that a no?"

"On the contrary. We expected the request."

"We'll work with you to set it up then." There was no use waiting, not when the entire alliance might hang on the reaction the two alphas had to one another.

"Very well." Emani's image swayed a little, then righted. "Rough seas?"

"Nothing unusual." Tapping at the comm controls on her desk, she looked at him and Kenji in turn. "While we are not yet allied, BlackSea would like to pass on some information in the spirit of cooperation."

Not waiting for a verbal response, Emani split her screen. "Two days ago, three of our members found a ship dead in the water off the coast of Sardinia—well outside their territo-rial waters, however." The empty half of the screen filled with the image of a sleek yacht that had to be at least one hundred feet long. Painted a gleaming black, it was shaped like a bul-let, the windows tinted. "As per our own internal rules, they shifted into human form to render assistance."

Riaz had no trouble believing her explanation. More than one stranded sailor or shipwrecked crew had been saved by those from BlackSea—the sea changelings might have been notoriously secretive, but they didn't hesitate when it came to a question of saving lives.

"All seven of the people on board were Psy," she continued. "They'd been dead long enough to cool, but rigor had not yet begun to set in." Seven crime-scene images appeared onscreen, replacing that of the yacht. "As you can see, they appear to have been executed."

"Suggests a team with military training," Kenji murmured before pausing and asking Emani to reorder the images a certain way. "No, not a team. Look at what I'd bet was the first kill—broken neck. The rest are all clean strikes with a laser weapon. Silent and efficient."

"We agree. It appears the individual responsible for the executions took the weapon from the first victim and proceeded to use it to eliminate the others."

And, Riaz thought, if the yacht had been found in the high seas, that pointed to the involvement of a second craft—no one but another water-based changeling could've swum to shore from that far out. In which case, BlackSea would've sunk the boat and its dead cargo in short order, no one the wiser.

"Our people," Emani said, breaking into his thoughts, "had enough time before a Psy team located the boat that we were able to gather a significant amount of data. One of the things we discovered was this scrap of fabric."

Riaz stared at the image of the ragged square, one half of it bearing an emblem of some kind. "I've seen that before."

"Yes, very likely." Emani input a command and the fragment re-formed into a whole.

Kenji hissed out a breath. "Son of a bitch."

ADRIA had just finished having coffee with Tarah and was heading back to the office she'd been assigned down the corridor from Drew when Shawnelle ran up to her. With an exuberant personality and wild bronze curls to match, the athletic fifteen-year-old was incredibly sweet, a gentle maternal submissive.

"You didn't forget?" the girl asked.

"No," Adria reassured her. "I was about to get my camera—you want photos, right?"

A bright smile against skin the shade of polished teak. "Do you think anyone will want to see?"

"Don't try that shy act on me," Adria teased, tugging on one of Shawnie's tight curls. "Walker's put me onto your tricks."

Shawnie giggled, protesting her innocence all the way to Adria's office, where Adria grabbed a camera capable of taking holographic images as well as high-definition two-dimensional shots. "I'm all yours."

Shawnelle led her quickly down the corridors, past all the busy sections, to a small room at the very back. Pushing through the door, she waved Adria in with excited motions.

Entering, Adria whistled. "You have a bunch of elves working for you?"

"The others helped," Shawnie said. "Especially Becca and Ivy."

Adria shook her head. The room had been four plain stone walls and a door when she'd assisted Shawnie make the request for a work space. The teen had been terrified of approaching Riley on her own, but she'd had the will. All Adria had had to do was provide moral support.

Now, the four walls were each painted a different color from lime green to blood orange to aqua-blue and crisp white, the paint remnants no doubt left over from when the maternals had redone the common areas of the den. Vibrant and alive, it suited Shawnie. The faded carpet on the floor was clearly a discard from someone's home, but it had been washed and dusted to within an inch of its life, its battered elegance imparting a warm coziness to the room.

Against one wall stood a long table on which were spread swatches of fabric, beside it a compact sewing machine, while there was a small curtained cubicle to the back. Walking to the cubicle, Shawnie whispered to the person on the other side—Ivy, from the scent—then glanced at Adria. "Ready?"

Adria held up the camera. "Set."

Taking a deep breath, Shawnie pulled the curtain back with a theatrical flourish to reveal her friend dressed in a beautifully worked black jacket that nipped in at the waist before flaring out gently just above Ivy's slender hips. It was detailed with funky beading on one shoulder—as if a colorful rain had fallen down the velvet of the jacket—and set atop a simple pair of blue jeans, strappy black heels completing the look.

Stunned by the beauty of Shawnie's work, Adria didn't say anything as Ivy held a number of poses to fully display the jacket. "Sweetheart, you're a star." She smiled at Ivy. "And you're on the way to being on a catwalk."

They both blushed, looking toward each other with huge smiles.

Adria snapped a photo, capturing the moment. "That one's for you two." Then she took a number of shots of Ivy displaying Shawnie's creation for SnowDancer's weekly newsletter.

"You really like it?" Shawnie asked afterward, her heart on her sleeve.

"I'd wear it if it was in my size," Adria said honestly, conscious that nurturing the juvenile's pride and self-confidence, while listed nowhere in her official mandate as Shawnie's trainer, would flow into every other aspect of the girl's life—including the defensive and aggressive moves Adria was teaching her.

As Shawnie bounced away to help Ivy change out of the jacket, Adria's wolf laid its head on its paws, its belly warm with contentment—like the human part of her, it knew this work was as important to the health of the pack as any battle victory, any security measure. Shawnie's bright spirit, Ivy's innocent pleasure in her friend's accomplishment, these were the things every dominant fought to protect.

KENJI met Riaz's gaze after Emani signed off. "How do you want to handle this?"

"I'll talk to Bo," Riaz said, referring to the security chief and effective leader of the Human Alliance, a man he'd taken care of to get to know after the Alliance's run-in with Snow-Dancer and DarkRiver.

"Hawke?"

"Not yet." The alpha had enough on his plate with the threat to Sienna—and he'd always trusted his lieutenants to work independently, part of the reason why SnowDancer had such strong men and women in those positions. "Let me see what I can find out first."

"I'll put out some feelers, too," Kenji said, his expression serious in a way that belied the reckless abandon of his chosen hair color.

"Call me on my cell if you hear anything." Logging off, Riaz decided to grab some coffee from the nearby break room before calling Bowen. He was frowning at the implications of the Human Alliance being involved in the assassination of an entire Psy team when he walked into the break room—to come to a complete halt, the scent of crushed berries in ice wrapping around him, delicate as the most fragile snowflake.

Chapter 36

ADRIA GLANCED AT him from the counter, her guarded smile familiar. "Hey." She held up the coffeepot, pouring him a mug when he nodded. "Milk?"

"No, black." It felt strange to be having this ordinary conversation with her, the undertone faintly awkward, when he'd been buried balls-deep in her only hours ago.

"Here you go." Passing it over, she began to add sugar to her own mug.

His eyebrows rose after the fourth teaspoon, the awkwardness dissipating into an amused affection that made his wolf prick its ears. "Sure you don't want some coffee with your sugar?" he asked when she began to stir.

"Everyone has their vices." A suspiciously bland comment, followed by, "Maybe you'd like me to fetch you a bar of dark chocolate."

He grinned, wondering how she'd figured out his predilection for the stuff. "I figured you were a strong-black-coffee type of girl." It intrigued him that he'd been so off base, made him aware of all the things he didn't know about this woman who'd shared her body with him. Especially when she poured in what looked like half a pot of cream, then took a gulp, shivering with pleasure.

His body hardened. The urge to touch her, to claim skin privileges outside the bedroom was almost overwhelming, but he grit his teeth and fought it. They'd set limits on their relationship, and he needed to respect that, not only for his sake, but for hers.

Adria leaned back against the counter. "You look tense."

Her color-drenched eyes, they saw too much. It was one of the first things he'd thought at their initial meeting, and regardless of how uncomfortable it made him as a man, her perceptiveness was a skill he could utilize as a lieutenant. "You know much about what went down with the Human Alliance a year ago?"

The Alliance had tried to plant bombs in San Francisco, attempted to kidnap Ashaya Aleine. Bo and his people, rebels from the group at the time, had made the stupid-ass mistake of kidnapping a young male from DarkRiver territory in an effort both to protect him and to gain the packs' attention. "About Bowen and his group?"

"Yes"—Adria took another sip of her coffee—"all senior soldiers were briefed. I know we've been working with the cats to build a functional relationship with them."

"It's been rocky," Riaz acknowledged, "but we knew we had to find some way to make things work." The Alliance's business standing had taken a hit immediately after the events in San Francisco, but as Hawke had predicted, it had rebounded even stronger.

Changelings have packs, the alpha had said. *The Alliance is the human equivalent—it not only represents humans as a group, it's powerful enough that people pay attention.*

Not a body to disregard, regardless of the fact that humans were so often labeled the weakest part of the triumvirate that was the world.

"Are they breaking their side of their bargain," Adria asked, "trying something in our territory?"

"No, but they've been implicated in a set of assassinations

in the Mediterranean." He pushed off the wall, decision made. "I'm going to call Bowen. Want to sit in?"

Blue-violet eyes streaked with gold widened at the corners. "Yes, I would."

Coffees drunk and mugs washed, they headed toward the conference room. "Does the Alliance have people with the training to pull off something so clean and, we have to assume, fast?" she asked after he finished summarizing the situation.

"Bo could've done it. He worked in covert ops in the military arm of the Alliance before he decided he didn't like where that arm was heading under the previous leadership." Into a violence as cold and self-serving as that of the Council. "If it was the Alliance, I'm more interested in the why."

Adria raised an eyebrow as they entered the conference room.

"Bo," he explained, "has been very carefully rebuilding the Alliance's reputation."

"And this kind of violence, if it got out," Adria murmured, "would bring up too many ugly memories in the wider population."

He reached behind her to shut the door. "Grab a seat out of camera range," he said, allowing her enigma of a scent to seep into his veins. "I want you to act as a second set of ears and eyes—Bo's very good at only giving away what he wants."

Choosing a seat that offered an excellent vantage point, Adria watched Riaz put through the call. His back to her, he couldn't see her, and so she allowed herself the indulgence of a lingering visual examination, her eyes drawn to his left shoulder and the jagged curves and lines of the tattoo hidden by his T-shirt. She loved the way the black ink looked against his skin, as she loved the muscled beauty of his frame, the way he moved when inside her.

It wasn't difficult to see why he intrigued her on the deepest level.

But though he was undeniably a sexy, handsome man, her wolf saw beauty through a different lens. It was drawn to his strength, his ease with himself—and with her. Riaz wasn't bothered if she lost control during intimacy and drew a little blood, didn't care if she wanted to take the reins at times.

When they'd worked together during the battle with Pure Psy, he'd given orders with cool, calm control even in the midst of chaos. The soldier in her respected him for that, while the woman found it another compelling aspect of his character.

However, she also understood that he'd be maddening in a relationship. He wasn't simply a dominant predatory changeling male, a lieutenant, he was a lone wolf. It was legend how incredibly possessive and insanely protective a lone wolf became with the woman he claimed as his own—as opposed to one with whom he'd agreed to build a friendship based on a storm of shared need . . . and shared pain.

"Two seconds," he said, those amazing eyes locking with her own. "Ready?"

Her stomach clenched in visceral awareness. "Yes."

"Who the hell is this?" a rough male voice asked, accepting an audio-only transmission after the call rang for a quarter of a minute.

"Bo, it's Riaz."

A pause, the sound of sheets rustling. "Christ, let me get out of bed," was the response, though it had to be midmorning in Venice.

"Late night?" Riaz asked.

"Unfortunately not the X-rated kind." A couple more seconds passed before Bo's face appeared on-screen. He'd shaved off his hair, so he didn't have bed head, but his face was rumpled on one side, the smooth caramel brown of his skin carrying a fine sunburn . . . as if he'd been out on the water. "That was quick." Somber eyes that watched Riaz with piercing intensity.

Riaz didn't blink. "You know what this is about."

"I can guess." Bo rubbed a hand over his smooth skull, the lines of his face masculine yet elegant—a man who'd be beautiful if not for the flinty hardness in his eyes, the ropes of muscle across his bare shoulders. "I can't say anything on this line."

"It's secure."

But Bowen shook his head, a stubborn angle to his jaw. "Has to be face-to-face, and I'm not planning on any travel right now."

Leaning back against the wall, Riaz folded his arms. "You're sounding paranoid."

"You would, too, if you'd just had the week I've had. It'll only take you what"—Bo frowned—"three hours on an express airjet to get here?"

"This isn't the best time for a SnowDancer lieutenant to leave the pack." Riaz held the Alliance male's gaze. "What priority is your intel?"

"High." No hesitation.

"I'll call you back."

"Trust me, Riaz. You want to hear what I have to say." Bowen signed off with those portentous words.

Waiting until the screen was clear, Adria said, "Why didn't you confirm a trip?" He was right about the timing, but it was doable, wouldn't affect the strength of their defenses.

"If he's on the mark about the comm being monitored," Riaz said, blue-black strands of hair falling across his forehead, "it's no use tipping off any listeners to the fact we'll be in the area."

Her pulse spiked. "We?"

"I'm going to need backup." Riaz saw Adria's eyes widen. "Situation like this, I'd usually ask my man already in the area, but he's got something else on his plate, and you speak fluent Italian." He knew it was the right decision, that her linguistic skill and status as an experienced soldier made her the perfect choice. He also knew he was treading a dangerous line.

But Adria, when she rose to her feet, showed no indications of having read more into his suggestion than he meant. "How do you know that? The fact I speak Italian?"

"It's my job," he said. "I keep track of anyone in the pack who has a skill that might come in useful internationally." Adria's CV had passed across his desk when she transferred. "What I can't understand is why you chose to learn Italian when Spanish would've been more useful in the region."

She didn't answer, her next words telling him her mind was on something else altogether. "I don't want to disrupt things so early on with my trainees."

"It should only be a day or two." He knew how heavily the juveniles relied on their assigned supervisors.

A slow nod. "That's manageable. I was planning to ask Riley to put me on a high-perimeter shift anyway." Catching his questioning look, she said, "They might be submissives, but constant oversight isn't good for any wolf's development."

"We'll leave early morning tomorrow," he said, wondering how a tough senior soldier understood SnowDancer's submissives so well. "That give you enough time to organize cover for your duties?"

"No problem." Then to his surprise, she did a funny little dance around her chair, singing, "I'm going to Venice. I'm going to Venice."

It startled laughter out of him, his wolf standing up in fascination at the unexpected and sweetly charming crack in Adria's sober facade. "If you're really good," he said when she stopped dancing to grin at him, "I'll take you on a gondola ride through the canals." Delight, bright and dangerous, cascaded through his veins.

Chapter 37

HAVING COMPLETED HIS research, Vasquez located the first three addresses fast enough, but it took hours of hacking through Net firewalls to unearth the second three and four days to complete the list. Psychically exhausted, he considered sending the one he served an e-mail with the update, but they had agreed on electronic and psychic silence. *Nothing* of their plan was going to leak and jeopardize everything they had set so meticulously in place.

Conscious that tiredness could lead to mistakes, Vasquez slept long enough to become functional, then made his way to the compound hidden deep in a rural sector of Ireland. "I have the coordinates and necessary images of the first set of targets."

"When can we move?" The voice was a rasp, a broken saw, issuing from a throat that had suffered second-degree burns when Henry Scott screamed as his legs were turned to ash, one of his arms sliced below the elbow by a whip of cold fire.

The medics had been working to repair the damage, but it was severe. Sienna Lauren's X-fire had cauterized the wounds, so they'd needed to be cut open vein by vein to allow for the regeneration aids to work. However, the worst damage had been done when a Pure Psy operative shoved his body over Henry's in an effort to protect him. That operative's weapon had melted into the former Councilor's flesh.

It was proving near impossible to excise the plas from his body, some of it appearing to have integrated into his organs. As a result, Henry remained hooked up to multiple devices, his body supine on a hospital bed inside a large chamber of sterile glass, his ruined voice issuing via a speaker. However, the fire had done nothing to his mind, and they were Psy. The mind was all that mattered.

"Are we in a position to strike?" Henry elaborated, his bloodshot eyes looking at Vasquez through the glass.

"I recommend waiting until we have at least ten complete sets." It would allow them to strike back to back, leaving no time or room for a counterstrike. However, it all depended on whether Vasquez could muster enough trusted personnel with the right abilities.

Loud, rattling breaths. "The Net is becoming weaker with each day that passes, filled with those whose Silence is flawed. We need to remind them of who we are as a race."

"Yes, but our chances of success rise exponentially if we act without any warning." Giving the enemy no time to prepare before the avalanche.

Henry took a long time to reply, his breathing so rough Vasquez knew this interview would soon end. "Five sets," the former Councilor said at last. "Five complete sets and one outlier."

"Sir?"

"A small location, a demonstration of what we can do ahead of the primary hits."

"A test to ascertain the validity of our refined method?"

Their earlier plan had proven to have a fatal flaw, so he could agree with the precaution, except that it risked tipping their hand.

But Henry said, "If those in the Net want to feel, then perhaps we should teach them the taste of terror."

Vasquez would never betray the only man who appeared to be taking the disintegration of Silence not as an inevitability, but as a disease that needed to be stopped, but he was also not a cipher who followed Henry's every command. "We chance losing the element of surprise," he said. "It could lead to the primary targets being sequestered."

"Would it not be better," Henry said, "if we did not have to act against those targets? Perhaps one demonstration is all that will be needed."

Vasquez considered the question, realized his leader was right. This strategy was not one they had agreed to lightly—it went against the founding tenets of Pure Psy. However, it was a proven fact that those who adapted to altered circumstances were the ones who survived. "One outlier," he said, already weighing up suitable possibilities. "If we are to hold to the timetable, I must get back to my duties."

"Go." A pause. "Vasquez?"

"Sir?"

"You have been loyal. I won't forget."

"Purity will save us, sir." Vasquez's ancestors before Silence had been murderers and sociopaths. Silence was his salvation. "I'll set things in motion."

Everyone, no matter their location or race, had a Psy neighbor, colleague, or business acquaintance. When Pure Psy rose this time, it wasn't only the Psy who would learn the meaning of fear.

Chapter 38

RIAZ STEPPED OFF the watercraft he and Adria had boarded to reach Venice after the airjet landed at nearby Marco Polo Airport, both of them carrying small duffel bags. It was temperate this time of year, the air around them dusky with the oncoming sunset, the soft light burnishing the old stone of the buildings that remained above the waterline.

As a result of changing water levels in the Adriatic and an undersea quake that had badly damaged the wooden foundations on which Venice stood, much of the jewel of a city was now underwater, though some of its iconic, graceful bridges survived, a few marooned in the midst of wide canals. However, instead of sinking into obscurity, Venice remained a vibrant, living city due to its complex network of biospheres below the waterline.

The spheres had been developed by a consortium of water-based changelings and put into place during the final decade of the twenty-first century. A large number of BlackSea's people still called Venice home, but Riaz's wolf found the old city claustrophobic, especially beneath the surface, where the biospheres acted as—to his mind—protective prisons.

"I've always been fascinated by Venice." Adria did a full circle on the "floating" roadway designed to rise with the water, her eyes taking in everything with unhidden wonder. "It's filled with so much history you can almost hear the city whisper it to you."

Painful though his memories of Venice were, it was impossible not to be affected by the infectious depth of her joy. "You should see it during Carnevale." It was just before the last Carnevale that he'd first seen Lisette, and he'd been

unable to stop himself from seeking her out during the
celebrations.

Standing in the shadows created by the alcove of a moss-
covered building, his face concealed by a half mask, he'd
watched her lithe figure swirl in her husband's arms, both of
them full of the wild energy that came from the beautiful
chaos of the festival. She'd been dressed in red and black, a
Spanish flamenco dancer transplanted onto Venetian soil, her
sun gold hair dyed a vivid black.

"It's on my list." Adria's slightly husky voice broke into
his thoughts, so very different from Lisette's French-accented
soprano. "Along with Mardi Gras in New Orleans, the Inca
Trail, the Taj Ma—" Her eyes connecting with his, she cut
herself off midstream, a slight wash of color on her cheekbones. "Sorry, I'm talking your ear off."

"No, tell me." Struck once more by how much he didn't
know about her, he found himself fascinated.

"How about you tell me," she said instead, cocking her
head a little to the side as they detoured to drop their bags off
at the hotel. "You were away for a long time. Tell me some
of the places you visited, the things you saw."

Riaz shoved a hand through his hair, thinking back.
Though he had been based in Europe, he'd traveled through
Asia and parts of Africa, had adventures that had thrilled and
changed him in different ways. "I once got caught in the
monsoon rains in India," he said, choosing a memory he knew
would make her laugh, because when Adria laughed . . . the
edges inside him gentled, hurt less. "The human part of me
loved it, but my wolf was not impressed." He shuddered, as
if flinging water off his fur.

Adria's laughter held her own wolf's amusement, the fine
streaks of gold in her eyes glittering in the deep orange light
of the setting sun. "I can imagine. Did you make it to Nepal,
see Kathmandu?"

He shook his head. "I was on my way there when I was
recalled to Rome to take care of some pack business." He'd
met Lisette not much later, and the ensuing months had torn
him bloody, until he'd had to go home to the den deep in the
Sierra Nevada mountains, where he could lick his wounds
surrounded by the warmth of his pack.

He still needed that warmth, that connection, but felt no lack today, though he was far from his heartland. It wasn't hard to understand why, with Adria walking long-legged and happy beside him, her pleasure in Venice as open and as unhidden as the heart of her wolf.

No ties. No promises.

Yet, in spite of the vow they'd taken, ties were forming. Ties of friendship, of need, of respect. Whenever this relationship ended, those bonds would remain. Riaz's wolf was pensive about that, but it didn't reject the idea out of hand—Adria wasn't just Pack now, wasn't just a lover with whom he'd shared skin privileges. She'd become someone who mattered to both sides of his nature, part of his own personal "pack" of people.

His to protect.

BOWEN was waiting for them outside an unassuming seventeenth-century building half submerged by the rising waters that had permanently flooded the Venetian lagoon, the bridge that had once linked it to another, larger building long gone, leaving it an island at the end of the road, the shimmer of water beyond. The leader of the Human Alliance held out a hand. "Riaz, good to see you again."

"Bo." Shaking the proffered hand, he said, "This is Adria."

Bowen's smile changed, into the kind a man gives a woman who'd caught his attention. "Welcome to Venezia, Adria."

"Thank you."

The cool remoteness of her response made Riaz realize how long it had been since he'd heard that tone from her. His wolf's smug pride had his lips tugging up at the corners.

"Come on in." Bowen led them through the doors of the apparently small building that housed the Alliance offices, down the carpeted front hallway, and into an elevator.

Riaz spotted six security cameras, five obvious guards, and at least three concealed ones he discerned only because of his sense of smell. That was on top of a laser-alarm system and the prettily dressed receptionist with the eyes of an assassin. He didn't even think before positioning himself so that

Adria was protected by the heavy bulk of his body. He saw her sharp look, caught the tiny nod. Rather than fighting his subtly protective stance, she focused her own attention on covering his blind spots.

"Expecting company?" he asked Bo once they were in the elevator.

The other man leaned back against the wall, folding his arms over a black T-shirt that said, "Just because you're paranoid doesn't mean they're not out to get you." The quote was amusing, the way he bared his teeth less a smile than a feral display akin to that of a wolf. "Something like that. We'll talk inside," he said as the elevator doors opened. "I had some food brought in."

Stepping out into the biosphere-protected part of Venice made Adria's shoulders slump in disappointment, though her eyes never lost their alert watchfulness. "It's no different from the aboveground city," she whispered in a sub-vocal murmur he had to lean down to hear, her breath a caress across his jaw.

"Be patient." He knew what was coming, his wolf quivering in anticipation as it waited to see her response.

"In here." Bo pushed open a door.

Adria froze in the doorway, her eyes huge.

"More like what you expected?" he murmured in her ear, nudging her forward with a caressing stroke of his hand on her lower back.

Clearly captivated by the meeting room that, at first glance, seemed suspended over nothing but water, she walked slowly inside. The Alliance building was on the very edge of the city, which meant it was possible to actually see the water lapping at the biosphere from a number of lower-floor rooms. Located in a corner, with three glass walls, this one was the most magnificent—it created the illusion of the clear blue-green water touching the glass, when the actual curve of the biosphere was several meters away.

As if putting on a show, a pod of sleek silvery fish darted across that water, their scales catching the sunlight from above.

Not saying a word, Adria crossed the deep green of the carpet to look through the glass into the water. Up close, Riaz knew the view was bisected on the right side by the remnants of neighboring buildings that had sunk and deteriorated pre-Restoration, as well as by the wooden pilings on which those buildings had once stood, but flawlessly clear on the side that faced out into the lagoon.

"She's damn beautiful," Bowen said, and it was a question.

Riaz's response was instinctive. "She's taken." Neither part of him cared that the agreement he'd made with Adria gave him no rights of possession.

"Lucky bastard, whoever he is." An oblique glance.

Adria turned at that moment, the light from the water playing over the clean angles of her face, the light-shot amber of her eyes a silent indication of her wolf's fascination with this strange city. "I'd go insane living here, but for a visit, yes, it's a sight."

"You should see the view during a storm." Bo walked over to the conference table already set with sandwiches, water, fruit, and cookies, urging them to take a seat. "Even some of the folks who live and work here can't handle it. The reminder that there's not much between Venice and oblivion cuts too deep into the bone."

"You like it." Adria's voice had thawed a fraction, her lush mouth soft with the faintest of smiles.

Bowen's cheeks creased into a deep smile in return. "Yes. She's a stunning lady, my Venezia."

Riaz's wolf bristled at the hint of flirtation in the male's voice, but he managed to remain polite as they each grabbed some food. "So," he said, once everyone had had a chance to take a few bites, "why the intense paranoia?"

Swiveling in his chair, a cookie in hand, Bo used a sleek black remote to bring up an image on the comm screen behind him. It was of a middle-aged man, a little pudgy and altogether harmless looking. "One of our senior comm specialists." He dropped the cookie onto his plate, his jaw a hard line. "We found out two weeks ago that the Psy broke and programmed him."

ADRIA pushed aside her plate, appetite lost. "Did he survive?" Brainwashing was hard on Psy minds from what she'd picked up from the Laurens, but it was *vicious* on changelings, involving as it did the shattering of their strong natural shields. With humans, it could go either way, since their natural shields were so weak as to be nonexistent—but their brains also weren't built to take that kind of psychic pressure.

"He's on life support." Bo's tone was bleak. "We're trying everything we can to give him a shot, but . . ." Rubbing his jaw, he took a deep breath, and when he next spoke, the bleakness had been replaced by anger. "He was—*is*—a good man, fought hard not to give in to the compulsions. The doctors say he had to have suffered constant nosebleeds, worse."

"You think he failed," Riaz said, his anger a quiet, dangerous thing that spoke to her own. "That he compromised your comm system from the inside?"

"Thing is," Bo said, "Reuben can't tell us what he did or didn't do—by the time we discovered what the bastards had done to him, he'd lapsed into a coma." He shifted his chair sideways, so he could see the comm screen and them at the same time. "We're in the process of ripping out and reinstalling every single piece of comm equipment on-site. Software and hardware. Until that's complete, we're in total shutdown on any but the most general conversation."

"Cell phones?" Riaz asked.

"We're replacing the whole lot—Reuben was the one who issued them to us." He shook his head. "New ones are supposed to arrive today for the techs to pull apart and check."

Adria agreed with the precautions, extreme though they might seem. Only a fool would consider the Psy race a nonthreat. "Do you have any idea who orchestrated the attack on Reuben?" It was easy to generalize the Psy as the enemy, but the psychic race ran the gamut from the innocent to the evil, same as changelings and humans.

Bo's expression turned brutal, stripped bare of any lingering trace of the charm he'd earlier displayed. A quick touch of the remote and the image of Reuben was replaced by that of a woman with cheekbones that could cut glass. Her hair was a deep, luxuriant mahogany, her skin slightly olive toned, her eyes an acute hazel-green.

"Tatiana Rika-Smythe." Ice in every syllable. "She's not as flashy as some of the other Councilors—this one's more like a snake in the grass."

"You sound certain." Adria had been in the upper hierarchy of the pack long enough to know that Councilors had a way of working machinations behind machinations.

Bo discarded Tatiana's photo for another image, that of the yacht that had started everything. It sat adrift in the ocean. "Ask me why I was on that yacht in the middle of the fucking Mediterranean with seven Psy guards."

Adria's claws sliced out, threatening to mark the gleaming wood of the table. "They planned to break you, too." It took conscious effort to retract her claws—Riaz had kept control over his own, but his eyes were a hypnotic, dangerous gold.

Bo took several minutes to reply, clearly fighting the rage that had caused white lines to appear around his mouth, carved into the warm hue of his skin. "We're starting to think that that's what happened to the old chairman," he said at last. "It would explain why he suddenly started making those bullshit calls—at the time, we all hated him. Now . . . I pity the poor bastard." Running a hand over the smooth curve of his skull, he grabbed a bottle of water, slugging back half of it before he spoke again. "One of them stunned me while I was walking home around nine at night. When I woke up, I was on the yacht."

It was a plausible story—especially since it involved a male who, like all strong men, didn't think anything could touch him, but something didn't ring true. "You're not the official head of the Alliance," she said, never moving her eyes off his face.

"The chairman position is now largely administrative." Bo shrugged off her implied question, his expression betraying nothing. "Just means Rika-Smythe has good sources of information."

"Are you telling me," she insisted, conscious of Riaz going very still beside her, "that you were arrogant enough to go out alone after dark when you'd already discovered what had been done to Reuben, knew the Psy might be out to mess with you?"

Bo's smile was slow and dangerous. "Smart and sexy—my perfect woman." He finished off the water. "We were working on the assumption that with Reuben down, someone else with his level of access to our systems would be a target. We made sure everyone who qualified was covered . . . except for me."

"Playing bait?" Riaz tapped his fingers on the table. "No way for you to know you'd be able to handle the operatives who captured you."

"I wasn't *stupid* bait," Bo said with an offended snort. "Had a GPS tracker implanted an inch below my armpit, where pretty much nobody ever thinks to check. We also had a team in the air above me the entire time."

The man had guts, Adria thought. Because air support or not, he'd been on his own on that yacht. "You weren't worried about psychic coercion?"

A small pause before Riaz whistled. "Son of a bitch." His tone was a mix of admiration and disbelief. "You did it, you actually figured out how to make that chip work."

Chapter 39

IT HAD BEEN after their first run-in with the Alliance that the pack had discovered the group had been experimenting with a chip that, once implanted, acted as a shield against Psy intrusion. Or that had been the official line fed to the Alliance's soldiers. In truth, the original chips had acted as remote kill switches.

Bo's smile was grimly satisfied. "Hell, yes."

Riaz was impressed, but he needed the answer to another question before he could ask Bo for more information on the chip. "Does Ashaya Aleine know?" The scientist was one of the most experienced people in the world when it came to neural implants, and had—when the dust settled after the aborted kidnapping—agreed to help Bo and his people fix the defective chip. If she, and by extension, DarkRiver, had known of the Alliance's success and not shared the information, the shit was going to hit the fan. Hard enough to cover everyone.

"No." Bowen sliced his hand through the air, his tone leaving no room for doubt. "Her help was critical, and not one of us will ever be anything but grateful, but she's not Alliance, wouldn't keep our secrets." A blunt answer. "The most recent prototype we sent her was created from one of the earlier designs. We figured we'd share the truth once we were ready for the packs to know."

"The yacht incident pushed things ahead of schedule," Riaz guessed, his wolf relaxing now that he didn't have to inform his alpha that a member of the pack that was their most trusted ally had breached their alliance. Beside him, he sensed the tension drain out of Adria, too.

"We voted to give Ashaya a twenty-five percent stake in the patent," Bo said after nodding an affirmative to Riaz's statement. "A patent we'll be filing for when hell freezes over, so Aleine owns a percentage in a design that'll never make any profit. The only important thing is getting the chip into as many humans as possible. Being protected from mental violation shouldn't be a luxury."

Riaz was unsurprised at the secrecy, but Bo's confidence in the success of the implant seemed premature.

Adria echoed his thoughts, the delicate wildness of her scent licking over him as she leaned forward over the table. "I don't see people lining up to be implanted."

"Lot of trust if they are," Riaz added, restraining the urge to run his hand slowly down the arch of her back, displayed so beautifully by her current position.

"You're thinking from a changeling perspective," Bo said, the passion in his eyes an inferno. "Humans . . . you have no idea what it's like to walk around knowing one of the Psy could slip into your mind at any time and take things, or plant things. It's rape and it's a violation committed over and over and over again against people who can't fight back." Flat, hard words. "A human makes a technological breakthrough, and the next thing you know, the Psy already have a patent on the invention. Just coincidence." His laugh was bitter. "That's if they choose to leave the human's memories intact so he or she even knows what's been stolen."

Fisting his hand on the table, he blew out a breath, his next statement not as drenched in anger. "The initial rollout was soft, limited only to Alliance personnel I personally vetted. Reuben wasn't on the list. If he had been . . ." He shook his head. "That's done and gone. Fact is, the Psy are going to find out about it sooner or later, so we've begun an Alliance-wide operation. Everyone who wants a chip gets one."

There was nothing Riaz could say to that, every word Bo had spoken an ugly truth. But the SnowDancer understood his sense of violation in a way the other man couldn't comprehend. Psy had broken so many of their strongest two decades ago, almost destroyed the pack. Riaz had been a juvenile, but he would never forget the blood, the loss . . . and the lethal determination in the eyes of the boy with hair of silver-gold who had become their alpha while barely more than a child.

Riaz saw the same unyielding determination on Bo's face. Whatever it took, whatever the personal cost, he knew Bo wouldn't flinch, not if it meant protecting his people. "Did you go first?"

"No way I was going to ask my men and women to do something I wouldn't."

Adria's husky voice brushed over Riaz's skin, snagging his attention. "I didn't see a chip in the back of your neck. Did you change the location?"

"It's there. Covered by a dermal patch that blends into my skin." He jerked his head toward Adria, challenge and flirtation both in the faint smile on his lips. "You can feel it if you like."

Once again, Riaz's wolf flashed its canines but held its silence, well aware Bo was jerking his chain. Nonetheless, his focus was acute and deadly as he watched the woman who was his lover walk to stand behind Bo's chair.

"Where?" she demanded.

"Here." Reaching back, he tapped a spot.

Unable to see any difference in the honey brown of his skin tone, Adria pressed the pad of her finger over the warmth of his nape. The hardness was slight, but when she traced around the area, she realized it formed a small square. Looking at Riaz, she nodded, startled by the way the wolf watched her out of those eyes. Throat suddenly dry, she had to break the eye contact, clear her throat, before she could speak. "Could be a dummy."

Bo shrugged. "I'm sane and alive after being taken captive by seven Psy. Think about it."

She had, and in spite of her words, her instinct was to believe him.

Riaz placed his arm on the back of her chair as soon as she retook her seat, his attention on Bo, but his fingers just brushing her hair. Her heart slammed into her ribs, because subtle though it might be, she understood it for a possessive display—it was the first time he'd ever done anything of the sort in public, a warning of the notorious lone-wolf tendency toward possessiveness. The thing was, Adria had never expected him to train that aspect of his personality on her.

She was still trying to work out how to respond to the unexpected act when he spoke, his voice creeping under her skin to touch parts of her it had no business touching.

"If you didn't ask Ashaya to help you test the implant," he asked, eyes that had returned to their human shade locked on Bowen, "who did you trust enough to do the testing?"

Bowen took his time answering. "We heard about the Laurens," he said when he did speak, his expression giving nothing away. "About how they've been alive all this time. How'd they do it? A familial net?"

Adria leaned forward in excitement, inadvertently breaking the contact with Riaz. "Another family of defectors?"

However, Bowen shook his head. "No." Another pause. "Let's just call them a well-organized group." His expression made it clear he'd share no other details of their identity. "They dropped out of the Net in degrees, changed their appearance, and blended into the population. No one would've been the wiser, except that one of them was injured in a freak accident six months ago—hit by bricks falling onto the street from a building undergoing maintenance."

Adria found herself sliding back into her seat, her skin burning at the renewed contact with Riaz's fingers.

"I saw him trying to limp away," Bo continued. "I'm certain he wouldn't normally have said a word, but he was concussed at the time and kept repeating 'no DNA profile' as I was leading him to the ambulance. I figured he had a criminal warrant out on him, but then he mumbled the word 'PsyNet.'" A shrug. "I did what any good security chief would do.

I brought him here, had him patched up, and interrogated him while he was still dopey."

A ruthless act—but then, from what Adria knew of him, Bo had never pretended to be anything else when it came to taking care of his people. The wolf in her respected that, even as it understood that the Alliance man would betray even the staunchest ally if it came down to a choice between that ally and those he considered under his protection.

"By the time his friends tracked him down," he said, "we knew who they were and that blackmailing them would be a very bad idea, so we simply suggested that our interests might mesh and let it go at that."

An intelligent and calculated decision, from a man Riaz had seen leak charm like a tap in a successful effort to divert people's attention from his cold-eyed intelligence. "You've got balls, I'll give you that."

Bowen's grin was a flash of canines. "The reason we know it was Tatiana behind the attack on Reuben," he said, grin vanishing as quickly as it had appeared, "was that the men who were sent to take me in didn't bother to hide the comm conversation they had with her once I was on board, even though the stun had worn off."

"Careless." Riaz traced circles on Adria's nape with the tip of his finger.

"They figured I wouldn't be in a position to say anything after she got through with me." Bracing his forearms on the gleaming wood of the table, Bo bit out his next words. "The bitch does her own reprogramming—she made it clear no one else was to touch me."

Considering the facts, Riaz made the tactical decision to share some knowledge. "Tatiana is thought to have the ability to penetrate almost any shield."

Bo's pupils contracted. "Shit."

"Yes. No way of knowing if the chip would've held her off, since it's technological, not natural," Riaz said, "but seems she can get into most minds without causing major damage."

"Less scars to hide," Adria said, and he heard the empathy in her, the soft heart she hid beneath the tough exterior.

"But," he added, cupping her nape gently with his hand,

"Tatiana's ability is noteworthy because of how unusual it is, so it doesn't change the impact of the chip. Still, your people need to make sure they don't get cocky."

"Noted."

"Once you take away their psychic advantage," Adria said into the silence that had fallen after Bo's curt nod, "Psy are very vulnerable."

As, Riaz mused, Bowen had proven with deadly efficiency on the yacht.

"They have a tendency to rely on their abilities," the human male agreed. "The ones I took down on the yacht were armed, but they paid so little attention to me it was the easiest op I've ever completed. A single guard on the door?" He snorted. "Soon as I had his weapon, it was all over. None of the others were on alert because they assumed their telepathic sweeps would warn them of an intruder."

"Why kill them?" Adria's question betrayed the inherent compassion of her nature. "Why not simply incapacitate?"

"A message," Riaz answered, the predator in him recognizing the one who sat three feet away. "He was sending a message. They fuck with the Alliance, you aren't going to take prisoners."

A small shrug from Bowen, his jet-black eyes steely with lethal purpose. "Leaving them alive would've been a sign of weakness, and Tatiana expects weakness from the 'emotional' races. What the bitch doesn't understand is that rage is an emotion, too."

Chapter 40

HAVING SPENT TWO hours with Bowen, going over the advantages the artificial shields might present the humans in SnowDancer and in the packs of their allies, Riaz reported in to Hawke via a highly secure satellite comm link set up using equipment at a small SnowDancer office hidden in Venice. Though the office was unmanned except for when Pierce was in the city, it had multiple layers of security not even a teleporter could breach without setting off a silent alarm. Not that they'd find much except some expensive comm equipment—the call history was set to erase itself the second after a user signed out.

"Bo says he couriered Ashaya the final chip earlier today, after making the decision to let us in on the secret," he told his alpha. "Have her test it as well as she can." Riaz wasn't certain how far the scientist could go without implanting it in anyone, but it was worth a shot. "No way I'm taking Bo's word on the effectiveness of the technology."

Hawke nodded, and Riaz could almost see him weighing up every possible variable before he said, "I also want to send Judd in, test the one Bo has in him."

"I figured. Bo's expecting it."

Hawke glanced to the side, his head cocked at a listening angle. Turning back to Riaz after a couple of seconds, he said, "Judd won't be able to get there until tomorrow night. You okay to stay?"

"Yes." He turned to the woman beside him. "You?"

Adria nodded and spoke directly to Hawke. "I cleared two days just in case."

"Even if you hadn't," Hawke said, the wolf's laughter suddenly in his eyes, "Riley's so happy right now, he's granting leave to anyone who asks. I'm half afraid to turn around and find the entire den has left for the Bahamas."

They all grinned at the idea of solid, stable Riley in a spin of joy. Riaz couldn't imagine it happening to a better man. "He drive Mercy to violence yet?"

"Not so far, but I have popcorn for when the show begins."

Signing off after another round of laughter, Riaz and Adria reset the office's security and left via an ingenious passageway that spilled them out into a small but busy shopping district.

The walk to the hotel was quick, the streets around them swathed in velvet darkness broken by the twinkling lights from several eateries spilling warm conversation onto the street. "Dinner on the balcony?" he suggested as they entered their second-floor room.

Adria lit up.

And something in him gentled, wild tenderness invading his veins. "What do you want?" He picked up the room service menu.

TIPPING the waiter at the door, Riaz took the food out to the balcony himself. The temperature had cooled but remained comfortable, the night below dotted with pretty colored lights from a nearby restaurant, the golden-hued windows of another small hotel, the old-fashioned streetlights. Not far in the distance, water danced black and silken through a canal.

Pouring two glasses of wine, he handed one to Adria. "To Venice."

She clinked her glass to his, her hair tumbling around her shoulders. "To Venice."

It almost felt as if they'd made a vow . . . but to what, he didn't know.

The food was simple but the flavor satisfied, as did the darkly romantic music lilting up from an evening busker. Wineglass in hand after they'd eaten, the wine midnight rubies in the muted light, Riaz watched Adria. She'd twisted in her chair to cross her arms on the curlicued metal of the railing, her face tilted into the soft wind and her ear cocked to the music. All her cares seemed to have vanished, the hardness created by life gone, until her beauty was exquisite, the lines of her face elegant and graceful.

This, he thought, this was who she was beneath the wariness and the hurt and the shields. A woman who, he suddenly knew, would tell him truths the other Adria never would. Dangerous though it was, this tightrope he was walking, he put down his wine and held out a hand. "Dance?"

A startled look, the gold streaks in her eyes vivid in the dark . . . her wolf coming to the surface. But she stood, flowed into his arms, one of her hands at his nape, the other locked with his own as he wrapped his free arm around her waist. She was tall enough that he didn't have to bend, didn't have to do anything but step closer. Their bodies aligned in sweet perfection, her head coming to just below his chin.

A faultless fit.

Drawing in the hidden notes of earthy warmth in her scent, he moved to the sway of the music, his blood hot, his body ready. But neither part of him was in any rush. He'd rushed too much with Adria, always been in too much need. Tonight, that need was tempered by the sexual pride of a dominant male, the desire to show her the lover he could be when his head wasn't messed up.

The fact it wasn't, even though he stood in Venice, where it had all begun, was because of her, this strong, guarded, complicated woman turned into a lazy-limbed goddess in his arms. He couldn't quite understand how it had happened, how he had come to trust that she would never betray his secrets, but he did. So when she lifted her face to his, long fingertips stroking his nape, he bent his head and met her kiss halfway.

Hot and lush and open, it was a languid tangling of mouths. The softness of her, the curves, the lean strength, it all intoxicated. Her scent was in his every breath, and he wondered if she was becoming embedded in his skin, becoming part of him. It happened with lovers—he'd fought the change, not wanting another woman's scent on his skin . . . but his wolf didn't claw away the idea this time.

Painful as it was, the wild heart of him had accepted what could never be, though he couldn't yet forget. But it wasn't simply that, would never have been enough. Man and wolf both, they were fascinated by the enigma of Adria. The courage he'd witnessed under fire was only a single facet of a complex gemstone. Already, he knew her harsh, prickly surface to be a facade, the woman underneath one who understood SnowDancer's most vulnerable . . . and who knew how to offer comfort to a broken male without unmanning him.

Spreading his hand on her lower back, he urged her closer. "Do you know what the words to the song mean?" he asked as the busker began to sing a song in Venesiàn, a language Riaz had made an effort to pick up during his time in Europe.

She shook her head, strands of ebony silk catching against his unshaven jaw. "It sounds beautiful, though."

Nuzzling at her, he began to translate, their clasped hands

held against his chest. Her sigh at the poignant emotion of the romantic ballad was eloquent, the lips she pressed to the dip at the base of his throat lush and inviting. It stroked a low, deep sound of pleasure from him, his body primed. "Stop that if you want me to keep translating."

A teasing feminine chuckle. "I'll behave."

Riaz murmured the words to her until the song ended, the busker's voice replaced by the sweet sounds of his fingers caressing the strings of his guitar.

"We should tip him." She moved the hand at his nape down to curve over his shoulder, her breath blowing a delicate kiss across his skin when she spoke.

"Do you want to go down?"

She looked up, violet eyes lit by amber. "Yes."

Fingers tangled, they left the room and made their way to the busker. The tip they dropped into his open guitar case made him grin. "Come," he invited with a flourish of chords, "dance!"

Adria's smile was shy. "Would you like to?"

Riaz had his arms back around her before he realized he was moving, the familiar cobbled streets of Venice made new by her laughter as she navigated the uneven surface high enough to have escaped the flooding, her fingers tightening on his hand.

"I've got you," he murmured.

His wolf, so long trapped in pain and confusion, pressed against her, happy. Sliding his hand down her back, he danced with her under the half moon, barely aware of passersby until an older Italian couple, the woman's hair a luxurious mink streaked with gray, her mate's face lined with age and life, swirled in to join them.

The dark truth he carried inside him struggled to awaken in the face of their unspoken bond, but the night was too beautiful to mar with regrets. Man and wolf, he focused every part of himself on dancing with the captivating woman in his arms. He didn't know how long they swayed in the sultry warmth, but when they drew apart, it was in silent agreement. Leaving the other dancers, they walked back to their room, the music following them upstairs.

He'd left the balcony doors partly open, and the gauzy

curtains floated in the gentle breeze. Keeping the lights off
to assure their privacy, he ran his fingers over Adria's cheek,
luxuriating in the warm smoothness of her skin. "No," he
said when she went to take off her T-shirt. "Let me." Running
his hand down the curves of her body, he drew up the soft
fabric with slow anticipation.

SHE was being seduced, Adria thought, as Riaz gripped her
hips and pressed a kiss to the bared skin of her breastbone,
her T-shirt having crumpled soundlessly on the rich cream
of the carpet.

"You taste like berries," he murmured, kissing his way up
the slope of her neck. "Ripe, lush, juicy."

Except for when he'd asked about her fantasies, he'd never
before spoken much in bed. The deep timbre of his voice
hazed her mind, his callused skin on her own threatening to
tangle what threads of reason remained. "You never told me
your fantasy," she whispered against his mouth.

He angled his face to rub his jaw delicately against her
cheek, his thumbs shaping the vee of her hip bones. "A strong,
sexy woman in my bed, mine to do with as I wish. *You.*"

"That's a very dominant-male fantasy."

Sensual amusement in his eyes, he just looked at her.

She laughed, though her pulse was a staccato drumbeat.
"Yes, why am I surprised?"

His kiss was as slow, as romantic as the night, the kind of
kiss a man might give to a new lover he was wooing into his
bed. "Let me," he whispered again, unhooking her bra to pull
it off and drop it onto her T-shirt before pressing her against
him again, big hands splayed on her back in a way that
shouted possession. "Let me." A kiss pressed to the sensitive
spot behind her ear.

Shuddering, she wove her fingers into the thick silk of his
hair, willing to be petted and caressed and adored enough to
surrender the reins to this man she trusted not to betray her
faith.

It had been *so long.*

"Yes." It was the barest whisper, but he heard her.

Fingers on her jaw, another gossamer kiss, his body so big

and hot. "Hold on." With that, he reached down and swung her up into his arms, carrying her to the bedroom . . . and to the bed made up with soft white linen on which some romantic soul had scattered rose petals. They were velvet bites against her back when he placed her on the bed, the faint light spilling in from the balcony the only illumination.

They were wolves. It was all they needed.

"We should turn down the bed," she said, her eyes on him as he reached back to strip off his T-shirt, baring a body she craved even more today than the first time they'd shared the most intimate skin privileges.

"No sheets," he said, kicking off his shoes and reaching down to tug off his socks with curt male efficiency. "I want to see you." He came around to get rid of her boots and socks as quickly, before prowling up over her, his hair falling across his forehead. "You are so beautiful." He sounded almost . . . surprised, as if he was seeing her for the first time.

Perhaps he was, because she didn't quite know this lover either. The one who touched her with sensual fascination and wanted to discover her every secret pleasure point. "Riaz," she whispered when he kissed his way down her navel, having tugged off her jeans and panties to discard them over the side of the bed.

"Mmm." A wet kiss pressed just above her pubic bone, his hands pushing her thighs apart, the roughness of his skin a shock that made her quiver.

It was the most intimate of kisses, his patience exquisite. Her soft cries lingered in the air, shimmered on the fine layer of perspiration that turned her skin into a mirage. And still he petted her with a slow attention to detail that made it crystal clear that while she was the one who trembled and broke, this was very much his pleasure, too.

His fantasy.

The realization was more intoxicating than any wine. Surrendering to the sensations, she was still gasping for breath when he finally made his way up her body to nip at her throat hard enough to leave a mark. All the while, he petted her breasts, her abdomen, the tops of her thighs with hands both proprietary and demanding enough that she knew his control wasn't as impeccable as it appeared.

She opened her mouth to his kiss, her legs to the jean-clad thigh he pushed in between. But he withdrew it after only a second, muttering, "Skin," before rolling away and stripping off his clothing to return to her, a big, dangerous predator who had decided to pet her to pleasure such as she'd never before felt.

This time, he settled himself over her, his erection pushing aggressively against her abdomen. He allowed her to close her fingers around the heated steel of him, the skin that sheathed him paradoxically soft. She wanted to taste him, please him as he'd done her, but tonight, she was his to do with as he wished. It wasn't in the nature of a dominant female to give in so utterly in bed, but Adria hadn't ever felt so treasured by a lover. It threatened to make her afraid, but she refused to submit to the insidious emotion, refused to taint a night she knew would become a memory she'd cherish.

His mouth at her breasts, licking and tasting. His hand between her legs. His fingers sliding deep into her, his way eased by the molten heat of her need. She squeezed, attempted to hold him, but he withdrew . . . and then he was nudging her thighs apart and pushing into her with the thick intrusion of his cock.

"Let me," he whispered once more, sliding one hand under her head to fist it in her hair, stroking her leg up over his hip with the other.

She could do nothing else, her body his instrument. Rocking home with a grunt, he claimed another kiss, this one hotter, more demanding, but continuing to hold that lazy edge that said he had all night to love her. And when he began to move, it was with the same languorous rhythm, their bodies locked in a slow dance that seared pleasure through to her toes.

Seduced . . . she was being seduced.

Chapter 41

HAWKE LOOKED ACROSS the cabin to where his mate sat curled up in bed with a datapad. She was reading a paper her lecturer had recommended, while he had Kenji and Riaz's joint report on the BlackSea negotiations. He'd rather have been in bed beside Sienna, but she'd barred him from it. "We won't get any work done otherwise."

Sprawled in the armchair he'd added to the cabin a couple of weeks ago, he tried to figure out why he was so damn happy when by rights, he should've been feeling a little surly.

Because she's here. My mate is here with me, safe, doing something utterly ordinary.

It was a gift he couldn't have anticipated a few months ago, and one he'd let no one tarnish with fear.

Sienna looked up at that instant. "You're not working." Touching her finger to the screen of her datapad, she primly turned a page.

"And you've been on the same page for ten minutes."

"Drat." Laughing, she put the datapad on the comforter and threw her arms apart. "As Ben would say, 'Hi! Want to play?'"

Always. "Not outside." It was raining, and while his wolf could function fine through snow and sleet itself, both parts of him liked being warm and dry.

"Some tough guy."

"Come here and say that." Putting down the report, he crooked a finger.

Instead of obeying, Sienna gave him a secretive, slightly guilty look. He'd seen that same look more times than he could count while she'd been a juvenile. Tempted to pounce on her, he said, "Do I want to know?"

"I want to make cookies."

He grinned. "Is that what they're calling it now?"

She threw a pillow at him. "I brought the ingredients in my backpack. So, can we?"

Lobbing it back, he cocked his head. "We have the night to ourselves"—a mission to accomplish even with the current relative peace—"and you want to make cookies?"

She was suddenly very interested in the pillow. "Lara does it and it looks fun. Marlee and Toby like it." She picked at the stitching of the pillowcase. "I'd like to know how . . . for the future."

In case we have children one day.

She could've asked Lara, Evie, Tarah, but she'd waited to ask him. It made him her slave all over again. "Another memory for your box?"

Her smile was the sun coming out of the clouds. "I have chocolate chips."

"Then I guess"—getting up, he held out a hand—"we're making cookies."

Determined to succeed, they pulled up recipes on the Internet, watched demonstration videos, and substituted cranberries for raisins, because neither one of them was a fan of "shriveled grapes."

The best thing that could be said about their maiden effort was that it was edible—and that Sienna had melted chocolate on the tip of her nose he had to lick off.

They managed to burn the second batch—in a no-burn oven.

The third batch, however . . . "These are mine." He made an imaginary line down the tray that put ninety percent of the cookies on his side.

Throwing her arms around his neck, Sienna kissed him, smiling all the while. "Fine," he murmured. "I'll give you two."

"Are you saying my kiss only rates a two?"

"I could be persuaded to reconsider."

Later, after he'd fed her warm cookies while she promised him all sorts of favors, they drank milk and brushed their teeth to make up for the sugar currently swimming through their bloodstreams, and got into bed facing one another. Rain continued to pound on the roof, a transient shield around their own private world that made the cabin seem even more snug.

"I had fun." It was a sighing comment from his mate.

Running a fingertip around the shell of her ear, he said, "I think we should try muffins next. I like banana bran." Because he'd had fun, too, the long-forgotten boy in him rising to the surface. He'd made cookies with his mom a lifetime ago, had lost the memory under the weight of the pain that had come later, but it was once again a radiant jewel in his mind.

"I was thinking marble cake," Sienna said, expression sparkling with excitement.

He whistled. "Ambitious."

Rubbing her nose against his, she whispered, "No one will ever know if we end up with a vaguely mud-colored cake instead."

He chuckled, grabbing her and turning onto his back so that she ended up lying along his body. "Look at us, we're talking about something so domestic." No guns. No enemies. No tension.

She beamed. "It's wonderful, isn't it?"

"Yeah, it is." Danger stalked his mate, but this moment, it was theirs, private and safe and with the scent of cranberries and melted chocolate in the air.

ADRIA woke up feeling better than she had in years. She'd spent the night tangled around a sexy, gorgeous man who'd laughed with her in the midnight hours, his voice a delicious rasp over her skin, and who'd made love to her again sometime before morning. He'd been more demanding the second time, but no less tender. She was feeling terribly petted and spoiled.

When she poked her head up from the sheets to see him walking into the room dressed in nothing but a towel hitched around his hips, a cup of coffee in hand, she simply stopped breathing for a second. "Come here," she murmured once she could speak again. He smelled of soap and man and coffee, and she wanted only to rub her face against his chest, indulge the deep sensory need he both created and filled in her.

Taking a seat on the bed, he put the coffee on the little side table with pretty curved legs. Her eyes locked on a droplet of water making its way down his chest, the dusky hue of his skin broken by a sprinkling of dark hair. "You missed a drop," she said, catching it on her finger.

No laughter, his expression reserved.

Fingers curling into her palm, she allowed her hand to fall to the sheet. "This changes things, doesn't it?" She'd known the night had been too beautiful not to, had been trying to ignore the inevitable truth, because this feeling inside of her, it was a fizzy joy she hadn't felt for so long it wasn't even a memory.

"Yes." A single rough word, but his hand, it closed over her own, warm and protective.

She spread her fingers, interlocked them with his own. "Do you want to end it?" The fact it hurt her deep inside to ask that question was an unmistakable sign she'd already started to fall for this man who could never give her what she needed.

"We should stop," Riaz said, eyes of pale brown shot with amber in the morning sunlight, "before it costs us both."

"You're right."

Yet neither one of them made the move to break their physical connection. Adria's wolf stood in silence, uncertain . . . scared. It was hard to admit that, to accept that in spite of her every promise to herself, Riaz had come perilously close to breaching the core she'd vowed to protect. Part of her wanted to wrench her hand from his, turn away. It would be the safer choice, allowing her to walk out of this a little bruised but heart-whole. And still . . .

Riaz cupped the side of her face with his free hand. "I'm a bad risk, Adria." Raw, his soul stripped bare. "A really bad one."

Untangling their fingers, she pushed up into a kneeling position, the sheet held to her breasts. "I'm worse." The scars she carried were invisible, and marked her to the bone. "I don't know if I'll ever again be able to trust a man with all of me." His honesty deserved her own. "I'm broken deep inside."

Almost able to taste the intensity of her pain, Riaz curved his hand over her nape. "I swear to God, I will hunt Martin down and rip him limb from limb." A dominant female's pride, her self-belief was her armor, something no male worth his salt would ever attempt to strip from her.

Startled laughter coloring the air, Adria tugged him down

until their foreheads touched. "There's no need. It took me longer than it should have, but I saw him for what he was—and I saw the mistakes I'd made, too."

But the damage done, he thought, was nothing that would easily fade, her scars as indelible as his own. As indelible as the feminine strength that had brought her out of the darkness. His wolf, its teeth still bared, took a single step toward her, halted. He felt as if he stood on the edge of a treacherous cliff. A single wrong move could send him tumbling down into a rocky gorge, shattering his bones, his mind, his soul itself.

He'd never expected to be here, facing this moment, with any woman.

A storm cloud deep within, the shadow of a past he was determined to lay to rest threatening to darken the morning, but as strong was the knowledge that he couldn't live in limbo forever without going mad, and that the flickering flame between him and Adria was something important, something worth fighting for.

Maybe, just maybe, two broken people could manage to create something whole. "Yes," he said and waited, his wolf's body quivering with a tension that kicked him in the guts with exactly how important Adria had become to him. And, his eyes on the mark he'd sucked on her neck, he knew he wasn't going to behave and walk away if she said no.

"Yes."

Her answer made his wolf lunge to the fore. He didn't fight the shift, because this decision, it was as much the wolf's as it was the man's. A lovely woman with wide violet eyes and hair of tumbled silk was kneeling beside him when he completed the shift to pad around and take a seat on the sheets, his body pressing against her knees. An instant later, the air filled with iridescent sparks of color . . . to form into the shape of an elegant silver wolf with an unexpected white flash on her tail.

Shaking herself as if to settle her new skin, she lay down next to him, her muzzle on her front paws, her body half the size of his in this form. He shifted to crowd her against the headboard. Snarling, she pricked him with her claws when he pushed too much. He nipped at her ear.

Amber eyes turned to him in a warning that had his wolf

nuzzling at her with wild affection that came from the heart of the predator. She wasn't the one who had made its soul sing in recognition when they had been in this waterlogged city before, but she was his friend, his lover, carried his scent. The wolf trusted her at his back, with its secrets, had no intention of letting her go.

IT was late at night, well past a seven-and-a-half-year-old's bedtime when Judd sat down next to William on a fallen log in the wooded area behind the home the boy's family had bought on the borderline of DarkRiver and SnowDancer territory. There was no longer any need for Judd to hide his presence, his cover well and truly blown, but he made sure his visits to see William stayed covert nonetheless—the instant the vulnerable boy was associated with him, he'd become a target. There were those, Psy or not, who wouldn't hesitate to take William, mold him into a tool of death.

Like Judd, the boy was a Tk-Cell. He could literally move cells within the body itself—which meant he could stop a heart and make it look like a natural death. Judd had had to teach William that ugly truth not only because the boy had already inadvertently killed a family pet, but also because William needed to realize and acknowledge every aspect of his ability so that he could gain control over it. However, they were taking the practical application of William's Tk-Cell strength in a wholly new direction.

Now, reaching over, he ruffled the boy's soft brown hair. "Bad haircut." It was as if someone had put a bowl on top of his head and sheared around it. Crookedly.

William propped his elbows on his knees, cupping his face. "Mom." Pure exasperation. "She says it'll grow out, but I have to go to school!"

With enough time and effort, William could learn to morph the cells of his own body—but the skill was a difficult and enervating one even for Judd, and he was much stronger than William. "Tell everyone you did it on a dare," he said, opting for a much more accessible and effective solution.

A grin. "That's smart." His eyes went to the inside pocket

of Judd's leather-synth jacket, revealed by the way Judd had braced his forearms on his thighs. "I like chocolate."

Judd pulled out the bar he'd picked up en route. "It's yours if you can demonstrate your proficiency with the technique I taught you last time."

"Like a test?"

"Yes." Some would say the boy was too young for such things, but those people didn't understand how a psychic loss of control could devastate. The accidental death of his pet had almost destroyed William. What would happen if he stopped his mother's heart or gave his father a stroke?

No. Better that Judd be a harsh taskmaster—though he had no intention of treating the boy as brutally as he'd been treated as a child, until he'd broken and been re-formed into an assassin. Hence the candy bar for a reward, as recommended by Ben, his personal consultant when it came to all things concerning small children.

"Okay," William said, jumping off the log. "I've been practicing."

Putting the chocolate bar back in his pocket, Judd took out a small pocketknife. "Ready?"

William rubbed his hands down the front of his jeans, took a deep breath and said, "Yes. Go."

"I need to monitor you telepathically." The only time he would ever invade the boy's mind without asking was if William lost fatal control—and William had made that request himself.

"So you can see if I'm following the correct process," William said, his tone a perfect imitation of Judd's when he'd spoken those words.

It made his chest grow warm, the smile building from within. "Yes."

"Here they go." William dropped his shields, but he was never vulnerable to an attack—Judd had already taken over the task.

"One, two, three." He slicked the blade of the knife across his palm.

Blood welled, thick and red.

Chapter 42

IT LOOKED IMPRESSIVE, but he'd made the cut shallow—this was about building William's confidence in his abilities. It didn't take long before he felt his skin begin to tingle, then tug. In front of him, William's forehead was scrunched up, his eyes glued to the cut until Judd wasn't sure the boy was even blinking. Sweat trickled down one temple, his small fists clenched so tight the light tan of his skin was bloodless.

Five minutes of fierce concentration later, William said, "I'm done," and swayed on his feet.

"Sit. Drink." He gave the boy the liter bottle of nutrient-rich sports water he'd placed by his foot. Only when William was steadier did he take a tissue from his pocket to wipe away the blood and reveal the faint pink line of a scar that looked two days old. "Very good." He passed over the chocolate bar.

William tore off the wrapper to take a big bite. "It makes me really hungry," he said after he'd swallowed. "And tired."

"That's because you're using your psychic muscles. You need to remember to refuel and rest." Young, his body developing, William's psychic reserves were low. That didn't negate his power. "You did an excellent job."

When William beamed and leaned into him, Judd felt another one of those cracks form inside him. The ones the people he loved kept making, showing him he had the capacity to feel even more than he believed.

William finished the chocolate bar and looked up. "Okay, I'm ready for the other stuff."

The "other stuff" was where Judd took the boy through his entire method, teaching him where he could be more efficient, stronger, or more careful. "Close your eyes and focus." Dropping his inner shields just enough to allow William to slide into a specific part of his mind, Judd showed the boy the psychic pathway he'd taken, asked him to critique his own performance.

William was smart and motivated—an excellent student.

Well done, he said after the boy figured out the solution to a niggling problem. *That's enough for today. Disengage, shields up.*

"I'm going to Venice," he said when William opened his eyes. "Do you know where that is?"

"No, but I know it has water, lots of it. And funny boats." A pause. "Is that why I had to take a nap this afternoon and meet you so late? Because you'll be gone tomorrow?"

"Yes," Judd said, because he didn't lie to children. "You're important."

"You are, too." William's hug was fierce.

Judd hugged him back before escorting the boy to the edge of his parents' property, where his mother and father sat waiting at a wooden picnic table. William ran to them, bursting to share his success. Only when the small family was safe inside the house did Judd turn and walk back into the woods . . . and to the men who awaited him. "Aden," he said, finding the Arrow seated on the same log he and William had used. "Vasic."

"We didn't think you'd spot him," Aden said as Vasic shifted out of the viscous shadows between the trees.

Judd took a seat beside Aden. "I've learned a lot about tracking from changelings." He'd sensed Vasic's presence because of the silence the teleporter had created in the tiny denizens of the forest.

It was Aden who next spoke, his gaze focused in the direction of the house. "The boy's one of us."

"Yes."

Vasic's next words were quiet. "I'll keep an eye on him while you're in Venice."

Judd had expected nothing less. If there was one thing that held true for every Arrow he'd ever known—except Ming LeBon, and he'd never truly been one of them—it was that they were loyal. Sometimes that loyalty was misdirected, given to those who did not deserve it, but it was never false and never for sale. "Did you track me down for a reason?"

"We always have a reason, Judd." Aden picked up an acorn, examined it with care. "Do you know about the others? In Venice?"

"No." He'd never heard a hint about other rogue Arrows.

"Good. That means we succeeded." The Arrow medic placed the acorn back on the ground.

"Size of the group?"

"A small percentage of those who officially died during missions over the past decade."

"How?" All Arrow bodies were retrieved, death confirmed by a pathologist who wasn't part of the squad.

"First the squad liberated certain corpses from mortuaries after they'd been processed for burial. Of the right size and height to fit an Arrow about to defect. Then the corpses were substituted in place of the Arrows in planned incidents where the bodies would be so damaged, the DNA so degraded, it wouldn't be difficult to fool the scans. Explosions and fires."

"Risky." The whole thing would've unraveled if a conscientious scientist decided to double-check his findings before the "Arrow" body was cremated.

"Yes, but possible with the previous generation of DNA scanners," Aden said, giving Judd another indication of the long-term nature of the plan. "The same procedure wouldn't work now. That's why we currently channel the majority of defectors through a facility in the Dinarides."

The Ghost, Judd recalled, had mentioned the Dinarides facility in connection with Arrows who had been taken off Jax.

Vasic spoke on the heels of that thought. "Ming told Aden to wean the Arrows at Dinarides off Jax to see if they could be restabilized—and a few weeks later, he told his medical staff to ensure none of them made it out alive."

Because Ming LeBon only wanted perfect soldiers. Fractures that couldn't be mended or that might leave a vulnerability made a man useless to him.

"He staffed the place with non-Arrows as a check on me," Aden added, "but he forgot I'm not just a field medic."

Judd wondered if Aden had used the telepathic skills he'd learned from Walker to subtly influence the minds of the medical staff who may as well have been lambs led to slaughter. "No reason then for Ming to question the eventual death certificates that came out of the facility."

Aden's expression didn't change as he said, "Especially when their bodies had already been cremated, the cremations verified by Keisha Bale herself."

"The head M-Psy," Vasic said when Judd glanced up in question.

"Do I know the renegades?" Judd asked, impressed by the scale of the deception.

"The first four defections occurred in the generation before ours—the initial two remained heavily shielded in the Net for almost two years after their 'deaths,' until a third defection could be successfully navigated," Aden said. "Three is the smallest group they wanted to chance in terms of a stand-alone network."

"A smart decision." The LaurenNet had initially had two adults, one teenager, and two children, and it had taken everything they had to maintain the fabric of the psychic network.

"After the third defection, followed quickly by a fourth, the program went into hibernation to ease any suspicion. It was reinitialized when I took over the field medic position."

That was when Judd made the connection. "Your parents both died after the small stealth boat they were on exploded while at sea." Aden had been a boy . . . but old enough to have become Silent, old enough to have learned to protect the secrets inside his mind.

The other man didn't confirm his supposition, but neither did he deny it. "I watched you after you got yourself taken off Jax," Aden said instead, "considered bringing you in, but you were such a perfect Arrow. I could find no way to prove that the Jax hadn't already done what it was intended to do, that you weren't one of Ming's reprogrammed puppets."

Ironic, Judd thought, that he'd done such a good job of hiding his intentions even his fellow Arrows had never suspected him of seditious leanings. "Krychek?"

"Better than Ming," was the short answer. "As for the rest . . . We will make decisions that benefit the squad and the Net. That is the single operative factor."

Never before, Judd thought, had the Arrows threatened to break so completely from the ruling powers of the PsyNet. For now, Aden and the others followed Kaleb Krychek, but only until he betrayed them. That had been Ming's fatal mistake. "Do you intend to eliminate Ming?"

"It's a possibility." Aden stared out into the forest. "The Net is already destabilizing. A number of the squad believe the impact of his death won't be as significant when the overall fabric is rippling, but I'm of the opinion it could be the tipping point that leads to a deadly rupture."

"Agreed," Judd said, having had an update from the Ghost as to the current situation. "The Council might be fractured, but the majority of the populace doesn't believe that yet." Though the rumors were going viral. "Ming's death would be a profound psychic shock."

Aden gave a small nod. "The squad will follow my lead on this, and I've said we wait. He'll die when he needs to die."

Judd knew it wasn't false confidence. He also knew Aden understood exactly how vicious an adversary Ming would be—his assassination would take careful planning, a precision strike. A single hint of warning, and Ming would turn it into a bloody showdown.

Vasic shifted a fraction, the leaves rustling around his boots. "The Arrows in Venice—they'd like to speak to you, but it can't be in public."

"Your face is too well known now," Aden said. "They can't risk anything that could compromise their cover."

Judd had no argument with that, understood why the Arrows needed to maintain this secret. "Do you have images of a private location?" He needed it for a teleport lock.

Aden pulled out a small phone, handed it over. "Photos loaded. Call the preset number when you arrive and one of them will come out to meet you. Connection is secure, can't be traced, even if hacked."

Taking it, Judd considered how many more of these defector cells there might be across the world, martial and familial. "You've laid the groundwork for a total defection from the Net." Houses, finances, alternate lives, the defectors had had years to put everything in place.

Aden took time to reply. "It's an option, but only if there

is no other. The squad has no wish to abandon the Net, but neither will we stand by and watch those in power use us up then discard us."

"Some of us are tired, Judd," Vasic added quietly, the gray of his eyes holding the darkest of shadows. "When this is all over, all we ask for is peace."

When this is all over . . .

Judd wondered if anything or anyone would survive when the civil war in the PsyNet began in earnest, whether Vasic would ever find his peace . . . or go to his death an Arrow to the last.

"DO we need to see Bowen today?" Adria said to Riaz as they finished breakfast on the balcony, wanting to suggest they spend their time walking around the city. A little space might ease the strange, painful tension that both connected and distanced them.

He shook his head. "Until Judd gets here to test the neural chips, there's not much we can do." His phone beeped at that instant, the number on the screen making him grin as he answered. "The deal done?" A pause, then, "Yeah, fine." His grin widened at whatever the person on the other end had said, before he spoke again. "Where? Right."

Hanging up without good-bye, he said, "Do you know Pierce?"

"Tall, ice green eyes, could be Italian, Indian, Eastern European, a combination of all of the above or none at all?" The man she was thinking of had visited with Matthias a couple of years back, having driven his mom and nephew over to see a show. "Senior soldier out of Alexei's sector?"

Riaz grinned at her description. "That's him. He's tied up the deal he was working on and is headed in to see us. I assumed you'd be okay meeting up with him."

"Of course." Even a lone wolf, she thought, needed contact with members of his pack, and if Pierce had taken over Riaz's duties, he'd been on his own for months.

"As for his heritage," Riaz told her, eyes gleaming, "Pierce told me he comes from a line of globe-trotting marauders turned traders who mated 'with men and women from every known country and some that no longer exist' over the centuries."

"Good story."

"From his track record, women obviously think so."

Pierce had apparently already been on a water bus when he'd called, and it was only fifteen minutes later that they caught up with the other man in the lobby of their hotel. Adria's wolf chuckled at glimpsing the sidelong glances of passing women—and more than a few men—who couldn't take their eyes off Riaz and Pierce. One woman almost walked into a column. Adria sympathized. Separately they were both sexy, dangerous men with dark hair and bodies that could make a woman whimper. Together, they were lethal.

Oblivious to the attention, the two men embraced in a typically male way, complete with slaps on the back and punches on the shoulders.

"You still fucking owe me a hundred bucks," was Pierce's opening greeting.

"I'll buy you an ice cream."

The exchange made Adria's wolf grin, because it was clear the two were close enough friends that they didn't bother to be polite. When Pierce turned to her, his crystal clear eyes narrowed for a second. "Matthias's sector."

"Excellent memory." Introducing herself, she took a backseat to the conversation as they headed out to explore, the men's quiet, deep voices a welcome accompaniment to her absorption in Venice.

Walking into a glass-smith's forge on the neighboring island of Murano, she lost herself in the colors and shapes created from the fire, while Riaz and Pierce prowled alongside her with lazy patience. The pieces created in that small workshop and the ones that followed were beyond beautiful, fragile dreams born of silica and painstaking craftsmanship. She stroked her hand over a flowing sculpture that sighed with sensuality, laughed in delight at the tiny glass birds perched on an indoor tree, was beguiled by the miniature chandeliers.

In the end, she bought a trio of birds with bright cobalt plumage. "For Tarah, Indigo, and Evie, plus this gorgeous necklace for my mom," she said to Riaz when he walked over from another corner of the artisan's store, showing him the lustrous beads of orange swirled with gold. "And these for me." She held up a pair of miniature hummingbirds, the earrings jewel green with a dash of scarlet.

"You sure you want those?" A solemn question. "You've only been in half the stores on the island."

"Go ahead," she said, "make fun of the new traveler."

He kissed her on the cheek instead, the warmth of his body a caress she'd missed. "I like seeing Venice through your eyes."

A tiny bud of hope sprouted in her heart. "Thank you for showing me this shop." It had been hidden, a secret treasure trove. "What's that?"

He held up two small glass boxes in different colors, tied with glass bows of silver. "I took my mother one last time and she told me she needed a set. And for her highness, Marisol, I'll be grabbing a big box of candy."

It was impossible not to adore a man who made no bones about how much he loved the women in his life. "Your niece is a lucky girl," she said, rising to drop a kiss to the corner of his mouth. "And your mother raised a good man."

His arm slid across her waist to settle on her hip. "Pierce found something he thinks you'll like." Tapping her on the nose, he nodded to the other end of the shop. "I'll have this wrapped for you."

"Thanks." The tiny bud within her grew a single whisper-thin leaf of vivid green: Sex was one thing, but giving and accepting such sweet affection—tender and public and playful—it took their relationship to a haunting new place. A place that might cause her terrible hurt, and yet one she knew she couldn't walk away from.

It was too late for that.

Chapter 43

CHEST TIGHT WITH the realization, Adria crossed over to Pierce and peered inside the glass case beside which he stood. The sculpture displayed within was frankly bizarre—it looked like someone had smashed up a hunk of puke-colored glass, then put it back together. Badly.

"Isn't it magnificent?" Pierce touched the case with reverent fingertips.

Not wanting to hurt his feelings, she scrambled for a response. "I can see it speaks to you."

"Oh, yes. The artistic flow is indescribable."

Adria wasn't sure quite what to say to that, but he was waiting for her to respond with such an expectant expression on his face that she knew she had to speak. "Yes, it's . . . ah . . . imaginative."

Pierce began to talk about the absorbing ambiguity of the shapes and how the power of the piece was a subtle fusion of light and darkness. It was almost two minutes later, just when she was plotting her escape, that she caught the glint in his eye and realized she'd been had. Intense, passionate, and intelligent Pierce was a playful wolf at heart.

"Yes, yes," she said when he paused, "you're so right. In fact, I think it'd be the perfect gift." Biting the inside of her cheek to keep from bursting out laughing, she took one of his hands in between her own. "I'm going to buy it for you—no, no, I insist. You've been so great today, so patient."

Distinct alarm. "No, there's no need. I already have—"

"I insist." Turning, she quick-stepped it to where Riaz was standing at the counter, the bag containing her souvenirs in hand. "Riaz, I found the best gift for Pierce."

"If you give me that monstrosity," Pierce growled from behind her, "I will regift it to you on your birthday."

A snort escaped Adria. Pierce's eyes narrowed. And then she was laughing so hard, she had to walk outside and collapse against the wall. Following her out, Riaz tugged on her braid. "Pierce is not amused." Deep gold, his eyes told her his wolf most definitely *was*.

Pierce's snarl made tears come out of her eyes. "Serves you right," she managed to get out to the glowering male.

"Hey! I was—" An abrupt pause. "I think that's my cell."

Adria hadn't heard anything, but perhaps he had it on vibrate. As he walked a few steps away to answer the call, she turned to Riaz. "Do we have time to sneak into the glass museum I saw?"

Riaz wrapped his arm around her shoulders, tucking her close. "Come on."

Wanting to nuzzle at his throat, she gave in a little and pressed a kiss to the hollow. His response was a teasing snap of his teeth by her ear.

We'll be okay.

The bud greened with health, but deep inside, she knew it would never be so simple.

TRAVELING under an assumed name, and with his features disguised to avoid attention, Judd stepped off an airjet at Marco Polo Airport late that afternoon, then caught a water bus to Venice. He could've teleported in and negated the need for the subterfuge, but there was no point in using up his telekinetic reserves without cause.

When he reached the island, he found a corner out of sight of passersby—and of security cameras, concentrated on the images Aden had given him, and teleported to the location where he was to meet the rebels. It proved to be a small indoor courtyard, the walls creamy with age and covered with some type of a dark green vine.

There was no need to make a cell phone call.

"I was told I was expected," he said to the armed man who watched him with the flat eyes of an Arrow, though he was dressed in faded denim jeans and a blue T-shirt.

The slightest hesitation, the man's eyes flicking to his hair. It was currently dirty blond, his eyes a pale gray. "Who sent you?" The other man didn't lower his weapon.

Instead of answering, Judd—having built up the correct focus—bent the muzzle of the gun downward, rendering it ineffective. The rebel Arrow threw it aside, hitting Judd with a telepathic blow at the same time . . . but Judd had his psychic hands in the cells of the male's heart. He shifted things enough to pinch a blood vessel.

The man paled at the warning. "Tk-Cell." It was a gasp, his hand up, palm out.

Judd released him, fixing the damage as he left. "I assume no further introductions are necessary."

The answer came from behind him, where he'd sensed a familiar presence. "I apologize, Judd," said the melodic female voice. "Alejandro has orders to incapacitate all unknowns who enter the courtyard."

Keeping Alejandro in his line of sight, he turned to see a petite woman in her late twenties with a face that was all soft curves, her lips lush. But it was her eyes that told the truth of her nature—the color of coal, they were like chips of ice. "Zaira." Born in Jordan and raised in an Arrow training facility in Turkey, she'd been lost in action five years ago.

Zaira's gaze shifted. A second later, Alejandro gave a sharp nod and left. Only then did Zaira turn and invite him to join her for a walk around the courtyard. "We did not expect you until this evening. That's why one of us wasn't on watch."

"Alejandro is damaged."

"His neural functions are fine, but he was given an overdose of Jax while on a mission. It's left him unable to veer from an order. Alejandro no longer understands subtleties."

"Is he safe?"

"So long as I don't give him a direct order, he won't kill." Zaira paused for a long second before continuing the walk. "I saved his life, and he . . . imprinted on me. It concerns me, but according to Aden, there's nothing to be done. His mental pathways are locked."

Judd picked up the nuances of deep emotion, wondered how much of it was truth and how much a mask created to blend into the human world. Arrows did not easily break Silence. He knew that better than anyone. "Why did you want to see me?"

"From what I've gleaned from the media reports, you appear to have carved out a stable life for yourself and your family. We want to know how you did it."

Judd glanced around the courtyard, aware he was being watched by more eyes than Zaira's. "You all live here, in this compound?"

"Yes."

"What do you do for income?"

"Diversified investments made over a number of years, including properties in various cities and localities." Zaira turned the corner of the courtyard, coming to a stop beside a curved archway. "Money is not what concerns us."

Judd asked one final question before giving the other Arrow the answer she sought. "Do you intermingle with the outside population?"

"Only as much as necessary. The rest of us aren't like Alejandro, who simply can't handle the stimulation, but we continue to grapple with being outside Silence." She looked at him with a directness that would disconcert most non-Psy. "I defected before you, as did a number of the others, but we are nowhere as integrated into the world."

Judd thought of the kiss Brenna had given him as he left the den, the hug Marlee had run after him to claim, the punch on the shoulder that had been Drew's way of saying "stay safe." "You have to accept," he said, "that you need the humans and the changelings, as they need you." His race had abilities that had once been greatly respected, not merely feared.

"Isolating yourself will simply further what they began in the Net." He'd had a family, had known that Walker, Sienna, Toby, and Marlee all cared if he lived or died, and still he'd been brutally close to the edge. The Arrows who lived here had only each other for family—and most Arrows didn't understand what a family was, much less how to create one.

Zaira looked up at a sky gone that hazy blue that preceded sunset. "We can't take the chance with any outsiders. Not yet."

"No," Judd agreed, because their task was to be a hidden escape hatch. "But change is coming."

Zaira's eyes reflected only the steel will that had made her an assassin without compare. "We are ready."

We are Arrows.

"COME on. Judd'll be here in a couple of minutes," Adria said, having showered and changed after their day out.

Riaz, his hair damp from the same shower, followed her out into the corridor, shutting the door behind them. "Pierce just sent me a message to say he's going to get you for that stunt."

"It was his own fault," she said with a laugh, feeling a warm affection for the handsome wolf who was Riaz's friend.

Riaz's response was unexpectedly serious. "Shower or not, you carry my scent in your skin." Watchful eyes. "That bother you?"

Adria waited until they were inside the elevator cage to answer, the frothy happiness of the day suddenly a lump in her chest. "The last time I had a man's scent in my skin, it nearly destroyed me," she said, tearing open a barely healed wound.

Knuckles brushing her cheek, the dark wood and citrus tang of his scent in her every breath. "We're not all bastards, Adria."

The doors opened, saving her from having to continue the conversation. Not that she didn't agree with his words. But the memories, they were raw, painful things that clawed and bit and threatened to steal her rational mind without warning . . . because it had started out tender with Martin, too.

Gut churning at the conscious acceptance of a dread that had been a noxious whisper at the back of her mind throughout the day, she almost walked past Judd where he stood against a column in the busy hotel lobby. It was his scent that cued her, that touch of ice that was a cool kiss. "You make a good blond."

"Brenna doesn't like it," he said as they headed out into the early evening light, Riaz on her left and Judd on her right. "She's already bought the neutralizer to get rid of the color once I'm back home."

If Adria had met him on the street, she'd have thought Judd sophisticated and aloof, but there was no missing the love in his tone when he spoke of his mate. "I have to admit," she murmured, "if I had a choice of you with chocolate brown hair or blond, I'd go with the brown every time."

"*Chocolate* brown?" Riaz muttered. "Why don't you just go ahead and call him a stud?"

Adria blinked at the edgy comment, belatedly realizing the lone wolf by her side was irritated by the attention she was paying Judd. She'd never been a woman who got off on making a man jealous, and that hadn't changed. Which was why she said, "Because I'm partial to pretty gold eyes."

Color streaked his cheekbones. "Judd, you're not listening."

"Listening to what?" The other male shot them a quietly amused look. "We have a tail."

"Alliance," Riaz said. "I think it's more of an escort."

Adria had picked up the three men as well. "Bo," she explained to Judd, "is acutely paranoid, but in his shoes, I would be, too." She explained his abduction, as well as the brainwashing of the comm technician, the suspected fate of the former chairman.

Judd didn't sound surprised. "Rumor is, Tatiana reached her position on the Council by killing her mentor. I know for a fact that she used psychic coercion to get certain contracts—she's one of the most dangerous and unscrupulous women in the Net. Bowen is right to be paranoid."

Further conversation stopped as they reached the Alliance building and were ushered inside to where a scowling Bo was waiting by the elevator. "We had all the routes into Venice tagged," he said, eyes on Judd, "full surveillance with facial recognition software, and yet you got through."

Judd's response was pragmatic. "There's not much you can do to stop someone with my training coming into your city."

Expression still dark, Bowen led them down to the same room they'd used yesterday. This time, the water was an invisible, inky blackness beyond the glass—it created the unsettling illusion of being cocooned in nothingness. Hiding her shiver, Adria glanced at the four people who sat waiting for

them around the conference table: a slender woman Bo introduced as his sister, Lily, along with three other males ranging
in age from midtwenties to early forties.

"I figured five test subjects," Bo said to Judd after they'd
all settled in, "would give you enough of a range to cross
natural shields off the list."

Not necessarily, Judd thought, not given the breadth of the
Alliance. If the conglomerate that represented human interests was playing some kind of a high-stakes game, it had
enough of a membership that it could have gathered five individuals with the rare type of shield. However, all he said to
Bo was, "Ready?"

The male nodded.

The instant he touched Bowen's mind—or attempted to—
he knew without a doubt that what stopped his intrusion was
no natural shield. Such shields had always felt like solid walls
to his psychic senses, but a wall that could bounce things
back, repelling any psychic probe. This was a storm of electricity. His probes got through . . . but were destroyed before
ever reaching their destination.

Riveted, he tried the most subtle telepathic tricks he knew,
including ones Walker had taught him during his clandestine
'ports to his brother when Judd was a half-broken teenager
in an Arrow training facility. They failed, all of them. The
shield was a masterpiece, powered by the electrical charge
of the brain itself, and calibrated to provide maximum
protection.

As with a changeling, the only way to disrupt it without
having long-term access to the victim would be to blast in
with brute power, which would likely result in severe brain
damage. Futile if data extraction was the target. The solitary
other option was the surgical removal of the chip. Unless—"Is
the chip fused to your brain stem?"

Chapter 44

BOWEN GAVE A short nod. "Any attempt to remove it once it's fully integrated will cause death."

Which meant extraction would be as pointless as violent force.

Considering other ways to get through the electricity, Judd turned to Lily. She went white, clearly less certain of the efficacy of the shield than Bowen, but nodded when he asked for permission to attempt to breach the shield. Hers, he found, was different from Bowen's—less "active" in some ways, the currents smoother, but it was just as efficient in degrading his probes.

"The test is complete," he said, retreating from the mind of the final subject.

Bowen indicated that it was alright for Lily and the others to leave, but they hesitated. The security chief looked at Judd. "They want to know if you were able to get in."

It was a desire Judd could appreciate. "No. Infiltration proved impossible."

Bowen continued to grin after the doors closed on the four volunteers, lines creasing the pale brown hue of his skin. "Do you have any doubts about the origin of the shield?"

"It's unequivocally mechanical," Judd said, speaking to Riaz and Adria as well as Bowen. "An extremely beautiful piece of biocompatible engineering." His admiration was genuine—as was his concern. "Is it safe?"

"We've done extensive tests." Despite the confident words, Bowen's smile faded into a look of grim resolve. "Now that we've authorized a general rollout, requests are far outstripping supply, even though we've been blunt about the risks. The fact is"—the Alliance security chief's jet-black eyes locked with Judd's—"even if it does blow up our brains in a few months or a few years, we'd still have had that time knowing that no one could come in and take what he or she wanted. Knowing our thoughts were private."

Judd understood the need. He'd felt the same helplessness as a child. His entire life had been out of his control, held in the hands of those who wanted only to use him. "Full integration—how long does it take?"

"A year according to the projections," Bowen said. "After that, the chip will, in essence, become part of the brain stem."

"So"—Riaz's tone was quiet, serious—"deciding to put in one of these is a lifetime commitment."

"Yes." Bowen rubbed the top of his head, the stubble rasping against his palm. "We did the first five two weeks apart. We're the controls. If something goes wrong with number one within that grace period, number two has a shot to get the chip out, and so on."

"You'd be the first to fall." Adria's husky voice.

"It's my job to protect my people." Pushing his chair back from the table, Bowen stood, hands braced on the table. "Share the information with your pack, and with DarkRiver and WindHaven. If you have human packmates who're prepared to take the risk, the Alliance is willing to let a certain number of them cut into the queue as a gesture of good faith."

SIENNA was sitting beside Indigo on the edge of the White Zone, supervising a group of two-year-olds playing in the sandpit while their minders had a coffee break, when the lieutenant said, "You need to start shadowing different members of the pack."

"Other soldiers, you mean?" Sienna asked, assuming it was an exercise of some kind.

But the taller woman shook her head, her long ponytail brushing against the back of the fitted Western-style white shirt with three-quarter sleeves she'd tucked into her low-slung jeans. "One person from every subgroup in the den, from maternal females to healers, to techs, to mechanics, to domestic operations. Soldiers, you already know. And, it's not an order," the lieutenant added, "but a suggestion."

Sienna took time to think through Indigo's recommendation, understanding the lieutenant meant far more than she'd actually said. "Like Hawke," she finally murmured, speaking more to herself than Indigo. "He knows every minute detail of every aspect of the pack."

"Yes." One arm hooked easily over the leg she'd drawn up at the knee, her back to a young green pine, Indigo paused to call out encouragement to two little ones who were struggling with their sand pails. "Hold on, I better go help before they bury each other."

Returning a couple of minutes later, sand on the knees of her jeans and the fading echoes of the wolf's laughter in her eyes, she settled back into her spot. "Tell me the reason why," she said, as if their conversation had never been interrupted.

"So I can be his sounding board." The person with whom he could discuss ideas he wasn't yet ready to take to his lieutenants. "So I can understand the nuances of the situations he has to handle day in, day out."

"Smart girl." Brushing off her knees, the lieutenant turned to look at her. "But that's not the only reason."

"It's for me, too," Sienna said slowly, grasping what it was Indigo wanted her to see. "To make the journey from novice soldier to . . . something like a lieutenant"—but not the same, her priority Hawke rather than the pack—"faster and smoother." Wolves respected strength, and she had that. But she needed more experience, and crucially, she needed the acceptance of the pack when it came to any change in her place in the hierarchy. "The more people I shadow, the more connections I make."

Indigo's shoulder brushed her own as the lieutenant nodded. "Every wolf likes to feel appreciated. Hawke does it instinctively—you'll have to do it more consciously, but in no way does that devalue the commitment you'd be making to know and understand the beating heart of the pack."

Spoken, Sienna thought, like the protector Indigo was. They were stronger, undeniably more lethal, but all dominants considered themselves in service to the vulnerable in the pack—because without those gentler packmates, there would be no one to protect, no reason for them to exist . . . no sense of a home colored in affection and warmth. It had taken her years of living with SnowDancer to understand such subtleties. "I think it would be a good idea to start with a dominant maternal female, don't you?" They wielded as much power as the lieutenants, simply in a different sphere.

Indigo's glance held open approval and a pride that made Sienna feel as if she'd been given the most lavish praise. "Yes. I think if you ask Lara, she'll set it up with Ava."

The tension Sienna hadn't been aware of feeling until that moment leaked out of her, her shoulders relaxing. She'd met Ava any number of times. Her son, Ben, was one of Marlee's friends, though the two had recently fallen out—and neither would say what the problem was. "I will." Drawing in long breaths of the crisp, clean air, she watched a pup in wolf form help his friend complete a sand castle, patting the sand into place with baby paws. "It feels like I'm building the foundations for the rest of my life."

"Do you mind that?"

"I'm so happy, sometimes I think I'll burst." The depth of her joy scared her on occasion. Never had she imagined she'd have a future, a *life*, beyond the fury of the X-marker. Now that she did . . . "I'm going to build a foundation so strong, so solid, it won't ever shake, no matter what the future brings." No one, not even Ming LeBon, was going to stop her living her life.

RIAZ and Adria joined Judd for the trip back to the den that night. The automated water bus from Venice to the mainland was empty, no chance of being overheard, so they spoke in quiet voices, the wind brisk against their cheeks.

"Do you think anyone will want to take the risk?" Adria asked, worry and empathy battling for space within her. Sam, strong, loyal, courageous, was both a dominant and human. It would devastate him if he fell victim to a Psy mental violation, the act a savage blow to the heart of his nature. "I can see why they would."

Bracing his forearms on his thighs, Riaz said, "I have to admit, I never really considered just how vulnerable humans must feel," a troubled expression marking the strong lines of his features.

"Yes," Judd said from her right.

It hadn't escaped her notice that the two had sandwiched her between them the entire time they'd been together. Her wolf was irritated, its hackles raised. She wasn't a pup to be protected, but a senior soldier, well able to get herself out of trouble. "Do you think Hawke will want the information circulated throughout the pack?" she asked, fighting the urge to snarl. It would be like trying to explain trigonometry to someone who'd never seen a math book. The words just would not compute in their testosterone-laden male brains.

"No." Riaz's answer was decisive, the dark masculinity of his scent twining around her in invisible threads. "Not until Ashaya's done exhaustive tests to confirm the chip is safe."

"It could be said"—Judd's calm voice—"that the humans in the pack should be given the information and allowed to make up their own minds."

Riaz glanced at the Psy male. "You know a pack doesn't work like that. It can't."

"Yes." Judd echoed Riaz's position, the wind rifling through the dirty blond of his hair. "Hawke is responsible for the health of the pack as a whole, and sometimes that means making hard calls when it comes to individual choice."

"Yes," Riaz answered. "If our human packmates decided to do this, and the chips failed, their deaths would rip the heart right out of SnowDancer. The gain is not worth the risk, not yet."

Riaz's statement echoed inside Adria.

She thought of the risk she was taking, with this passionate, loyal lone wolf who might never fully belong to her, knew she might just be setting herself up for the hardest fall of all. But, as she'd told Riaz, she wasn't exactly undamaged goods. And . . . she didn't ever want to look back and regret what could've been.

Life might hurt, might bruise, might forever scar, but it was for living.

"If you think about it," Judd said as the fierce thought passed through her mind, "the PsyNet is structured more like a pack than anything else, with the Council in place of an alpha."

Adria shook her head, her wolf rejecting the idea. "There's

a big difference—Hawke's every decision, whether or not it's democratic, is for the good of the pack, while the Councilors have a way of using up their people until there's nothing left." It angered her to the core that it was the ones who were meant to protect, who were doing the most harm.

"This generation, yes." Judd's agreement was solemn. "But Councils pre-Silence *were* focused on the strength and health of the race as a whole. Ironically, it's that desire that led to Silence, but I think the seeds of hope are there, buried in the darkness."

As Riaz responded to Judd, the low rumble of his voice raising the hairs on her arms, she found herself thinking that Riaz was, in many ways, more similar to Judd than he was to another wolf. It would take him time to trust a woman enough to fully open up to her, but once he did, he would be devoted.

Adria didn't expect such devotion . . . wasn't sure she could handle it if it happened, her wolf panicked at the idea of the possessiveness that would be part and parcel of that kind of love. It made her wonder how Brenna handled it with Judd—the other woman wasn't a dominant, and had been terribly wounded when she and Judd had first gotten together.

But that wasn't the only thing she wondered. "Do you ever regret being mated?" she asked Judd after they'd made their way from the water bus to the airport and grabbed seats in the gate lounge. Even as she spoke, her eyes followed Riaz's muscled form as he walked over to the coffee stand to grab them drinks, his hair glinting with hidden highlights of copper and bronze.

Judd gave her an unreadable glance. "An unusual question from a wolf."

"Wouldn't it be easier," she clarified, "to do the work that you do, to walk into danger, if you didn't have a mate whose heart would break if you were hurt?"

Judd took his time answering, his gaze on the wide concourse and the people walking and running to catch their airjets. "It would be more . . . convenient," he said at last. "But it wouldn't be easier—Silence is based on the precept that emotion is a weakness, but what I feel for Brenna makes me stronger. I fight harder, dirtier, and rougher, *because* I know any injury to me will rebound on her."

"Sounds like a serious discussion," Riaz said, handing Judd the bottle of water he'd requested, before passing over Adria's hot chocolate. "With marshmallows." A smile that creased his cheeks, made his eyes flicker gold, wild and compelling.

Her wolf awakened at the sight of his own, the happy memories of lying beside him on the bed in their hotel room making it rub up against her skin in primal affection. It was all she could do not to nuzzle her face into his neck. "I can tell you're drinking your usual sludge." The scent of his coffee was rich, potent.

"It'll put hair on my chest." Lips still curved, he settled into his seat, draping his arm along the back of hers. "So"— his thigh pressing against her own as he pushed into her space in a very male way—"what are you two discussing?"

"Whether emotion makes us stronger or weaker," Adria said before Judd could mention mating, her heart twisting at the idea of stealing the smile from Riaz's eyes. "What do you think?"

Taking a gulp of his no-doubt scalding coffee, Riaz said, "I'd say it's what makes us human in the wider sense. Without it, we might as well be machines."

"Regardless of their problems," Judd disagreed at once, "the Psy in the Net aren't inhuman."

"Because in some deep part of themselves," Riaz argued, "they *do* feel."

"Yes." It was an unexpected response from a man Adria guessed had gone through the most stringent conditioning in the Net. "Silence was never as watertight as the Council's propaganda machine would've led us to believe." He nodded toward a mother and child walking down the concourse, the child's hand held tightly in the adult's.

It was clear by the cool lack of expression on their faces, the subtle stiffness of the woman's walk, that they were Psy. "A Councilor would say she holds the girl's hand because it's a practical method to ensure her genetic legacy is not lost or harmed."

At that very second, Adria saw the woman shift to block a suitcase from banging into the child, taking the bump herself. "Perhaps it's even what she believes," Adria murmured, "but there's more there." A protectiveness that had the woman tucking the child closer to her body, her hand cupping the back of the small blonde head.

"Not for all Psy." Judd stared at a luggage cart about to roll away from an elderly woman, and it came to a gentle, seemingly natural stop. "It's too late for some, the damage done by the conditioning too deep."

"Airjet Express BD21 to San Francisco now boarding."

Finishing off her hot chocolate, Adria gathered up the rest of their garbage and took it to the recycle slot. Riaz and Judd were up and waiting for her when she returned, with Riaz having slung her duffel over his shoulder, along with his own. She had no problem with that. But when the two of them went to fall in on either side of her, she halted. "I do not need bodyguards."

A confused look from both.

Her wolf flashed its canines. "I *knew* it wouldn't compute."

Chapter 45

RIAZ SEPARATED FROM Adria when they reached the den late afternoon San Francisco time. Showering, he pulled on his most well-worn jeans, the fabric soft from repeated washing, and a T-shirt, then made his way to her door. Her scent was damp and warm when she opened it, her hair sleek and shiny from her own shower, her body covered in soft gray pajama pants and a faded purple tee bearing the picture of a depressed cartoon donkey.

A raised eyebrow. "Yes?"

His wolf narrowed its eyes at her continued irritability.

Neither he nor Judd had been able to figure out what had put her back up before they boarded the airjet. He'd let her stew in silence during the trip, but now stepped into her space and nipped sharply at her lower lip. "Why are you acting snippy?" He kicked the door shut with his foot.

Glaring at him, she rubbed at the lip he'd bitten. "I just am. Get over it." She walked over to flop down on her back on the bed. "And go away so I can sulk in peace."

He fought his smile. Letting it out would be suicidal with a dominant female in this mood. "I have something for you." He held up the small bag he'd carried over.

A startled light in the brilliant hue of her eyes. "You got me a present?" She scrambled up onto her knees, holding out her hands. "Give!"

He walked across to sit on the bed. "I don't know if I should give it to someone so bad tempered." Playful as a pup, his wolf grinned.

Bracing her hands on his shoulders from behind, she closed her teeth gently over the tip of his ear. "I bite, so be careful."

"So do I." He snapped his teeth at her.

A delighted laugh, her claws kneading his shoulders. When she shifted around to sit cross-legged beside him, he put the bag in her lap. The wonder on her face as she took out and opened the velvet-lined box was worth all the trickery it had taken to buy, then hide the gift from her. He owed Pierce one.

"*Oh.*" She balanced the glass figurine on her palm—of a wolf with its eyes closed, its tail curled around itself. "The detail . . ." Gesturing for him to hold it, she retrieved the three other figurines with gentle fingers. They were even smaller—pups frolicking around the sleeping guardian: one growling at a wildflower, another eye to eye with a crow, the third crouched down in a sneaking position.

Closing the box, she arranged all four on the lid, placing the sneaking pup behind the adult wolf. As if the pup was planning to pounce on the guardian's tail. He chuckled. "I remember trying to do that to Dad."

Adria didn't answer, simply looked at the tableau, stroking a finger over one of the figurines once in a while. "This isn't fair." It was a whisper, her eyes gone huge and damp.

He'd bought the mischievous set for her because he'd thought it would make her smile . . . and he loved the way Adria smiled when she was deeply happy. He'd glimpsed that smile only once, when she'd first looked up from the sheets the morning after they'd danced on the balcony, had come to realize he wanted to see it again and again. But instead of joy, his gift had put tears in her eyes.

Cupping her jaw, he rubbed his thumb over the elegant arch of her cheekbone. "Hey."

She shook her head, pulled away. He didn't like that, but he let her get up off the bed and place the figurines carefully on the small vanity tucked into a corner. When she returned to straddle him in a single smooth motion, his body responded like a match to a flame, the sexual connection between them white lightning. Her lips were soft and wet as they seduced his, the taste of her an addiction that fought to steal his senses.

Not right, his wolf growled, *this isn't right*.

"Adria." Chest heaving, he wrenched her away with a hand fisted in her hair.

In response, she dug her claws into his shoulders and pushed, her eyes a pale, dangerous amber. It would've taken him to the bed if he hadn't been ready for it. Blood scented the air, sharp and metallic. Snarling, he ripped her hands off him, braceleting and pinning her wrists behind her back with one hand. It didn't induce her to desist. Thighs locked around him, she angled her head with predatory focus.

He gripped her jaw when she would've snapped forward to sink her teeth into his neck, squeezed. *"Behave."* This was a challenge, and he had to win it, or they'd never move past this moment.

A soft smile, eyes wolf-sly. "Riaz." Moving her body in a sinuous curve that enticed, she broke his hold on her wrists with a single wrenching move, went to slam her claws into his chest. But he wasn't stupid, and he knew damn well who he was dealing with—a trained and honed predatory changeling female out to win. Mercy was not something she understood. Not here. Not now.

Twisting at the last moment, he used her own momentum to pin her to the bed on her front. He manacled her wrists on either side of her body before she could catch her breath, pressing down on her with his much heavier frame. She was smart, she was strong, but in a contest of sheer brute strength, she would never win.

When he sank his teeth into the smooth curve of her shoulder, she bucked. He continued to hold her until she stilled, her entire body quivering with tension. Releasing his grip on her shoulder, though he continued to pin her wrists, he licked at the mark, then nuzzled aside her hair to press a kiss to her jaw, her face turned sideways on the pillow. "Say it."

The sound of teeth grinding.

Driven by possession and grim determination both, he allowed more of his weight to fall on her as he licked at the mark he'd made, using slow flicks of his tongue. It was a taunt, and the growl that rumbled up from her chest told him she knew it. But he had her good and pinned, and regardless of how much she strained, she couldn't throw him off.

"I yield," she finally gritted out.

Not quite trusting her—not in this mood—he released her wrists one at a time before bracing himself above her on one forearm. Using his free hand, he brushed aside the damp tangle of hair from her face and neck, baring the clean line of her profile. "Want me to get off you?" He continued to run his fingers through her hair, petting her to calmness.

A slight pause before she shook her head.

"Tell me when I get too heavy," he murmured, easing his lower body into the lithe curves of her own.

Her lashes came down over eyes that remained a haunting wild amber, then rose again. "It feels good."

Sliding his hand to her shoulder, he rubbed his thumb gently over the bite mark before reaching up to massage her nape, her scalp. Long, slow minutes passed, but she relaxed at last, going boneless under him. Pressing a hotly possessive kiss to the curve of her jaw, he squeezed her neck. "We're not just sex."

Riaz had made up his mind to pursue this indefinable, wonderful thing that had grown between him and Adria when neither one of them had been looking, and he wasn't going to allow the damage done to her by another man to destroy that. "Are we?" It was a question heavy with demand, his fingers tightening.

She dug her nails into the sheets, her jaw set. He knew she wasn't physically scared by him being on top of her—they both understood he'd release her the instant she made it clear she wanted out. No, her fear had an altogether different cause, her panic one he could taste in her skin when he licked out at her, the sheen of perspiration that covered her a fine sparkle. *"Adria."*

ADRIA jerked at the unrestrained dominance in that command. For the first time, she realized exactly how careful he'd been with her in their sexual encounters to date—he might have been tender, passionate, and urgent in turn, but he hadn't allowed her to see into the heart of the black wolf within. This man, the one who was speaking to her in a soft tone that was a hot blade over her skin, *this* was the primal core of him.

His fingers moved against her neck, a silent reminder that he held the reins. Her wolf wasn't happy with that . . . yet it was. The confusion of it caused a chaos of emotion inside her. So long she'd been with a man who had forced her to silence and stifle her true self in a hundred small ways because he hadn't been strong enough to handle her. Now, she was with a man who not only didn't have a problem accepting her strength, but who was also strong enough to overpower her in every way that mattered to a changeling.

Panic burned her gut like acid. *She* was the one who had always been in control, the one who could stop things before they went too far, before they pushed her too deep into painful emotional territory. "I changed my mind," she said, her tumult a smoldering blaze inside her skin, swamping all rational thought. "We need to break it off."

Releasing her nape, Riaz began to stroke his hand through her hair again, slow and easy and unmistakably, unbearably possessive. "I can scent your panic." A kiss on the mark he'd made when he'd bitten her. "Talk to me about it."

She couldn't do it, couldn't expose the naked, vulnerable girl inside the skin of the woman. However, when she went to turn her face away, he lifted his body off her. Another kind of panic stung her, the sense of loss devastating. But she was being turned onto her back before she could react, Riaz's heat covering her once more as he brushed her hair out of her eyes with his free hand, his other one braced by her head.

"I saw a cactus in the desert once," he said, his voice low and deep and a hum over her skin. "Called Queen of the Night. It had this exquisite creamy flower, and the scent, it intoxicated my wolf. But it only opened at night—you had to be patient to see it." Eyes of beaten gold. "I'm very patient." Suckling her upper lip into his mouth in an unexpected kiss, he tore her T-shirt on one side with his claws and—holding her gaze—shaped his hand over her bare rib cage.

Shivers raced over her frame. She tried to arch into him, sliding her hand around his body to push up his own tee so she could touch the hot, muscled skin of his back. "Please."

But he shook his head. "Sex is easy." He rocked against her, the hot steel of his erection pushing against the slick, needy flesh between her thighs. "I breathe your scent and I'm ready."

"Then why are you doing this?" she whispered, one hand fisting against his chest. "Let's keep it easy, as it was." No demands, no expectations, no heartbreak. Because she'd been wrong—she wasn't brave enough to chance more scars, more bruises. Not when this time around, she knew the agony would be so much worse.

Her wolf had never adored Martin as it adored the black wolf with the golden eyes.

Leaning down until his face was a bare inch away, his breath hot against her skin, Riaz said, "Because it's too late for that, and you're not the casual type. You never have been. Just like me." Crushed rocks and broken glass in his voice.

It was instinct to curve her hand over his nape, to pet him as he'd petted her. He let her touch him, let her claim skin privileges that were becoming ever more complicated. She'd thought she'd figured everything out in Venice, but tonight, what he'd done, it had touched the secret, idealistically hopeful part of her she'd allowed no one to reach for so long, it was a forgotten memory. The fact he'd already done so, when their relationship had hardly begun, it had her stomach in knots, her heart thumping against her ribs.

And then there was his dominance.

He spread his hand on her throat just then, curving it in a

gentle hold. "What're you thinking that's got your wolf so wary?" he asked in a low murmur, rocking once against the molten heat of her.

She twisted up in instinctive response, had the pleasure of hearing him hiss out a breath between clenched teeth. But though he stroked his hand down to lie possessively over her unfettered breast, he didn't take the next step, the one that would've left them tangled and sweat soaked. "I got used to bending," she admitted, fighting her pride to expose what a fool she'd been.

"With Martin. I had to bend to make him happy." It had taken place so slowly, she hadn't understood the corrosive ugliness of what was happening. Small things, she'd thought, things that didn't really matter—after all, the man had risked everything to save her life. Until she'd realized she'd begun to bury Adria to please Martin. "He was nowhere near as strong as you."

Riaz snorted. "You've been busting my balls since the instant we met—I sure as hell don't think you're suddenly going to flutter your lashes and simper at my every word."

Wolf and woman both blinked at the ridiculous image. "It's not that simple." She tried to find the words to explain. "Martin made me weak . . . No. That's not fair." There had been two people in that relationship. "I weakened myself to make him happy. I'm terrified I'll do the same with you." That was her flaw, no one else's.

Molding her breast with strong fingers, Riaz leaned down to take her lower lip between his teeth, releasing it oh-so-slow. "So you want to end things before they begin?" A harder squeeze, a deeper hint of teeth along her jaw. "That's the real weakness."

She dug her claws into his back when he bit her again. "Do that one more time and I'll give you a nice new tattoo."

Lips curving against her neck. "Yeah." His clean-shaven jaw was smooth over her skin. "I'm not real worried about you bending for me." Pushing up into a kneeling position straddling her hips, he ripped off his T-shirt and threw it to the floor before coming down over her, hands on either side of her head. "Open your mouth for me."

"Is that a request or an order?"

A lazy smile that reached his eyes, his mouth capturing hers in hot demand. She rubbed her tongue against his, felt him growl deep in his chest. Shuddering, she pressed her hands to his chest, his muscled body hers to explore. But when she ran her knuckles down the tantalizing line of hair below his belly button and to the top of the jeans that hung sexily low on his hips, he only allowed her to open the top button before tugging away her hand.

"I get to play first."

He'd ripped her T-shirt to shreds and was tugging off her pajama bottoms and panties before she realized *she* was his intended toy. Not resistant to the idea and with a few of her own, she pressed a foot to his chest the instant she was bare to the skin. "Get naked." Very much an order. "I want full skin privileges." She craved the sweet, hot slide of his body against hers, the hard male angles and delicious weight of him.

A kiss pressed to her foot, and suddenly, she was being flipped onto her front, the cold metal of his zipper biting into her as he settled his weight over her, his cock a hard outline. "No." Hot denial in her ear, one big hand shoving under her body to tease and tug at her nipple. "I think I'll be the boss today."

Chapter 46

"*RIAZ.*" IT WAS a warning, her claws slicing into the sheets.

Chuckling, he laved a kiss on her nape and—to her surprise—obeyed her unspoken demand, rising onto his haunches, his thighs on either side of her hips. Just when she was about to turn over, he put his hands on her back and began to massage downward from her shoulders, his hands strong, his fingers knowing. She moaned.

By the time he got to the base of her spine, she'd given up even the vaguest thoughts of rebellion. "You have two dimples here." A wet, luscious kiss to each that made her moan.

Apparently fascinated by the spot, he licked each dimple, rubbed his cheek against her skin. "I shaved especially for you."

Her toes curled. "I appreciate it." Though she was in no way averse to the rough scrape of his stubble, it melted her that he'd taken the time.

"Don't worry, I'll get my payment."

Her heart thudded, every inch of her very aware she was in bed with a big, dangerous wolf who wanted to do distinctly erotic things to her. When he lifted his head, silken strands of hair sliding over her skin, she expected him to get off the bed, remove his jeans, but he stayed in place, moving his hand down to shape and caress her lower curves. "I can scent you, so wet and ready."

The musk of the woman beneath him acted as a drug on Riaz's senses, the slickness of her pure provocation when he circled the entrance to her body with a single finger.

"Riaz." Not a warning this time. An invitation, her sweet curves rising to follow his touch.

Loving her so soft and pleasured, he shifted to kneel lower down her body, unzipping and shoving his jeans down enough to release his cock with a hiss of pleasure-pain. Squeezing his turgid flesh, he fought for control, found enough to caress his hands over her hips. "Up, Empress."

"Empress?" She brought up her knees in a fluid slide, rising so her back pressed into his chest at the same moment.

The blunt head of his cock already bathed in her slickness, he simply flexed his hips and pushed into her with slow, exquisitely pleasurable deliberation. "Queen," he grit out, fingers digging into her hips, "doesn't seem enough."

"Sweet talker." His lover's nails made tiny half-moon crescents on his thighs, her breathing ragged, her back arched, thrusting her breasts forward in sensual display.

Growling, he reached around to close his hands over the plump mounds. "Do what you will."

She moved on him, squeezing and releasing, and he knew he wasn't going to last much longer. Flicking one taut nipple in a way that always made her clench around him, he slid a hand down to fondle and tease the slippery nub of her clitoris.

"Riaz!" She spasmed around him in a burst of molten pleasure that ripped a scream out of her. But when she tried to ride him to completion, he dropped his free hand to grip her thigh, halting her.

"You're my toy, remember?" This wasn't just about sex, and he wouldn't allow her to forget it.

"Then play with me." She turned her face to demand a kiss.

Pleased at her trust, he gave her that kiss, and more, petting and caressing and indulging before he dropped his hand to her clit again. Playing with the hard little bundle of nerves until she was grinding her body against him in wild need, her breasts heavy and sensitive to his every touch, he took hold of her hips.

"Slow"—he lifted her off his cock, teeth clenched against the need to pound—"and deep"—he slid her back down to her long, hot moan—"and so wet."

This time he lifted her until the head of his cock popped out. Pushing past her passion-swollen entrance made her come around him, her muscles clamping down in feminine demand. Hands rising to squeeze her breasts, he thrust deep, riding out the hot pulses of her pleasure. But he couldn't come, not yet. Kissing her nape, he stroked his hands down her body to push her gently forward.

Ending up on her forearms, she shot him an amber-eyed look over the shoulder he'd bitten, her eyes hazy. That's how he wanted her today. Pleasured and marked and knowing exactly who held the reins. Because while Adria was a dominant, she couldn't be one in this bed. It would never work, not for either of them.

Fisting his hand lightly in her hair, he held her gaze as he pulled out, thrust again. And again. And again. Until she screamed and orgasmed so hard around him that her entire body trembled. Only then did he surrender, the orgasm all but ripping him in two.

. . .

HAVING left Naya with Lucas at the Chinatown office, Sascha glanced at the jaguar who'd driven her up when he brought the SUV to a stop near the den at around a quarter to six that night. "I think," she said, "we all agree I no longer need a bodyguard here." It was an implied question.

"It's not about trust," Vaughn responded. "It's about showing strength. Our alliance doesn't change the fact that we're two predatory changeling packs."

Sascha felt her lips curve into a rueful smile. "Just when I think I know everything there is to know about changelings."

The amber-blond male wasn't one of the more tactile sentinels, his reserve part of his nature, but now he rubbed his knuckles against her cheek. "Don't worry, we won't take back your pack membership."

Laughing at the sly feline humor, she got out of the vehicle, her telepathic senses alerting her to the fact they were being watched the entire way to the den. Another show of strength, a quiet reminder that SnowDancer had its lethal reputation for a reason. Lara met them at the entrance, her corkscrew curls in a ponytail, the pale lemon yellow of her shirt skimming the curves of her body. "It's good to see you." The healer embraced Sascha with a warmth that was genuine.

"I'm sorry I wasn't able to make it earlier." An issue had arisen with a juvenile, something she'd had to handle in her position as mate to the alpha. "The spike in Alice's level of consciousness?"

"Slight but holding." Stepping back, Lara smiled at Vaughn, the fox brown of her gaze warm in the way of healers—of all the people in a pack, they were the only ones who had no trouble interacting with, or being welcomed by, other packs, even those who might otherwise be the enemy. "Hello, Vaughn. How's Faith?"

"She wanted me to thank you for the photos you sent."

Lara waved away his words. "She saved the lives of those pups with her prediction—she's got a claim on them now."

A quiet nod from Vaughn.

"Do you want to come with us, or head out to catch up with the soldiers?"

"I'll come."

Nodding, Lara led them to the infirmary, updating Sascha on Alice's most recent readings as she did so. "The single bit of good news," she said as they walked into the infirmary, "is that minor shift in her level of consciousness, but it *is* so small we have to accept it could be a natural fluctuation." She gestured to the open door of a patient room. "Alice's."

"I'll wait here," Vaughn said, taking a watchful position outside the door.

Leaving the jaguar to his post, Sascha followed Lara inside. As always, Alice lay silent, her body covered by a soft sheet, her skull by a fine computronic skullcap that monitored her cerebral functions, while a number of other thin tubes ran out of her body. However, she was breathing on her own, her chest rising and falling in so gentle a rhythm, it would've been easy to miss had the rest of her not been so very motionless.

Sascha's attention locked on the fine bones of Alice's face. Marked by faint lines of tension, that face wasn't peaceful in repose, as if Alice was fighting from within, struggling to get out. "I can sense her. The emotional resonance is faint, but it *is* there." Sascha intended to strengthen it even further, having been mentally honing her ability to amplify, after reading about the technique in the groundbreaking book Alice had written more than a hundred years ago.

> One of the strongest and most unique gifts of a cardinal empath is the ability to dampen emotions. This study has briefly mentioned how that ability can be—and has been—utilized to control riots, but the same skill can be used in reverse to heighten emotions. However, the latter usage has the effect of draining the E, and even cardinals can only actively maintain it for a span of minutes, ranging from three to seven.

Alice hadn't described *how* E abilities worked on the psychic level, the thrust of her thesis more an anthropological study on empaths as a designation. As a result, Sascha had been left with tantalizing clues but no practical guidance. When she had first tried to control a volunteer "crowd," she'd exhausted herself in minutes.

Only later had she realized she'd actually been attempting to force emotion into the crowd rather than dampening their own. It had been a start. While she still hadn't cracked how to dampen emotions, she did think she could heighten them. "I wish I had a teacher instead of stumbling about in the dark." It frustrated her at times like this, the power within her that she had no idea how to shape.

"You already know more than any other E-Psy on the planet—give yourself a little more time." Squeezing Sascha's arm, Lara moved to the control panel at the end of the bed. "The readings don't show any problems. You can start whenever you're ready."

Exhaling quietly to center herself, Sascha took one of Alice's thin, pallid hands in her own and closed her eyes. However, before she could begin, she had to identify the other emotions that lingered in the vicinity so she could establish a baseline: Lara's intense focus, her concern; Vaughn's alert watchfulness and curiosity; the tenor of a deep friendship emanating from two changelings in another patient room.

Baseline laid, she narrowed her attention to Alice.

Frustration.

Clean, clear but so faint she had to strain to sense it. Isolating the emotion with meticulous care, Sascha began to do what she'd theorized. Instead of bluntly pushing emotion into Alice, she instead "hummed" an emotional note that resonated with Alice's frustration.

If it worked as she thought it should, it would change the depth of Alice's frustration, bring it to the surface of her consciousness. Once there, it should continue to resonate at the higher frequency, stimulating Alice's mind until the human woman had the strength to break free. Sascha didn't know how long she'd been humming the note, changing the psychic range to find the perfect pitch, when something "clicked."

"I'm seeing a blip." Lara's quietly excited voice came from a distance. "I think it's working."

TWO days after their return from Venice, and Adria had no idea what she was doing about to walk into the Delgado house in San Diego. Riaz had caught her around four that afternoon, just after she'd completed her second session with a unit of Indigo's novices who wanted to learn the style of martial arts at which Adria was proficient. Sienna Lauren, who'd been the first to sign up, was turning out to be well suited to the discipline.

"It's the underlying order of it," the young woman had said. "I like the fact the entire art is built on a base of hundreds of set moves that the fighter puts together in unexpected ways."

It was Sienna she'd been chatting with when Riaz appeared on the edge of the outdoor training area. "I managed to get two tickets on the high-speed train to San Diego," he'd said when the younger woman had taken her leave. "Departing in two hours."

Startled, it had taken her a moment to figure out what he meant. "We can't take off again so soon after Venice," she'd said, heart in her throat.

"Return trip tonight—we'll get back into the den around two a.m. You're done for the day, right?"

"Yes, but I was planning to catch up on some paperwork." Like all dominants in charge of minors, she made sure to keep their parents updated with weekly reports.

"Do it on the train." He'd tapped her cheek with his finger. "Come on, Empress. I want you to meet my family."

She'd been hit sideways by the emotional import of the request—the fact Riaz had invited her so close to the heart of his personal pack . . . it made a thousand butterflies awaken in her stomach.

"The gardens are stunning," she commented now as they stepped out of the taxi, one hand unobtrusively on her abdomen in an effort to soothe the fluttering within.

"You have wonderful taste, dear!" The same small, curvy woman she'd seen at Hawke and Sienna's mating ceremony appeared unexpectedly from around the side of a sprawling rosebush, hands held out and a huge smile wreathing her face. "I'm so glad to meet you, Adria."

Adria leaned down to accept Abigail Delgado's hug, the scent of her a mix of spices she couldn't name and a sweet floral note. "Me, too," she said, suddenly tongue-tied.

When Abigail stepped back, Adria looked up to see Riaz, dressed in jeans and a chocolate dark shirt with the sleeves rolled up to the elbows, being hugged by a tall man who had such strikingly similar features it was clear they were father and son. The only difference was that the thick black of Jorge Delgado's hair was faintly threaded with silver, the fine lines at the corners of his eyes and around his mouth adding a quiet depth of character. "God," she said without thinking, "Riaz is going to get even more beautiful as he grows older."

Abigail's delighted laugh made Adria color, but Riaz's mother tucked Adria's arm into her own and squeezed. "It's a terrible cross we have to bear, sweetheart."

Meeting those twinkling eyes at the whisper, Adria burst out laughing, the butterflies taking flight to leave her wolf happy on an elemental level. Later that night, when Riaz tucked her to his side as the train punched through the opaque veil of night, she knew the dinner had been akin to the possessive dominance of his loving after Venice—her lone wolf was claiming her in his own quiet, determined, and inexorable way.

Her heart stuttered, jubilant and terrified in equal measures.

Chapter 47

KALEB FOUND HIMSELF at a dead end in the Net, but instead of backing away and attempting to navigate around the section, he examined every aspect of the blockade. It was a black wall. No fractures, no data. Dead space, the Net truncated.

Such barricades formed naturally in areas with low population densities. The NetMind shunted the individuals in the zone into the nearest active channel in an exercise in efficiency most people never realized—because the NetMind augmented the Net link of the affected to ensure those men and women felt no strain at being psychically positioned outside their geographic area.

The problem with this truncated section was that it was *almost* but not quite far enough away from a relatively dense population matrix. Any gain in efficiency resulting from shifting the minds in this sector wouldn't have been enough to justify the NetMind's output.

Which meant the neosentient entity hadn't created this roadblock.

It took him three hours to wedge open a small doorway in the wall of black without tripping the inbuilt alarms. Slipping through, he closed it behind himself, concealing the doorway for later access. The barricade proved to have been nothing but a firewall meant to discourage anyone from continuing to follow the trail—because it was hot again on this side.

Even as he swept through the slipstream in search of his target, part of his brain continued to sift and sort the millions of pieces of random data that floated past. Rumors, whispers, business information, snippets of fading conversation, it was all filtered out so it wouldn't clog his mind. Until a single fragment made him pause.

. . . pushed the anchor down the steps, but his death . . .

Not halting his psychic pursuit, he touched the NetMind's curious presence, asked it to follow the fragment. The vast neosentience returned to him in a split second with the report that the fragment was all that remained. The rest of the conversation had degraded, its energy absorbed back into the Net.

Regardless, only one anchor had died in that manner in the preceding weeks. And since the mode of his death had not been made public, the fragment appeared to infer the male had been murdered. What Kaleb couldn't reason out was why. As he and Aden had discussed, the death of an anchor offered no one in the Net any advantage.

Following that logic, it was likely the murder was tied to something that had nothing to do with the victim's position as an anchor. That other reason was often cold, rational money—the anchor's heirs might simply have wanted to hasten the speed of their inheritance.

Kaleb sent Aden a telepathic message, taking care not to disturb the trail in front of him. It glowed a faint silver to his psychic senses, and he was almost certain this was it . . . when it disappeared with total abruptness.

I'll follow up. Aden's telepathic voice.

Kaleb responded automatically. *Contact me as soon as you discover anything.* He scanned his surroundings for any hint of the silver thread. But it was gone as if it had never existed.

Chapter 48

FIVE DAYS AFTER the visit to his parents, Riaz watched Adria jog past with a small group of her kids. Perched as he was on top of the jungle gym part of the training run, he had an excellent view, knew she was teaching them one of the emergency evacuation routes they might one day have to utilize to protect the pups, should all the dominants be needed to hold back an invading force.

Man and wolf both stopped what they were doing to watch the woman who, he was slowly beginning to see, was as much a nurturer as an aggressive protector. An unusual combination, rare in the hierarchy. While she was undoubtedly a dominant soldier with impressive offensive capabilities, there was a gentleness about her that was more akin to that of the maternal females. It was an aspect of her personality he'd brushed up against more than once without realizing it—and it made his protectiveness toward her intensify, until he knew he'd have to be careful not to cross lines that would most definitely annoy his amber-eyed wolf.

As if sensing his scrutiny, she turned to look over her shoulder, her expression softening. "Hey," she mouthed.

"Hey," he mouthed back.

Lips curving, she returned her attention to the teenagers around her, disappearing under the thick canopy of the trees not long afterward. His wolf stretched its neck, trying to catch a final glimpse of her, but it didn't snarl when the trees continued to block its view—it knew she'd return to him, the bonds between them no longer cobweb fine. What had happened after Venice had changed things on a fundamental level.

He'd made his decision, made his claim.

Adria hadn't rejected his possession—not the same as acceptance, but as he'd told her, he was a patient man. Smiling at the way this skittish wolf was beginning to trust him with pieces of her heart, he turned his attention back to the obstacle course that was the training run. The soldiers had begun to learn the old pattern, which meant it was time to reconfigure it into a new one, which he was doing, with Judd's help.

The other lieutenant, his hair back to its normal chocolate brown shade—Riaz's wolf snorted—teleported him a wrench when he called out for it. "Thanks." He twisted a stubborn bolt into place, his mind going through the issues to be discussed at the upcoming lieutenant meeting. "Heard anything from Ashaya?"

"Just an update on how long her initial tests will take," Judd called out from under the structure. "Approximately a month. Ashaya's very dogmatic and detail oriented in her work."

"Good." Unscrewing a small piece, he snapped it into a new position on the right. "Bowen—what's your take?"

Judd came out from under the structure to look up at him, wiping his forearm across his sweat-damp forehead and leaving a streak of grease behind. "He is, in a sense, an alpha. The Alliance looks to him for direction and protection—seen that way, his actions may be ruthless, but they're for the good of his pack."

"Spoken like a true wolf."

Judd caught the wrench he threw down, waiting until Riaz's feet hit the ground to say, "As Drew would say, if you can't beat 'em . . ."

"Yeah, too late to back out now. We know where you live."

Judd's response was to put the wrench with the other tools and raise his eyebrow. Of course Riaz couldn't turn down the challenge, and they were scrambling over the modified jungle gym in seconds. It dumped Judd on his ass two minutes in. Riaz lasted another ten seconds. "Damn," he said with a satisfied laugh. "Got us both. Excellent." No one was going to learn to beat this configuration in a hurry.

Eyes narrowed, Judd stared at the structure as if at a mortal enemy. Slapping his fellow lieutenant on the shoulder, Riaz said, "Don't even think about it." A pissed-off telekinetic versus the complex metal pylons and tubes of the jungle gym—the results would not be pretty.

Judd glanced at his watch. "I'll destroy it later." Cool as ice, but Riaz caught the glint, knew the Tk would be back until he'd beaten the obstacle. "We'd better get to the meeting. It's almost two."

Heading in, they put away the tools and quickly washed up before walking into the special conference room set up for lieutenant meetings. Hawke and the other lieutenants—via comm link and in person—were all present. Indigo, her feet propped up on a second chair, her legs crossed at the ankles, said, "You're late," without looking up from her datapad.

That datapad was suddenly hovering several inches in the air . . . before it zipped to a stop in front of Judd. Taking it, he said, "And you're playing Wolf versus Leopard."

Everyone laughed as Indigo threatened Judd with bodily harm, but the Psy lieutenant continued to study the datapad. "You have an excellent territorial strategy—though it appears this game skews to favor wolves. Was the developer a wolf?"

"I confess!" Tomás threw up his hands. "It was me."

Nudging the datapad back to Indigo, Judd twisted a chair around to sit with his arms braced on the back. "If you want cats to play it, too, you have to even out the playing field."

Tomás's eyes gleamed. "I think you just volunteered to be my impartial test player."

"Fine. As long as I get a share of what are certain to be huge profits, taking the competitiveness of wolves and leopards into account."

Tomás tapped the side of his nose as more laughter filled the room. "I'll have my people talk to your people."

Hawke leaned back in his chair, tipping it so it balanced on two legs. "His 'people' is Brenna, so watch out or you'll be lucky to come out of it with the shirt on your back." Hands linked behind his head, he glanced at Riley. "Okay, what's on the agenda today? Any attempted mini-strikes by Pure Psy I don't know about?" It was an irritated question. "It's like that mole game where they keep popping up."

"Nothing in the last four days," Riley replied to a round of applause. "And Sam is leading the trap-detection pool with an impressive nine points."

"Four days," Indigo said in a musing tone of voice. "That's the longest gap to date. Strain on their limited personnel beginning to show?"

"Moles reproduce very quickly," Judd said dryly.

Jem almost snorted out the water she'd been drinking. "Enough with the moles, let's not give them the satisfaction of sucking up more of our time."

"I now declare a mole moratorium." With that solemn statement—which made Cooper choke—Riley picked up the datapad in front of him. "BlackSea's first on the list. Kenji, Riaz, give us an update."

Riaz nodded at Kenji to answer.

"We had a bit of back-and-forth, but they're now happy with the contract." Pushing his shockingly sedate black hair out of his eyes, Kenji glanced at Hawke. "They made their decision about the alliance before they ever approached us. It was just a case of working out the details."

Riaz had to agree. "It's going to come down to the meet." He and Kenji, as well as Riley, would accompany Hawke to the face-to-face with Miane Levêque, while BlackSea was sending along Emani and two other representatives of their ruling board with Miane. In deference to BlackSea's preference to be near water, the meeting was set to take place in a waterfront building owned by DarkRiver. "Still no hint on why they're suddenly so keen on an alliance."

"We get an answer at the meet, or we walk." The alpha's smile was all teeth. "Beautiful Garnet. Report."

Jem rolled her eyes. "Nothing new. I've still got the steady trickle of Psy coming into my sector. I think the majority are continuing on to San Francisco."

Frowning, Indigo said, "City's going to start having a population and housing issue if this keeps up."

"It's not that bad yet," Riley replied. "Cats are keeping an eye on the situation—there are enough apartments in the general area for the time being. The Psy coming in are staying clear of den territory and DarkRiver's territorial borders."

Coop, who'd touched base with Riaz just yesterday, the two of them bullshitting over the comm, had nothing to report. Neither did Matthias, but Alexei was sporting an impressive black eye and a scowl. However, all he said was, "All quiet here."

"No way, Sexy Lexie," Tomás said, earning a deadly look, "fess up. Where did you get that shiner?"

"Dominance challenge."

Hawke's hands dropped, the legs of his chair slamming to the ground as his expression grew dark. "Another one?"

"Don't worry—I took off the kid gloves." White grooves bracketed his mouth. "He's alive . . . barely. I don't think anyone else will want to try their luck."

"Good." Hawke's tone was without pity. "We might've gained two or three strong soldiers as a result of the challenges, but it's a waste of your time dealing with them."

"Did you even put ice on that?" Jem asked, wincing at the damage to Alexei's face.

The young lieutenant shrugged. "Wasn't time—I didn't want to give him a chance to heal up before we delivered him to his pack."

The message, Riaz thought, his wolf in complete accord, had to be brutal, unmistakable. "I think," he said, when Riley turned to him and asked for an update on the Human Alliance, "it might be time to revisit the idea of a permanent liaison with them."

The sound of teeth grinding. Nobody had forgotten or forgiven what Bowen had done the last time he'd been in the area.

Coop was the one who broke the silence. "Riaz is right. The Alliance is too big to simply ignore."

Hawke shoved a hand through his hair, asked for opinions. Everyone had one, but they finally decided to feel out some kind of a liaison arrangement.

"Can you handle that?" Hawke glanced at Riaz. "You've got BlackSea as well."

"Kenji can take most of the load there," he said, receiving a nod from the other lieutenant. "And this isn't a full alliance negotiation." He caught Judd's eye. "I might need your input now and then." The other man had access to the PsyNet, and Riaz knew there were powerful people in the psychic network keeping an eye on the Alliance.

"No problem."

"The possible civil war inside the Net," Indigo said to Judd. "Any news on that front?"

"Close to ignition—all it needs is a single match." A chilling prediction. "I've gotten the word out among the Psy in the city. The forewarning may save some of them."

Some, Riaz thought, *not all*.

CLOSING the door to her office after completing the day's session with the kids, Adria wiped her hands on her jeans, took a deep breath, and put through the call. It was answered on the second ring, her mother's vivid blue eyes filling the computer screen, the honey brown of her hair tumbling over her shoulders—it was Cullan Morgan who had given his daughters the ebony of their hair, but Tarah's and Adria's eyes came from Felicity.

"Adria." Heartfelt smile on her face, her mom reached toward the screen as if to touch Adria, then dropped her hand with a rueful smile. "How are you, my baby girl?"

Adria's heart clenched at the love that sang in her mother's every word. She'd kept her distance from her parents for too long, driven by a caustic mix of shame and anger, and her wolf ached to feel the fierceness of her mother's embrace, the rough affection of her father's touch. "Good. I went to Venice."

"Oh, how lovely. I know you always wanted to." Felicity beamed, glanced over her shoulder. "Cullan, come here! Your pumpkin's on the comm."

Adria laughed, knowing that regardless of her age or rank, she'd always be their surprise baby. "Hi, Dad," she said when her father's handsome face filled the screen.

"I should spank you, Adria Morgan," was his growling response, his beard sprinkled liberally with silver. "When are you planning to visit your parents?"

"Soon as I can get three or four days of leave in a row." Her parents were based in Los Angeles as a result of her mother's position at the university, her father in charge of SnowDancer's construction arm in the city. "Riley's in a very good mood, so I might be able to swing it in the next few weeks."

"Oh, I heard," her mother said with a delighted grin. "He'll make a wonderful father."

"That he will," Cullan agreed. "Always had a steady head on his shoulders—even when he was making trouble with Hawke, Cooper, Riaz, and the others when they were younger."

Adria had decided to keep her silence on her deepening relationship with Riaz. It wasn't that she didn't want to share her family with him, didn't want her parents to meet the intelligent, passionate lone wolf who was twining ever stronger bonds around her heart, but that she had to be dead certain. Never again did she want her mother and father to worry and hurt as they had when she'd been with Martin.

No, the next time she introduced a man to her family, it would be because she knew he loved her with his heart and soul, his devotion unflinching.

Chapter 49

SIENNA'S NERVES WERE shot by the time she shoved into Hawke's empty office and sprawled in his chair late that afternoon. The scent of him surrounded her, but it wasn't enough. Scowling because she wanted to sulk *with* him, she got up, deciding to track him down like he so often did her.

It didn't take long—because she knew who to ask.

"I saw him, Sinna!" Ben volunteered when she interrogated the kids in the White Zone. "He's fixing a car."

"Thanks, Ben." She kissed his cheek—and the cheeks of all the other pups who'd gathered around—then made her way down to the garage.

Hawke wasn't, in fact, "fixing a car." He was discussing a rugged all-wheel-drive vehicle that looked like it had been taken apart piece by piece, with the head mechanic. Staying out of sight, she didn't interrupt what seemed to be an important conversation, but she knew he was aware of her, his wolf rubbing against the mating bond in a primal hello.

She didn't know how she knew which part of him she was talking to at any given time. She just did. And she'd learned to stroke the wolf through the bond, did so now. When Hawke finished his conversation and walked across to her, he just tapped her on the cheek and said, "My office," having clearly sensed her mood.

The instant they entered it, he raised an eyebrow. "Someone's been sitting in my chair."

She slumped in it again. "The maternal females hate me."

Pale, pale blue eyes suspiciously bland, Hawke leaned back against his desk in front of her and looked down to meet her no-doubt temper-foul gaze. "I'm guessing shadowing Ava didn't work out."

"Her baby was fussy today, so she arranged for me to shadow Nell instead." Cocking her fingers, she pretended to shoot herself in the head. "Do you know how many times I was pulled up in front of Nell as a juvenile? Well, she does. Has a memory like a steel trap."

"I see."

"Stop laughing," Sienna muttered, glaring at her mate though he hadn't made a sound. "This is serious."

An infuriating chuckle before he used his foot to push the chair away, then pull it back in so she ended up between his legs. "Tell me exactly what happened."

"I showed up to meet Nell in the nursery, and we spent an hour with the pups. That was nice." She loved the innocence of the babies, the way the toddlers shrieked in delight, their joy guileless and forthright. "It was when we left that Nell decided to wander down memory lane. Her 'favorite' "—she hooked her fingers to create air quotes—"one about me is from that time my class was camping in the mountains, and I convinced the girls to steal and hide every single stitch of clothing owned by the boys. She said she was impressed by the precision timing involved in the raid."

Hawke remembered the incident and the punishment he'd meted out to all those involved—fighting the urge to congratulate the girls on the sheer audacity of the stunt the entire time. "Nell probably *was* impressed." He sure as hell had been.

Responding with that adorable growling sound he loved, Sienna pushed herself back until his chair pressed against the wall, her legs kicked out in front of her. "She then made me sit through a discipline session with two of the younger teens—it was like a bad rerun of my life. Later, she took me to a meeting where the senior maternal dominants all worked around a quilt. I can hardly sew enough to complete emergency repairs in the field!"

Hmm . . . "Did she invite you back?"

A grumpy nod.

Delight had him hooking his foot under the chair and rolling her back toward him. "Ask me the name of the reigning champ of trouble in the den before you came along?"

Sienna's continued black mood was apparent in her muttered, "Who?"

"Nell."

That got her attention. *"Nell?"*

"Yes. And she held the title for ten years. So"—he leaned down with his hands braced on the arms of her chair—"I'd say it's definite that she was impressed by that raid."

Biting down on her lower lip, his mate said, "The quilting meeting?" in a small voice.

"It's where the maternals get most of their business done. And they don't invite just anyone."

"Oh." Sienna rubbed a hand over her face. "To be honest, the meeting was painless in comparison to the time I spent with Nell—I felt like I was being raked over the coals."

"How did you respond?"

"I treated her with the respect due to her as one of the most senior people in the den." Lashes down, back up. "Though I did get a little irritated when she pushed too hard—and I might have pointed out that I'm an adult female now and not particularly interested in rehashing my past exploits. That's when she took me to the quilting."

"Good," he said, claiming a hard kiss before rising to his full height once again. "If you'd let her walk all over you, you'd never have been invited to the meeting." Slender Nell might appear young and almost fragile, but the leader of the maternals had a spine of titanium and appreciated the same in others. "The fact you can't sew is irrelevant—they bloody well give me a needle and thread when I attend."

Sienna spit out a startled laugh, the stars returning to her eyes. "What do you do?"

"Remind them I'm alpha." The wolf snarled. "Then I sit and I listen." Because the maternals were the backbone of the pack, the ones who made them family, gave them heart.

"I made myself useful cutting pieces for the quilt," Sienna said, "but mostly I listened, too." A long, shuddering release of breath. "So . . . it wasn't a disaster?" Hesitant, quiet, a request for reassurance.

It fucking killed him each time she exposed the depth of her trust in him, this woman who, as a scared, lonely child, had been taught not to trust anyone. "Not even close," he said, crooking a finger. "I'd call it an unmitigated success."

Rising, Sienna pressed her body to his, her fists tucked

against his chest. Cuddling her close, he rubbed his jaw against her temple. "You're doing beautifully." He knew she was walking this road not simply for herself, but for him, for SnowDancer, so the pack would know they could have faith in the strength of their alpha couple.

Pride and love vied for space inside him, collided in a powerful punch of emotion. "Come on," he said, running his hands down her back. "Let's sneak into our quarters for an early dinner." He wanted to touch her, pet her, adore her, hold her.

CAUGHT up on work the next day, and with her and Drew's next climbing tutorial not until later, Adria found herself a sunny seat on a giant boulder in the White Zone just before lunch. She wanted to sit and fiddle with a small computronic engine part the mechanics had discarded as too much trouble to fix. It was, but she liked the challenge. She was almost sure she'd figured out a partial workaround when she caught a scent that was now embedded in her very skin.

Her wolf rose, padding to the surface of her mind, and she dropped the hand holding the part to her thigh to focus on him, this lone wolf who was becoming her own . . . though he would never be *hers*. His stride was confident, a man sure of his strength. But he wasn't unbending, was capable of a tenderness that threatened to make her fall so deep, she'd never recover.

Reaching her, he glanced at the engine piece, angled his head in a silent question.

"It's a hobby," she said, sliding the piece and her miniature tool set into a pocket of her buff-colored cargos, feeling oddly shy. As if this were their first date and he'd caught her playing like a child. "A puzzle to solve."

Placing the brown paper bag in his hand on the boulder, he reached into his own pocket to pull out a small, polished wooden carving of a leopard mid-prowl. "My hobby," he said, standing the leopard on her palm. "It's not finished."

Astonished and charmed, she ran her finger along the back of the incredibly lifelike animal. "When do you do this?" She was fascinated. "I've never seen you."

"Here and there, when I'm thinking."

"Can I have it?"

A glint of gold in the pale brown, the wolf's delight. "When it's done." Plucking it from her fingers, he slipped it back into his pocket. "Show me what you were doing with the part."

Retrieving it, she explained, while he stood between her parted knees, one of his hands on her thigh, his hair shining blue-black in the sunlight. It was a subtle intimacy, and it wrapped her in silken chains—she had to concentrate to get the words out, wasn't sure she breathed until he said, "That looks like fun," in an intrigued tone. "I want to take one apart with you."

A laugh bubbled out of her. "Alright."

Stealing her laugh with a kiss that was pure hot, wet demand, he squeezed her thigh before reaching to get something from the bag he'd brought over. "Here."

It was a sandwich. "Chicken and avocado," she murmured, another piece of the hard shell around her heart falling away. "My favorite."

"And your sugar and cream with a dash of coffee." Placing the thermal cup and his bottle of water on the boulder, he took out his own sandwich.

The sun warmed her shoulders as he turned to brace his back against the stone, her thighs on either side of his bigger, more muscular frame. When she pressed an impulsive kiss to his nape, he made a low, rumbling sound in his chest, a wolf pleased. All of her—body and soul—trembled in primal response.

Dangerous, she thought, this was so dangerous. Too many pieces of her in his hands. She had to hold something back, some part of her that would protect her against the nights she woke to find him lying awake, a faraway expression on his face. Because it would happen—no matter the passionate tenderness growing ever deeper between them, she was second best, would always be second best.

The harsh truth of it bruised her heart. Putting down her mostly uneaten sandwich, she rubbed her hand surreptitiously over the organ. She didn't know if she was trying to quell the ache or contain the wild fury of what she felt for Riaz. But she had the sinking feeling it was too late. Perhaps it had been too late the instant her wolf first responded to him, the attraction visceral.

Having finished his sandwich, he turned to grab his water, saw hers. "Eat the rest."

Already on edge, she bristled. "Since when do you get to give me orders?"

Eyes of pale gold met hers, lashed by black silk. "Since I realized you have a tendency to not eat properly." Picking up the sandwich, he held it out.

She took it, placed it back down. "Don't try to control me."

Riaz's voice was a deep rumble. "I will not let my woman mistreat herself. Eat the sandwich or we'll be here all day."

My woman.

Her throat choked up, until she couldn't speak, every part of her hotly conscious of the hand he'd placed once more on her thigh. A couple of inches higher and he could slide that big hand to cup her with the same intimacy he'd done last night, in the hushed dark of her bed. The rough heat of his body so close, the dusky bronze of his skin an invitation to her lips, it stole her mind, made it impossible to think.

Pushing aside his hand, she brought her legs up to crouch on the boulder—then jumped off the other side. "Maybe I'll eat the sandwich later"—her heartbeat punching into her throat—"if I feel like it." This had nothing to do with the sandwich, they both knew that.

Narrowed eyes. "You really want to challenge me over this?"

His tone raised her wolf's hackles . . . and shot adrenaline through her body. "You know, why don't you eat it, since you seem to like it so much." With that, she turned and sauntered into the forest, ensuring her hips swayed in a way designed to further arouse his most dominant instincts.

RIAZ stared into the trees where Adria had disappeared, his wolf at snarling attention. If she thought he'd just let her go after that kind of provocation, she had no idea who she was dealing with. Taking the sandwich, he wrapped it up in the paper bag and slid it into the pocket of his jeans. It was going to be squashed all to hell by the time he ran her down, but his empress would damn well eat it.

A grim smile on his lips, he was on his way into the forest when a small body barreled into his legs. "Whoa!" Grabbing the pup, Riaz set him upright.

But the boy wobbled, his face screwed up in a childish effort not to cry.

"Hey." Crouching down, Riaz checked the pup over, discovered a sprained ankle. "Come on, little buddy." He took the boy into his arms. "We'd better go see Lara."

The distraught pup attached himself to Riaz like a limpet and wouldn't let go until his mother arrived at the infirmary, by which time Adria had a fifteen-minute head start. However, Riaz was a lieutenant and one of the best trackers in the pack. It took him only two minutes to pick up the crushed berries and ice and wild musk of her scent, another thirty seconds to realize two very important things.

One, Adria had run full-tilt the instant she was out of his sight; and two, she'd made an attempt to cover her tracks, so she clearly understood the consequences of the gauntlet she'd thrown in his face. His blood turned hot, the chase suddenly a very adult game . . . until her tracks, no longer concealed in any way, showed that she'd slowed down to a walk.

He bared his teeth.

Adria thought he'd given up. That was her second mistake. Her first had been to taunt him in the first place. Stalking her in silence, he tracked his quarry to a natural pool fed by two streams, taking care to remain upwind. A pile of discarded clothes lay on the bank, but that wasn't what drew his eye.

Sleek and wet, she rose up out of the clear water, reaching back to squeeze the excess moisture out of her hair. Her nipples were hard, bitable points from the chill of the wind, her skin cream licked with gold. Flexing and unflexing hands that wanted to stroke and pet and possess, he dipped his gaze to the dark triangle between her thighs, his body rigid with the need to drive his cock into the molten tightness of her.

No more running, my stubborn, beautiful soldier.

Chapter 50

ADRIA FINISHED WRINGING out her hair and considered whether or not to use her T-shirt to blot her body dry. She could always shift and return home in wolf form. It might be best if she did, because she wasn't sure she could hide the painful depth of her disappointment otherwise.

The chase had been a test, a game put in motion by the wolf that lived within her, wary and hopeful and with the courage to roll the dice. She'd needed to know Riaz cared enough to be pissed off, enough to follow. Changeling males who'd claimed a female were touchy about the kind of challenge she'd handed down, *never* simply allowed one to pass. That he had made it clear that though he'd called her "his" woman, it was only the shallowest of commitme—

"I like what you're wearing."

She was hauled back against a hard male body, one of his hands splayed possessively on her navel, the other cupping her breast to pluck at her nipple before the import of that deep voice registered. Her pulse turned into a hammer, her breath coming in soft gasps.

"Sorry I'm a little late," he murmured in a way she knew meant trouble. "Pup emergency."

Relief and exhilaration threatened to make her melt against him . . . but she was a dominant female wolf. Slicing out her claws, she went to break his hold, but he'd read her intent—she found herself being spun around, her wrists imprisoned behind her back. He was using only one hand, but his hold was unbreakable.

"That wasn't nice." He gripped her jaw hard enough that she couldn't use her teeth against him, and bent to take a bite out of the side of her breast.

"That hurt!" She clenched her thighs, the delicate folds between her legs slick with a moisture that made lie of her attempt at a snarl. *"Riaz."*

Hot, wet laps of his tongue. "You liked it." He squeezed her jaw in warning when she growled low in her throat, eyes of wolf gold looking into her own. "Behave."

She might not have been a lieutenant, but neither was she a submissive. Not telegraphing her actions in any way, she brought up her knee at the same time that she snapped forward her head.

Rearing away, Riaz blocked the groin strike, but the dual attack distracted him enough that she was able to free herself. Slashing out with her claws before he could regain his balance, she scored four perfect lines across his chest, shredding his tee. Red seeped into the edges of the white fabric, but the cuts weren't deep. Only enough to remind him that he was playing with a strong, dangerous woman, not an untried girl.

Tugging off the torn T-shirt, he threw it aside. "Now," he said, stalking her with slow, prowling steps and an unblinking stare, "I'll have to do more than just bite you."

Oh, God. Seeing his nostrils flare, the tang of her arousal thick in the air, she fought the primal urge to pin him to the earth skin to skin, and shot him a deliberately provocative smile. "I don't see you anywhere near me."

He laughed . . . right before he lunged at her. The solitary reason she got away was because she danced left and into the deep pool created by the convergence of two streams. Coming up a second later, she saw him crouched on the verge, watching her, his head angled in a very wolfish way. "I don't want to get wet."

"Good, I'll stay in here then."

Thick black lashes lowered to hood his eyes. "I just saw an eel swim past."

She jerked. "No you didn't." Except what was that brushing her leg? Yelping, she jumped a fraction to the right, glared at him when he chuckled. "You're making it up."

A grin that was all teeth. "Come out and I'll only bite you a little."

She shuddered against the impact of him so playful and

more than a tiny bit dangerous. That was it, she was a goner. Dead and buried. *Don't give in.* It was a command from her wolf—who understood that the male stalking her was having fun. So was she.

Treading water, she shook her head. "Thanks for the offer, but I don't think so."

Shrugging, he dug his now-bare feet into the grass and settled in, watching her with that same unwavering and unquestionably predatory focus. "It's right behind you," he said a minute later, the tension between them a thrumming bowstring. "With a friend."

She spun around, backed up. "Lia—"

"Gotcha." He hauled her out of the water and pinned her to the soft grass in a single powerful move.

Nipples rubbing against the exquisite friction of his chest hair, she wrapped her legs around the possessive intrusion of his hips. "You just wanted me close enough to grab." She scratched lightly at his shoulders with the very tips of her claws.

Arching into the caress, he said, "I'm a wolf. What did you expect?" He slid his hand between her thighs with a boldness that intoxicated. "Let's play a different game now." Thumb and forefinger slick with the creamy evidence of her welcome, he rubbed the taut bundle of nerves that was her clit.

Shuddering, she said, "Yes," and tugged his head down for a kiss that ended with his tongue in her mouth and his fingers pushing inside her in hard male demand. "Let's."

AN hour later, Riaz's hand trembled as he stroked it over the damp silk of Adria's hair, her face peaceful in sleep. His beautiful, prickly, wounded Adria had fallen asleep in his arms after the playful dance of their loving. He understood what that meant, knew he'd reached a part of her most people didn't even realize existed.

It was only fair.

Because she'd reached deep into his soul, too, to places he'd thought would remain forever barren. Quite simply, he was happy. Cautious eyes, claws and all, Adria made him happy. He'd worried his wolf would fight him, fight how hard he'd fallen for her, but the predator in him was delighted with the lover who had become a friend . . . and who now owned a great big chunk of his heart. It nuzzled against her as he indulged his bone-deep need for skin privileges by caressing the sweep of her back.

"You're mine, Adria Morgan."

It was a punch to the throat, the discovery that he was still capable of such a visceral depth of emotion. Finding then losing Lisette hadn't withered away the part of him that felt a wild possessive tenderness toward the long-limbed goddess in his arms, and where once he would've seen his feelings for Adria as a betrayal, he now saw them as a gift. He'd been given a second chance.

Her lashes fluttered up at that instant, sleepy eyes of mountain-sky blue streaked with veins of precious metals, looking up at him. "Was I sleeping?"

It was instinct to play with her. "You snore adorably."

Laughing, her voice even huskier with sleep, she pretended to pull his nose. "You don't."

"Snore?"

"Snore adorably."

He bared his teeth at her. She bared hers back. Filled with affectionate joy, the brick that had been a crushing weight on his soul crumbling away to nothing, he drew a line in the sand. Never again would he look back.

Lisette was his past, Adria his future.

RILEY finished his cell phone conversation with Kenji in relation to the BlackSea meet and glanced over to where his mate stood at Nate and Tammy's kitchen window, her eyes trained on something outside. They'd driven down because he'd needed to return some tools he'd borrowed from Nathan, and since she'd been off shift, Mercy had come along to catch up with Tamsyn—and take the opportunity to "dress like a girl."

Having chosen a strappy dress patterned with bright yellow sunflowers, she'd pulled her red hair back in a high ponytail and slipped her feet into simple white flip-flops decorated with a single daisy at the toes. She looked sunny and pretty and girly—and he knew damn well she'd worn those shoes because she could kick them off in a second and haul ass, should it be necessary for the protection of the pack.

Smile widening, he walked over to slide his arm around her waist and nuzzle a kiss to the creamy slope of her neck. "What's so interesting?" he murmured in a sub-vocal whisper, conscious of Nate and Tamsyn teasing one another at the table on the other side of the kitchen bench.

"Faith is having hysterics."

Wolf immediately on alert, he followed her line of sight to see the spectacle of tranquil, graceful Faith NightStar doubled over in the DarkRiver healer's backyard, laughing too hard to reply to whatever it was her bemused mate was saying. She and Vaughn had swung by fifteen minutes earlier to drop off a box of medical supplies they'd picked up for Tamsyn, had ended up staying for coffee.

Now, the F-Psy finally stopped giggling long enough to say something to Vaughn. The jaguar's grin could best be described as shit-eating.

Mercy's claws hissed out.

Riley squeezed her waist. "Do you want to know?" His wolf paced in excitement—man and wolf both liked knowing things in advance, but Riley was aware Mercy preferred surprises. He'd go with her choice on this, since it was highly unlikely he'd be able to keep his mouth shut if Faith had foreseen what he thought she had.

Because right before Kenji's call distracted him, Riley had caught Faith staring at Mercy, cardinal eyes huge. A second later, the F-Psy had developed a sudden cough, strong enough that she'd had to step outside. Clearly, Mercy had already connected the same dots he just had.

"I love surprises," she whispered, retracting her claws and placing her hand on the as yet flat curve of her abdomen, "but I think this time, for our sanity, we'd better find out what she's seen in our future."

Riley rubbed her lower back. "Probably a hellion redhead."

"Or perhaps a stubborn wolf pup who likes to get his own way."

Grinning at one another, they turned to Nate and Tamsyn. "We'll be back in a second," Mercy said, tugging him toward the door.

It took them only seconds to reach Faith and Vaughn. "Spill it," Mercy ordered the instant they were close enough.

The F-Psy wiped tears from her eyes, her smile the sweetest innocence. "What?"

"Don't make me beat it out of you, Faith NightStar. Just tell us—is our child going to drive us *that* insane?"

For some reason, the question set Faith off again. She laughed so hard she ended up sitting on the ground, Vaughn crouched beside her. Rubbing her back, the jaguar attempted to look solemn. He failed miserably, his cheeks creased in a rare grin. "You know," he said, "the future is mutable, subject to change."

"I'm guessing from Faith's response that this particular aspect of it is pretty much set in stone." Folding her arms, Mercy tried to breathe past the bubbles of incipient delight in her bloodstream. "Our baby's going to shift into a wolf, isn't he?" Adorable, she thought, their pup would be downright adorable, his cute face a miniature copy of Riley's.

"Hmm." Faith pursed her lips together.

"Into a leopard?" Riley's delight was transparent. "With Mercy's pattern of spots?"

A spurt of laughter before Faith said, "Hmm," again.

"Faith." It was a shared growl.

Sharing a cagey look with her mate, the F-Psy said, "I think Tammy handles her boys real well, don't you?" in a musing tone of voice.

Mercy's legs collapsed under her. "Nu-huh," she said, aware of Riley coming down beside her. "I am not having twins."

"No, I'm sure you're not." Faith's immediate response was strangely disappointing when the idea of twins had been such a shock. "You know how foresight works—things are never crystal clear, and multiple births are rare." Rising to her feet, she held out a hand to Vaughn. "Let's go drink that coffee."

Mercy's head was so turned around, it took her brain until after the other couple had left the yard to process what Faith had actually said. "Multiple births." Her no-doubt punch-drunk eyes slammed into Riley's. *"Multiples."*

"But she's sure we're not having twins." Riley looked alternately ecstatic and dazed. "Changelings have a lower birth rate than Psy or humans, but *within* that, we do have a higher rate of multiple births than the other races."

Mercy stared at him. "How can you be so calm?"

"Because I can't wait to kiss the babies you give me, kitty cat." Taking her into his arms, he nipped her affectionately on the jaw. "One or three or five, I hope they all have their mama's spirit."

"My mother always said my punishment for giving her countless gray hairs before she was thirty would be little terrors of my own." Stealing a kiss from those firm lips, she said, "Hopefully, your genes will balance mine out, and we'll get gorgeous, well-behaved auburn-haired babies who listen to their mother."

Riley stared at her . . . and then they were laughing and kissing and holding on to one another, happy and scared and nervous all at once.

ALICE

FROM: Lara<lara@snowdancer.org>
TO: Sascha<sascha@darkriver.net>;
Ashaya<ashaya@darkriver.net>;
Tammy<tamsyn@darkriver.net>;
Amara<amara@sierratech.com>
DATE: Sep 22, 2081 at 1.21 p.m.
SUBJECT: Patient A

I wanted to give you an update on the results of Sascha's visit.
Patient A's mental activity has increased at an acute rate, and
I have to say she's significantly more "alert." However, there are no
signs of her rising to consciousness.

FROM: Amara<amara@sierratech.com>
TO: Ashaya<ashaya@darkriver.net>
CC: Lara<lara@snowdancer.org>;
Sascha<sascha@darkriver.net>;
Tammy<tamsyn@darkriver.net>
DATE: Sep 22, 2081 at 1.38 p.m.
SUBJECT: re: Patient A

It may be the optimal time to inject her with the new serum.

FROM: Ashaya<ashaya@darkriver.net>
TO: Lara<lara@snowdancer.org>
CC: Amara<amara@sierratech.com>;
Sascha<sascha@darkriver.net>;
Tammy<tamsyn@darkriver.net>
DATE: Sep 22, 2081 at 3.45 p.m.
SUBJECT: re: re: Patient A

I agree with Amara. However, we'll need another seven to ten days
to complete our final calibration of the serum—some of the tests
take time to show results. Call me if you see any sign the patient is

regressing. I'd rather not inject her with the serum as is, but if it's a choice between taking the risk and her life, then I will.

Why do you make me use this archaic method of communication? I am not a primate only capable of tapping out primitive messages on a keyboard.

Because you need to learn to communicate with others.

Why?

Amara, you said you'd try.

Very well. Have you completed your analysis of section 2B3 of the Alliance neural chip?

Yes. It appears stable and secure. Your conclusions?

I concur. Let's move to section 2B4.

Agreed. Amara . . . how are you?

Stable and secure.

Amara.

There is a male in the labs who speaks to me. I do not know why— he has nothing of relevance to say.

Perhaps he likes you.

Then he's being irrational. I can't like him back.

Talk to him anyway. You might find it an interesting interaction.

Unlikely, but I will consider it another step in my "rehab."

Do you feel any different?

I no longer have psychopathic thoughts as often. I believe that could be termed progress.

You're not a psychopath.

Or perhaps you simply don't want me to be.

Chapter 51

HAWKE SLAPPED RILEY on the back. "Hell yeah." His wolf was as proud of the other man's news as he'd be if he were the father.

Riley raised his beer in a cheer. "To redheads."

Hawke clinked his bottle to Riley's, both of them seated on the steps of Hawke and Sienna's private cabin. While the place was meant to be off-limits to the rest of the pack, they'd realized they enjoyed inviting friends over at times.

"Wait," Hawke said, before taking a sip. "Which redhead are we saluting? My redhead, Mercy, Faith, or your future spawn?"

"All of them." Riley spread his arms expansively. "And I'll thank you to call my spawn pups or cubs, or pupcubs."

"Pupcubs." Hawke mused. "I like it."

From her chair on the porch, Mercy shook her head at Sienna. "The boys are drunk."

Sienna was fascinated. "I've never seen Hawke drunk. Or Riley."

"This," Mercy said, her tone that of a wise teacher, "is celebratory drunkenness. Witnessed at times when men rejoice in their own prowess."

Riley glanced over his shoulder to grin—actually *grin*—at Mercy. "I gave you multiple pupcubs. I have prowess."

Eyes dancing, Mercy walked to sit behind him on a higher step, so he could lean against her chest. "Yes, you did, and yes, you do."

Sienna realized she was grinning, and when Hawke shot her a wolfish smile, she couldn't help but obey the silent order to sit with him as Mercy was doing with Riley. Later, the DarkRiver sentinel pulled her aside for a second. "These two are both hardheaded," the other woman said, the words affectionate, "but after this much celebration, even his Alphaness will have a hangover. Be gentle."

Sienna certainly didn't have to be gentle that night—Hawke was in a mood, and oh her body liked it. With energy to burn and then some, he exhausted her into limp incoherence before tucking her possessively against him, nuzzling his face into her neck and falling asleep.

He didn't move for eight hours.

Showered and dressed after she managed to wriggle out of his embrace by promising him all sorts of lavish things she wasn't sure he heard, she sat down on the bed with a mug of coffee and brushed back his hair. One eye opened the merest slit. Closed. A groan sounded. "Shut the curtains."

"They're not open." Given the unpredictable effect of alcohol on Psy abilities, she'd never been drunk, but she'd seen her friends in the condition, kept her voice to a whisper. "I have coffee."

"Grr." He refused to move.

Laughter bubbled in her chest. "It's my special blend." Breathing deep, she took a sip. "And you have a comm-conference in forty-five minutes." He could do it from here, but he needed to be conscious for it.

"Tell Riley to handle it." Spoken into his pillow.

"Riley was more drunk than you and is probably still comatose." Putting the coffee on the bedside table, she snuggled back into bed beside him.

Eyes remaining closed, he flung an arm around her waist and hauled her against him. "I can hear you thinking." Grumpy.

"What if when we do decide to have children, I only conceive one?"

Another slit of husky blue. "I have no idea what you're talking about."

"I just . . . Is it better to have twins or triplets?" He and Riley had been so delighted by the news. "We could ask the medics to ensure that." Though, the leopards had been as overjoyed at Naya's birth, and she was a single baby.

Hawke closed his eye. "I love you, but I have a hangover and you're talking crazy."

She scowled. "I'm just trying to understand."

Giving a deep, complaining groan, he opened both eyes. "How many makes no difference—me and Riley, we'd have gotten drunk sooner or later. He's the first one of *us* to have a kid. Get it?"

Oh. "Like if it was Evie or Maria or someone else in my group." She did get it. "It's a milestone."

"And it's fucking hilarious that Riley, without whom the den would fall apart, is half terrified at the fact he's about to become a father."

"Only a best friend would find his nerves hilarious."

"God, you're adorable, even when you're talking loud enough to wake the dead."

"I'm whispering," she pointed out with another scowl, and, rubbing her hand against the bristles on his cheek, got up. "Drink this coffee or I'll open the curtains." Energetic and busy as he was, she'd never had to deal with him so surly in the morning—it was fun discovering this unexpected facet of his personality.

"Don't give me orders. I'm the alpha."

"I don't care."

"Come here."

"Do I look like it's my first time tangling with a wolf?" Reaching down, she pulled the sheet off him, exposing the nude length of his body, his skin golden even in the dim light.

Oh my.

Really, he had no right to be so gorgeous.

Painful as it was to turn her back on the delicious man in her bed, she went to the curtains. "You now have thirty-five minutes, and these curtains are . . . open."

No sound.

She turned to find he had a pillow over his head.

Laughing, she bounced onto the bed and kissed her way down his spine. "Fine," she said, utterly in harmony with the world, "let's stay in bed all day."

"Teasing wench." He got rid of the pillow. "Who am I comm-conferencing with?"

"Selenka Durev in Moscow." The two packs had an informal arrangement to share information, and this was a "touching base" kind of a chat. "You know how quick-tempered she is—she might take it as an insult if you're late." A kiss to his nape. "I'll turn on the shower." As she got out of bed and did so, she realized she was smiling. No matter his mood, there was no man she'd rather wake to find next to her.

When he walked into the shower and asked her to remind him of the points he was meant to go over during the comm-conference, she felt the tie between them grow deeper, more nuanced. He hadn't asked her because she was a novice soldier. He'd asked her because she was his mate, and he needed the reminder. Just as he'd allowed her to see him hungover. A simple thing, a small vulnerability, but it meant everything coming from an alpha wolf.

IT was a terrifyingly happy week after that interlude by the pool that Adria found herself toe-to-toe with Riaz. "Don't give me an ultimatum." Martin had thrown too many of those at her during their years together, until even the hint of one made rage erupt in her bloodstream.

"It's not an ultimatum," Riaz said, his tone a silky threat. "It's a warning. I've let the issue of shared quarters slide a hell of a lot longer than I should have. You're mine. You live with me. End of story."

Her wolf bristled. "It's not an inevitability." And it wasn't as if they ever slept apart.

"Fuck that. If I wanted to live alone, I wouldn't *be* in a relationship." Twisting her braid in his hand, he held her in place. "So your thinking time has just run out."

She dug her claws into his chest, saw him wince. "Let go or I'll rip this T-shirt, too."

Respect on his face. "I'll let go . . . after this." The kiss was hot and angry and refused to allow her any distance.

She was still growling in fury when she ran into Indigo not long afterward. "Don't ask," she snapped the instant the other woman went to open her mouth. "Not when I saw you making kissy faces with Drew five seconds ago."

Indigo held up her hands in surrender. "Hey, we fight. Drew just makes it damn hard to stay mad at him. Do you know what he did today?" She answered her question before Adria could respond. "He lined the dashboard of my vehicle with miniature teddy bears with sad faces. I mean, come on! Not fair."

Adria laughed despite herself—because Indigo was holding one of those adorable tiny bears as she gesticulated. "You have it so tough, boo-hoo."

Indigo mimed throwing the soft toy at her. "See? I never get any sympathy." Tucking the bear into her jeans pocket, where it watched them mournfully, she said, "So?"

Adria shook her head. "I'm going for a run."

"I'll come with you."

"Go away," she muttered. "I want to be alone."

"Get over it. You're in a pack."

They ran in silence for over half an hour, ending up on a high mountain meadow dotted with wildflowers and huge broken rocks thrown around as if by a giant's hands. Taking a seat on one of those rocks after quenching her thirst at a fragile waterfall hidden nearby, she said, "Sorry for being snippy."

Indigo, seated on the ground with her back to the sun-warmed rock, reached over to pat her on the shin. "You're allowed. What did Riaz do?"

"He's demanding I move in with him."

"Hardly surprising," Indigo said, stretching out her legs. "He's a wolf. Pack is everything, and his woman is where it begins."

Those words again—*his woman*. "I made the decision to be with him," Adria whispered, "but I never thought I'd fall so hard, so deep, until his name is written on parts of me Martin never touched." It was the first time she'd consciously accepted that fact . . . and the fear that came with the knowledge. Martin had hurt her, but Riaz, he could savage her. "He does these things and they take my breath away, make my chest hurt."

"What kind of things?"

"Yesterday, he disappeared with my boots and came back with them resoled because he'd noticed they were damaged." When she'd thanked him, he'd run his knuckles down her cheek and said it was his job to care for her. "I found a shawl in my quarters the other day, soft as air, and the precise color of my eyes." Golden threads woven into the exquisite blue.

"And he's always feeding me," she said, bewildered by the unexpected tenderness. "Cupcakes and homemade pizza and my favorite spaghetti." Then there was the most wonderful thing of all—the wooden sculptures she kept finding in her pockets. Her favorite was a tiny dragon, its expression fierce, its claws out.

"Protectiveness is part of the package," Indigo said. "You know that. I'm more dominant than Drew, but he still finds ways to take care of me." She took the sad bear out, smiled, and kissed its face before tucking it safely back into her pocket.

"I know. I just never expected Riaz to be like that with me." She didn't have to explain why, didn't want to speak of the unknown woman who was Riaz's mate.

Twisting, Indigo looked up at her. "I get why you're hesitant. I guess the question is, do you think you'd be happier without him?"

"I can't bear to think of being without him." The hurt was bone deep . . . and that was her answer.

Coming down to sit beside Indigo, she said, "It's no use trying to keep a physical distance between us, is there? When I already belong to him here." She rubbed a fisted hand over her heart, knowing that regardless of how much it terrified her to trust her love to a man whose own would never belong to her, keeping it stifled did an injustice both to herself and to the lone wolf who had made her feel so cherished. "I have to have the courage to love him without conditions."

Chapter 52

VASQUEZ WENT OVER the most recent report cataloguing the acts of attempted sabotage on SnowDancer land. The incidents had dropped off markedly in the past two weeks, and none had caused the wolves any problems, but planning and carrying them out was keeping the majority of Pure Psy's remaining forces occupied.

Good, he thought, sending a telepathic message to the ringleader to continue. So long as they were engaged in the pointless task, he could set up the warning "outlier" strike without having to concern himself with anyone getting too curious. No leaks could be permitted. Not now.

Not when the time had finally come.

"There is one problem," he said to Henry when they met that night. "Though I have a unit ready to move on the secondary targets, I still have only one operative I trust with the primary task." Making back-to-back strikes impossible, though—and not counting the outlier—he had five complete sets of confirmed locations. "However, I do not recommend waiting. The Net is becoming further infected with those whose conditioning has fractured."

"You have permission to move as soon as you see an open window," Henry replied, his broken voice short of breath. "We will succeed, Vasquez."

"Yes, sir. We will." No one and nothing had the power to stop them. Not this time.

Chapter 53

TWO DAYS AFTER Adria moved in with him, Riaz was a happy wolf. He loved having her in his space, loved that her scent was everywhere—and that his was all over every perfect inch of her. And he was definitely smug about the fact that though their request for quarters in the couples section hadn't yet gone through, she hadn't made any noises about his room being too small for the both of them.

Wiping the smile off his face since it totally destroyed his hard-ass rep, he put through a call to Bowen, needing to talk

through some final details about SnowDancer's permanent
liaison arrangement with the Alliance. The security chief
asked him to organize clearance for the liaison to fly to San
Francisco for a sit-down discussion within the next few days.
"I think I have the perfect candidate, but I want to discuss
her with Lily. She's taken over Human Resources, knows our
people inside out."

"Hold on." Switching lines, Riaz made a quick call to his
counterpart in DarkRiver—Nathan—and got the clearance,
the city very much leopard territory. Back on the line with Bo,
he said, "You've got permission," then set out the conditions—
basically dealing with how much freedom of movement the
liaison would be permitted. "You coming along?"

"I'll try. Depends on the security situation."

"Any further aggression from Tatiana?"

"Nothing obvious. Covert surveillance is likely." A beep
in the background. "That's my cell phone. I better get it—link
up with you later in the week to confirm flight details."

Hanging up, Riaz swung by Indigo's office to discuss a
personnel matter. The other lieutenant gave him a considering
look across her desk after they were done. "Adria told me
about the rose petals."

He knew when a wolf was fishing. "Did she?"

"Damn it. She mentioned rose petals and then she blushed.
Adria never blushes."

Sprawled in her visitor chair, he just smiled. "So, you and
Drew are heading to take over Alexei's sector in a month."

"Only caretaking," Indigo clarified. "You know how good
he is. Needs a bit more seasoning is all. I'm taking most of my
novices and younger soldiers along," she added. "Good for them
to learn to work with dominants from other sectors. The ones
I'm leaving here are those with an aptitude for weapons—
Alexei's going to do sessions with them while he's here."

Knowing Alexei's strength in that area, Riaz knew the
novices had lucked out. "He had any more problems with
challenges?"

"No, but there has been an interesting development as of
last night—the wolves in the pack that kept challenging him?"
At Riaz's nod, she continued. "Turns out they're in a bad way.
Their alpha passed two months ago from old age, and while

the lieutenants were able to keep it quiet and hold the pack together, they're all comparatively young and weak."

In a situation where a pack had no successor to their alpha, Riaz thought, a strong lieutenant who had the backing of his fellow dominants could ensure the pack's continued health. But it needed to be someone of Riley's caliber—a man every wolf in the pack could respect and whose strength was unquestioned.

Without that, the natural aggression of the dominants would spill over, disintegrating the pack from the inside out. "Is that why all the challenges?" he said, seeing the weaker pack's plan—a clever one, if only they'd had someone who could take Alexei. "They wanted one of their people in a position of power in SnowDancer?"

Indigo nodded. "They're desperate to merge with us, but it's a tough ask for them to bring in their people under someone they don't know and trust. Especially given our reputation."

A reputation that, Riaz knew, had been carefully cultivated in the years after Hawke took over as alpha. No one else, that young boy had declared, would *ever* see SnowDancer as easy prey. Each and every dominant in the den had backed that reputation up with teeth and claws and blood, until even the most aggressive packs steered clear of SnowDancer territory. "Alexei's show got their attention," he guessed.

"Yeah—and since pretty much every dominant in their pack was there when he returned their man, they had a chance to judge him for themselves. They've made a formal request to be permitted to move in under SnowDancer's banner, bringing their territorial lands with them."

"This pack know what that means?" SnowDancer expected total and absolute loyalty, had executed one of their own not long ago when he proved a murderous traitor.

"They will—and if it goes through, our region swap might have to wait a bit while our new packmates get settled in under Alexei." Indigo glanced at her watch. "It's time for you to leave for the meet. Make sure the octopus doesn't get you."

"Funny," he muttered, but part of him was intrigued by the idea of changeling octopuses. Or should that be "octopi"? BlackSea was so secretive, it was impossible to separate wild conjecture from fact.

Hawke and Riley met him in the garage. The three of them—and Kenji—had debated dressing in suits, but had settled on their usual jeans and T-shirts. This was who they were, and if BlackSea didn't like it, there wasn't much hope for a functional alliance.

"Who's going to drive?" Riaz asked, reaching the vehicle.

They all looked at one another . . . then stuck out their fists for a game of rock, paper, scissors. Riley won, with Riaz losing and ending up in the backseat. In a good mood, he wasn't fussed, his mind filled with thoughts of the woman who had brought him back to life, branded her claim on his heart. His tough, prickly, generous Adria, who wasn't so tough or prickly after all.

Last night, he'd had her in giggling fits after finding a ticklish spot and taking merciless advantage. He'd felt as young as a pup as they twisted and tangled in the sheets, her giggles erupting between stern admonitions and breathless threats. Wolf grinning at the memory, he talked to the back of Riley's head. "How's Mercy doing?"

The senior sentinel caressed the steering wheel through a turn, sliding the vehicle gracefully onto the highway beyond den territory. "She hasn't snarled at me yet." Pure disbelief in every syllable. "I turn up out of the blue while she's working, and she smiles, gives me a kiss, and lets me hang around as long as I want."

Hawke turned to look at Riley, suspicion writ large on his profile. "We're talking about Mercy the sentinel? The one who'd kick your ass if you dared baby her?"

"Maybe it's the pregnancy?" Riley sounded hopeful.

Riaz winced. "Pregnancy usually makes dominant females meaner, not nicer." It tended to take very careful petting to calm one down once she got her fur ruffled. "Are you sure she's happy to see you?"

Riley gave him a *look* in the rearview mirror.

"Right," Riaz muttered. "Mating bond." The scar inside him stretched, the wound throbbing, but it didn't bleed. Because the thing was, he knew when his empress was happy, too, his wolf attuned to her own.

Hawke rubbed his jaw. "I'd say enjoy it while it lasts," was his thoughtful advice. "Sooner or later, she'll turn into a she-demon."

Riley's growl filled the vehicle. "Don't insult my mate or I'll have to stop this SUV and beat you dead."

Hawke's hair caught the light coming through the open sunroof as he shook his head, the strands gleaming white-gold. "I can take you."

"Bullshit."

"After the meeting, you and me. Riaz will referee."

Well aware the two men were the best of friends and often took each other on in combat, Riaz interlocked his fingers behind his head and looked up at the clear blue sky visible through the sunroof. "Dolphin changelings—what do you think?"

Riley was the one who replied. "That one, I could give credence to. Any number of humans and nonwater-based changelings—even Psy in some cases—report being saved from drowning by dolphins. The survivors always mention how intelligent the creatures seemed."

"That," Hawke said, "assumes humans, changelings, and Psy are the only intelligent species on the planet. Pretty arrogant of us."

"Jellyfish," Riaz said, after considering the other inhabitants of the sea. "Seriously, there *cannot* be jellyfish changelings."

Hawke turned to look over his shoulder. "What the hell have you been smoking?"

Riaz shrugged, his mood undampened. "It was green and leafy." He made a note to discuss the subject of possible sea changelings with Adria—intrigued as she was by puzzles, she'd find it as fascinating as he did. "There's Kenji." His flight delayed, the lieutenant had asked them to swing by the airport and pick him up.

Jumping in sans luggage, Kenji and his magenta hair took a seat beside Riaz. "A teenage girl screamed and asked for my autograph—thought I was part of some boy band from Japan."

"I told you so," Hawke said. "Did you give your fan an autograph?"

Kenji grinned. "It would've been such a shame to disappoint her."

The rest of the drive was taken up with a quick discussion about the upcoming meeting, which Hawke would lead, the rest of them providing backup and security as needed.

Riaz tapped Riley's shoulder when they hit the Embarcadero, pointing left. "That building." Squat and wide, it fronted the pier, the shimmer of the Bay visible in the small gap between the warehouse and the fence.

Parking, they got out to find Nathan waiting for them. The senior DarkRiver sentinel took them through the empty space Riaz had already checked out with him earlier in the week. Nate went over all the exits and entrances once again, as well as anything that could be a possible blind spot in a fight. Because of its shape, the warehouse didn't really possess any shadowy corners, part of the reason Riaz had chosen it.

"We've disabled the surveillance equipment as you asked," Nate said to Riaz, "but one of the techs is standing by if you want anything functional."

Hawke shook his head, crossing the cavernous space to slide open the wide door that led out onto the pier. "No, we'll lose their trust if they figure out they're being monitored."

"In that case, the place is all yours. Call me once you're done and I'll send someone to lock it up. Good luck." The DarkRiver sentinel left with those words.

Riaz and Kenji followed Riley and Hawke out onto the pier. Seagulls cawed overhead, the scent of brine and fish pungent in Riaz's nostrils, the wind rifling through his hair. Taking a deep breath, he scoped the area one more time. While it allowed easy access to and from the Bay, once on the pier, their guests would be blocked from the view of the other warehouses by the high fences on both sides.

Given BlackSea's preference to stay under the radar, he and Nate had even rigged up a temporary boathouse, ensuring Miane's group could go straight from their boat to the pier. Nate had suggested BlackSea might simply swim in, but Riaz didn't think they'd be anything but besuited, polished professionals.

He was proven right.

"Here they come." The sleek craft cut through the water with the grace of a dancer, its engine near silent. Unsurprising—BlackSea's shipbuilding arm was considered to be peerless, its craftsmen and craftswomen artists.

The vessel slipped into the temporary boathouse and docked. And then Miane Levêque was stepping onto the pier with two unfamiliar men and Emani. Dressed in a neat skirt suit of deep green, Miane was a woman of medium height with translucent hazel eyes uptilted a fraction at the corners and stick-straight hair of ebony, the black too soft to be called jet.

That hair was cut into a blunt fringe above her eyes, throwing them into sharp relief. Her skin was a shade that placed her ancestry in Northern Africa or the Middle East, or possibly part of South America. Riaz didn't have to guess—he'd done his research, knew she'd been born in the port of Cairo to an Algerian mother and an Egyptian father.

"Hawke." She held out a hand that bore scars from more than a few nicks and cuts, though her nails were manicured and polished a glossy shade Riaz thought might be called oyster.

Hawke shook it, holding her cool, almost cold gaze. Riley introduced himself a second later, giving Miane a reason to look away. It was an almost ritualistic dance when two alphas met for the first time. Left to their own devices, they'd stare until one of them either backed down or drew first blood.

Riaz remained in the background with Kenji, his attention on the men who'd come with the BlackSea alpha, both clearly there for her protection, regardless of any status they held in the Conclave. That wasn't an insult—he and the other lieutenants were here for Hawke's protection. None of them would drop their guard at any time, in case this was a giant double-cross and BlackSea was aiming for the assassination of the most powerful alpha in the country.

"Please," Miane said, taking a small step back, her feet encased in black leather-synth heels that made a clipping sound on the plascrete, "join me on my vessel. The stateroom is more than adequate for this meeting."

A gracious offer meant to put them off their game, their

wolves having a strong dislike for the motion of the sea. They could bear it, but it would fray tempers, reduce concentration.

"Thanks, but I'll decline." Hawke bared his teeth in a smile that was a silent warning. "If you prefer not to enter the warehouse, we can talk here."

Miane considered it, one of her men whispering in her ear at a sub-vocal level. "Malachai says it will be easier to spy on us outdoors, use audio equipment to pick up our voices. The most secure place would be out at sea."

Hawke just waited. He'd made his intentions clear, and now it was up to Miane to accept or walk away. After a tense pause and another muted discussion with the hard-eyed male named Malachai, the leader of the BlackSea Conclave inclined her head, and Riaz knew she'd decided to trust them this much at least. "Let's proceed inside."

Riaz left the doors open behind them. Intercepting a glance from Emani, he said, "We can use audio disrupters to make certain the conversation remains private," and produced the small, round devices from a flat case in the back pocket of his jeans.

Emani checked the disrupters with a handheld scanner and nodded. Together, they set out and activated four of them, one in each corner of the warehouse. No one spoke until they'd returned to stand behind their respective alphas.

"We," Miane said, "have been pleased with SnowDancer's willingness to work with us on an agreement."

Hawke watched her without blinking. "Let's cut to the chase—the only remaining questions are whether we can work together on the ground, and the real reason why you're suddenly so keen on an alliance."

A slight widening of her eyes was the sole indication of Miane's surprise. "Blunt."

"We worked with you on the contract because it made sense with your people being so spread out," Hawke said, "but that's not who we are, and that's not how we function. Better you know that now than be surprised by it later."

A faint hint of warmth in the cold intelligence of Miane's eyes. "Did you know that changeling sharks are so rare," she said, "they're considered a myth even by some of the change-lings in BlackSea?"

Hawke's responding smile was razor sharp. "I'm guessing you don't believe the same."

"As to that, I'll keep my own counsel, but I will say I understand predators."

"In that case, let's talk."

Chapter 54

HAVING BEEN ASSIGNED to a shift at the infirmary at the last minute, Adria lifted a questioning eyebrow at Elias when he joined her. "Last I checked," she said, "we didn't have any dangerous criminals in here."

"They're hoping to wake Alice Eldridge." Elias kept his voice low. "Hawke wants extra security until Lara can get a read on her while she's conscious—there's no way to know what she was programmed to do before being put to sleep."

Shifting slightly, Adria glanced into the patient room. While access to Alice was strictly controlled, Adria had seen the comatose woman in the aftermath of the battle, when she'd helped move Alice's bed to the side to make room for injured SnowDancers. Alice lay as she had done then, ashen and motionless. Around her stood three women, each with a frown of concentration on her face, their voices overlapping as they talked over last-minute adjustments.

Lara, Adria knew and respected. Ashaya Aleine, too, was familiar after that dinner at Mercy and Riley's, her tight curls pulled severely off her face into a neat bun, her blue-gray eyes startling against the rich brown of her skin. The third woman, with her soft curves, honey-toned skin, and cardinal eyes, was no one Adria had ever spoken to, but recognized nonetheless.

Sascha Duncan, mate to the DarkRiver alpha, and an E-Psy. Adria's wolf wasn't quite comfortable being around a woman who could sense its emotions—especially when those emotions were so painfully deep and complex. Living with Riaz, it was *nothing* like living with Martin. The man was dominant and pushy and arrogant enough to want his own way, but he was also perverse enough to be delighted with her when she snarled at him.

The thought made her lips twitch for a fleeting second, before darker emotions rose to the fore. In spite of the realization she'd had on the wildflower-strewn meadow in the mountains, a desperate kernel of self-preservation kept warning her to keep a piece of herself separate, apart. Not to hurt him . . . but because she wasn't Riaz's mate, never would be, their relationship unbalanced on the most fundamental level.

PERIPHERALLY aware of Eli and Adria in the doorway, Lara glanced at Ashaya. "Yes?"

The scientist nodded. "We've done as much as possible without injecting her."

Conscious the M-Psy was profoundly concerned about the damage they might cause, Lara said, "If we do nothing, she'll die. Her body is failing."

Ashaya's head snapped up from the panel at the end of the bed. "I told you to warn us if she went downhill. We could've moved faster."

"I spoke to Amara," Lara said, thinking of the woman who was physically identical to Ashaya, but so very alien in her thinking. "She told me that if we injected Alice with the uncalibrated serum, the risk of failure rose by seventy percent. I made the decision to wait."

Ashaya gripped the top of the panel, her bones pushing white against her skin. "My twin has a way of being right while hiding things, Lara. You know that. You should've double-checked with me."

"I didn't want to distract you at such a critical stage." Ashaya herself had told Lara the final calibration would take precision work—so much so that the scientist had spent two days away from her mate and son, in the dedicated lab DarkRiver had built for her.

"No harm done—the serum *wasn't* ready." Ashaya went as

if to shove a hand through her curls, realized they were bound, and dropped her hand back on the bed. "For future reference, though, my twin is very, very smart, but she has no moral compass."

Sascha made a small sound in the back of her throat. "I didn't like Amara when I met her," she said, clearly still troubled by what she'd described to Lara as an overwhelmingly hostile response. "Even now, she sends a chill through my bones because of the *lack* in her, but that lack isn't as total as it once was. I don't think she'll ever be capable of the normal range of emotions, but she may be showing a stunted kind of awareness of the emotions of others."

Ashaya's face held painful hope. "You're not certain, though?"

"No, I'm sorry." Sascha touched the other woman on the arm. "I have such a strong reaction to her that I find it difficult to get a clear read, and as you said, her intelligence is unquestioned. She's fully capable of manipulating her responses."

Smart enough, Lara thought, to fake empathy.

"But," Sascha added, "there *has* been a change in her, that much I can verify. It might simply be the effect of being in a clean psychic network—there's no DarkMind in the Web of Stars, no hidden miasma that's seeping into her brain."

"I'll take that." Swallowing, Ashaya returned her attention to the computronic readout on the panel in front of her. "Unless either of you disagrees, I think it's time we spoke to Alice."

Lara and Sascha both nodded at her to go ahead.

Pressure injector in hand, the scientist looked to where Sascha's fingers now intertwined with Alice's. "Are you sensing anything?"

"Frustration again," Sascha said, three deep vertical lines between her eyebrows. "But there's something else." Lashes lowering, she squeezed the bridge of her nose between the thumb and forefinger of her free hand. "Determination." Her eyes flicked open. "I'd bet my life she's trying her hardest to wake up."

"That's enough for me." With no more hesitation, Ashaya pressed the pressure injector to Alice's neck, punching the serum into her bloodstream. "The effect should be apparent within two or three minutes if it works as it's supposed to."

No one said a word, the silence so pristine Lara could hear the hushed breaths of everyone in the immediate area, including Eli and Adria. If the room had boasted an old-fashioned ticking clock, she thought, every tick would've sounded like a bomb.

One minute.

Checking the data coming in through Alice's computronic skullcap, Lara shook her head at the others.

Two minutes.

It was Ashaya who checked this time, her fingers flying over the panel. "No change."

Three minutes.

Four.

Five.

Disappointment a heavy rock on her chest, Lara squeezed Ashaya's arm in silent sympathy, and they walked to stand across from Sascha. However, the cardinal empath paid them no attention, her eyes gone a midnight that denoted either strong emotion—or a powerful use of her abilities.

Exchanging a taut, hopeful glance with Ashaya, Lara maintained her silence.

"Ashaya," Sascha said almost half a minute later, her voice muted, as if her attention was elsewhere, "do you have more of the serum?"

"Yes, but a second shot could kill her." Ashaya fiddled with the settings on the injector, paused for a second. "Amara's confident we can safely give her another eighth of a dose."

Recalling the other woman's earlier warnings, Lara turned to her. "You trust her on that?"

"This is a challenge." Ashaya's answer held a clarity that said she saw her twin's faults and flaws as well as her gifts. "Amara doesn't like failing, and Alice's death would constitute failure."

"I can feel her struggling," Sascha said, her fingers now locked so tightly with Alice's that the warm honey of her skin was bloodless. "She knows she's trapped—there's panic, fear. God, it's like she's suffocating from the terror of being entombed inside her own body."

Clearly shaken by the report, Ashaya put the injector to Alice's neck. "Are you sure, Sascha?"

"Yes. Quickly."

A press of Ashaya's thumb and a one-eighth part of the serum blasted through the permeable barrier of Alice's skin.

Alarms blared a second later, Alice's body arching so severely off the bed that she almost bent herself in half before falling back onto the sheets in a jagged spasm. Scanning the alarms, Lara grabbed the oxygen mask and placed it over Alice's mouth and nose. "Ashaya, stats!"

"Rapid spike in her mental activity. Irregular heartbeat, insufficient oxygen being absorbed."

Slapping Sascha's hand over the oxygen mask to keep it in place, Lara reached for another injector and pressed it to Alice's upper arm. "Now?"

"Heartbeat is stabilizing." Ashaya tapped the screen. "Oxygen levels reaching optimum. Brain activity continues to be erratic."

"Alice," Sascha's gentle voice turned somehow ruthless, it was so intent. "Alice, you're safe. *Focus.*"

That was when Lara looked down and realized that Alice Eldridge's eyes, so rich a brown that pupil and iris were near impossible to differentiate, were wide open.

HAVING returned from the meeting with BlackSea to be told the news about Alice Eldridge, Riaz spent several minutes talking with Ashaya and Hawke. It wasn't simply about the human woman that they spoke.

"I've been focused on Alice," Ashaya said, "but what I've studied so far of the Alliance chip hasn't raised any red flags. However, that's not saying much—I'll begin intensive work on it as soon as Alice is stable."

Waiting until after the scientist had returned to the infirmary, Hawke said, "When's Bo getting back to you about his liaison?"

"Next few days." Riaz folded his arms. "What do you think about the BlackSea situation?" The secretive changeling group had finally shared why it was they needed Snow-Dancer as an ally.

Hawke's expression was grim. "They're a valuable group to have as friends. We help them as much as we can—Miane knows I won't do anything that'd leave SnowDancer vulnerable."

Riaz had had the same thoughts. "Do you want me to set up another meeting to finalize the alliance?"

Hawke took a second to think about it, shook his head. "I'll talk directly to Miane, make sure there are no misunderstandings. Can you take some of Riley's load? I figure he's earned a rest . . . and some spare time to stalk Mercy."

Riaz's lips twitched. "Not a problem." As a result of arranging things with Riley, as well as staying late to take several calls from the men and women in SnowDancer's international network, Riaz didn't get a chance to speak to Adria until after nightfall. Unable to find her in the den, he shifted and began to check out her favorite spots in the forests one by one.

He found her at the third location, the full moon a spotlight across the large clearing dotted with young saplings that had come up after a storm felled many of the mature trees a couple of years back. Silhouetted against the midnight blue of the night sky, their slender profiles added a haunting beauty to the scene.

And there was his empress walking through the saplings, her head lowered in thought.

He watched for a long, motionless moment, his hunger satisfied now that he'd found her. She was magnificent. Strong and lithe and lovely. And his. Even if she wasn't quite certain she wanted to be—Adria thought he didn't know about the apprehension that haunted her, but of course he knew. He noticed everything about her.

He'd been patient, but it was time she accepted he wasn't ever letting her go.

ADRIA caught the woodsmoke and citrus of Riaz's scent on the breeze, but it took her several seconds to locate him—in the end, it was those golden eyes that gave him away. If he closed them, he'd be a black shadow in the dark. When he brushed himself against her legs, she ran her fingers through his fur. "What are you doing here?"

He didn't shift into human form, just pressed more heavily against her in silent demand. Comprehending, she continued to stroke him, his wolf more than big enough to reach halfway up her thigh. When he looked up, caught her gaze with the night-glow brightness of his own, she felt her heart stutter, kick-start in a faster rhythm.

That look, it was of the hunter.

And she knew this silent dance between them would be decided tonight, one way or the other. Either she tore down every one of her defenses and accepted his claim to the soul, or she walked away. Except she didn't think the latter was an option.

Nerves and anger collided.

He was pushing her, but of course he would. That was who he was. Like she was a dominant who knew her own strength. Breaking contact, she shifted, not bothering to strip. Her clothes disintegrated off her as the agony and ecstasy of the change took over, sparks of light blazing in the lush mystery that was the night.

A heartbeat later, she stood on four feet, her head angled toward the black wolf who was so much bigger and stronger, but who she knew would never cause her physical harm. That knowledge, it was enough for the wolf, but the woman needed more, needed the devotion she knew he would offer only one woman his entire lifetime.

He nuzzled at her, but she danced away, racing through the willowy shadows of the trees and across the silent music of a moon-silvered stream. He was fast, so fast, but she was clever, and she tangled and twisted around trees young and old, over jagged rocks and across sleepy flowers to cross another stream, splashing downstream to conceal her scent before coming up on the other shore.

The black wolf was nowhere to be seen.

She wasn't fooled, knew he was stalking her. Padding quietly along the verge, she kept her eyes on the other side of the stream . . . and caught a glimpse of feral gold. He lunged across the water, but she was already racing to put distance between them, squeezing through gaps he wouldn't fit, skating under fallen trees that wouldn't accommodate his size.

The next time she halted, her heart thumped a pounding beat, the wolf's exhilaration mixing with the woman's. The air was a treasure trove of scents, the night full of song. It intoxicated. Knowing she needed to think with a clearer head, she shifted back into human form, her hair tumbling around her as she crouched on the forest floor, her head angled to the wind.

Dark, of the forest, kissed with woodsmoke and a wild bite of citrus.

All around her. In her skin. Against her tongue.

His lips smoothed over her neck, his hand gentle on her hip, but she knew she was caught. Turning, she watched him with the wolf's eyes. His own hair fell over his face, his gaze luminous. This time, those eyes said, he wouldn't let her run. But she wasn't a wolf because she gave up. She twisted to the left without warning.

He was there almost before she moved, taking her body to the earth. She shivered at the cool kiss of the dew-laden grass, but he didn't let her up. "I have you." His voice was gravelly, dark with the determination of the predator inside him. "And I'm keeping you."

She lifted a hand to his cheek, the tenderness within her an endless river. How could she have ever thought to keep any part of her heart safe from him? It was an impossibility. She was caught, well and truly. Tears burned her eyes, trickled down the sides of her face and into her hair.

"Shh." He kissed the salt-laced sadness away, rolling onto his back and taking her with him, one hand cradling the back of her head, the other stroking down the curve of her spine. "Don't cry, sweetheart."

His gentleness twined another tendril around her heart, until she was so entangled in him, she knew she'd never break free. For the first time in her life, her wolf had chosen. And it had chosen this lone wolf. "You have me," she whispered. *All of me.*

Chapter 55

KALEB WAS AT his home office when Silver called. "A. V. is Vasquez," she said, "of that my family is as certain as we can be without having his DNA. He also appears to be running things as far as Pure Psy is concerned. However, the rank and file believe he speaks for Henry."

So did Kaleb. The NetMind and DarkMind both had had too calm a reaction to Henry's "death." Kaleb had attempted to use the twin neosentience to track the former Councilor, but they had been acting increasingly erratic of late, and he'd been unable to focus them on the target. That bespoke a profound problem in the Net, the depth of which perhaps he alone understood—Henry's fanaticism and the continued deterioration of Subject 8-91 were simply symptoms of a more dangerous malaise.

Concluding the conversation with his aide, he rose from his desk, playing a small platinum star through his fingers. The metal was warm from his touch, but his mind worked with ice-cold precision as he decided what was to be done with Henry. *Aden.*

The telepath's reply was crystal clear. *Councilor.*

Kaleb will do. The Council is no longer in existence except in the minds of the populace.

Kaleb.

Henry will continue to be a problem if he lives. Do you have any issue with eliminating him? Kaleb needed to know how much of the Arrows' loyalty was his.

No. His policies are not good for the Net.

Kaleb rubbed his thumb over the shining surface of the star. *Then regard it as an authorized mission.*

Noted.

Telepathic connection severed, Kaleb considered those who'd remain after Henry's demise. Shoshanna, he didn't waste time on. Henry's "wife" had flaws that would make it easy to manipulate her. Nikita would leave Kaleb alone so long as he didn't attempt to violate her territory—or harm her child and grandchild. The other Councilor hid it well, but Kaleb could glide through the Net without causing a single ripple. He saw everything. Nikita's conditioning might be flawless, but she wasn't Silent.

Not in the way he was.

Nikita's protective instinct was her Achilles' heel, but Kaleb had no reason to exploit it. Not as long as she didn't attempt to get in his way. If she did . . .

His eye fell on the star. He halted his movements. And knew he had his own weakness, one Nikita would never guess at, and so he still had the advantage in his dealings with her.

As for Anthony, Kaleb didn't think there would be any problems—he had no desire to encroach on NightStar lands or capture Anthony's stable of F-Psy. No foreseer could stop him once he'd decided on a course of action.

That left Ming and Tatiana. Both would have to die when it was time. There was no other viable option. Kaleb would not chance them coming at him from behind.

The star sparked in the light from the lamp on his desk.

Caught, he stared at the small charm, wondering what its owner would make of his thoughts of assassination. Soon, he would discover the answer. Because he'd just breached another layer of security, unearthed the oldest part of the trail. It was fragile and fragmented, but it was there.

Soon.

Chapter 56

RIAZ CALLED ADRIA to ask her to come along to the meeting with Bo and the liaison three days later and discovered that she was already in San Francisco with Indigo, Tarah, Evie, and another woman who had a familiar scent but looked nothing like she should—from her height, to the color of her hair and eyes, even the shape of her face, the latter apparently altered using high-tech gel pads Judd had procured from who knows where.

As he pulled away after picking up Adria, the other four women waved at him from the café where they were eating large pieces of cake slathered in frosting. "How in hell did Sienna talk Hawke into letting her out of den territory?"

Adria gave him an arch look. "I have no idea. Didn't ask." Scooping up a bite of the apple pie she'd had packed to go, she fed it to him. "However, she *may* possibly have pointed out that she's an adult female with the right to make up her own mind."

He bit back a grin at her tone. "Yes, she *may* have done that, but Hawke is newly mated and there's a high probability she's in Ming's crosshairs. Hawke might be intelligent, but he's not that rational, not when it comes to Sienna."

Eating a bite of pie herself, Adria made a "hmming" sound in her throat. "You know, you're right. Though, until you picked me up, she was with a lieutenant, a senior soldier, and a woman who thinks of her as another daughter. No one was going to get to her."

Riaz had to concede that point. Forget about Tarah being submissive—maternal wolves would fight to the death to protect their young.

"Buuuuut," Adria drawled, "five minutes before I left, I

got a call from Simran and Inés. In the area. Shopping. Heard we were nearby, said they'd come join the group." A narrow-eyed look, but her tone was admiring. "The man is devious."

Riaz chuckled. "Of course he is." Brute strength alone did not the alpha of a pack make. "You think Sienna's figured it out?"

"From the little smile she got on her face when Simran called, yes. She wasn't mad—I think she realizes exactly how hard this must be for Hawke."

Riaz's wolf growled in disagreement. "If she did, she'd have stayed safe in our territory."

"And if she was the kind of woman to do that," Adria responded, "she wouldn't be strong enough to be mate to an alpha." She fed him another bite of pie. "There's a difference between taking sensible precautions and tucking your tail between your legs."

It took conscious effort to think past his protective instincts, to understand that when a man chose a strong woman for his own, he made a commitment to nurture and respect that strength. Adria would never allow him to coddle her—but as Sienna didn't fight Hawke's need to ensure her safety, Adria allowed Riaz to hold her, trusted him to take care of her in a hundred small ways that soothed his wolf.

There was no longer any hint of distance between them, that night under the moon having forged a bond that was young, raw, and hauntingly powerful. He couldn't imagine waking without her, loved to fall asleep with his legs tangled in her own, her husky voice the last thing he heard. He knew that when the urge to roam isolated reaches awoke again within his wolf, he'd coax her to go along. Solitude would be no fun without her.

Picking up her hand, he pressed a kiss to her knuckles. "Thank you for being mine."

A startled look, followed by a smile that lit up her eyes. "Ditto."

He was still smiling when they walked into the light-filled lobby of the art deco hotel where they were to meet Bo and his liaison. That was when Riaz took an emotional kick to the chest that knocked all the air out of him.

. . .

ADRIA'S wolf punched to the surface the instant she sensed the sudden tension that gripped Riaz's body. On alert for a security risk, she followed his gaze to where Bowen stood with a woman of about five-two, maybe three, her hair a shining gold she'd pinned into a neat roll, her body clothed in a fitted aquamarine shift that set off eyes of gentle gray.

No weapon. No threat. Only a lovely woman . . . from Europe.

A horrible sick feeling in her stomach, Adria looked from the stranger to Riaz, saw the shock that had turned his eyes wild, and she knew. She *knew*. But the woman and Bo had seen them, were walking over, and somehow, she managed to make it through the introductions. Yet even through the ringing in her skull, the nausea choking her throat, she noticed that Riaz never touched the woman—Lisette, her name was Lisette—never even looked at her properly.

"Lisette used to be the business manager for another company," Bo said to Adria, "but she's taken up a permanent position with us." Smooth as silk, not even a hint that that other company was a front for the Alliance. "Her specialty is in communications—the perfect choice for a liaison."

Riaz folded his arms. "Is Emil with you?"

Adria caught what she thought was distress in Lisette's expression before the other woman smiled and replied in French-accented English. "No, he had some business in Berlin." Glancing at Adria, she said, "Riaz and my husband worked together on a project while Riaz was in Europe."

God, Adria thought, how that must've killed Riaz. Her pain for him was endless, her own anguish a cavernous darkness inside of her. To know and accept that the man she loved had a mate, and to come face-to-face with that mate were two different things. It ripped away the rose-colored lenses she'd put on since the night under the moon, slapped her in the face with the reality of her status as nothing but a substitute for the woman Riaz really wanted.

She didn't know how she got through the meeting, but neither she nor Riaz said a word about it until they were in

SnowDancer territory. "So . . . she's the one." A statement
that was in reality a question, because she needed to have it
confirmed, to hear it from his mouth. Yet, some small part
of her was a child, wanting to hear him say, "No," and tell
her she was imagining things, even when the truth was a neon
sign in front of her.

Riaz brought the car to a halt. "It changes nothing between
us." His response was harsh, the hand he placed against her
cheek rough with warmth. "You're the one in my heart."

No, I'm the consolation prize. They both knew he was
only with her because he couldn't be with Lisette. Pride
choked up her throat, but she didn't shove his hand aside,
didn't tell him to get the hell away from her—she'd come into
this with her eyes wide open. To punish him for something
over which he had no control, to walk away at this moment
when she knew he had to be suffering the most vicious
pain . . . no, she couldn't do that to her black wolf. Love, she
realized at that terrible moment of truth, could be incredibly
unselfish, even when it hurt until she bled.

Unclipping her safety belt, then his, she crawled over to
straddle his lap, wrapping her arms around him. "I'm here."

SHE broke him, Riaz thought, his arms clenching around the
sleek muscle of her body, his heart thundering. Unable to
speak, he buried his face in her neck, drawing in the strange
delicacy of her scent, so complex and unique. It anchored his
shocked and newly wounded wolf, calmed the man.

He'd expected fury, had thought he might find himself out
in the cold when he needed her more than ever. The one thing
he'd never expected was this generosity of spirit, and he
should have, because she'd shown him over and over that she
wasn't only a tough-skinned soldier, but a woman of empathy
and heart, a woman any man would be proud to call his own.

Pressing a kiss to the beat of the pulse in her neck, he felt
her hand stroke through his hair. His wolf basked in the tenderness. "It was the shock more than anything," he said, her
skin so soft under his lips. "I'll be fine now."

Adria rubbed her cheek against his before she drew back.
"No pretence, Riaz," she said, holding his gaze with the

unflinching honesty of her own. "You tell me if this isn't working for you."

He fisted his hand in her hair, shock obliterated by possessive fury. "It damn well is." Maybe he'd gone into this relationship needing the comfort of a packmate's touch, but now? Now he'd staked his claim. "You're mine." The wolf growled in agreement. "I am never letting you go."

Chapter 57

VASIC WAS IN a remote, night-shrouded part of Nunavut, Canada, talking with Aden about their progress in tracking Henry, when a shudder rocked him. Initially, he thought the Cape Dorset region had experienced an earth tremor.

Then Aden shook his head. "Something's happened in the Net."

A split second later, having opened his psychic eye, Vasic dove into the slipstream of the PsyNet as Aden did the same. The Net was the biggest data archive in the world, millions, trillions of pieces of data uploaded into it each and every day. But rather than the relatively smooth rivers of information Vasic was used to seeing, this section of the Net was twisted, crumpling in on itself.

Shield! he telepathed to Aden.

Around them, the star-studded black of the Net was literally collapsing, taking the hundreds of minds anchored in this section with it. He expanded his shields to protect as many minds as he could, but while he was a powerful Tk-V, Aden was the stronger telepath, able to shield a far greater number.

Straining in his physical body, he focused on holding the shields on those he'd managed to grab from the edges of the disaster zone, not thinking about the ones who'd been caught in the collapse. Severed from the Net, they would've died a quick and violently painful death.

Aden, he telepathed when he saw the edge begin to expand in a rippling wave. His telepathic abilities weren't enough to hold back the continuing cascade of destruction and protect at the same time.

I've called the others.

But someone else arrived before the rest of the squad, and his power was so vast it blinded. He single-handedly built a buttress around the collapse, sealing up the breach, until Vasic could release the minds he'd protected.

Krychek's not only a cardinal Tk.

A dual cardinal, Aden replied. *Impossible.*

Except that much telepathic power was nothing less than cardinal level.

"It's holding," Krychek said on the psychic plane, the conversation protected from leaking into the PsyNet by shields of impenetrable black. "Can you get into the collapsed section to check the extent of the damage? I need to maintain this suture until the Net seals itself."

Aden checked with Vasic, got a risk assessment identical to the one he'd made. "Yes."

"I'll leave this small window open for you." Kaleb indicated the coordinates. "Go."

Diving into the twisted wreckage, Vasic at his back, Aden maintained heavy shielding as he navigated broken pathways that threatened to cut and shove into his mind, the blackness of the Net somehow jagged and devoid of life. "Stop." He made Vasic check his biofeedback link, as he did the same.

Only when he was satisfied that their link to the Net was holding, regardless of the fact they were now in a "dead" section, did they continue. It didn't take them long to find the locus and the cause of the unprecedented network failure. The Net had imploded into a sharp point at that location, as if the psychic fabric had been sucked into a vortex.

"The anchor for this region," he said to Vasic, "is dead."

"His death alone wouldn't have caused this. There are multiple fail-safes." Vasic went closer to the frozen vortex, the mangled fabric of the Net having created a natural plug . . . too late to save the men, women, and children caught within. *We need to find the body.*

Returning through the window Krychek had left, they informed him of the lack of survivors, watched him start to finalize the seal. "The anchor is dead," Aden said. "We'll work to locate the body."

Dropping from the psychic plane, he waited for Vasic to open his eyes. The Tk-V brought up something on the computronic gauntlet on his arm as soon as he did so. "I'm accessing the anchor files for this region."

Aden waited, aware Vasic was searching for an image he could focus on for a teleport.

"There." An instant later, the Tk-V teleported them directly in front of a two-story cottage on the edge of Cape Dorset. The lack of neighbors was unusual for a Psy—but not for an anchor. Many members of Designation A craved isolation.

It was because, an anchor had once explained to Aden, they were constantly surrounded by others on the Net. Unlike with ordinary Psy, an anchor could not shut off that awareness—it was an inbuilt component of their ability to hold the Net in place. Their relative seclusion on the physical plane was a psychological coping mechanism.

Light spilled from the cottage, and when Aden made his way to one of the windows, using the shadows outside to his advantage, he saw no hint of danger. *I'll ring the doorbell.*

Wait until I'm inside.

Vasic heard the clear tones of the bell echo through the house a second after he teleported into the room visible from the window. When there was no other sound or movement, he let Aden in. Working in practiced silence, they checked the first floor and found nothing, before heading up to the second.

There. Aden nodded at a drop of what looked like blood on the carpet that covered the steps.

Halting, Vasic looked more carefully and saw two other drops. *Whoever did it, passed this way.*

The body was in the corner room the anchor had used as his office. From the dents and the blood splatter, he'd been flung violently against the wall at least twice. "This is the

work of a Tk," Vasic said out loud, after scanning the room
for listening devices, the scanner—able to be adapted to many
tasks—built into his gauntlet.

Aden didn't say anything until he'd walked over and
checked the anchor's throat for a pulse. "Death confirmed.
His skin, however, is warm. Fits with the timeline."

Vasic ran his eyes over the dents the anchor's head had
made in the wall. There was blood, yes, but the killer had had
enough on him to drip, which meant he'd been up close and
personal with his victim. "Catastrophic fracture in Silence?"

"You're certain it was a Tk?"

"Pattern of the victim's injuries added to the high-impact
damage to the wall makes it highly probable." He looked at
the blood-splattered mess on the desk where it appeared the
anchor had been working prior to the attack. "Either the
uncontrolled violence is stage dressing, or someone is using
an unstable Tk for his or her own purposes."

A flicker at the corner of his eye. Swiveling, he found
Kaleb Krychek in the room with them. Though the fact wasn't
well known, the former Councilor was one of the rare Tks
who could go to people as well as places, and he'd obviously
zeroed in on either Vasic or Aden.

Dressed in a pristine suit, his face bore no marks of strain
as a result of the power he'd expended on the Net. "The information I was able to gather from the NetMind," he said, taking in the carnage, "indicates the fail-safes were all murdered
seconds before the anchor's death, by killers who broke into
their homes armed with laser weapons. It happened so fast,
the NetMind couldn't stabilize the fracture."

Aden rose from his crouching position beside the body.
"That would require a coordinated effort. The names of the
fail-safes aren't broadcast, and while their security is nowhere
near that of an anchor"—the reason why non-teleport-capable
assassins had been able to breach their homes—"each is pas-
sively monitored."

Which is why, Vasic thought, the entire network had been
eliminated around the same time. Any warning and contingency plans would have come into play. The Psy had backups
upon backups when it came to anchors—Designation A was
the foundation of the entire psychic framework that kept their

race alive, the Net far too big to be stable without them. Kill the anchors and the Net would suffer a total collapse, taking everyone with it.

ADEN watched Vasic begin to move around the office. Quiet, calm, icily focused. "Could this be the work of one of the other former Councilors?" he asked Kaleb.

"It would make no logical sense—fracturing the Net fractures their power base."

"An individual who knew the parameters of the failure ahead of time could ensure the safety of his allies and the deaths of his enemies."

Kaleb's eyes, living pieces of the PsyNet, locked on Aden's face. "Yes. However, such indiscriminate carnage better fits the tenets of Pure Psy—my fellow ex-Councilors tend to be much more targeted in their assassinations."

Aden thought of the lack of support the group had received in the Net after their recent humiliating defeat at the hands of the coalition of changelings, humans, and Psy—most of the population believed Pure Psy shouldn't have stepped out of the Net, that the aggression contravened their stated aim of Purity. Given Pure Psy's increasingly extreme ideology, that lack of support might well have been taken as sedition.

"Even with depleted numbers," he said to Kaleb, "the group has the capability to organize such an attack."

"And their general has the discipline." Kaleb turned from Aden to Vasic. "Have you found it?"

"No." The other Arrow looked up from the transparent computer screen he'd brought up. "There's no message here, and nothing on the Net from anyone claiming responsibility or threatening more violence."

That, Aden knew, didn't mean further murders weren't planned. Kaleb's next words made it clear the cardinal telekinetic had come to the same conclusion. "Protecting every anchor across the world is a statistical impossibility."

"Agreed." There were too many of them, strong and weak, critical and peripheral. "However, we can send out an alert to each region, advise the authorities in charge of the anchors to beef up security."

"Warn them of the possibility of a strong Tk being involved," Vasic added, his eyes on the bloody dents in the wall. "At least 8 on the Gradient."

"That's going to be problematic. There are very few people stronger than a Gradient 8 Tk."

Kaleb was right—which meant more anchors were going to die unless they ran the architect of this attack to ground. "If this is the start of a Pure Psy campaign," Aden said, considering how to narrow down the possible targets, "certain regions are more likely to be hit." Nikita Duncan and Anthony Kyriakus hadn't only been part of the coalition that had defeated Henry's fanatics, they'd also been vocal in their anti–Pure Psy views. More crucially, their region was becoming a magnet for those whose Silence was fractured or otherwise suspect—anathema to Pure Psy's aim of absolute purity.

"This location would seem to argue against Pure Psy involvement," Vasic pointed out. "It has no strategic or political importance."

"I'd theorize this was a training run in a quiet region of the Net." Aden acknowledged his theory had a flaw, in that it required the aggressors sacrifice the element of surprise, but that didn't disqualify it—not when irrational behavior was becoming a hallmark of Pure Psy operations. "We shouldn't discount it being the work of an unknown group, but it's reasonable to give Nikita and Anthony specific warning."

Kaleb nodded. "I'll take care of it."

Vasic broke his silence. "Preliminary reports are coming in—four hundred and seventy confirmed dead so far."

And the region that had collapsed, Aden thought, was tiny, with a sparse population. A single sector collapse in San Francisco would take tens of thousands of lives with it.

"At least eighty-five of the dead are children."

Aden met Vasic's eyes in a silent warning, but Kaleb wasn't paying attention to the Arrow who was both Silent and broken. "I have to go," the former Councilor said after a ten-second pause. "Release the general security notice, Aden." He blinked out in the next breath, his power so vast the teleport took him little to no effort. The only other person in the Net as fast was Vasic, and he'd been born with the ability. Kaleb had learned it as a Tk.

"He could have done it himself," Aden said, staring at where the cardinal had stood. "We'd never know with the speed he teleports."

"Yes."

KALEB teleported into Nikita's office to find Anthony Kyriakus already there. Since Anthony was a telepath with no teleport-capable ability, that meant he'd either used one of his Tks to arrange an immediate 'port . . . or he'd been with Nikita at the time of the attack. Very late for a political meeting.

Unbuttoning his suit jacket, Kaleb took a seat beside Anthony, on the other side of Nikita's desk. "A de facto Council?"

"I have no reason to want the Net to suffer a catastrophic failure," Nikita said instead of answering, her ruler-straight black hair brushing her shoulders. "Neither does Anthony. Neither do you."

"So certain?"

"You want to control the Net, Kaleb. Broken, it's useless to you."

He said nothing to that, betrayed nothing. Nikita thought she understood how his mind worked. She didn't, but it was to his advantage to let her misapprehension continue. "There's still no sign of Henry, and Shoshanna has bunkered down somewhere in England behind heavy shields." None of which would protect her when the time came. "Tatiana and Ming are the wild cards." Kaleb had his suspicions about Ming's involvement in the Pure Psy assault in California, but the military mastermind had been very careful to bury his tracks.

"There are others who have reason to want to damage the Net," Anthony said, and the three of them went through much the same conversation he'd had with Aden and Vasic.

Aden, he thought with a corner of his mind, was the center around whom the Arrows rotated. While the telepath wasn't the most powerful member of the squad in terms of raw psychic ability, he was the one the rest of the Arrows looked to for leadership. He also had the support of Vasic, the only teleporter in the Net faster than Kaleb himself. To own the squad, Kaleb would have to have Aden's loyalty. And he would. Because Kaleb had plans Nikita couldn't even guess at, and having a squad of lethal assassins behind him would make things both deadlier and smoother when he played his endgame.

"Now that the violence has a shape, will your foreseers be able to predict the next strike?" Nikita asked Anthony.

"I've given the order, and I'll forward any pertinent information, but chaos on this scale skews and warps the timeline." Anthony glanced at Kaleb. "We'll ensure our anchors are well protected."

"I can offer you a certain number of my troops." He knew the two ex-Councilors had limited military resources of their own, would find it near impossible to cover the anchor network in the area.

"Thank you," Nikita said, "but I'll decline."

Anthony's response was much the same. Kaleb hadn't expected anything else—if he were on the other side, he wouldn't trust himself either. "The offer remains on the table, should you change your mind."

Rising, he buttoned up his suit jacket at the same time that he soothed the panic of the NetMind. The neosentience was scared, and while Kaleb didn't feel, he had learned to differentiate the moods of the DarkMind and NetMind both. Now he gentled the NetMind and reined in the DarkMind, the darker sentience stronger in the wake of the murderous violence. "If you'll excuse me. I need to return to my own region."

A second later, he teleported into another room on another continent. "Ming," he said. "Tatiana, I see you've heard about the attack."

Chapter 58

AFTER A NIGHT spent curled around the woman who had healed something broken in him, then held him as the wound tore open again, Riaz woke with his world back in focus.

"Good morning," he said, brushing aside the inky strands of hair that clung to Adria's cheek.

"Morning." A faint smile, the caution hidden but present.

He felt like he'd been punched all over again, but he told himself to be patient. His not-so-tough soldier had had a shock, too. Leaning down, he nibbled at her lower lip in a playful kiss, one hand splayed over her rib cage, his other arm braced above her head.

She ran her own hand up his chest and around to his nape, petting him with the same affectionate laziness, her smile growing deeper. "This is a nice way to wake up."

"Yes, it is." He went to say something else, but the comm beeped, Riley summoning him to an urgent lieutenant meeting.

He didn't want to go, wanted to love Adria sweet and slow, show her who she was to him, but he was a lieutenant as she was a senior soldier. Dashing into the shower, he walked out to find she'd scared up a cup of coffee for him. "I hope it's not another attack," she said, eyes of blue-violet dark with worry.

Cupping her cheek, he pressed his forehead to her own for a single, precious moment. "I hope the hell not. I'm guessing whatever it is, the seniors will all be briefed soon as we're done."

She nodded. "Go on." A quick kiss, the warmth of her lips still with him when he walked into the conference room a few minutes later.

"Is that coffee?" Indigo groaned as she walked in behind him.

Putting down his mug, Riaz poured her a cup from the carafe on the table, aware the other lieutenant had worked until nightfall with Felix's team, then returned to supervise her novices in a night training exercise. Riaz had offered to handle the latter, but Indigo had wanted to personally judge their progress since a couple were edging toward full soldier status. "Don't tell me your boy toy isn't treating you right," he said as he handed the coffee over.

Indigo swigged half of it before saying, "I shall deal with you later," in an ominous tone stripped of its menace by a jaw-cracking yawn. "Do you know what this is about?"

"No." Grabbing a seat, he turned toward the monitors as

Alexei's and Jem's feeds came online. "You two have any idea what's happening?" he asked.

"My guess—something's up with the Psy," Jem said. "I went for a street run this morning like I sometimes do, and I don't know how to describe it; there was this eerie quiet on the face of every Psy I passed."

"Whatever it is," Alexei pointed out, "if we're having a meeting and not going into emergency mode, it's probably not an imminent threat to the pack."

Tension level dropping a notch because the young lieutenant was right, Riaz went to ask Alexei about the wolves who wanted to merge with SnowDancer when Hawke entered with Riley and Judd. Conversation stopped for a minute as the other lieutenants started to come online. Kenji, Tomás, Matthias, and Cooper all snapped into focus one after the other. Coop was as bright eyed as if he'd been up for hours, and Kenji appeared to have come in from a night shift, but the others didn't look impressed.

"I thought the war was won," Tomás groaned, a giant mug in his hand. "This was my sleep-in day."

"I thought that was yesterday," Cooper said.

"Shut up. Just because you're getting laid on a regular basis doesn't mean you have to be smug about it."

Coop's smile was slow and definitely smug.

Tapping the table with a finger on the heels of that smile, Hawke called the meeting to order. "Judd, Lucas, and I," he said, "had a very interesting conference call with Anthony and Nikita a few minutes ago."

Everyone quieted. The pack's relationship with the two powerful Psy was shaky at best. There was no doubt both had done their share of the heavy lifting when it came to protecting the city from Henry Scott's army—they'd provided combat-ability troops, used their own considerable telepathic powers to repel the intruders. However, that didn't mean they could be trusted.

"Good news is," Hawke said, "it's highly likely we're no longer target numero uno as far as Pure Psy is concerned."

"Why aren't you celebrating?" Indigo asked, reaching for the carafe and pouring herself a second cup of coffee, topping up Riley's when he held it out.

Hawke's expression was grim, the words he spoke even grimmer. "Because the civil war in the Net isn't a possibility—it's begun. The most recent casualty count is five hundred and seventeen."

"Shit." Matthias rubbed his face, his dark skin gleaming in the light of the little table lamp he hadn't yet turned off. "An explosion of some kind?"

Judd was the one who answered. "Part of the Net collapsed last night."

A shocked hush.

"The victims' separation from the Net was so violent," he continued, "they would've had no chance to attempt to reintegrate. Men, women, children . . . entire families wiped out."

"Angry as this makes me," Coop said, his scar white from the force of his emotions, "we can't affect the Net. Why did Nikita and Anthony contact us?"

"The Net collapsed because the anchor in the region was murdered, as were all his fail-safes," Judd explained. "Anchors are protected on the psychic plane by permanent shielding that's close to impossible to break. However, they're still mortal."

Riaz saw it then, what Nikita and Anthony wanted them to do. "They need our help to protect the anchors in the territory." It was a historic request . . . especially when Riaz thought it through and realized the two Psy were willing to trust SnowDancer with the locations of people who were the greatest vulnerability of their race.

"Yes." Judd pushed his hand through his hair, a rare physical betrayal of his emotions. "Before we make up our minds on that, there's something I'm not sure you all realize."

"Wait," Indigo said, pushing over a cup of coffee. "Drink this first. No offense, gorgeous, but you look like hell."

Judd gave Indigo the faintest of smiles, obeyed the order. "Ever since the discovery that SnowDancer protected Marlee and Toby from rehabilitation," he said, after drinking a good third of the cup, "a lot of the Psy in the area are looking to DarkRiver and SnowDancer for some kind of leadership. At the heart of it is the knowledge that you protected the defenseless their own leadership sought to destroy."

"Changeling packs," Riley said in his measured way,

"have managed to retain our sense of identity, to survive being sucked into the Psy machine, because we're careful about who we call our own."

Changelings would fight to the death to protect the pack, Riaz thought, but gaining the trust of that pack was a hard thing—as Judd himself knew. However—"It doesn't sit right with me that we turn our backs on people who trust us to help."

"With me either," Riley said as the other lieutenants nodded. "At the same time, our wolves would go insane trying to protect such a large 'pack.'"

Because once a dominant took responsibility for a group, he took *full* responsibility.

"Hell of a mess," Matthias muttered.

Having tipped his chair back on two legs, Hawke now brought it down on all four. "Putting that aside for now, first we need numbers. Judd?"

"Twenty anchors across the state," the lieutenant replied. "Two hundred backups—ten per anchor."

Tomás whistled. "That's a damn low number on which to pin the lives of millions of people."

"There are others, like Sophia Russo, Max's wife, who also help stabilize the Net, but they can't hold back a collapse, so they aren't targets." Judd drank the rest of his coffee. "Three of the twenty are cardinals and technically the only true anchors in the network. However, the secondary anchors, trained since childhood, are just as integrated into the psychic fabric of the PsyNet, have the same vulnerabilities. While the cardinals control exponentially larger areas, taking out a single secondary hub will mean tens of thousands of deaths."

Alexei leaned forward, his blond hair tied back with a piece of string. "How long would we have to maintain the watch?"

"Not long," Judd said to their surprise. "There are very, very few Tks who can teleport to people rather than places. The odds are excellent that the telekinetic behind the anchor murder doesn't have that ability. Which means he needs images of his targets' living spaces—and those he's probably sourcing from the 'in case of emergency' files kept on anchors."

"Anthony and Nikita are arranging new bolt holes," Coop guessed. "Clever, simple, and effective."

"We can do it," Riley said, having had his head together with Indigo while the rest of them spoke. "Factoring in Dark-River, the Rats, and WindHaven, along with certain trained humans we know we can trust in the city, we have more than enough people to cover all the anchors and backups twenty-four/seven."

"Will it leave the territory vulnerable?" Hawke asked, the question that of an alpha whose primary goal was to keep his people safe, even if that meant making a ruthless choice.

Indigo shook her head. "No, we're in very good shape."

Hawke's pale eyes scanned the room. "Yes or no. The decision will affect every single sector of SnowDancer territory, and if we say yes, it puts us on one side of the line in this civil war."

Riaz's wolf knew there was only one choice. "Like it or not," he said, "as the most powerful group in the area, we have a responsibility to the region now." As Riley had pointed out, changeling packs were insular for a reason, but they were not and had never been, blind to the outside world.

"Riaz is right." Cooper's voice. "We can't just look away while our neighbors are slaughtered."

"That's not who we are." Jem's statement was echoed by every single lieutenant in the room.

Hawke's nod held a quiet pride that said he'd expected no other answer. "But, it can't be permanent." Implacable words. "Our wolves aren't made for that kind of political maneuvering—and I have no desire to rule this region or any other. We protect, and when the dust settles, we help the Psy population find their feet."

An immediate round of agreement, and then they got down to the hard question of exactly how they could protect themselves and the anchors from a Tk. Judd had a simple answer. "Attack with deadly force as soon as they 'port in. No warning."

HAWKE walked into his office to find Sienna standing to the right of his desk. Her attention was on the wall and the map that showed the land currently in the process of being replanted—work that was set to hit completion this week.

Knowing how it haunted her, what she'd almost done to Snow-Dancer, the lives she'd taken to protect the pack, he didn't offer her any platitudes. Instead, tugging her against his chest, he rubbed his chin over her hair, his wolf soothed by her mere proximity. Her arm came around his waist in return, but when she spoke, the words her voice shaped were unexpected.

"Judd gave me the latest update on the deaths in Cape Dorset." Quiet. Solemn. As she'd been when he'd woken her to tell her the news. "If they obliterate an anchor point in this region, the casualty count will be catastrophic."

He should've learned by now how good she was at ignoring her own emotions to focus on harsh reality, but she still surprised him at times. Would continue to do so, he thought, as long as he lived. There was nothing predictable about Sienna . . . except for the love he saw in her eyes every single morning, his own personal dawn. "We've agreed to help with the protection detail."

"I want to—"

"No."

Pulling away, she frowned. "I know you're worried about Ming, but he's got to have other priorities right now. I can wear a disguise like I did when I went out with Evie and her family."

He folded his arms. "That disguise only worked because of the context." It was the sole reason he'd been able to let her go—because no one would expect Sienna Lauren Snow, cardinal X, to be walking around the city shoe shopping. "You think the people planning to attack an anchor won't scan the area? The instant after they figure out you're Psy, they'll know who you are." They'd also know the value of that information to those who sought to harness the fury of an X.

Stubborn tension marked her jawline. "I can't hide forever." She folded her own arms, feet set slightly apart. "I'm strong enough to take on even a cardinal telekinetic."

"And I should just forget about the big fat target on your back?" Anger crept into his voice, his wolf's hackles up.

"Oh, you mean to match yours?" Narrowed eyes. "I'll stay if you'll stay."

Blowing out a breath, he growled.

Sienna stepped closer instead of farther away, dropping her arms. "I thought we already worked this out?"

He'd permitted her to go into battle, permitted her to put her life on the line. That didn't mean he'd liked it. "Did you forget the fact that I'm a dominant wolf as well as your mate?" He was not sane when it came to the idea of her being hurt.

She rolled her eyes at him, then smiled. One of those sudden, brilliant smiles she gave him every day, smiles that made him feel ten feet tall even as they cut him off at the knees. And when she cupped his face and tugged him down to rub her cheek against his own, her breasts pushing against his folded arms, man and wolf both knew they were sunk.

Unfolding his arms, he ran his hands down her back as she pressed a line of kisses along his jaw. "Not yet," he whispered, his voice stripped to the core.

Sienna drew back, lines between her eyebrows. "Hawke?"

He was wolf, was alpha. Revealing vulnerability, even to his mate, didn't come easy. "I almost lost you," he said, the memory making him want to rage, as he relived how close he'd come to never again seeing Sienna's smile. "I need—" He couldn't complete the sentence, his emotions too raw.

Cardinal eyes devoid of stars stared back at him. "I understand," she said, and he felt the depth of her perception along the mating bond. "We, both of us, need a little more time to convince ourselves we made it." Stroking her hands over his chest, she wrapped her arms around him to rest her cheek against his heart.

He hadn't expected it, that she'd surrender to the violent depth of his need to hold her safe, if only for a fleeting whisper of time. And he knew he couldn't allow her to do it, couldn't steal her freedom to assuage his need. "Go," he said, forcing the words out, "speak to Riley. Ask him to pair you with someone senior and experienced."

Pushing away from his chest so she could meet his eyes, Sienna touched her fingers to his face. "Beautiful man."

His claws pricked the insides of his skin, his wolf fighting the human's decision.

"I'll stay." Her palm against his cheek, her eyes luminescent with emotion. "It's the logical choice."

When he cocked his head, she said, "If I go out there, you'll be half insane with worry and of no use to the pack." She pressed her fingers to his lips to stop him from speaking. "I'd be the same if it was you." A crooked smile. "I'm making this choice not for you, but for both of us—I'll have other chances to help the pack in that way. This time, I'll help by being one of the ones who'll remain behind to guard our territory."

Taking her hand, he kissed the slightly rough skin of her palm, that of a soldier, a fighter . . . and of a woman who understood him in ways no one else ever had, or ever would again.

Chapter 59

I AM NEVER letting you go.

Adria held Riaz's passionate words to her heart during her first watch on anchor detail. But it was hard, so hard, when she knew he had a meeting with Lisette this afternoon. He'd asked Adria if she wanted to accompany him, and the feral wolf in her had swiped at the chance, but Adria wasn't a jealous, angry woman, wouldn't allow herself to become one.

So she'd reined in the urge and said no, trusting him to honor her faith.

But she was still a woman who loved. It hurt to imagine him speaking to Lisette, until her every pulse was a razor cutting her from the inside out. Part of her pain was for him, for the agony that had to be tearing him to pieces. To be so close to the one meant to be your mate, only to be denied. It was such a cruel idea, it made her chest ache. Or perhaps the ache was for her, a symptom of her knowledge that this truth would never change—she would never be who Lisette was to Riaz.

At that moment, she could almost envy the Psy their Silence.

The older man she guarded, his hair a dusty gray, his eyes near the same shade, looked up from the papers he was grading. He was a teacher at the university. Anchors didn't need to work, and often couldn't because of the mental discipline required of them on the Net, but Bjorn Thorsen was a mathematical genius. "It makes no rational sense," he'd told her, "to have my knowledge die with me."

Now, he said, "A wolf in my study. The world has changed indeed."

Adria liked Thorsen. There was something about him—as if in spite of his mathematical bent, he had the capacity to see the most nonnumerical of subtleties. "Yes," she said. "This is the last thing I ever expected to be doing."

"I'm eighty-five years of age." He brought up his computer screen, showed her an image of himself as a much younger—and stiffer—man. "At the start of my lifetime, changelings weren't even a blip on the Council's radar. I've watched your people's power grow ever stronger, and I've watched my people make bad choice after bad choice. This latest state of affairs, it's no surprise."

Startled, she turned to lean her shoulder against the wall. "You expected someone to begin murdering anchors?"

"It's only logical, Adria." Putting down the pen in his hand, he met her eyes, his gaze holding a fierce power. "If you control the anchors, you control the Net."

"But they're killing, not controlling."

Thorsen shook his head, his face holding the wisdom of someone who had lived well more than twice her lifetime. "Do you not see? Once they have shattered a larger, more critical section of the Net, the ones behind this will make it known they'll break other parts, murder other anchors, unless those anchors swear fealty to them."

Adria frowned. "What advantage would that give them? As I understand it, you stabilize the Net, nothing more." The answer came to her as the last word left her lips. "If you stabilize the Net," she said, realizing the true level of cold intelligence behind the sadistic plan, "you can destabilize it." That destabilization had the potential to affect thousands, tens of thousands at a time. "What better way to control the masses than to let them know their very lives hang in the balance." One step out of line and the Net itself could be collapsed around them, their lifeline extinguished. And unlike the Laurens, most ordinary Psy likely didn't know *how* to defect into a smaller network, much less have the psychic and psychological strength to pull it off.

"Excellent," Thorsen said, sounding like the teacher he was. "Of course, such a practice can't be maintained long term. The reason anchors themselves don't destabilize the Net and hold everyone hostage isn't only because it would be an irrational act, but because we're so deeply connected to it, any damage we do rebounds back on us. I might survive it once or twice, but beyond that . . ." He rubbed at his temples.

Her wolf went on alert. "What's the matter? Telepathic attack?" If so, she had Judd on standby. He could teleport in and hopefully disrupt the process.

Lines of pain radiated out from the professor's eyes. "No. Dissonance programming—it appears I am not meant to talk of such things." He dropped his hand, his breathing rough. "It's excruciating on one level, but I've become somewhat numbed to it over the years."

"Because a man of learning," she said, pouring him a glass of water from a nearby jug, "doesn't like having his thoughts truncated." He wouldn't call it bravery, wouldn't even call it an emotional decision, but he'd made a stand in his own quiet way. "What do you think you'll see in the next decade of your life?"

His eyes were calm, his answer brutal. "War."

RIAZ halted in the doorway of the meeting room on the lower floor of the same art deco hotel in San Francisco. "Where's Bo?"

Looking up from the other side of the small oval table, Lisette said, "He flew back to Venice an hour ago," in that distinctive clear tone of hers. "There was another attempt to take Alliance personnel. Everyone's safe, but he wants to be there on the ground. He assumed you'd be fine working out the final details with me."

"Of course," he said, making a mental note to follow up on the attack with her later in the day. As liaison, Lisette should have the most up-to-date information. "Have you gone over the communication protocols I e-mailed through? Any problems?"

Lisette's smile was soft. "Won't you sit?"

He took a chair across from her, and it was the first time he'd really looked at her since her arrival in the country. The impact was . . . unexpected. The primal draw he felt toward her hadn't disappeared, but it had dulled to background noise, leaving him clearheaded and in control. What had him taking a deep, quiet breath was that his wolf, too, showed no desire to wrench at the reins, to lunge at her. It lay quiet, watchful.

Lisette lifted a hand in a graceful motion, the fine gold bracelet around her wrist sliding lower down her arm. "I have no issues with the protocols. I should've told you that in my e-mail, but I . . . wanted to talk."

He took in the shadows under her eyes, the paleness of her skin, felt his protective instincts stir. "What's the matter?"

"I'm sorry." She swallowed, shook her head. "I don't know why—" Another head shake before her face crumpled.

"Hey, hey." Walking around the table, he crouched down beside her, taking her hands into his. "Tell me what's wrong."

It took her several minutes to catch her breath. "I haven't spoken to Emil in a month," she whispered, her eyes red.

"Ah, Lisette." Rising, he pulled her into a hug.

She held on tight to him. "I don't know why I can speak to you about this, why it feels so easy." Bewilderment. "I haven't told anyone else."

Riaz's wolf understood why she felt so comfortable with him, yet he knew to his bones that she wasn't the one he'd go to if he was hurting as badly as Lisette was now. There was only one person he trusted enough to lower his guard, leave himself defenseless, only one person to whom his wolf would speak its secrets. The knowledge was another piece settling into place, another filament in the bond between him and his empress.

Squeezing Lisette tight, he released her and nudged her back into her chair. "Why?" he asked after getting her a cup of coffee. "I know you're crazy for one another."

"Something happened and he just stopped talking to me," she said in an almost sub-vocal tone. "I can't believe he's having an affair, but what else could it be?" She wiped off another rush of tears. "I said I was leaving him, hoping the shock would get through to him and he'd finally tell me what was wrong . . . and he said he wanted a divorce."

MERCY wasn't the teensiest bit surprised when Riley turned up that night to join her on her security patrol of the city. Her leopard butted up against his scent, playful and affectionate. Riley's returning touch was careful, almost . . . tentative.

Tilting her head to the side, she said, "What's up, my personal and very sexy big, bad wolf?" Riley was never tentative. Though quiet, the man had steamrollers beat. He'd have made mincemeat of the little submissive he'd once dreamed about—Mercy had forgiven him for that, but she still liked to jerk his chain about it now and then.

Not tonight, not when he looked so solemn.

"You're being sweet," he said, the tentativeness replaced by frustration. "I keep waiting for a hiss and a swipe with your claws, and instead you pet me."

Laughing softly, she pressed her body to his. "Riley, my Riley." So solid and strong and stable, he was her port in the storm. No matter what happened, she knew she could come home to Riley, his love as enduring as the mountains themselves. "I know what it does to you to have me vulnerable."

The fact she carried a child—*children*—in her womb, meant she was no longer as fast or as lethal, cognizant as she was about not doing anything to injure their young. It was the reason she'd asked to be put on routine patrols. "I *know*." Claws kneading gently at his shoulders, she spoke with her lips against his. "It doesn't make me crazy when you check up on me." His deep need to care, to protect was patent in every shimmer of the mating bond. That's who Riley was, and she loved him for it.

"Honest?" he said, stroking his hand around to her nape.

"Honest." Sealed with a kiss. "Are you going to stay?"

He gave a sheepish nod. "I put myself on shift here. I know it's doubling up, but we have enough people that no one will notice."

And Riley, she thought, had earned the time. He was SnowDancer's rock, too, had been for as long as Hawke had been alpha. "Come on. Let's go neck on the pier—Zach will cover for me." Her partner was being very discreet on the other side of the street.

Riley laughed; it was one of her favorite sounds in the universe.

Chapter 60

"IT'S AS I expected," Vasquez said to the man inside the sterile chamber. "The anchors in the California region are now under heavy guard."

"Can we get to them?"

"Yes, but we may jeopardize our primary operative." Too late, Vasquez realized that he shouldn't have given ground on the Cape Dorset strike. "We should change the focus of our next planned hit from San Francisco to another major center with the potential for high impact."

"We aren't mindless anarchists," came the rasped-out response. "The populace must see we do this for a reason. To cleanse the Net of those who have failed to maintain their Silence."

"The risk is high. Nikita and Anthony have changeling support."

"Which only displays their weakness." His judgment was one Vasquez shared. "It's time we demonstrated that. San Francisco remains the target."

Every part of his training told him the move was a foolish

one, but he also knew Henry was right. Violence alone was not the answer. The message must be heard. "I'll begin the preparations." It would take extensive reconnaissance and extreme patience, but Vasquez had never yet failed in his task.

Chapter 61

ADRIA HAD BEEN coping. She hadn't interrogated Riaz about his meeting with Lisette the previous day, hadn't picked and prodded at the unspoken truth that hovered between them, conscious that doing so would only create a wound that would fester. Instead, she'd made the decision to cherish the tender and passionate tie that had grown between them, to bask in the wild affection of his wolf, and not obsess over the primal bond they'd never have. So she didn't know how this had happened, how she'd ended up alone with the woman who made it impossible to think about anything else.

"Thank you so much for this," Lisette said, strapping on her safety belt. "I truly wasn't hinting at a ride when I ran into you."

"It's not a problem." Having dropped off some papers at DarkRiver HQ for Hawke, Adria had been walking back through Chinatown to her car when she'd run into Lisette coming out of a souvenir shop. "Buy anything interesting?"

The woman laughed, and it was a sweet, gentle sound. In spite of her perfect makeup and hair, her pristine tangerine-colored dress that looked both professional and summery beneath a neutral-toned trench coat, Lisette gave off a warmth that was genuine. Now, she rustled in her bag and came out with a small jade statuette. "The storekeeper said it would bring me good luck—I'm going to ask DarkRiver and Snow-Dancer for permission to set up an apartment in the city."

Adria's heart stuttered. "You'd continue to be the liaison?"

"Yes. It might actually work better if the packs have me here on the ground."

The other woman's words made too much sense, speaking as they did to the changeling preference for situations where they could judge the other party's mood, his or her scent. "Have you and your husband decided which part of the city you'd want to live in if you get the okay?" The question was a reminder to herself that Lisette was happily married, had no desire to press a claim on the lone wolf who was Adria's.

A long silence from the passenger seat, so long that the hairs stood up on the back of Adria's neck, her mind working a hundred miles an hour. "Your husband's not moving," she guessed, knowing she shouldn't pry but unable to let it go.

"No." It was a whisper. "We've separated."

Adria's wolf felt as if it had been kicked with steel-toed boots, was broken and bleeding as her world crashed down around her, but her voice sounded oddly calm. "I'm sorry." She understood the hurt that came with the collapse of a long-term relationship, couldn't not feel compassion, even toward a woman who threatened to steal everything from her. "It's final?"

Lisette turned her head toward the window, her hair a pale gold in the sunlight. "The last words he spoke to me were about a divorce." A bleak confession. "I never knew how easy it was to dissolve a marriage."

The other woman's despair was a black wave, and Adria knew Lisette's love for her husband hadn't died, just been badly bruised. Riaz deserved more, deserved a woman who'd give him everything . . . but Lisette was his *mate*. And she was now free.

Adria wasn't sure how she managed to function the rest of the drive to Lisette's hotel. Her good-bye was curt enough that the Alliance liaison gave her a concerned look, but Adria was barely keeping it together—she didn't have enough goodness in her to be gentle with the other woman's pain. Leaving before Lisette could ask her what was wrong, she drove with single-minded focus to SnowDancer land, parked the vehicle in a heavily wooded section, braced her hands on the steering wheel and screamed . . . until her sobs robbed her of breath, shattering her to pieces from the inside out, the pain in her chest nothing to the one in her heart.

No matter if Lisette remained in love with her husband, she was Riaz's mate. Adria would've fought for her black wolf with everything in her against any other opponent, but that single fact couldn't be altered, couldn't be wished away. It wasn't coincidence that Lisette found herself wanting to settle in California, her actions colored by a connection she didn't consciously understand or realize. Riaz had to feel it, too, feel that primal draw that was the greatest gift of a changeling's life.

But he'd made a promise to Adria, and he wasn't a man who reneged on his promises.

So she'd have to be the one who broke her own heart.

JUDD walked into the infirmary just after twelve, aware Walker had taken Lara off to lunch. It was easy to skirt Lucy's attention—the nurse was involved with a young girl who'd come in with broken ribs after tumbling out of a tree, her tearstained face red, though she was making a valiant effort to fight back the sobs. Still, she was only seven.

Fighting the instinctive urge to help, he slipped unseen past Lucy and the pup and into the room occupied by Alice Eldridge. He made sure the door shut with the softest snick at his back before he turned to take in the patient. She lay with her eyes closed, her hands on top of the sheets, her head angled to the side. Though no longer hooked up to a feeding tube, she continued to wear the thin computronic skullcap.

Her chest rose and fell in easy breaths, her lashes dark against the dull brown of her skin. That skin needed the sun, needed to be burnished. Brenna had found some old photos of Alice Eldridge hidden online, including one taken by her rappelling partner as she came down beside him. Her legs had been gently muscled as she braced herself on the wall, her smile brilliant, the unexpected blonde-kissed brunette curls exposed under her helmet shiny with health.

Nothing like the wasted woman in the bed.

Yet her eyes, when they opened and zeroed in on him, were the same. Ebony, so dark the pupil was difficult to distinguish from the iris. He waited for a reaction, and it wasn't long in coming. "Arrow," she said. "Former."

"You remember." He hadn't been certain she'd recall anything about their fleeting conversation.

"I thought," she said, her voice rough with disuse, "you were a dream."

Walking across the room, Judd grabbed a chair and sat down beside the bed. "Your memories from before?" Lara and the others had become frustratingly closemouthed now that Alice was awake, citing the trust a patient needed to have in her physician. But this woman had incredible knowledge locked inside her mind—knowledge Sienna would need going into the future. Alice was the *only* authority on X-Psy in the world.

A deep breath, ebony eyes shifting to the right.

Following her gaze, Judd saw the water bottle. He picked it up and held the straw to her lips. She took a sip, two, before halting. Waiting until he'd put the bottle back, she said, "A broken kaleidoscope. Those are my memories."

"Yet you know what a kaleidoscope is."

A faint smile on that too-wide mouth. In the photo, her mouth had seemed perfect for her face, her smile huge. But here, her face all jutting bones, the lushness of her lips didn't fit. "Yes," she said. "Strange place, the mind. I've lost me, but I've retained the world."

Her intelligence was clear, even now, when she was so damaged. It made him wonder who Alice would be if she ever again regained her full self. "Do you know when you are?" A hundred years, more, had passed since the beginning of Alice's forced sleep.

"Yes." Such loss in that acknowledgment. "I had parents. I remember them. They're gone." Simple words to describe an ineffable truth.

"I'm sorry." There was something about Alice that made him think "she's one of us," though the scientist was human, and from a time long gone. Perhaps it was because she had tried to study the most outcast of all designations.

The sorrow in Alice's expression was replaced by a quiet knowledge as she watched him. "You wanted to break me," she said. "Any Arrow would."

"I needed the knowledge in your mind."

Alice's lashes came down, lifted, her chest rising and falling. "Strange how I remember the Arrows."

"Perhaps we were the last thing you saw." His historic brethren could well have been the ones who had taken her.

A frown, the smooth skin of her forehead wrinkling. "No," she whispered. "Zaid wouldn't have allowed them to put me in a box."

Za-eed.

Alice's pronunciation of the name, Judd thought, was perfect. It was her acquaintance with it that surprised him. Zaid Adelaja had created the squad, been the first Arrow, a telepath with a ferocious ability in mental combat. "You knew Zaid?" It wasn't impossible—if Judd was right about the date of Zaid's death, the other male's lifetime would've intersected with Alice's.

Her hand fisted on the white sheet. "I think so."

Shattered memories, he reminded himself, certain she wasn't healthy enough to lie. "You'll remember."

"You sound more certain than the lovely healer with the black curls." A pause, her fingers rising to touch the computronic skullcap that covered her shaved head. "I had curls. So many colors in there—as if my father's blond and my mother's black hair collided in me." Dropping her hand, she stared at the wall, her gaze distant.

He wondered what she saw, but he kept his peace for now. Force would not make Alice remember, regardless of how important it was that she did. Rising, he returned the chair to its spot against the wall and was about to leave when Alice spoke again.

"All I remember before you," she whispered, "is sadness, such terrible sadness. It made my heart tear in pain, until the agony took over my world. Zaid . . . Zaid was there."

ARRIVING back in the den four hours after she'd dropped off Lisette, Adria might've allowed herself a little more room to breathe, hope struggling to find a ray of light in the darkness, but then she saw Riaz walking toward her and knew time had run out.

Riaz's smile reached his eyes. "Hello, Empress."

"Hey you." Flowing into his arms, she let the strength and heat of him surround her one last time. "Do you have time to talk?"

"A few minutes," he said, wrapping the long tail of her hair around his hand as he had a way of doing. "I have to head in for a discussion with Hawke about BlackSea."

"Something come up?" Such an everyday question. Such a quiet intimacy she'd never again experience. The next time they met, it would be as senior soldier and lieutenant, not lovers who had become friends . . . more.

"No." His chest rumbled against her. "Just a case of setting up a permanent communications line. We're thinking Kenji for the liaison, since I have the Alliance."

A sharp lance of pain, and she thought, perhaps it was better to do this here. If they went behind closed doors and he fought her, she might give in. But out there, with pack-mates at the far end of the corridor, and the exit not far behind her, she was, in a strange way, protected from her own weakness where he was concerned.

Drawing back until she could look into his face, she said, "I saw Lisette—she told me she's getting a divorce from her husband."

No surprise on his face, just the intense determination of a dominant who intended to get his own way. "It doesn't change this, doesn't change *us*."

"It changes everything." Her voice a harsh whisper, she stepped back, breaking the connection between them.

He didn't like that—she saw it in the flash of temper in eyes gone pure wolf.

Breath a jagged blade in her chest, she shook her head. "Don't tell me you don't wonder, don't th—"

"I fucking don't!" He grabbed her upper arms, held her in place, the raw fury in his voice a wild thing. "I made my choice, and I chose you. *Don't you do this*. Don't you destroy us."

It was so tempting to give in, but she knew that in spite of what she'd tried to convince herself, the idea of his mate would always be a painful silence between them. Still . . . she wasn't that self-sacrificing. She wanted to keep him, and if he wanted to stay, surely it was all right?

Agony seared her blood, her wolf howling in bone-deep sorrow.

And she knew she loved him too much to steal this joy from him. "Go," she whispered, and it was torn out of her. "Be happy."

The sound that came out of Riaz's throat was that of a mortally wounded animal. Gripping her nape, he hauled her against him. *"No."* A single brutal word spoken against her ear.

Tears burned in her eyes, choked up her throat. She wanted so desperately to hold on, just hold on, but in her head played the nightmare of waking up one day to find that he hated her, as Martin had hated her. Her former lover had resented her strength, but Riaz would have a far deeper reason to hate her.

No, she wouldn't do that—to him, or to herself.

She was worth more. She was worth being the first, the only. Not second best, not the one who'd caught this incredible man when he was hurting from a loss a changeling alone could understand . . . not just a trusted friend he couldn't bear to hurt. "Go," she whispered again, brushing her lips over his jaw in a final caress that held her heart. "She's yours. You need her, and she needs you." Ripping herself out of his arms, she shoved through the nearby exit and began to run.

Her feet pounded the earth, her blood thudded in her veins, and her heart . . . it splintered into a million fragments.

RIAZ stared at the exit. He could catch her—the crushed berries and ice and hidden warmth of her scent was embedded in his every cell. He could track her through wind and hail and snow. But he couldn't go after her.

Not now.

Not when he didn't know the words to say to convince her of a love that had come to define him, a love that bore the name of his prickly, generous, beautiful Adria.

"Fuck." He slammed his fist into the stone wall of the den, scraping the skin and leaving a streak of blood behind. It barely registered. Instead of howling with possessive fury, he grit his teeth, reined in his wolf—who clawed at him in a confusion of rage and pain—and strode out the same door Adria had used.

He needed to think, to plan. Because no way in hell was he letting her go. She was his, had given herself to him. He wasn't a generous man when it came to his empress, wouldn't return her heart. It goddamned belonged to him and he was keeping it.

Fighting his most primal instincts, he ran in the opposite direction from the one she'd taken, pushing himself so hard that his powerful changeling chest hurt with the force of his breaths. Still he ran. Until he was in the thinner air of the higher elevations, the sky riotous with the fiery dance of sunset, and his body forced him to stop. Bracing himself with his palms on his thighs, he gasped in the crisp, clean air, his heart pumping hot and rapid.

It wasn't as much of a surprise as it should've been to see a huge silver-gold wolf materialize out of the trees. Hawke wasn't alpha simply because he was stronger and faster than the other wolves in the den—he was alpha because he knew his people. Shoving a hand through his sweat-damp hair, Riaz jogged over to the edge of a stream fed by the mountain snows, and threw water onto his face. The chill of it shocked.

When Hawke shifted beside him, Riaz didn't look at his alpha. It wasn't the fact the other man was nude—such nakedness after a shift was an accepted part of a changeling's life, nothing to be remarked upon—but because he had no desire to talk to anyone. "I need to be alone." It was only Adria he'd allow close to him whenever she wanted. Everyone else could get out and stay there.

Hawke's response was resolute. "Nell saw you smash your hand into the wall—she thought you probably broke a bone and never noticed. What the hell happened?"

His rage simmered, needing an outlet. "I said, *leave me alone.*" Deciding to make his point explicit, he shifted into wolf form, lips peeled back to flash his canines.

Hawke changed between one heartbeat and the next, his eyes staring Riaz down. Except Riaz was in no mood for a dominance display. Snarling, he launched his body toward Hawke's, claws out.

They met in a clash of fur and blood and fury.

Chapter 62

TEN MINUTES LATER, he threw water on his face again, winced. The cut over his eye had bled plenty, and his cheekbone felt as if it was crushed, though it was probably just a heavy bruise. The only consolation was that Hawke hadn't come out of it unscathed—though he had managed to slam Riaz to the ground at the end, sink his teeth into the scruff of Riaz's neck.

"You were fighting angry," the alpha now said. "Made you sloppy."

Blowing out a breath, Riaz flexed his hand. "Nell was wrong by the way. Nothing broken." Though his hand was red and raw, his knuckles scraped.

"You ready to talk now?"

"You usually beat your lieutenants to get them to talk?"

Hawke's bark of laughter was genuine. "Ask Riley sometime." Running his hand over the fur of one of the wild wolves who had come to stand guard while they fought, the alpha met Riaz's gaze. "Adria?"

Riaz wasn't a lone wolf just because he liked solitude. He didn't trust many people with his innermost thoughts, was happier keeping his silence. Except this time, he knew he needed his alpha's help. Taking a quiet breath, he began to speak.

"Shit, Riaz," Hawke said when he finished. "Hell of a mess."

"Tell me you have the answer." Hawke was the sole person in the den who might. "You're the only wolf I know who found his mate twice."

"Have you?"

Riaz sucked in a breath, the pain in his chest stabbing

deeper. "Adria is mine." He would not budge on that, not now, not ever. She'd just have to get used to that fact. "But the mating tug, it's towards Lisette." Though it was no longer a feral, possessive rush, but a gentle knowing at the back of his mind, in itself a strange thing, given that he was a predatory changeling male—then again, nothing about this situation was "normal" in any way.

Hawke's hair caught the light as the other man shook his head. "If I told you I had the answer, I'd be a liar."

"Yeah." There was a single critical difference between his situation and Hawke's—the child Hawke believed would have been his mate had died when Hawke had been a boy. "If Rissa had lived . . ."

"I wouldn't have been the same man," Hawke said simply. "I'd have been mated for years before I ever met Sienna, and that life would've shaped me in a wholly different way." A wry smile. "Who knows, I might even have been a nice guy."

Unexpected amusement threaded through the tangled knot of Riaz's emotions. "I can just see you baking cupcakes."

For some reason, that made Hawke howl with laughter before his alpha shifted and padded into the stream, the wild wolves following in his steps. Riaz's own wolf stretched inside him, wanting out. He surrendered to the need, following Hawke across the stream and even higher up into the mountains. Their small pack loped at an easy pace, the wind rippling through their fur, the scents in the air sharp and brittle with cold.

The beauty of the Sierra Nevada hit his heart anew, and he wondered how he could've ever left this place of mountain and forest, lakes and rivers. It hurt his heart, the love he felt for this land. Scrambling up onto a small hillock formed by fallen rocks, he lifted his head and sang of his joy at being home . . . and of finding the one who was meant to be his. His pack joined in his song, and it was good.

Padding back down, he ran again.

When the pack halted, it was beside a mirror-perfect lake. Riaz assuaged his thirst before shifting, his mind if not calm, then at least a fraction less disordered. Sparks of color beside him denoted Hawke's own shift. Neither of them spoke for long, quiet moments as the early evening wind rustled through the trees, the fiery sky above curling with an edge of indigo blue.

"Are you in the mating dance with Lisette?" Hawke asked at last, scratching the head of the wild wolf that had curled up beside him. "Because if you are, your wolf's made the decision for you and trying to fight it will destroy you."

"No." Neither man nor wolf wanted to be in the dance with Lisette—the idea of it felt wrong on every level, a betrayal so vast, it made his wolf snarl in defiance. "All Lisette and I ever had between us was a possibility." And he knew in his gut that the time for that possibility to come to fruition had passed, regardless of any accepted rule. "Have you ever known a wolf in a relationship to find his mate?"

Hawke took time to reply. "I've known couples who've been together for years to suddenly develop a mating bond. I've always thought that perhaps the human's choice influences the wolf's, or maybe two people come into perfect sync after that time together—kind of like Indigo and Drew knowing each other for so long before they mated."

Riaz understood what his alpha was saying, had seen the same thing himself, but—

"That's not the question I asked."

Husky-pale eyes locked with Riaz's. "The answer is no. Love without the bond, where the wolf *accepts* the lover, rather than being neutral about it, seems to stop the mating bond coming into play with anyone else." Pausing, he added, "Simplest explanation is that the commitment takes the place of the mating bond."

"So if I'd met Adria first"—fallen so fucking hard for her first—"I wouldn't have to deal with this." A situation where the woman he adored thought he was meant for another.

"Yeah, likely." Hawke patted the side of the wolf whose head he'd been scratching, and it reluctantly made room for another. "Dalton might know more about this than either one of us," the alpha said, naming the pack's Librarian, "but there is something else I can tell you."

Riaz waited.

"The choice isn't yours—it's always the woman who accepts or rejects the bond."

"Hell it isn't." Riaz's claws sliced out of his skin. "The

female might accept the bond, but I damn well bet you the male's got to be willing. This one isn't." Once, he would've sold his soul to be Lisette's, but something fundamental had changed in him, his soul reborn from a crucible of shattering pain. He'd survived, come out of it scarred, altered, stronger, a man who loved a soldier and had no desire to turn back the clock.

"It's Adria's face I see when I think of home." Adria's eyes of blue-violet that looked back at him from the faces of the children he'd started to imagine since that night in the moonlit meadow where she had become his. "Adria who holds my secrets."

"You'd walk away from the woman meant to be your mate?"

"Yes." Maybe it wasn't a choice any other wolf would ever make—hell, the idea might even horrify—but no other wolf had lived the life that had led up to this moment. "I've found the woman who's meant to be mine." The woman who had his wolf's wild devotion.

"Are you sure?" his alpha asked, though he'd just given his answer.

Riaz met the other man's gaze, his anger so deep he knew his eyes were those of the predator that lived within him.

But Hawke didn't back down. "You're talking about Adria's life," he said. "You have to be certain you're never going to turn around and see a lack in her."

Riaz wasn't even aware of reacting. He just knew he had his clawed hand around Hawke's throat, his alpha's hand gripping his wrist in a punishing hold.

Pale blue eyes met his own, Hawke's own wolf calm.

Growling low in his throat, he withdrew his hand, his claws slicing back into his skin. "I died, Hawke." Brutal words. "When I first saw Lisette and realized she'd never be mine, I broke into so many pieces I was the walking dead when I returned to the den."

It was Adria who'd forced him back to life, who'd challenged, fought, and played with him until he wasn't only alive but wildly, gloriously so. "I trust Adria on a level I don't even trust you." As was right. A wolf should trust his mate more than any other . . . yet Adria wasn't his mate, except in his heart. "My wolf trusts her." He let that wolf rise to the surface, let it color his eyes and his voice.

Hawke blew out a breath. "As your mate, Lisette has the potential to earn an even deeper trust."

Riaz snorted, conscious the alpha was playing devil's advocate. "And you have the potential to take up knitting." The wolf thought in far more concrete terms, and it had given its loyalty and its heart to Adria. That someone else *might* be a better fit, even when that someone else promised to be its mate? It was a pointless consideration.

A quiet nod, an acceptance. "What're you going to do?"

"Convince Adria I mean what I say." He'd accept no other outcome.

ADRIA made certain she swapped tasks and shifts to ensure there was no chance of running into Riaz. Her skin hurt, her bed a cold place she hated, her entire body aching with a loss that made her feel as if she'd been beaten. She wasn't sure she could stop herself from reaching for him if she saw him.

So when she walked into her room the day after their last painful encounter and found a powder pink box bearing his scent on the bedside table, she thought the rawness of her need had made her hallucinate. Touching the box with wondering fingers, she jerked when it didn't disappear. Neither did the cupcakes within.

"Strawberry cream, red velvet, banana berry, and apple spice." A knot in her throat, she picked up the apple spice one and licked up a fingerful of the frosting. The sweet delicacy melted on her tongue . . . the taste merging with the salt of the tear that kissed her mouth.

She didn't remember telling him her favorites, but she must have.

Collapsing on the bed, she put the cupcake back in the box, her shoulders shaking with the force of her emotions. Good-bye, she thought, he was saying good-bye with the sweetest tenderness. It would've been easier if he'd been angry, or if he'd simply ignored her—*God, that would've hurt*—but he'd sent her cupcakes and made her fall in love with him all over again.

"I hate you," she whispered, dashing away her tears, and it was the biggest lie she had ever told. The lie she told later that day, as she gave three of the cupcakes to Shawnie, Becca, and Ivy, was only a tiny one by comparison. "I tried, but I couldn't eat them all." The truth was, she still had the one she'd tasted, couldn't bear to finish it. It would feel like she was accepting his good-bye, and she wasn't ready.

Three hours later, she glared at the polished little wooden box sitting in the middle of her desk. "Look!"

Indigo stared dutifully. "It's lovely. Plain, but I hear lone wolves are sometimes a bit odd with their idea of gifts."

"Plain?" Incensed—with who, she didn't know—Adria began to take the box apart.

Indigo leaned in close to watch the demolition, her eyes wide. "It's a puzzle!" Delight had her reaching for a piece.

Adria slapped away her hand. "You have to do it in the exact order or . . . you won't see this." A miniature representation of the Colosseum hidden in the center, complete with carved archways and the suggestion of tiered internal architecture.

Indigo rubbed her finger carefully down the glossy wood. "This is . . . wow. I've never seen a wooden puzzle this complicated."

He'd created it for her, Adria thought, because he knew she liked puzzles, had to have been working on it for a while.

"Why Rome?"

Empress. "Never mind that," Adria said, reassembling the box under Indigo's fascinated gaze. "He's not listening to me." The stubborn wolf wasn't saying good-bye with dignity and grace, he was *courting* her. Outrageously.

"Adria, darling," Indigo said slowly. "You do realize you're talking about a dominant male? Since when do they listen to anyone once they've made up their minds?"

"You're not helping."

"You know"—a look of glee—"now I understand why everyone had so much fun watching Drew drive me insane."

Grabbing the cupcake she'd brought to the office, Adria took a big bite. If Riaz thought she was going to soften and melt under his charm offensive and forget the painfully real chasm that divided them, he didn't know her . . . but he did apparently know of her love of Italian opera, a vaguely guilty secret she'd shared with no one, and the very *un*sensible reason why she'd learned the language.

Two tickets to *La Bohème* greeted her that night, tucked into the corner of her vanity mirror. Her heart leapt, but determined to make him see reason, she took the tickets and pinned them to the board in the senior soldiers' break room. No one made any effort to claim them, in spite of the fact they were for highly coveted seats.

"None of us are insane enough to piss off a lone wolf," Simran said when she found Adria glaring at the tickets the next day. "Especially when said lone wolf made it a point to say he'd hunt down and bury the person who dared take any gifts meant for you."

Ignoring the fact the other woman's eyes were bright with humor, Adria ripped off the tickets and stalked to Riaz's office. He wasn't there—she wasn't sure if she was relieved at not having to test her strength of will where he was concerned, or cheated at being robbed of the knock-down, drag-out fight she'd been anticipating.

Borrowing a hammer from Walker Lauren, she pounded the tickets into the office door with a nail. Hawke, passing by, helpfully held the tickets in place while she hammered the nail. He didn't say a word, his expression so bland it was clear he was highly amused.

Riaz didn't say anything either.

He just snuck back into her room and tucked the abused tickets back in place. On top of the vanity, he left a gaily wrapped box. Unable to resist unwrapping it, she found a shiny new tool kit, complete with a personalized purple hammer. Her wolf was so charmed, it took her a second to focus and see what he'd done.

The hammer was personalized all right—with the name "Adria Delgado."

"Oh, Riaz," she whispered, "what're you doing to me?"

Chapter 63

KALEB KNEW THE Arrows had a discreet watch on him, but he had long ago perfected the ability to move through the Net undetected, and he used that ability now. He was too close to locating his target to allow any obstruction or delay.

Anyone who tried to stop him would soon discover that unlike the others who had once been Council, he didn't mind getting blood on his hands.

Chapter 64

DEEPLY SATISFIED WITH the fact that he'd forced Adria to play with him, even if she might not see things in the same light, Riaz went looking for Dalton the next morning. Hawke's thought was a good one—the Librarian carried the pack's history in his mind, might well know of an analogous situation, information that could aid Riaz in his campaign to convince Adria that what they had was right, was true. He'd take all the support he could get if it would help him court his empress back into his arms.

When he arrived at Dalton's study, it was to find a note on the elder's door saying he was at his "lake office." Smiling, Riaz jogged down to the edge of the lake nearest the den, aware Lara's grandfather liked to sit not on the pebbled shore, but up on the grassy verge, beneath the spreading branches of a thickly leafed oak.

"We're contemporaries of a sort," he'd once said to Riaz, patting the trunk of the still-growing tree. "Though I fear she'll outlast me."

Now, he raised his fox brown gaze as Riaz appeared out of the trees. "Ah, there you are," the Librarian said, as if he'd been expecting the visit. "Come and talk to me, Mr. Delgado."

Riaz's wolf sat straight up, reminded of a hundred childhood scrapes. "You only ever used our last names when we were in trouble."

Dalton's dark skin shimmered with warmth, his eyes dancing. "You have the same look to you today," he said. "What have you done, pup?"

Taking a seat beside the elder, Riaz told him everything, aware he couldn't hide the truth if he wanted Dalton to understand a situation that should've been an impossibility. After he finished, Dalton sighed, his gaze on the lake. "Look at it, so smooth, with only the faintest of ripples."

"The wind's calm this morning."

Dalton said nothing for a long time, until those who had not grown up with his presence would have believed him asleep. Riaz knew better, understood the white-haired elder saw everything with those bright eyes he'd bequeathed his granddaughter.

"The Territorial Wars were a storm," Dalton said at last, "creating a thousand ripples. Shattering everything that should be."

Including, Riaz understood with a painful burst of raw hope, the normal rules when it came to courtship and mating.

"Records from that time are fragmented at best," Dalton continued. "Many Librarians were killed in the fighting, while others made the choice to begin anew when the postwar packs were founded."

Riaz thought back to his history lessons as a boy, recalled that decimated by the bloodshed, a number of packs had amalgamated across the country, each group choosing a new name to represent their varied membership. "So a lot of the records made during the wars may have been destroyed?" Regardless of his intense frustration at coming up against the roadblock, he could understand the survivors' desire to leave the horror of war in the past—especially when some of those who had amalgamated had once been bitter enemies.

"Yes." Dalton put his hand on Riaz's shoulder, squeezed. "But some believed as I do, that the past must not be forgotten, no matter if it is the Librarian alone who knows the truth. Those records exist." Squeezing again, his fingers strong despite their apparently gnarled state, he dropped his hand back into his lap. "Even in war, the rejection of a mate was a rare thing. More often, when it happened to combatants on opposite sides of the line, the choice was made to come together, to attempt to effect peace. Sometimes, it worked. Other times . . ."

"They failed, were executed," Riaz guessed.

"No," Dalton answered, to his surprise. "Mating is so precious a gift that even warring alphas would not execute those of their packs who bonded with the enemy—but such bonded could not be allowed to remain in either pack. The mated can keep no secrets from one another."

Riaz thought of Mercy and Riley, and the impossibility of the pair remaining part of their respective packs if Snow-Dancer and DarkRiver went to war. "It would've been hell." To walk away from your pack was no easy thing, not for a wolf.

"Especially for the most dominant, the wolves the packs desperately needed to protect their vulnerable. The one unambiguous case I know of where two changelings who felt the mating urge chose to reject one another involved enemy lieutenants."

Riaz's wolf lowered its head, comprehending the agony that had to have torn those two apart. Mating was a joy every changeling hoped for, but protecting those under their care was as primal a drive. No dominant could walk away from that duty and live with himself—the guilt would poison any relationship. "What happened?" It was a crucial question.

Dalton rubbed a fallen oak leaf between his fingertips. "The records aren't as clear on that, but there are hints the nascent bond may have broken under the force of the dual repudiation."

The ember of hope within Riaz flared brighter—Lisette's

continued and deep love for Emil was as much a rejection as Riaz's conscious one, their situation not so very different from Dalton's lieutenants. "So they were able to bond with other people?" To have the chance to mate with Adria . . .

Dalton's smile was sad. "We'll never know—they both died in the final battles." Glancing at Riaz, he shook his head. "Such disappointment. You wanted a road to follow, but all I give you are ghosts and shadows."

Shoving his hands through his hair, Riaz rose to his feet, paced across the pebbles and to the water's edge before walking back to crouch beside Dalton. "There is no *reason* for the female to have a choice if it means nothing," he said at last, because while Dalton would share information, he had always made his students find the answers to their own questions.

"Yes." Wrinkles fanned out from the corners of the Librarian's eyes. "Perhaps you will be the one who solves this riddle, eh, Riaz? It is ever the lone wolf's task to journey into the unknown alone."

"I'm not alone," Riaz said at once, the words requiring no thought. "Adria walks beside me." Even if the stubborn she-wolf didn't see it yet.

Dalton smiled. "So."

And Riaz understood that while a mate bond would be an incredible happiness, the lack of it did nothing to diminish his love for Adria, his wolf's devotion absolute. "Call me a fool and be done with it then," he said to the elder who saw the present and past both with crystal clarity.

Reaching out, Dalton instead patted Riaz's cheek as he'd once patted the tree trunk. "Go court the one you have chosen, pup, and leave an old man to his ruminations."

IT wasn't until Adria walked into the garage that night—two days after Riaz began his relentless pursuit—that she realized she'd been outflanked. "I thought I was on watch with Sam." The tiny carving this obstinate wolf had left sitting in her locker earlier, of a hilariously drunken skunk, burned a hole in her pocket.

"I'll only give you so much space," Riaz said, his smile dangerous, "and you've used up your quota."

She didn't tell him he was an arrogant S.O.B. who had a store of impossible charm, and she didn't wrap her starved body around him until nothing hurt anymore. Instead, she got into the SUV and said, "I didn't have a chance to read the entire brief." Three of her kids had been pulled into the principal's office—proof that being submissive didn't mean good behavior. She'd spent the past two hours getting to the bottom of things. "Anything I need to know about this particular anchor or the location?"

"No, it's standard." A pause. "Hold on." The SUV shuddered over a hole in the road.

Ignoring the jolt, Adria pulled out her mini datapad. "I better scan it anyway—I'd tell off my trainees if they skipped homework." She focused, managed to absorb the material, but when she tried to carry on and catch up on the pack-wide senior soldiers bulletin, it proved a failed effort. She couldn't turn off her wolf's awareness of the male in the passenger seat, the one who *did not belong to her*, regardless of the unexpected, wonderful battle he was waging.

"I saw Lisette yesterday," he said without warning.

The words in front of her blurred. "How is she?"

"Not in love with me." The words were hard, making it clear that courtship or not, his anger had in no way dimmed.

It somehow hit her deeper, that even though he was so mad at her, he continued to want her, continued to court her.

"Which is great," he added, "because I'm not in love with her either."

"Give it time." Love and the mating bond were interlocked for every mated couple she'd ever met—she wasn't going to fool herself by pretending they would be the exception that proved the rule.

"God you're obstinate." It was a snarl. "Must make me a masochist that I like that about you."

Her wolf bared its canines, charmed but trying not to allow it to matter. "I only get worse the more you know me. Consider it a lucky escape."

The smile Riaz shot her was feral. "I'm not the one thinking of escape—and just in case you haven't figured it out, I'm not about to let you succeed."

With that warning, he brought the SUV to a stop in the

drive of a small home tucked neatly in the Presidio, enough land around it that the place must've cost a substantial sum.

Stepping out of the vehicle, she circled around the front. Riaz met her there, curling his fingers around her upper arm when she would've moved past. She jerked, the spark of contact explosive. "I'm not going to leave," he murmured, his breath hot against her lips, "and I'm not going to change my mind, so get used to having to deal with me."

Hope was a tiny light in her heart she no longer had the willpower to stamp out. "We have a job to do." Practical words, but her voice held a vulnerability that terrified her—especially when she saw Riaz's eyes turn night-glow and knew he'd heard it, too.

SIENNA stopped on a promontory, looking out over the land below. It was her second day in a row on the routine task of running perimeter security—though Riley made sure her routes remained erratic—but she didn't mind. As she'd said to Hawke, this time around, it was how she could help the pack.

"Anchor watch isn't much more exciting," Riordan had said to her as he left tonight to act as backup to two senior soldiers, no novices having been posted as main guards. "Mostly they just sit there working or reading or sleeping."

"Maria said you had a good story about your first anchor."

"Oh yeah, that's the one who kept watching me as if she was waiting for me to grow fangs and try to eat her. I couldn't help it—I used my claws to scratch my nose. Her eyes almost popped out of their sockets."

Smiling at the memory, she wondered if those in the PsyNet would have offered another group such help. Once, she would've said no. But now . . . Though Nikita Duncan and Anthony Kyriakus might have helped defend San Francisco out of their own self-interest, stories had come in, in the aftermath of the battle, that told of ordinary Psy helping their fellow man, regardless of race.

A DarkRiver soldier had fallen in combat, been dragged inside by two elderly Psy women while they held back his attackers using their combined telepathic abilities. One of the humans DarkRiver knew well had told of how his son, a curious little boy, had snuck outside and down a block to peek at the jet-choppers dropping Pure Psy operatives from the sky.

Out of his mind with worry, his father had been getting ready to head out into danger to search for the missing child when a Psy neighbor—one of three students sharing an apartment—called to say he was safe. They'd snatched the boy off the street and hidden him in their home, protecting his mind from the psychic strikes the operatives had thrust out as a defensive measure while they landed.

It would've been safer for those students, the elderly twosome, to stay inside. After all, neither an injured soldier nor a small child could offer them any tactical advantage. But they hadn't remained behind closed doors, safe. They'd helped for no reason except that it was the right thing to do.

A brush of fur against her leg, that of the wolf who'd appeared out of the trees.

Hawke didn't have much time with everything that was going on, but he always found her during her shifts, even if it was only for a few minutes at a time.

Crouching down beside his proud head, she ran her fingers through the silver-gold of his fur. "When I think of the stories that came out of the battle, it makes me proud to be Psy."

The wolf angled his head, his eyes piercing in the dark. She laughed, able to read the affronted expression on his face as if he'd spoken. "Yes, I'm a SnowDancer," she said, because this was her family, her pack, her home, "but I'm a Psy Snow-Dancer."

The wolf considered this before turning his muzzle and nipping very, very carefully at her jaw, those lethally sharp teeth not even bruising her skin. Laughing again, she rubbed her nose against his. "Thanks so much, Your Wolfiness," she said, knowing that had been his way of saying her decision to call herself a Psy SnowDancer was acceptable.

A growl rumbled out of his chest, and she immediately recognized that it wasn't the playful one he used with her when he wasn't serious. This one was very, very, *very* serious. Every sense on alert, she rose to her feet, telepathically scanning the area at the same time.

"Intruders," she said a second later, moving with as much

stealth as possible beside her wolf as he padded toward their prey. "Psy mental shields."

"Wait." Crouching again, she used another sub-vocal whisper to convey what she'd sensed. "They're scanning the area. They have to know I'm here." Not her personally, but a mind with a Psy fingerprint. "I'm not sure if they know about you." Sienna could sense the subtle but critical differences between the mind of a feral wolf and that of a changeling, but she'd been in SnowDancer for years—most of her race didn't have that advantage.

The pale eyes of a husky or a bird of prey met hers, the glance both protective and adamant. They'd been mated only a short time, hadn't yet learned all of each other's subtleties, but she understood the unspoken message. And she disagreed. "Whoever it is will know I can destroy him in a split second the instant he sees me. I'll go in prepped."

Hawke's lips lifted to display his canines.

"This is my area of expertise," she said, holding his gaze, because he *would* stare her down and get his own way if she let him.

This time, the bite on her chin was a fraction harder, a warning not to get herself hurt or she'd be in a hell of a lot of trouble. Running her hand through his fur once more, she watched him become a shadow indistinguishable from the trees as she made her way to the small clearing where three Psy minds waited. They were shielded, but she knew deep in her gut who it was that had come for her before she ever glimpsed him through the trees.

The birthmark on the left side of his face was a red splotch, a pigmentation error he'd once told her his parents hadn't had corrected because they'd believed it would make him more resilient if he had to overcome such a thing in a society that prized perfection. Ming could've taken care of it once he was no longer a minor, but he hadn't. A badge of pride, she'd always thought, or perhaps a way to gain a psychological advantage over other Psy, all of whom were taken aback the first time they met him face-to-face.

But Sienna felt no shock. She knew every line and pore of that face, was intimately acquainted with the evil that lived within Ming LeBon.

I'll burn him up and watch him die . . .

Her own words, as true today as when she'd spoken them to Hawke. Aware the two men on either side of Ming, their hands touching his shoulders, had to be teleporters, she considered how exactly to kill the man she hated beyond all others without injuring his guards. They had done her no harm, and she would not judge them when she herself had been forced to be Ming's protégée.

"Sienna," Ming said into the silence, his voice calm, in control, cold enough to burn. "I know you're out there."

No, she thought, he didn't. He was simply taking a calculated risk that the mind he sensed was hers, having no doubt used satellite surveillance images to narrow down the range she might be present in tonight. From the lines of strain on the faces of his teleporters, this wasn't the first spot they'd jumped to in their attempt to pinpoint her location.

Keeping her silence, she continued to work out the most efficient way to kill him.

"The world is changing," he said, his military haircut exposing the narrow bones of his face. "While there was no room for an X of your toxic capacity in the previous one, there is now. The Psy will need a new ruling council after the dust settles, and you're already considered a hero by many."

Sienna would have laughed at his arrogance, but she had no laughter in her where Ming was concerned. Eyes narrowed, she lifted her hand and looked sideways to meet the gaze of the wolf who had shifted out of the shadows so she could see him. There was no censure in his gaze, only the approbation of a fellow predator.

Nodding, she turned . . . and set the cold fire free.

Ming teleported out the instant before the fire would've hit him, and it smashed into the tree opposite, turning it into ash between one breath and the next. "Bastard's men were primed to 'port." It must've been brutal, holding their minds on the brink of a teleport for that long.

Hawke shifted in sparks of light and color, the wolf transforming into a male who took her face in his hands and said, "You'll get him next time."

It was exactly what she needed to hear. "Yes, I will."

Her mate wrapped her in his arms, the soft pelt of silver-gold that covered his chest a sensory pleasure as she held him tight.

"He actually thought I might go with him," she said, the insult violent.

"If you had, it would've ended his problems." Hawke's voice was not entirely human. "Now, he has to find a way to kill you."

Recalling her dark emotional response when she'd seen Hawke in danger on the battlefield, she stroked his back, his skin hot silk. "Ming," she reminded him, "will have to get through you and the pack to get to me."

"He'll never succeed." It was a growl.

"No, he won't." The wolves might not have psychic power, but as Henry Scott had learned, it wasn't only the mind that mattered when it came to war.

Pushing away from him just a fraction, she stood on tiptoe to reach his mouth. "I didn't get a kiss tonight." He needed the contact and so did she—to wash Ming's poisonous words from her mind, to remember she was so much more than he could ever imagine.

"I don't know if you deserve a kiss," her mate said, his chest rumbling under her spread palms. "Seeing as you ignored my order to get the hell away from Ming."

Sliding her hands up over his shoulders when he bent to make it easier for her, she linked her fingers behind his neck. "Are you going to bite me very hard?" she teased, using words her young cousin, Marlee, had apparently once spoken.

"Smart-ass." Moving his hands down to that ass, he slid them into the back pockets of her jeans.

Hard and dominant though he might be, she thought, surrendering to the hot, wet caress of a kiss he laid on her, her man had a vein of tenderness she was certain no one else, except perhaps the pups, ever saw.

"We have to continue the watch." It was a rough murmur.

"I know," she said, though all she wanted was to have him inside her, branding her, loving her. In the lazy, possessive mood he was in right now, he'd rock in so slow and easy, make her feel every thick inch. "I wish it was a few hours later."

He reached up to pet and fondle one of her breasts with a

proprietary hand, not helping to get her arousal under control. "Patience." Releasing her aching flesh, he stepped away a couple of inches. "You know you like it slow."

"No, that would be you." Already keenly missing the wild heat of him pressed up against her, she watched as he shifted, the beauty of it stunning her anew. "I like it fast."

The wolf huffed with laughter, and then they were running again, the night wind rippling through his fur and kissing her face. In spite of the enraging confrontation just past, Sienna had never felt so content.

Chapter 65

DISMISSING THE M-PSY he'd called to his quarters, an older female who knew the value of discretion, Ming walked to stand in front of the mirror. The flesh-colored thin-skin bandage the medic had placed on his chest hid the majority of the diagonal wound, but he could still see the blistered, red edges.

He'd been only minutely brushed by the whip of cold fire, but it had succeeding in frying through his skin and thin layer of subcutaneous fat to melt muscle and score bone. A second's delay and he would no longer have internal organs, his body cavity filled with ash.

As it was, he now bore a scar that made it appear as if someone had dug a furrow through his skin with a viciously sharpened spoon. The M-Psy assured him the injury could be repaired, filled in, but Ming had no intention of taking her up on it.

Not at least, until Sienna Lauren was dead.

The girl had just proven she was too dangerous to keep alive, even on a leash.

. . .

STANDING on the edge of the property that housed the primary target, Vasquez looked at the Tk who was, at present,
his most prized operative, both their faces covered by black
balaclavas. Low-tech, but effective as a method to obfuscate
identity. Though the Tk would not wear it during the op
itself—it compromised his peripheral vision, and there were
never any witnesses to worry about after he was done.

Are you certain you can evade the guards? The changelings had proven more dedicated sentries than he'd anticipated,
leaving no obvious vulnerability. *The organization can't
afford to lose you.* However, they had to strike soon, before
the impact of their first strike dissipated into nothing.

The Tk took time to study the house, the movements of
the outer guard, the second guard hidden from view in a
windowless inner room, along with their target. That largely
unused room hadn't been photographed as part of the security
file on the anchor, so it was clever of the changelings to move
the target into it—but Vasquez was smarter. He and the Tk
beside him had run reconnaissance on this property before
the Cape Dorset operation, taken their own backup images.

As they had of a number of anchor homes in the region.

The reason they hadn't planted a transmitting camera
inside was because the anchor's home, like those of her brethren, underwent a deep security scan every week. Vasquez
couldn't risk that the bug would be found, the transmission
tracked back to him.

I only need a second to disable the animal inside, the Tk
said at last. *The one outside will not make it to the room in
time.*

I can provide a distraction. He took out a gun. *Will that
be sufficient?*

A nod. *Wait until I give the signal.*

Chapter 66

RIAZ HAD PULLED rank and taken the inside watch on the anchor—since they were dealing with a Tk, chances were high Adria would be safer on the outside perimeter. Of course, he hadn't been stupid enough to actually say that. "You look like you want to bloody me," he'd muttered, deliberately ruffling her fur. "Walk it off before you scare our charge."

Narrowed eyes, the violet tinged with amber. "I know what you're up to. Stay in one piece or I really will hurt you."

When multiple gunshots hit the side of the house, he thought he'd been proven horribly wrong.

Adria!

Even as the rage of anger and terrifying worry blazed inside his mind, he caught a flicker out of the corner of his eye. Claws out, he was moving before the assassin fully materialized. He slammed into the man's body, trusting the anchor to react as they'd practiced and duck under her desk, cell phone and laser scalpel in hand—it was deadly when used as a weapon, especially in close quarters, as well as being the only offensive option that didn't make this particular anchor turn green.

"Identify!" he yelled at the instant of impact, because there was a very slight chance this was a friend not foe.

In answer, the intruder shoved Riaz back with vicious telekinetic strength, crashing him into the heavy desk hard enough to fracture the wood, but Riaz had already dug his claws into the attacker's abdomen. Their violent separation had the effect of ripping the other male's stomach open. Clamping one arm over his torn flesh in an effort to keep his intestines inside his body, the Tk thrust out a bloody hand and invisible fingers gripped Riaz's throat in a choking hold.

Spots colored his vision, his chest screaming at the lack of air even as his ears registered more gunshots outside. *Don't you dare get hurt, Empress.*

Not bothering to try to pull off hands he couldn't see or touch, Riaz went for the weapon in his pocket. His fingers closed on the barrel, spasmed, and for an instant, he thought he was going to shoot himself. God, that would piss off Adria. Spurred by the thought, he managed to grip the weapon and pull it out.

"Useless animal." The Tk used his ability to smash it out of Riaz's hand.

But that, Riaz thought, was all right. Because even though he had no air, he could scent crushed berries in ice, embers of hidden fire.

One.

Two . . .

The murderous bastard's brains exploded in a spray of blood and bone as Adria took him out from behind, her weapon held with rock-steady hands.

Coughing and gasping in the air rushing back into his lungs, he crawled his way around the desk to ensure the anchor was safe. She swiped out with the laser scalpel, just barely missing his face.

Good, he thought, realizing at the same instant that the spots in front of his eyes were merging into pure black. *Shit.*

ADRIA wasn't fast enough to catch Riaz before his head slammed to the ground. Ignoring the mess she'd made of the assassin, she ran to crouch beside her wolf, her fingers searching for his pulse. "Sonja, you're safe," she told the anchor. "Did you make the call?"

"Y-yes." The young woman peered out from under the dented and now blood-splattered desk. "They said they'd—"

Sensing the air move at her back, Adria swung around with gun pointed . . . and recognized the two men who'd teleported in from Judd's descriptions. "No," she said when they went to examine the dead assassin. "Check Riaz first. The bastard was trying to choke him." Ugly, mottled bruises had already formed on the dark tan of his flesh.

It was the Asian male with the sharp cheekbones who came to kneel beside Riaz. "I'm not a changeling medic," he said in a voice that was arctic in its lack of emotion, after running a slim-line scanner over Riaz. "But he appears unharmed. He should recover consciousness soon."

It wasn't what the Psy male said, but rather the fact she could feel Riaz's back rising and falling under her stroking hands, his color returning, that had her pressing a relieved kiss to his temple, his face turned to the side as he lay on his front. "Sorry you didn't get your captive," she said, knowing they would've preferred to interrogate the assassin. "I had to shoot to kill."

"Understood." Rising, the black-clad man walked to join his similarly clothed partner, a tall dark-haired male with gray eyes so haunted, she wondered what he saw when he closed them.

Riaz groaned at that instant, putting a hand to his forehead as he pushed himself up into a sitting position against the side of the desk. "I have the headache to end all headaches."

She wanted nothing more than to yell at him for scaring her, then pepper his face with kisses. "You're alive," she said, her game face almost crumbling when he gave her a smile that said he saw right through her tough act, "so don't complain." Forcing herself to leave him, she helped the anchor out of her hiding place but told the young woman to stay seated on the floor behind the desk. "You don't want to see what's on the other side."

The anchor's gaze was strangely vacant when it met hers. "Okay."

Shock, Adria realized. Unlike the two cold-eyed men who were examining the fallen Tk, and in contrast with Bjorn's quietly mutinous independence, most anchors were coddled and protected, never came this close to harsh reality. "Aden," she said, using the name she'd been given for the medic.

His head lifted, and she realized how handsome he was— if you liked your men icy enough to give you hypothermia. "Yes?"

"I think you need to ensure your anchor isn't . . ." *about to crack.* Biting off the words on the tip of her tongue, she just said, "Check her."

Aden rose with an almost feline grace to circle the desk and crouch beside the anchor. Who froze, her eyes locked on his uniform, on the single star that decorated his left shoulder. "Arrow Squad. I thought you were just a story."

Aden didn't reply, checking the woman over with an efficiency that said he saw her only as a living, breathing machine. He didn't speak, but Adria knew he and the other Arrow had to be communicating telepathically. Finally, he took out a pressure injector and punched the medicine into the anchor's body by pressing it to her neck.

Sonja slumped.

Catching her, Aden laid her down on the carpet. "We can't afford for her to destabilize the Net," he said to Adria. "Her mind will continue to maintain things as they are while she sleeps. When she wakes, she'll have the appropriate medical support."

Adria didn't like the fact he'd acted without asking the anchor's permission, but then, she didn't know if he'd telepathed to Sonja, and the PsyNet wasn't her field of expertise. More important, Judd had said this man and his partner were to be trusted, and Adria had absolute faith in the lieutenant. "We're charged with her safety," she said in response, checking Sonja's pulse herself to make sure she was okay. "I can't release her to anyone other than you two."

"Vasic will teleport her to a medical facility." With that, he returned to his partner.

Pricking her ears as Riaz rubbed at his face a foot away from her, she tuned in to their low-voiced conversation.

"Yes," Vasic said. "Confirmed."

"You're certain."

"Yes."

Realizing the two Arrows were either cognizant of the acute nature of changeling hearing, or so used to communicating telepathically that they weren't going to let anything slip, she met Riaz's gaze. He gave a small shrug, and she knew he'd been attempting to listen, too. Shifting closer, she said, "Let me check your eyes." It was a ruse—she needed to touch him, settle nerves that had been shredded when he collapsed.

"Thanks for the rescue." He sat patiently while she used

the mini-torch in her pocket to determine that his pupils were reacting properly. "Good shot."

Her wolf would've happily gutted the bastard who'd hurt him if Riaz hadn't already taken care of that, but she said only, "You're my partner. No thanks required."

"The gunshots." Eyes of palest brown scanning her body with protective intent. "Are you hurt?"

"I don't think the shooter had ever targeted a changeling before—he was too slow." Tucking the torch back into her pocket, she kept her face turned away from the carnage, but there was no way to avoid the fact that her clothing was splattered with flecks of things she didn't want to think about. Her face, she'd wiped on the clean T-shirt she wore under her sweatshirt, but she desperately wanted a shower, the scent of death clogging her nostrils. "Here."

Ripping off a clean part of her T-shirt, she wiped off the blood that had hit the side of Riaz's face, his clothing relatively unscathed because of the angle of the shot.

His hand touched her hip, startling her enough that she froze. Holding her gaze, he stroked gently. Not a sexual caress, she realized, simply comfort from one changeling to another, one wolf to another. Swallowing the lump of emotion in her throat, she threw the torn fabric into a small metal trash can probably meant for office detritus, and lowered her voice to a sub-vocal level. "Not here, not yet." She couldn't afford to break down, to crawl into his arms and give in to her own rippling shock.

Cutting the contact, he nodded, and they both pushed up to their feet. Riaz was a fraction unsteady, but it only lasted a couple of seconds. In front of them, the two Psy males got up from their crouching position beside the body, the quiet one walking across to the desk to pick up Sonja and teleport out. His speed was stunning to witness, especially when he teleported back less than ten seconds later.

"The Tk wasn't working alone," she said to them both. "His partner shot at the house, then at me when I realized it had to be a distraction and headed inside." Bypassing the front door, she'd smashed her way through a lower-floor window. "I'm pretty sure he was standing in the shadow of the stand of eucalyptus trees out front."

"One minute." Vasic left for the corridor and—Adria guessed—the window from which he could see the trees. He returned not long afterward, holding several blackened pieces of grass. "Yes, he was there. As was what appears to be a jet-powered motorcycle. The scorch marks on the grass make it clear he left in a rush."

Knowing there was nothing they could do to help track the shooter if he'd departed on the high-speed vehicle, Adria nonetheless made a note to see if she could pick up a scent by the trees. It might come in useful later, if they had to identify a suspect. Beside her, Riaz said, "I'll talk to Dark-River, see if the shooter blew past one of their security patrols. Long shot, but worth a try."

"An analysis of the weapon's signature might provide some clues," Adria said, but knew the chances were their quarry was too clever to have used a conspicuous tool.

Vasic's next words proved her right. "Generic projectile gun, mass-produced," he said, glancing at the black screen of the computronic gauntlet that covered his left forearm.

Riaz shoved a hand through his hair, messing up the already tumbled black strands. "We can continue to watch the perimeter while you work."

Aden shook his head. "There's not much to be done here beyond the cleanup. We'll take care of that and secure the house." He sounded as if the task was a simple case of spilled milk, not bone and brain matter drenched in blood. "We appreciate the assistance."

Adria wondered how often one of these men said that to anyone.

ADEN stood at the window in the corridor and watched the two SnowDancers get into their vehicle after spending several minutes by the eucalyptus trees where the shooter had stood. He was interested in whether the male would insist on driving, regardless of the fact he'd been unconscious not long ago. Predatory changeling males had a reputation for irrational behavior. However, this one bent his head toward the tall, beautiful soldier female—her eyes a shade Aden had never before seen—before laughing and allowing her to take the driver's seat.

It made him wonder what the woman had said that she'd provoked the emotional response from a man who had watched Aden and Vasic with a predator's stealthy focus since he regained consciousness. "This isn't the first time the changelings have helped Psy," he said, watching their taillights disappear into the night. "And yet we have never assisted them."

"The point is moot," Vasic said from inside the room where the body lay. "The changelings do not ask for help."

True—the packs were very insular. "It seems all three races have faults." The Psy were arrogant to the point of not seeing the reality in front of them, and the humans, they had allowed themselves to be subjugated and treated as weak for far too long.

Leaving the window, he returned to the body. "One of Henry's. Confirms the Pure Psy connection." Visual identification made impossible by the fact the SnowDancer's kill shot had obliterated the Tk's face, Vasic had accessed the Council's main Tk database, confirmed ID via DNA. An Arrow who had infiltrated Pure Psy had then provided verification of the dead male's continued political allegiance to the group.

"Have you had any success in tracing Henry?" Vasic asked.

"No. However, I have something in progress that may give him to us before the night is out." It was a bold prediction, but Aden knew his own abilities, as he knew Henry's. "He can't be shielding himself—he doesn't have the skill." Henry was high-Gradient, but it wasn't always about power, as much as how the power the individual had was *used*.

"Vasquez must have arranged it through a more gifted telepath." The squad had zeroed in on Henry's general even before Kaleb Krychek made him a priority, been attempting to flush him out. "He continues to be a problem—I've been unable to track down any images of him since his official death." The man had scrubbed the Net clean of his presence.

Vasic walked the perimeter of the room, and Aden knew he was calculating the work to be done. "Did you discover why he was removed from the training program for the squad?" the teleporter asked as he turned a corner.

"He failed the psychological evaluation." It was a difficult test to fail—sociopaths made the perfect assassins after all. "A high level of instability."

"The psych eval may have been wrong in this case." Vasic returned to the center of the room. "He has run things with military precision for Henry."

Aden watched Vasic lower his head, flex his hands. "He is also a zealot."

"Some would say so are Arrows." Blood droplets began to peel off walls and out of the carpet, coalescing into a single red stain above the dead man's body. "We very much were at the start, when Adelaja created the squad."

An elite unit formed to protect Silence, that had been their mission statement. For over a century, the Arrows had ensured no one dared raise his or her voice against the Protocol, believing it was Silence that had saved their race. Now they knew Silence had consequences that could lead to the extinction of their people, and that war was inevitable. After it was over, they would have to find a new reason for being.

The giant "drop" of blood mixed with smears of brain and bone grew bigger and bigger as Vasic collected minute traces from the carpet, the walls, the air itself. If the anchor decided to return to her home once the danger was past, she'd find no evidence of violence.

"Where shall I take it?" Vasic asked, his tone indicating no emotional disturbance at the grim task.

However, Aden had known the other man nearly his entire lifetime, understood how close Vasic was to the final edge. "Biohazard container at the Arrow morgue," he said, and watched as, instead of teleporting the biological material out, Vasic teleported one of the containers in. The blood and brain matter poured easily into the floating receptacle, not a drop spilled, and then the container was capped and teleported away.

Vasic next lifted the body off the ground and cleaned up the blood trapped beneath, while Aden rechecked the room for any covert surveillance devices the Tk might've planted in advance of his attack. He knew Nikita and Anthony's people had already done a pass, as had the changelings, but an Arrow took nothing on faith.

He found no sign of a bug.

Satisfied, he turned off the mobile disrupter he'd switched on when Vasic 'ported them in.

"The room's clean," Vasic said into the silence, the corpse floating a few feet in front of him. "The morgue?"

"Yes."

Chapter 67

"IF I'M UNDERSTANDING how the anchor network works," Adria said, a sudden chill invading her veins as they drove through the light drizzle that had begun to fall, "then the fail-safes connected to this anchor have to be dead."

Brutal comprehension darkened Riaz's expression. "I hope to hell you're wrong."

Thankfully, it turned out she was.

"It looks like Pure Psy decided to reverse the order," Judd told them when they met the former Arrow in the White Zone on their return to the den, his jaw tight with contained fury, his hair damp from the misty rain. "Murder the anchor, then use the ensuing chaos to eliminate the backups. But there's a second, worse option—that they intended to go directly from anchor to anchor in the state."

"Kill enough of the linchpins," Adria said, the surface proximity of her wolf apparent in the amber tinge to her eyes, "and the support structure would've started to crumble."

Judd took in the blood that stained the bottom of Adria's torn T-shirt, her sweatshirt bunched up in her hand. The soldier had tilted her face toward the rain, and he knew she wanted only to wash off the stink of blood and death. "The fail-safes are backups, *not* anchors," he said, confirming her guess. "They can't maintain the PsyNet on their own over an extended period, and even if other anchors stretch their zones of influence to cover the gap, the fabric would eventually stretch too thin, begin to tear."

Riaz's gaze connected with Judd's. "I thought I got it earlier," he said, "how big this is, but I didn't, not until now. Anyone who knows the locations of every anchor across the world, or in a large enough region, can annihilate the PsyNet."

"Yes." The reason no other race had ever been able to use that weakness to wipe out the Psy was a lack of knowledge—only a Psy in the Net, one with access to classified information, could gather data on the identities and physical locations of the anchors and their fail-safes.

Adria blew out a breath. "My God . . . the trust they've put in us."

"Whether or not other Psy do," Judd said, "Nikita and Anthony both understand there are certain lines DarkRiver and SnowDancer will not cross." That core of honor was one of the reasons Walker and Judd had risked defecting into such dangerous changeling territory—the idea of "acceptable collateral damage" was anathema to the packs. Children and innocents *were not* to be harmed, and a Net collapse ended lives with pitiless impartiality. "Regardless, it's only a temporary trust—soon as the anchors are moved, we'll no longer have that information."

"Why are the safe houses taking so long to organize?" Riaz asked, blinking away the water beading on his lashes. "These anchors are sitting ducks right now."

Judd's own frustration echoed the other lieutenant's. "They can't be moved too far." It was a critical limitation. "Not if they'll be staying in that location for a while, and we have to assume they'll be there for the duration." The anchor population needed to remain evenly distributed—too many in one area, or anchors moved too far outside the region, would warp the fabric of the PsyNet. "It makes it harder to find safe bolt holes."

Riaz swore low under his breath, grim understanding in

his expression. "Because the assassins know they only have to search a limited area."

"Yes." Anchors also had a high need for stability, so they couldn't be shifted to a temporary location, then moved again without negatively impacting the Net in this region. "However, the latest update from Nikita and Anthony gives an estimate of forty-eight hours before the relocations begin."

"How bad is it going to get?" Adria said after Judd finished speaking, fighting the urge to wrap herself around Riaz and just breathe in the living heat of his skin until the chill left her bones. She didn't regret killing the assassin, but the violence had shaken her nonetheless—she wanted to kiss away the ugly bruises on her lone wolf's neck, to cuddle into him and allow her guard to drop.

"Bad," Judd said in response to her question. "Pure Psy might've lost this Tk, but they'll find another." Unspoken was the reality that Judd's designation was one of the most unstable in the Net, vulnerable fodder for a group that promised peace. "There is a high chance they'll move on to random targets . . . to people we can't protect."

Bleak and dark, his words made it clear just how many Psy might die in the coming days and weeks, perhaps months. "They won't win," she said fiercely. "We won't let them."

Judd touched his fingers to her cheek in an unexpected caress from this most remote of males, his skin cool from the rain. "You helped save an anchor today, and in doing so, protected thousands of innocents. It's a start." He nodded toward the SUV they'd driven up in. "I'm going to see if I can find out anything further."

A sudden shiver quaked Adria's frame as the Psy lieutenant got in and started the engine. "I need to shower."

"Come here." Eyes night-glow in the mist turning to fog, Riaz went to tug her into his arms.

"No. I'm all—"

He hauled her close, squeezing her nape and bending to rub his cheek over hers. Stubbled, his jaw was like sandpaper, but she didn't care, his skin an inferno. All she wanted was to crawl into him and never come out.

"I damn well am not letting you be alone right now," he growled. "So don't you *dare* send me away."

She had to, of course she had to, but she was weak enough that she clung to the solid strength of him for long minutes before allowing him to walk her back to her room. But when he would've come in, she put her hand on his chest and held him at bay. "No." It was so hard to get the single word out past the violent need choking her up.

Eyes of Spanish gold slammed into hers, the fury in them tempered by a tenderness that killed her. Ignoring her hand and her declaration both, he walked in and closed the door behind him.

"Riaz—"

But he was already spinning her around and tugging off her damp T-shirt. Gripping it in one hand, his other splayed on her abdomen as he stood behind her, he said, "I will never forgive you if you don't let me take care of you tonight." It was the vow of a predatory changeling male driven to the brink.

To her shame, she wasn't strong enough to push him away a second time. Instead, she let him strip her with gentle hands, let him join her in the steamy warmth of the shower and tend to her with a wild affection that broke her heart. There was no longer any anger in him, only a possessive gentleness that branded her as his.

Snuggled in a towel afterward, she sat while he dried her hair, then held on to him as he picked her up and carried her to the bed. Where he cuddled her close and ran his hand down her spine until she knew that held safe in his arms, the woodsmoke and citrus bite of his scent in her every breath, she'd have no nightmares.

"Te amo."

She was on the verge of sleep, her eyes heavy, but she heard the words of love he spoke, her beautiful black wolf . . . and she knew this night would break the last remaining fragment of her heart.

Chapter 68

VASIC WAS A killer. It was what he'd been programmed to be since he was a child pulled into the Arrow Squad. He'd been so confused, so scared. Because he'd still felt then, had known even as a four-year-old that the people who'd come for him weren't people he wanted in his life.

He'd escaped them, too. Multiple times. No security could contain a Traveler. That was why he'd been placed in the "care" of another Arrow, the only other Tk-V he'd met in his entire lifetime—and the only one who had understood how Vasic's mind worked well enough to trap him.

"Don't you feel anything?" It had been an innocent question from a child to the man who would become his father, trainer, and jailor.

"Emotion is a weakness. You'll be Silent soon enough, then you'll understand."

Vasic hadn't simply become Silent, he'd become even more an Arrow than his mentor. Patton had been on Jax, the drug used to control Arrows, so long that he'd become a weapon that was aimed, pointed, and told who to kill. And when his performance began to slip, he'd been put down like a dog.

Vasic hadn't been on Jax anywhere near as long as Patton, and so, in spite of what many believed, he could still think for himself. Jax might create perfect soldiers, but it also eventually numbed the minds of those soldiers. Vasic's mind remained razor sharp, his abilities honed to a lethal edge—after all, as a Traveler, he was part of Designation Tk, teleportation not his only skill.

Now, Vasic turned from the view of the Pacific afforded by this remote headland, the grass reaching the tops of his combat boots, and said, "You have Henry?"

"Yes." Aden's gaze was on the horizon, the sky a pale gray that merged into the black lick of the sea, sunrise at least an hour away.

"How?"

"I didn't look for Henry," Aden answered in an apparent paradox. "I looked for medics trained in treating severe burn injuries who'd disappeared off the grid."

And that was why, Vasic thought, Aden led the Arrows. "Send me the markers for the teleportation lock."

A quiet knock on his mind, a request for entry. When he opened the telepathic channel, Aden sent him detailed images of the sterile glass chamber in which Henry lay, his body scarred by X-fire. *The medic from whose mind I took the images will not sound the alarm—he has no awareness that I infiltrated his shields.*

"Henry," Aden added aloud, "has never thought long term, so the fact he left his medics unshielded was a foreseeable error, but I expected better from Vasquez."

Vasic considered what they knew of the man who was Henry's general, weighed it against his acts to date. "No matter what he believes, reason alone doesn't drive him." And such a man made mistakes. "What about Ming?"

They both knew Henry had had help in his more recent military activities—the former Councilor wasn't creative enough to have come up with strategies such as the sonic weapon that had turned the changelings' sensitive hearing against them. It was impossible to prove if Ming had also had a hand in the evolution of the idea to cripple the Net by murdering anchors, but the likelihood was high.

"We risk a fatal Net cascade if we eliminate two former Councilors so close together," Aden said, his hair lifting in the salt-laced wind coming off the crashing waves.

Not every Council death, Vasic knew, had such an impact. It depended on the surrounding circumstances. Marshall Hyde's assassination had caused a minor ripple at most. However, right now, the devastation in Cape Dorset had the populace reeling. Another shock could shatter a number of fragile minds. However— "Henry is already dead as far as most people are concerned."

"Exactly. His execution should leave the Net relatively unscathed."

"When do you want me to finish the job?"

Aden's eyes met his, the dark brown irises having a sense of life in them that Vasic no longer saw in his own. "I'm not your controller, Vasic. If we're to do this, we'll do it together."

"That's not rational. It heightens the risk of discovery."

"Perhaps," Aden said quietly, "we shouldn't always be so rational. Judd wasn't rational when he gave up everything on the slim chance that his family would find sanctuary with SnowDancer, and he has a life."

While they existed.

Vasic knew he would never have a life like Judd, was too damaged, but Aden had a chance. "I'll get it done," he said, and teleported out before the other man could stop him.

Arriving at his quarters, he pulled a black cloak around his body, the hood over his head, tugging the cowl forward until it shaded his face to dark invisibility. There was no need to give Henry's men, Vasquez in particular, a specific target—the more confusion, the less effective Pure Psy would become.

A heartbeat of concentration on the images Aden had retracted from the mind of the burns specialist, and he was standing beside Henry's sleeping form, the teleport so precise the air didn't stir, the proximity alarms quiet. Shadows filled the muted light of the room, until he was simply another part of the darkness.

The technician beyond the glass had no inkling of an intruder, his eyes on a monitor. Teleporting behind him, Vasic disabled the older man with a simple, painless nerve pinch that would keep him under for approximately an hour, before returning to the glass room filled with the hushed pump of the machines that kept Henry Scott's mangled body alive, his breath a harsh, repetitive wheeze.

X-fire wasn't like normal fire, the damage it caused so extensive and deep it wasn't always possible to totally repair. Henry, he saw, had lost his legs, part of an arm. The limbs must have been brushed by the cold fire and disintegrated before the former Councilor was 'ported out. Part of his stomach was visible through the medical gown, the teak color of his flesh appearing to be merged with the melted and bubbled black of some kind of plas. His face was relatively unscathed—except for the burn across his cheek and mouth that had taken his lips. Perhaps enough of a change to stop a teleporter who locked on to people as well as places, if Henry's shields hadn't been so strong.

Seeing this would disturb Sienna Lauren.

It was an abrupt thought, about a girl he'd met only once—when he'd reported in to Ming as an eighteen-year-old newly minted Arrow. She'd been a child, with a look in her eyes he'd recognized on a visceral level. His response to her had been one of the first signs that he wasn't Patton and never would be, the knowledge a gift that had allowed him to survive this long.

Now, having been watching the heart monitor, he glanced down . . . to see the former Councilor's eyes staring up at him.

"No," Henry rasped, his vocal cords clearly scorched.

"Any chance that we may have let you be," Vasic said, "was lost when you attempted to destroy the Net itself." The Arrows would not let *anyone* shatter the Net.

Reaching out with the part of his mind that wasn't as elegant as his teleportation ability, but worked as well, he snapped Henry's neck even as he unplugged the machines monitoring the other Psy's broken body. The use of Tk was negligible, the effect catastrophic. Henry died in the silence he'd wanted to create in the Net, and Vasic stood guard until the former Councilor's body was cold to the touch, with no hope of revival.

He teleported to the headland to find Aden seated on a bench someone had placed there so long ago, it had become part of the landscape. "It's done." Shoving back the hood of his cloak, he walked to the very edge of the cliff, the shimmering fire of the sky speaking of a luminous sunrise. "We must find and eliminate Vasquez to completely disable the Pure Psy machinery."

"Vasquez is smarter than Henry."

"We'll find him." Arrows always found those they hunted.

"I won't let you die, Vasic." Aden's voice was quiet.

Vasic didn't answer, but they both knew Aden couldn't stop him. Once Vasic had paid his debts, once the Net was safe, all he wanted was peace. Forever.

Chapter 69

EMOTIONALLY BATTERED BY a tender, haunting night that had been followed by the possessive wildness of her lone wolf's loving when morning broke—a loving she hadn't been able to resist, even knowing it was wrong—the last person Adria anticipated seeing when she opened her door to a knock a few hours later was Martin.

Too stunned to speak, she just stared at the sandy-haired man who had once been her lover. She didn't know what she'd expected if they did ever meet again, but it wasn't this muted sense of loss, slivers of memory floating through her mind. As if he'd been part of another lifetime.

"What are you doing here?" she finally asked, searching for but not finding whatever it was that had drawn her to him so long ago. In spite of the pain he'd caused her, she knew that in the final calculation, he wasn't a bad person—it was simply that there was no strength in him, and she needed that in her man.

"I wanted to talk," he said in a hesitant voice, his hazel eyes uncertain. "I won't blame you if you say no, but I'm asking."

Stepping out, she closed the door behind herself, the cell phone she'd returned to the room to retrieve in hand. "Let's walk outside." No matter what the status of her relationship with the black wolf who refused to allow her to set him free, she couldn't, wouldn't, have Martin's scent inside her room. It would be a betrayal.

Martin didn't say anything until they were in a part of the forest that overlooked the lake closest to the den, its waters smooth as glass today. Several packmates walked along the water's edge, played in the shallows in wolf form, or sat on the pebbled shore, but there was no one nearby, no chance anyone would overhear their conversation.

Leaning up against a sturdy young cedar, she ran her gaze over Martin. He was . . . different, the changes subtle but present. As if he, too, had been broken and put back together, his face holding a maturity it hadn't had the day she'd slammed the door in his face. And his eyes, they were turbulent with emotion when they met her own. "I came to say what I should have a year ago."

Still unsure about where this was going, she simply waited.

"I'm sorry, Adria." Stark words, his expression devoid of pretence, of the stiff dignity that had always been his armor. "Sorry for being a bastard and sorry for not having the guts to face up to what I was doing to us."

It wasn't anything she'd ever expected to hear, but she had the words to answer him. "Thank you for saying that." It meant something that he'd made the effort to find her, to speak an apology she knew couldn't have come easily. "But it wasn't all your fault—I played my part."

"Don't," he whispered. "Don't absolve me of blame I full well know I deserve."

"I'm not," she said, because she understood the courage it took to face your own failings, and she would not belittle Martin's.

"But"—she held his gaze, let him see the truth in her eyes—"it's done with, nothing you need to carry like a millstone around your neck." Her life right now might be a turbulent storm, but the chapter with Martin she'd closed long ago. It was part of a past that had shaped her but no longer caged her. "I hope you find happiness." The wish was a genuine one, for a man who had once made her laugh.

Closing the distance between them, he touched a hesitant finger to her cheek. "I never knew what I had until you were gone." An unspoken question, his eyes shadowed with loss and a tormented guilt both.

"We're a piece of each other's history now, Martin," she

said gently, the strength to be kind coming not from her aggressive soldier instincts, but from the part of her that understood compassion did not have to mean weakness. "In the past."

His gaze betrayed a regret that silvered the most poignant emotion through her, but found no twin. As Riaz had seen what seemed like a lifetime ago, she had never loved Martin the way a predatory changeling female should love her man— until it was a wild howl in her blood, a near-painful craving and a tenderness that burned. Still, they had not always been adversaries, so she didn't hurt him by rejecting his embrace before he left.

"Good-bye," Adria whispered as his back disappeared into the trees, knowing she had laid the final ghost to rest, even if Martin continued to wrestle with them. There was calm in making peace with her past, but that peace was overwhelmed by an anguish that went to the soul, as if a chunk of her self had been ripped out and the wound wasn't healing.

Because this time, she'd loved true.

Until, in spite of the silent promise she'd made not to ask him for what he couldn't give her, she couldn't bear to be with Riaz knowing she wasn't his one, his only. Yet . . . the way he loved her, the way he branded her with his kiss, the primal possession in the rough, beautiful words he spoke to her—it made her want to believe his heart bore her name, not Lisette's.

The tumult of her opposing thoughts had her wolf clawing and snarling, no longer sure which choice was the right one.

WHEN Riaz returned to den territory late that afternoon after handling something in the city, he was determined to continue where he'd left off with Adria—to discover she'd requested a change in her duties that saw her stationed up in the mountains for three days, on one of the high perimeter watches no one but the lone wolves much liked, they were so isolated. The soldier she'd replaced was ecstatic and more than happy to take Adria's shifts on anchor detail.

He knew the only reason she hadn't volunteered for an even longer stretch was that she was too loyal to her trainees to leave them scrambling. As it was, she'd organized two special sessions for them with the lone dominant who had the gift of not intimidating even the gentlest submissive—Drew—and taken a sat phone with her, in case the kids needed to get in touch. A sat phone she'd apparently pick up for everyone but Riaz.

His wolf snarled, but he bided his time, because when he went after her, he wasn't coming back alone. First, he had to take care of another matter he'd been working on in the background—and, given the shifts he was doing with the anchor protection squad, as well as his duties as the lieutenant in charge of SnowDancer's international business interests, it took him until the end of the following day to put all the pieces in place.

It was on the morning of the day after that he drove down to San Francisco.

Lisette smiled at seeing him at the door to her hotel room. "This is a nice surprise."

"We have to talk." It was past time. "About us."

Her smile dimmed. "Riaz, I sensed something the first time we met, but—"

He pressed a finger to her lips, feeling an affectionate tenderness toward her, such as he might feel for a cherished friend. "I know. I don't love you either." It was as simple as that, regardless of the promise of the mating bond that existed with Lisette. His heart, the heart of a lone wolf, belonged absolutely and indelibly to a stubborn violet-eyed woman who was going to make him chase her up into the mountains. No potential chimera of a future could hold a candle to the incandescent happiness man and wolf both felt simply being in Adria's presence.

"Oh good." Lisette's laugh was a bit teary. "Because I'm stupid in love with a man who doesn't want me."

Stepping inside the room, he closed the door and tugged her to the window that looked out over the parking lot below and the quiet street beyond. "You're angry."

Lisette's hand tightened on his. "Furious would be the better word. I know I left Emil, but he was supposed to *fight* for me! How could he just let me go?"

"Look down." He pushed aside the lace curtain.

Lisette's breath released in a soft whisper when she saw the slender blond man standing beside a silver rental sedan in the parking lot. "You called him?"

"He's been in the city since the day after you arrived." Emil was a good man, one who loved his wife so much, he'd thought to set her free when he'd been diagnosed with a rare genetic disorder that would mean years of arduous hospital visits to cure, therapy that might leave him in agony—something he knew would cause Lisette brutal pain. Except he couldn't bear to be without her, had followed her across the ocean and kept a watch on her. "He loves you."

"He sent me divorce papers!" Clearly outraged, Lisette fisted both hands . . . though her eyes continued to drink in the sight of her husband.

"Cut him a little slack. He was thinking crazy." Riaz had tracked Emil down with the intention of getting to the bottom of things, of making the other man see how badly he was hurting Lisette. However, it turned out Emil had already made up his mind to reclaim his wife and trust in the strength of their love to get them through the test to come.

"When I spoke to him today," Riaz continued, "he was planning to storm the defenses, but he agreed to give me a few minutes with you first." Only because Riaz had promised to try to soften Lisette's mood—though until right this second, he'd had no idea she even had a temper.

"Hah!" Lisette kicked the wall with a foot clad in a flimsy peach-colored heel, trying to push up the locked-shut window at the same time. "He thinks he can get me back just by turning up?!" A rapid storm of indignant French as she gave up on the window and stalked to the door.

Opening it so hard it slammed into the wall, she headed out.

Emil wasn't looking at the hotel when she stomped out, but he turned a split second later. Expression lighting up, he went to take Lisette into his arms. At which point, his sweet, loving, cultured wife punched him on the jaw, hard enough that his head spun. After which she cradled his face in her hands and kissed the life out of him, before stepping back and gesticulating in unrestrained fury.

Then she reached down, took off her shoe, and threw it at his head, oblivious to the small crowd of fascinated bystanders. Ducking the missile, a laughing Emil grabbed her around the waist, pinning her arms to her sides. But Lisette had enough freedom of movement to tug up the skirt of her knee-length shift and attempt to unman her husband.

Riaz winced, then grinned, knowing the other couple would be okay. The sophisticated and elegant Lisette the rest of the world knew would never cause a scene of such fiery proportions—clearly it was only with the man she loved that she let her shields fall. Just like his Adria would never allow any man but Riaz to reduce her to giggling fits as she wiggled across the bed in an attempt to escape his tickling fingers . . . or to hold her when she was at her most vulnerable. "I'm coming, *amada*. And I'm not leaving without you."

ADRIA knew it was beneath her wolf to have run, but she'd needed space to think. Something Riaz made it impossible to do when he continued to court her with such unyielding focus. After her talk with Martin, she'd walked into her office to find a potted plant waiting for her, big red bow around the pot.

Queen of the Night. For my empress. Let's plant it and see if she blooms for us.

Adria still had the note in her pocket, wrinkled and soft from constant handling.

Now, as the night closed in on the mountains, a purple-hued twilight, she ran to base camp and shifted into human form, the first watch complete. Dragging on jeans, a long-sleeved T-shirt in plain black, and a gray sweatshirt, she settled down in front of the laz-fire.

The other wolf on watch up here had his base camp at the opposite end of the route, would run the second watch, but Adria had to be rested for the third in a few hours. Even knowing that, she felt no desire to sleep, her mind a chaos of need and want and impossible choices. She had only tonight before she had to return to the den, and she had no answers to the questions that tormented her.

When she caught the dark woodsmoke and citrus bite of

Riaz's scent as she moved, she moaned, realizing it was coming from the sweatshirt. She'd thrown it into her pack from where it had been lying on top of the dresser, forgetting she hadn't worn it since the morning after the midnight meadow . . . the night she had given herself to him.

Now the mule-headed wolf was holding her to her word, contrary to every rule in the book when it came to mating. Emotions fluctuating between frustrated fury, black despair, and a passion that burned, she pulled the sleeves of the sweatshirt over her fingers and hugged her arms around herself, even knowing it was no way to clear her head.

Another whisper of that dark, hotly masculine scent . . . too strong, too fresh to come from the sweatshirt. Rising to her feet, her heart in her throat, she turned toward the trees. Either she was going mad, or the stubborn lone wolf of a male had come after her. God, but she *loved* him. "You have a mate." It was a desperate reminder to both of them, because her willpower . . . it was crumbling to so much dust.

"I have you." Rough, determined words. "An aggravating woman who asked the man I all but stole the Queen of the Night from to babysit it! I'll probably have to tie Felix up to get her back."

Adria shook her head, taking a physical step backward. "Don't be charming." Every wall she tried to put up was melting, every shield cracking. "I won't steal your chance at mating." It would poison their relationship one corrosive drop at a time.

Riaz continued to walk toward her, slow and relentless. "I gave it away of my own free will," he said, his eyes flickering dark gold in the light from the laz-fire. "I love you to distraction, Empress."

Her lower lip quivered, her traitorous heart slamming against her ribs. A lone wolf didn't say those words to just anyone, his devotion a gift he'd give only to the woman he called his own. "Riaz . . ."

He gripped her arms when she would've taken another step back, dragging her to his chest to hold her tight. "Don't." A husky whisper that was more wolf than man. "Don't walk away from me again. I couldn't bear it."

Her entire body shuddered as she fought the need inside

of her and lost. "You'll hate me," she said, her arms locked around him because she couldn't not hold him when he was close. "One day, you'll hate me." It was the thing she most feared.

Hand fisting in her hair, he pressed his forehead to her own, his eyes night-glow in the dark. "I will love you until the day they put me in the earth."

Tears lodged in her throat at the fierceness of his vow. She felt suddenly brittle, as if she was made of the same glass as the tiny figurines Riaz had brought her from Venice. But when she parted her lips to say something—she didn't know what— he covered them with his own. It was no ravaging, possessive brand, but a slow, sweet seduction, a persuasion.

Arrogance, force, dominance, she might've withstood, but this tenderness . . .

"Adria. Adria. Adria." His voice a rough murmur, he kissed a path down her neck, back up to her mouth. "My Adria."

She was only a woman. A woman who loved this man with the heart of the wolf within. She'd fought so hard, walked away even when it threatened to forever break her, had given him a choice. That he'd chosen her . . . no, she wasn't superhuman enough to resist that, even though deep inside, she knew the choice she was about to make might one day savage her. "I love you," she said against his mouth.

"Promise me you won't *ever* walk away from me again." A demand, his callused hand cupping her face, one of his thumbs brushing possessively over her lips.

"I promise." She kissed him when he would've returned the promise, loved him until he forgot what he'd been about to say.

Chapter 70

SIENNA SURVIVED ANOTHER meeting of the maternals to crawl into bed under the fluffy sky blue comforter she'd bought online. Patterned with white snowflakes, it felt so soft around her body that she felt as if she was floating on a cloud. Until it was tugged away sometime later, to be replaced by a far heavier, hotter blanket. "You're late," she murmured sleepily.

Nuzzling kisses along her neck, strong hands caressing the curve of her waist. "A kiss to my many spies, you went to bed at eight thirty." A kiss pressed to her breastbone. "Maternals make your head hurt?"

"A fraction less this time." Pushing her fingers through the thick glory of his hair, she tugged him up for one of those long, lazy, sexy kisses she adored from her wolf. "What did Lucas say?" With anchor detail having wound down as Nikita and Anthony began to shift the anchors into permanent safe houses in earnest, Hawke had gone down to DarkRiver territory with Riley for a meeting to finalize the inter-pack dating rules.

"That we should just shoot ourselves in the head now." Parting her thighs, he settled in between. "I like finding you naked in bed, all sleep-warm and silky."

Lips tugging upward at the satisfied statement, she wrapped one leg around his waist. "My friends gave me some very pretty lingerie as a mating gift." The intimate present had caused her to blush—making Evie, Maria, and the rest of her lunatic friends howl with laughter. "I'm scared to wear any of it," she told the wolf in bed with her, "in case you tear the satin and lace to pieces."

Nipping at her lower lip, he ran one hand up to pet and

fondle her breast. "You can do a fashion parade later—after I'm suitably sated."

"Arrogant man." She nibbled on his jaw. "You woke me up from a very nice dream."

A gleam in the wolf blue. "I'll make it up to you."

He did. Twice.

Lying happily exhausted across his chest, she stroked the muscled heat of him and spoke of something that had been on her mind since the confrontation in the forest. "Ming's not going to let it go."

"I know." Hawke didn't sound worried—his voice was that of a predator in hunting mode. Cold. Focused. Without mercy. "Which is why I'm going to kill him."

Pushing up on his chest, she looked down into his face, her hair creating a ruby red curtain around them. "*Excuse* me. I think you must've accidentally used the wrong pronoun."

The growl that rumbled up out of his chest was loud enough to rattle the water glass on the bedside table. "Fine, you can stand in the corner and cheer while I kill him."

She burst out laughing, and it was the last thing she'd have ever thought she'd do while talking about Councilor Ming LeBon, telepath and a monster who had turned her childhood into a torture chamber. Unlike the man in bed with her, the one who'd taught her to play and who treated her like she was a gift he'd been waiting a lifetime to open.

"If you're imagining me with pom-poms," she said, glimpsing the renewed gleam in his eye, "stop right now." The effect of her order was somewhat diluted by the laughter that continued to dance in her blood.

"Or what?" Unrepentant, he tumbled her over onto her back, but in spite of the wickedness in his expression, his next words were deadly serious. "He's going to die, Sienna. No one threatens my mate and gets away with it."

Ming had been her private nightmare for a long time. That was before she'd been claimed by an alpha wolf who had a ruthless will when it came to protecting those who were his own. Sienna understood that part of him—because it lived in her, too. Anyone who dared hurt Hawke would beg for mercy by the time Sienna was done with them.

"We have to have a plan," she said, speaking to the wintry-eyed predator that watched her out of the man's face. "One so good, Ming's abilities won't save him." The Psy male was a telepath specializing in mental combat, could slice through minds as if he had blades in his hands. "You and I will have to work as a team and trust certain others to assist—the most critical problem we have to solve is how to dispose of him without impacting the innocent in the Net."

Hawke's hand closed around her throat, the possessiveness of his hold echoed by the raw demand of his kiss. "You are so perfect for me"—hot words against her lips—"I'd steal you if you weren't already mine."

Surrounded by the strength and heat and wildness of him, she had never felt so ready to take on a nightmare. "I think we should call it 'Operation Ming Is a Dead Man Walking.'"

A feral grin on his face, Hawke leaned down until the night-glow of his eyes was only a centimeter away. "He won't be walking for long. *We'll* make sure of it."

RIAZ knew he had Adria's heart and her commitment as he accompanied her down to the den the next afternoon. She would never again try to leave him. Not that he'd allow it, he thought with an inward growl. But he also knew she hid within her a deep vein of wariness, and he hated that she was unsure of his love on any level. *Hated it.*

Patience, he counseled his wolf, but when it came to Adria, he wasn't patient. Like any lone wolf who had made up his mind about his woman, he was pitiless in his determination. "I never canceled our request for couples quarters, and it came through two days ago," he told her, feet set apart and hands on his hips, ready for the fight she was no doubt about to give him. "We're moving."

A stiffening of her jaw. "Nice to be asked."

Hackles paradoxically flattening at the acerbic edge in her voice, he snagged her around the waist and kissed her until she bit at his lip to get some air. Grinning at the sting that told him his empress was back, he said, "I'll let you pick the sheets."

She snarled at him, letting him feel her claws, but, to his surprise, cooperated in the move. Since the anchor detail was now at a low pitch, they had time to do it that day.

It was around nine at night that Adria gave a very welcome laugh and said, "You're a menace."

A slow grin spread across his face as he saw she'd found the bear he'd carved sleeping belly-up, a big smile on its face and a bottle of beer in one paw. "He had a party with the skunk."

Adria put the bear next to the drunken skunk on the shelf he'd put up for her to keep her mechanical puzzles. "You have more, don't you?"

He made a noncommittal sound . . . and found himself pounced on, as she tried to threaten the answer out of him. Turning the tables, he had her in giggles, and then he had her sighing and arching underneath him, her body molten with welcome. Afterward, she lay with her hand on his heart, his thigh pushed between her own.

Nipping at her ear, he said, "Are you ever going to admit to the fact you're a maternal dominant?" It happened once or twice in every generation, a maternal female with such aggressive protective tendencies that she chose to train as a soldier. But nothing, Riaz thought, could change the steely core of compassion that made the maternals who they were, that inherent kindness intertwined with strength reflected in Adria's every action.

Her laugh was husky. "What kind of lieutenant would you be if you couldn't figure it out, hmm?" She wrote her initials over his heart, as if marking him. "Nell was faster than any-one else to peg me—she wants me in the maternal cabal."

Grinning at her description of the power at the heart of the pack, he tucked her hair behind her ear so he could see her face. "Interested?"

"I dunno—it's like the mafia. Once you're in, you can never get out." A smile that danced with mischief, but her next words were thoughtful. "I chose to train as a soldier because it suits my wolf—I'm too aggressive to be a full-time maternal."

"You're great with the submissives." Ensuring the health of their young was only one aspect of the complex duties undertaken by the maternal females, but it was an important one.

"Yes." Another design on his chest, this one more aimless. "Working with pups and juveniles fulfills the other side of my nature. So the setup I currently have is about perfect . . . though, I might open a channel with the cabal." Another wicked grin. "It'd be nice to get their input on some things, plus since I'll have a foot in both camps, it'll be a way to make sure nothing slips between the cracks when it comes to the children."

"Do you think Riley had that in mind all along?"

"It wouldn't surprise me—even dopey over Mercy, he thinks ten steps ahead." Stealing a smiling kiss, she settled herself more closely against him and closed her eyes. "Go to sleep. We have to get up early."

"Good night, Empress."

"Good night, Golden Eyes."

He smiled, nibbled at her ear again. "Say that in public and you'll be sorry."

"Now you've gone and dared me. Don't you know never to do that with a maternal female?"

Riaz growled playfully at her. He was happy deep in his heart . . . but not content, because this laughing woman who had his wolf's devotion, a woman he adored beyond life itself, expected him to leave her, maybe not today or tomorrow, but one day. It was a hidden shadow in the violet-blue, a darkness he only glimpsed when she thought he wasn't watching. . . . and it eviscerated him.

He refused to allow her to hurt that way. Fucking refused.

JUDD was unsurprised to see Aden on the back steps of Xavier's church a week after the attack on Sonja. "The anchors in this region are safe," he told the Arrow. Each and every one had been moved, their locations known only to Nikita and Anthony, no backup files kept either on the Net or outside. But to everyone's surprise, the telepathic file containing images that could be used for a teleport lock in an emergency had also been sent to Sascha.

"My daughter's flaw," Nikita had said during the meeting,

staring right across at that daughter, "makes her the lone individual we can trust absolutely not to use the information to cause harm."

Sascha's reply had been as frank. "I'll share it with Judd— he's the only person who'd be able to get to the anchors in an emergency."

"The decision is yours," Nikita had said. "As an E, you have the capability to judge whether or not a former Arrow will use the information to kill."

It was, Judd knew, the first time Nikita had ever acknowledged that Sascha wasn't a failed cardinal, but a powerful one. And because he, Sascha, Lucas, and Hawke all knew that even if the civil war in the Net turned brutal and threatened to engulf the packs, none of them would seek to collapse the Net, to murder indiscriminately, he held the file inside his mind, tucked away in a section that would immediately and automatically degrade if his shields were ever breached.

Only the people who had been at that meeting, as well as Walker and Sienna, knew that he and Sascha carried the files. The information was too explosive, too dangerous, could make them both targets if it got out. Unless an anchor in the relevant area sent out an emergency distress call, no one would ever know.

"The same is being attempted in every region across the world," Aden now said, "but the task is massive, and the majority of cities don't have the resources of two Councilors. For the time being, we're recommending the anchors move their furniture around in unexpected ways and never go unarmed."

No Tk ever used the layout of furniture as a lock—it was too transient. And all teleport-capable Tks had an inbuilt space-sensing ability that meant they would never materialize in solid matter. Unless there was a psychic failure, the teleport would abort at the obstruction. However, if a Tk did 'port in, the unfamiliar layout could grant the anchor an extra few seconds in which to run or use a weapon. "It's a smart move."

"Henry is dead."

"You?"

"Vasic." A pause. "We can't trust him, not after this is done."

Judd didn't misunderstand the warning. "The children in the Arrow schools," he said, instead of responding directly to the statement, "who's watching out for them?" Even with the darkness swallowing the Net and the Arrows' attention, Aden would not have forgotten their youngest brethren.

"The most stable of us each have a group we monitor." Aden passed Judd a small black data crystal. "The names and addresses of the children. If anything happens to us, they are the ones you must protect." A pause. "Trust it to Walker—he'll understand and be able to help them better than you or I."

Judd put the crystal into the inside pocket of his leather-synth jacket, the act an unspoken promise. "Does Vasic monitor a group?" Vasic might not feel, but he had a conscience, would never damage a child by abandoning him. That conscience was why the Tk-V hated himself, though he would not put it in those terms.

"No." Aden looked out into the night. "He doesn't trust himself not to kill if he sees a teacher hurting a child—we can't yet intervene. It risks giving everything away before we're in a position to take total control of the training system."

"How close are you?"

"On the verge. Unlike Ming, Kaleb appears to have no inclination to take a direct hand in the schools." A long pause. "Even when we seize the reins, total liberation will be impossible."

"I know." Without the mental discipline forged by his rigid Arrow training, Judd's abilities might have self-destructed long ago. "But the process doesn't have to be cruel." A young boy's arm didn't have to be broken over and over again until he stopped screaming.

"Some would say such a stance will destroy the foundation of the program."

That pain was a state of mind, to be overcome. "And perhaps we'll discover it makes us stronger."

Aden didn't say anything for a long time. "I have to go. There has been an explosion at a Psy research facility in Belgrade."

Judd watched the other Arrow disappear into the darkness

before rising and entering the church to take the second pew
from the back. He felt the slightest brush of air as the Ghost
slid into the pew behind him a minute later. "Do you know
about Belgrade?" Judd asked while they waited for Father
Xavier Perez, the third part of their unexpected triumvirate,
to finish speaking with a parishioner in his office.

"Of course." No arrogance, simple fact. "It was small and
is being contained, no fatalities."

"Luck or a lack of planning on the part of the attackers?"

"The latter. The facility is privately funded, and about
to begin a critical assessment of the Silence Protocol—
somehow, their mission statement leaked into the Net twenty-
four hours ago."

The fact that any group had gained permission to conduct
such a study was momentous, though Judd had a very good
idea of how it had been done. As he had about the leak. "Pure
Psy acted in the heat of the moment." Judd knew what the
Ghost knew about Vasquez, and so he knew this act was out
of character. "Henry's death may have severed the leash that
kept Vasquez rational." He had no doubt his fellow rebel was
aware of the ex-Councilor's demise.

"Perhaps." No concern. "It's time, Judd."

Yes, the dominoes had begun to fall, unstoppable and
inexorable. "Is the violence necessary?"

"Some things need to be broken to become stronger."

The Ghost left thirty seconds later, called away by something urgent.

Sitting alone in the peace of the church, Judd thought of the
murders perpetrated by Pure Psy, the violence done tonight,
the blood that would be spilled in the future. Instead of
reminding the populace of the value of Silence, the aggression
was nudging awake long-buried emotions, fear so dark and
from so deep in the psyche that not even the most painful
conditioning could keep it imprisoned.

Silence was one crack away from total failure.

Some things need to be broken to become stronger.

"He does not understand friendship," Judd said to Xavier
later, "but I do."

The priest's dark skin glowed in the light from the candles
that were the sole illumination now that he'd turned off the

lights. "Is it mercy to end the life of a friend savaged by torment, or is it a sin?"

"Those are your questions, Xavier. Mine is only this: if he proves too unstable"—willing to extinguish the Net in a rippling wave of endless death—"will I have the strength to execute a man who is a mirror of who I might've been in another life?"

Chapter 71

TWO WEEKS AFTER the attempted assassination of the San Francisco anchor, and a week after the flurry of bombings on a number of Psy research centers and institutions of learning, it felt to Adria as if the entire world was holding its breath. Seven days had passed with no more signs of a civil war that could devastate the planet, but with Judd Lauren having shared what he knew with the senior members of the pack, Adria knew the lull was nothing but the calm in the eye of the storm.

It was all going to come crashing down, sooner rather than later.

As a soldier, she worked with her packmates and their allies to prepare the pack and the region—and to some extent, other parts of the world. Through their allies' connections, and their links with the Human Alliance, the BlackEdge Wolves, the water-based changelings, and less formal relationships with other groups, SnowDancer had a worldwide network that disseminated and shared information in an effort to provide people with the means to protect themselves when the storm blew in.

However, within herself, where no one could see, she fought a far more heartbreaking war. Her love for Riaz had come to define her. She knew that no matter what the future brought, she would never again feel this glory, never again burn with such vibrant passion and wild tenderness. It gave her incredible joy to live with him, to laugh with him, to fall asleep in his arms . . . and every day, she woke up and for a single painful second, wondered if this was the day he'd look at her and realize what he'd given up.

She'd learned to hide that instinctive dart of pain, and today, as they sat on a bench in Golden Gate Park, watching the people out for a stroll among the flower beds on this piercingly bright fall day, she could almost believe that everything was as it should be, that she was with a man who was meant to be her own and no one else's.

"Are you ever going to talk to me again?" Riaz demanded, his tone that of a man at the end of his patience.

It puzzled her. "Didn't we just have a conversation about the toy dog we saw in that woman's purse?" The little yapping thing had gone silent when the woman walked past them, its big eyes watching Riaz and Adria as if it expected to be eaten.

It had made them both laugh.

But no laughter colored Riaz's voice when he spoke again. "We talk about everyday things, inconsequential things." Eyes of palest brown met hers, shimmering with a film of heated anger . . . but his words, they held raw pain. "You've shut me out of your heart, *amada*, and it's shredding me to pieces."

It made her blood turn to ice, her breath catch until she had to get up, to walk, so she could find air again. He didn't try to hem her in, her black wolf, didn't do anything but watch. When she came back down to sit beside him, she gripped the edges of the bench. "I didn't mean to." It was instinctive, this withdrawing into herself, a defensive measure she'd learned in the years she'd been with Martin. "I didn't even realize I was doing it." Hurting him in the same horrible way she'd once been hurt, something she'd vowed never to do to anyone.

Devastated, she willed him to believe her. "I never meant to—"

"I know." He reached out to tuck a flyaway strand of her unbound hair behind her ear in a sweet, familiar intimacy. "And I'm trying so goddamn hard not to push you, but I need you to be mine. Because I'm yours."

Simple. Unguarded. A lone wolf's heart in her hands.

Her chest ached. "I'm so afraid," she whispered, tearing her soul open because his honesty demanded her own. "I try not to be, but I'm *so* scared you'll regret letting her go. The fear chokes me up sometimes."

Riaz didn't do anything she would've expected from a dominant male. He didn't take her into his arms and try to convince her it would be all right, didn't growl or snarl until she relented. Instead, he said, "Look over there."

Following his gaze, she found herself looking across the large flower bed in front to focus on an elderly couple who'd been sitting on the bench opposite them for some time. Adria had watched them take snacks out of a small lunchbox, pass each other coffee from a silver thermos, and hold hands. As they were doing now. "They're beautiful together." Their love was age worn and familiar, a groove worn into their lives and hearts. "You can tell they're a unit." Like a mated pair, one wouldn't long survive the other.

"They're not changeling."

"Human," she said. "Must be a hundred and twenty-five at least." Fit and healthy, though they'd allowed their hair to turn snow white, their bodies to soften. Age sat on them with the warmest elegance.

"It's their hundredth anniversary today," Riaz said to her surprise. "So they decided to re-create their first date."

Wonder bloomed within her. "How do you know?"

A small smile curved his lips, brought that light into his eyes she so adored. "I was eavesdropping when the park was a little quieter. The wind carried their words."

"That's so romantic," she said, her face stretching from the depth of her smile. Maybe one day, it would be her and Riaz on this bench, a hundred years from now.

The dream was one she wanted with her every breath . . . and one, she understood in a moment of crystal clarity, that she had the power to make come true. As she had the power to destroy it, burying it under the cold darkness of fear until nothing remained.

The realization wiped everything else aside to leave her with a single blinding truth: their future had never been, and was never going to be, Riaz's choice alone. He'd fought so hard for her, her lone wolf, and she would fight for him, too, to the last beat of her heart. Never again would she step gracefully aside. Forget about setting something free if you loved it—she would goddamn hold on to her man. Her wolf growled in agreement, its bruised spirit infused with steel, a door crashing open inside her that she hadn't even been aware was locked shut.

"They're not changeling, Adria."

Her determination a hot pulse in her skin, she turned to look at him, his profile strong. "I know." It was a frustrated statement, because all she wanted to do was touch her black wolf, hold him, make it up to him for having been such an idiot for so long.

"What does that mean?"

"Riaz."

He slipped his hand to her nape, squeezed. "Look."

Still scowling, she glanced up to see the man lean over to kiss his wife before he turned on the tiny music player he'd put on the bench. He held out his hand and she flowed into his arms. The song was an old one, from the time of their youth, and while their feet moved a little slower than they might have on that long-ago first date, the love between them was so luminous, it made every single person around them halt, stop breathing.

Adria, too, didn't take her eyes off the couple until they finished dancing and packed up their things to walk away, hand in hand. "That's . . ." She had no words for the sheer beauty of what she'd seen.

"They're not changeling," Riaz said again. "They don't have the mating bond. Whatever they feel for one another can't be what one mate-bonded changeling feels for another."

"How can you say that?" She swiveled to face him, incensed that he'd try to lessen the wonder of what they'd just witnessed. "I dare anyone pry them apart."

Riaz said nothing, his eyes a brilliant dark gold that glowed.

And she heard what she'd said, what he'd said. "We're not human," she whispered, hope an incandescent burst of sunshine in her blood.

This time, he did take her into his arms, into his lap, uncaring of who might be watching. "Does that mean we love any less?" Rough words from the heart of the wolf.

Shaking her head, she wrapped her arms around his neck and held him tight. "I love you to madness." She pulled back, his face cupped in her hands, giving him the words, the courtship, he'd given her. "Until I wake up early some days just to watch you sleep, until it hurts to be separated from you for even a day, until I steal your sweatshirts so I can rub my face against your scent."

His arms squeezed her till she knew she'd carry bruises, but she didn't care. When he would've spoken, she stopped him with a kiss, fisting her hand in his hair. "No more chances, Golden Eyes. You're mine and I'll draw blood to enforce my claim." She didn't care if a hundred women claimed rights—Riaz belonged to Adria and she was keeping him. "I'm through with being reasonable and accommodating and stupid enough to ever let you go. So get ready to tangle with a very possessive dominant female who considers you hers."

A slow smile, the eyes of the wolf looking out at her. "I thought you'd never say that." He nipped at her jaw, his wolf rubbing up against her own with an affection that made her want to shift and play with him through the flower beds. "You're my one and only, too, but you already know that."

Yes, she thought with a joyful laugh, she did. It was in his every touch, every glance, every caress, the pulse of it arcing through her bloodstream. They might never have the mating bond, but they'd created their own bond, and she dared anyone to break the wild beauty of it.

Then he spoke again and the joy splintered into a near-unbearable tenderness. "Heart of my heart, that's who you are, Adria Morgan. Chosen and forever." Picking her hand off his cheek, he pressed a lingering kiss to her palm before placing it over the strong, steady rhythm of that very heart. "Wolf and man, you own every part of me."

Turning her hand to curl her fingers around his own, this lone wolf who wore his love with such pride, unafraid to show his vulnerability, she whispered, "Heart of my heart . . . my Riaz. Chosen and forever." Smile tremulous, she traced his lips with her fingertips and surrendered the final vestiges of her own defenses. "And we're even . . . because you own every part of me, too."

His mouth moved under her touch, his smile creasing his cheeks. "I guess we'll have to take good care of our gifts."

"The best." Laughter bubbled inside her, the sheer depth of her happiness seeking an outlet. "We need to dance."

A raised eyebrow.

Passion melding with tenderness, she kissed him until his heart thundered, until he grinned in wolfish delight and asked her to do it again. "So," she said after granting his wish, "we can do it on our hundredth anniversary."

Her black wolf smiled, rose . . . and spun her out in an outrageous curve before spinning her into his arms again, her back to his chest. "Where you belong," he said, pressing a kiss to her pulse.

Yes.

Retrieval

KALEB HAD FOUND the first clue eight months ago, a psychic tracker he'd constructed and released into the Net. Of the thousands he'd sent out, only one had returned to him. It had been old and crumbling, but it had carried a viable information payload.

A name.

A direction.

It had taken him months of painstaking tracking through the Net to pick up the trail. The last weeks had required hours of intense concentration every single day, the blind alleys and shields formed to confuse a pursuer having had years to mature and morph until they created a twisted psychic jungle. Enough to halt even the most highly trained operative. But . . . no one had expected Kaleb to come hunting.

No one knew they had taken what belonged to him.

No one alive anyway.

Because he'd made it through, and now stood silent and motionless, certain he was so close to his target that he was in danger of setting off multiple psychic trip wires.

Touching the NetMind and the DarkMind, the latter identity still stronger than the former, he asked them to tell him what they saw. His mind filled with an overlay of fine lines across the star-studded skies of the Net. Those were the "blood vessels" of the network, conduits for the rapid transfer of information. He disregarded them to focus on the finer red lines below—psychic alerts someone had rigged in a section of the Net that appeared uninhabited.

Skirting the trip wires with the flawless mental grace of a cardinal with lethal combat training, he continued toward his target. There were more trip wires, more traps, until he glimpsed the minds of the guards at last. But they didn't see him. Cloaked in psychic invisibility, his shields impenetrable, he passed right by them. To find himself in front of the doors of a locked psychic vault disguised as dead space. It had been constructed by a telepath of considerable skill, its effect to create a prison around a particular mind, ensuring no trace of that mind leaked out into the Net.

Kaleb had waited too long to make a mistake now. He circled around the vault to check for hidden alarms that would alert the ones who monitored it. He found five. Dismantling them took four hours of unremitting concentration. Only when he was certain no other alarms remained, did he "break" the psychic seal of the vault and step inside. He stayed two seconds, just long enough to take a telepathic imprint of the mind within.

Dropping out of the Net after leaving the guarded and rigged area with the careful stealth he'd used to enter it, he teleported at almost the same instant, using the imprint of that imprisoned mind as a telekinetic lock. This was the rarest possible method of getting a lock, because to get it, you had to rip apart the shields of the mind being used as a lock, effectively laying the brain open—but the mind he'd seen in the vault had already been stripped, its shields destroyed.

Completing the teleport, he found himself in a small white cell, the walls padded, the glare from the single ceiling lamp cutting. No windows. No natural light.

He ignored the irrelevant factors. Only one thing mattered.

He'd found her.

Turn the page for deleted scenes
from Nalini Singh's

Tangle of Need

Mercy and Riley's News

Author's note: This scene didn't make it into the final draft as it didn't contribute directly to the main storyline, but I think it's a lot of fun. I adored seeing the whole family together, and I hope you do, too!

"Yeehaw!" Bastien picked Mercy up in a bear hug the instant after she and Riley announced the news of the pregnancy to their siblings and their mates, as well as Dorian and Ashaya.

Her parents, whom they'd told before everyone else arrived, and their respective alphas—who had both *guessed* the instant they saw Mercy that morning—were also present in the living room of her parents' home. With the other sentinels and lieutenants scattered over various areas and duties, Mercy and Riley planned to contact them one by one after the breakfast Mercy's mom had put together.

"Hot damn, Merce," Bastien said. "You're having a freaking baby!"

Sage shoved him aside to snatch her away—though neither male was as rough as he'd usually be with a sister long considered an honorary boy. "How about Sage II for a name?" he said, squeezing her tight. "Has a nice ring to it, don't you think?"

She didn't even get a chance to roll her eyes before her youngest brother, Grey, demanded his turn, his embrace warm, his grin mischievous. "I bet your cub likes me best."

"Get in line, shrimp," Drew said, kissing her on the cheek as Indigo grinned and wrapped her in a delighted hug. "He's going to be a wolf."

"Hell, yes," Hawke muttered from where he was standing shoulder to shoulder with her father, a quietly amused Judd leaning on the wall beside them.

Lucas snorted from the other side of the room. "Kid's going to have the good sense to shift into a cat."

"Damn straight." Dorian pushed through to take her into his arms. "You did okay for a skinny redhead, Bikini Babe."

Smiling at the quiet murmur, she cupped his face, nodding

to where Ashaya and Keenan stood with Bastien. As she watched, her brother swung the laughing boy up onto his back. Keenan was familiar with the entire family as a result of Mercy's and Dorian's friendship. "You didn't do so bad yourself, Boy Genius," she said as Ashaya walked over, her tight curls electric around her head.

"I'm so happy for you, Mercy." The other woman took her hands, squeezed, her joy apparent, no matter that she was more reserved than their exuberant packmates.

Snagging his mate to his side, Dorian grinned and held out a hand to shake Riley's. "I don't know whether to congratulate you or pity you the gray hairs you're about to gain."

Mercy threatened to kick him, to Dorian's unrepentant laugh, just as Brenna came over to throw her arms around Mercy and Riley both. "Thanks in advance for my first niece or nephew, who I plan to spoil until you want to muzzle me."

And it hit Mercy all over again.

I'm going to have a baby!

The thought was stunning and beautiful and so wonderful she could hardly breathe. Hugging Brenna back, she said, "I've got it covered. I ordered a family set of muzzles." As the first child born into either the Kincaid or Smith families, their baby was going to be surrounded by doting aunts and uncles.

Brenna laughed and released her just as Mercy spied someone else walking toward them. Leaving Riley and Brenna with Sage—who'd swung by with glasses of celebratory grape juice rather than wine in deference to Mercy's pregnancy—she walked over to meet Sascha in the middle of the room.

Naya, cradled in her mother's arms, batted a fisted hand at Mercy with playful intent. Mercy grinned, letting one of those soft, fragile hands close over her finger. When Naya brought it to her mouth to gum it, Mercy reached out to rub that tiny nose. "You're going to have a little friend in not too many more months, Miss Naya."

Leaning in close, Sascha murmured, "Maybe our children will mate with one another," in a considering tone of voice.

"Don't give Luc and Hawke ideas," Mercy cautioned, sotto voce, "or they'll be drawing up an arranged marriage contract before you know it."

Sascha's eyes sparkled with laughter just as Sienna

appeared at her elbow. "I think Naya wants to come play with me," the young Psy woman said, and made away with the baby.

"Hey!" Mercy protested.

"You'll have your own soon enough!" Sienna called out, making a beeline for Lucas.

"Smart girl." If Sienna had gone toward her own mate, Lucas would've reclaimed Naya an instant later. It wasn't something he could control; his protective instincts were too powerful, regardless of the fact that every person in this room knew Hawke would spill blood to keep a child safe. The wolf alpha clearly understood—in spite of his own primal urges as a newly mated male, he didn't prowl over to join Sienna while she had Naya in her arms. "What does your kitten think of all this commotion?"

"She's a changeling. She loves being around Pack." Sascha's affectionate gaze took in the happy chaos inside the room. "As for the wolves, I think she's still a bit confused about them, but she definitely likes Sienna."

Glancing across to where Sienna stood with the baby, Mercy saw Naya kicking her legs in delight as Sascha added, "Sienna had me show her the telepathic games I play with Naya to teach her the basics of shielding. She's really patient and she enjoys the games as much as Naya, and I think Naya can sense that."

Mercy nodded, then checked to make sure no one else was too close before asking, "How are you doing with the whole baby thing? Tell me it's instinctive."

"Some of it is. The rest of the time, I just hound Tammy for advice." A pause. "I had a mini-breakdown the other day when Naya refused to feed and wouldn't stop crying. I decided I was the worst mother on the planet." Sascha made a self-deprecating face. "Tammy talked me down from the ledge."

"Oh good."

"Thanks for the sympathy."

"Hey, I was scared you'd say you knew everything from day one." Mercy took a deep breath to settle her stomach. "I'm terrified half the time and delighted the other half."

"Normal." Sascha's face was suddenly wreathed in a smile that could only be described as goofy. "Naya just reached out to check I'm still here. Lucas said changeling children do the same thing, but they do it by demanding physical contact. She does that with him, won't sleep until he places her against his chest, where she can hear his heartbeat."

"I remember when Grey was a baby. My parents carried him skin to skin as much as possible." Smiling at the idea of her child up against her heart, against Riley's heart, she felt her eyes burn. "Crap. I'm not supposed to get emotional for a few months."

The scent of warmth, of home, her mother's arm sliding around her waist. "Well, I don't care about crying." A beaming smile from red-rimmed eyes. "I'm finally getting a grand-baby." Lia held out a cell phone with a video call already in progress. "Now that your grandmother and grandfather have told every single person they could find, they'd like to talk to you about maybe coming for a visit, say, for nine months."

Mercy glanced down at her mother's suspiciously bland expression. "No throwing me on Gran's mercy while I'm in a delicate condition."

Lia's eyes teared up—with laughter this time. "God, sweetheart, you'll probably be running patrols into your eighth month. Delicate!" Still laughing, she started to relay the conversation to Mercy's alpha grandmother.

As the sound of her voice merged with the other conversations in the room, Mercy sought out and found Riley standing solid and calm in the eye of the storm. Sliding into his arms, she said, "Our baby will have a great family." Blood and pack.

Riley's smile was slow and deep, the one he saved just for her. "Kid's already got a head start with you for a mother."

Of course then she had to kiss him. Catcalls from her hellion brothers or not.

Hawke and Sienna

Author's note: This small scene was edited out of a larger one featuring Hawke and Sienna.

"Smart-ass." Moving his hands down to that ass, he slid them into the back pockets of her jeans and suckled her upper lip into his mouth.

Breasts pressed up against him, she demanded more, got a nip on her lower lip, followed by a wet, hot open-mouthed tangle of a kiss that had her tunneling her fingers into his hair even as she tried to become tall enough to cradle the erection she could feel against her abdomen.

Chuckling at her frustration, Hawke shifted his hold to the backs of her thighs and lifted so she could wrap her legs around him. He took a couple of steps until her back touched the trunk of an old pine. "Better?"

"Much."

Her hands roamed possessively over his shoulders and chest as their mouths met again, while he braced one of his palm down beside her head, his other on her thigh.

Hard and dominant though he might be, she thought, surrendering to the lazy caress of a kiss he laid on her, her mate had a vein of tenderness she was certain no one else, except perhaps the pups, ever saw.

She'd been exhausted the other day, lying limp in bed, when he'd come in. Prowling up over her, he'd nudged her onto her front, and given her the most luxurious massage of her life, all hot, slow strokes and strong fingers.

She'd been jelly by the time it ended, her bones melted.

And then he'd done her front.

Thighs clenching around him at the memory of how that massage had ended, his fingers and his mouth playing her like the most delicate of instruments, she sucked on his tongue, delighting in the taste of him. When they drew apart, it was only to gasp in a breath.

Turn the page for a preview of a
new story from Nalini Singh

Declaration
of Courtship

Part of the *Wild Invitation* anthology
coming in 2013 from Berkley Sensation!

Chapter 1

COOPER HAD BEEN good.

Very good.

More good than he'd ever been in his life.

He'd stayed away from his sexy new systems maintenance engineer for over six months. *Six* months. It might as well have been a decade as far as he was concerned. A dominant predatory changeling male did not do patient when he decided on a woman, but circumstances had forced patience on him, and it was a patience that had worn his wolf's temper to a feral edge.

With her curvy body and that soft ebony hair he wanted to fist in his hands while he used his mouth, his teeth, to mark her creamy skin, she spoke to his every male instinct. The wolf who was his other half was in full agreement. Both sides of him wanted to claim her until no one had any doubts that she belonged to him.

However he'd gritted his teeth and fought the primal urge, aware that as the lieutenant in charge of the satellite Snow-Dancer den located on the northern edge of the San Gabriel Mountains, Grace was under his protection. His status wouldn't have put the brakes on his pursuit had she been even a moderately strong dominant, but Grace was one of the most submissive wolves in SnowDancer. Cooper knew damn well submissives didn't automatically obey dominants, but the impulse was a visceral one.

Added to that, Grace had been deeply vulnerable immediately after shifting into a new den. Cooper had known he couldn't go after her until she'd formed new friendships, created a support system that would give her the strength to reject him if his courtship was unwelcome.

His claws pricked the inside of his skin at the thought, but man and wolf both knew that if she said no, he had to back off. At once. Because where a dominant female might run to incite a man to chase her in a challenge that came from the wild heart of her wolf, if a submissive ran and it wasn't open play, she was trying to escape.

Don't run from me, sweetheart, he thought as he took the final steps to her. *I only bite a little.* Not quite true, but he was planning to be on his best behavior until she trusted him enough to handle the aggressive sensuality that was an integral aspect of his nature. "Grace."

GRACE felt her heart kick against her ribs at the sound of that deep masculine voice as darkly delicious as it was dangerous to her senses.

Get a grip, Grace. You're being ridiculous.

It was the same thing she'd been telling herself over and over since her first day in the San Gabriel den, when Cooper had welcomed her to the region. Big and deadly and gorgeous as he was, it wasn't hard to see why he'd knocked the breath out of her at first sight. The man was a living, breathing aphrodisiac. If they'd been alone, she wasn't sure she'd have survived that meeting without doing something very stupid.

Like attempting to claim skin privileges from a male she was certain no one dared touch without his explicit permission.

Yet even in her stunned state, she'd known the attraction to be a wild impossibility. While dominants mated or bonded with submissives often enough that it wasn't considered unusual, the dominance gap between her and Cooper was *too* wide. They were literally at opposite ends of the hierarchy— her wolf knew Cooper could chew her up and spit her out without noticing.

And still, every time he came near her, her entire body went taut with expectation.

"Hi," she said, without looking up from her kneeling position in a corner, beside a heating conduit that needed a minor refit.

Akin to the den in the San Rafael Mountains where she'd

spent her teenage years, and on a smaller scale than the central den in the Sierra Nevada mountains, this den had literally been carved into and below a mountain, then reinforced with stone walls. The tunnels were wide and spacious, the rooms generous, but underneath the raw natural beauty of the stone pierced with threads of glittering mineral lay a highly complex technological heartbeat, one that Grace helped maintain.

"Has there been a malfunction in one of the critical systems?" she asked, guessing that was why Cooper had taken the time to personally track her down. With both the chief and deputy chief of her department away at different tech conferences, Grace was currently the one in charge. "I can look at it straight away—this isn't urgent."

"No, everything's fine." Cooper crouched down beside Grace, immediately taking up all available air in the vicinity.

Concentrate on the job, Grace ordered herself, attempting to focus on the digital wrench she was using to remove a fried tube . . . but her entire body was attuned to his every breath, her muscles strung tight.

"How's it going in this section?" he asked, his voice pitched at a level she recognized as "careful."

She fought the suicidal urge to throw a tool at his head. Her place in the hierarchy didn't determine her entire personality. As with every other dominance level, submissives could be shy or exuberant, cheerful or moody, sensual or reserved. Grace might be quiet and a little shy in comparison to the majority of her packmates, but she could handle loud voices just fine—growing up with two older adoptive siblings, dominants who'd inherited a hair-trigger temper from their father, she'd heard more than her share.

"We're about halfway through the overhaul," she said, wishing he'd forget her place in the hierarchy and just see her as a woman . . . a woman he wanted.

If he did, what would you do?

Probably run very fast in the other direction.

She twisted the wrench a fraction too hard and almost broke the tube. "Damn." Cheeks burning, she flexed her fingers, took a deep breath, and completed the extraction with care, hotly conscious of Cooper's watchful gaze. "There. We can recycle the components."

"Removed without a scratch. Impressive." He picked up the component. "Did you get the new shipment you wanted?"

She tore her eyes away from his hands, face heating even further at the raw images that had formed unbidden in her mind—of those big hands on her body, on her breasts, his skin exquisitely rough against her own. Never had she responded to a man on such a primal level, and that it was a man whose mere presence made her wolf acutely uncomfortable? Surely, fate was having a good laugh at Grace's expense.

"Yes," she managed to say in response to his question. "I did. They were high quality, as promised." Hearing a gentle click as he returned the component to the floor, she put down the wrench and went to pick up a—

"Grace." Fingers curling around her wrist.

Her pulse spiked as she stared at that strong, dark-skinned hand so warm and gentle, the calluses on his palm a sensual abrasion. She couldn't speak, the rush of noise inside her head too loud, drowning out all else.

"Grace." Softer this time. Coaxing. "Look at me."

Swallowing, she chanced a peek, her wolf at rigid attention. If he'd commanded, she would've obeyed at once, her nature such that defiance of an order from a lieutenant stressed her on a primal level. The fact that she was changeling rather than a wild wolf meant she *had* the capacity for such defiance, but it would require bone-deep disagreement on her part, enough for the human side of her nature to override the powerful instincts of her wolf.

But Cooper hadn't commanded. He'd requested . . . in a way that made everything female in Grace come to trembling attention. Now, her eyes met the intense near-black of his, skated away. When he did nothing but wait with a patience she'd never expected from him, she lifted her lashes again, her gaze locking with his.

It sent a thrill through her wolf. To hold the gaze of a lieutenant was a bold move for any wolf, but for a submissive, it went far beyond that. In any other circumstance, it could've been dangerous—just as she had her instincts, dominants had theirs. If one interpreted the eye contact as a challenge, it could end badly. The fact that in the majority of cases where such a thing had happened both parties had been in wolf form did nothing to negate the danger of triggering an inadvertent violent response.

Because a submissive would *never* come out the winner.

Cooper's thumb brushed over the skittering pulse in her wrist. "There you are." The low murmur touched her in a caress so intimate, it felt as if she was bare to the skin, exposed and vulnerable.

Inhaling a jerky breath, she broke the shocking eye contact, tugged gently at her wrist. When Cooper's fingers tightened for an instant, her heart stuttered. He released her before the next beat. Not certain of anything, she fell back on what she knew, picking up another one of her tools to do . . . something. Except her thoughts were a scramble, a burn of lingering heat around her wrist. She began working on a random non-essential section of the duct, where she could easily fix any errors later.

Beside her, Cooper shifted a fraction, the single inch he closed between them enough to have her wolf quivering and alert; anticipation, desire, and a good dose of panic all mixed in.

"You don't ever have to fear anything from me." It was a rough murmur, a verbal pet of her senses. "If you want me to stop anytime, anywhere, the only word you ever need to use is 'no'. Okay?"

She jerked her head up and down, her throat as dry as the shimmering sands of the Mojave.

"But," he continued, "I don't intend to go away until you tell me to do so. I'm planning to court you."

The tool fell from her nerveless fingers to clatter to the floor. Reaching over, Cooper picked it up, put it back into her toolbox. "I'll leave you to your work . . . but Grace? I'll be seeing you again soon." With that promise, he rose and was gone, his powerful body moving with a wild strength kept in fierce check as he strode down the relatively narrow access corridor and out into the den proper.

Heart crashing against her ribs hard enough to hurt, her breath jagged in her throat, Grace collapsed against the smooth stone of the wall. "Oh, God. Oh, God. Oh, *God*." Her chest rose and fell in a harsh, uneven rhythm as she attempted to take in air, clear her head.

The effort failed.

Reaching blindly for her water bottle, she swallowed.

The cool liquid wet her throat, but did nothing to calm the fever in her blood.

"I'm planning to court you."

Never in her wildest imaginings had she thought Cooper would speak those words to her. The furthest she'd dared had been improbable erotic fantasies that left her sweat-soaked and aching for completion, fantasies in which they lay skin to skin, her lips on his throat, his hands gripping her hips as he pinned her under him in readiness for his possession. In real life, she'd almost certainly panic if she was ever in that position, her wolf seizing her mind to present quiescent submission to the predator in bed with her. But the hard reality of the hierarchy didn't matter in her fantasies.

Had Cooper invited her to his bed, those fantasies may have given her some kind of a foundation on which to ground herself, ephemeral though it would've been. However, a changeling male didn't use a word like "court" when he was welcoming a woman to share his body and his bed, whether for the night or longer. No, he was *serious*.

Big, dangerous, beautiful Cooper wanted her as his.

Chapter 2

ALMOST READY TO believe she'd imagined the whole thing, Grace lifted the inside of her wrist to her face, drew in the wild earth and dark amber of Cooper's scent from her skin. The complex notes made her want to nuzzle her nose into his throat and breathe deep, until she could separate out the elements that made up the decadent whole.

Even now, the lingering whisper of it caused her skin to prickle, her mind cascading with sensory memories of the dark heat of his muscled body, the deep bronze of his skin, the black hair he'd taken to shaving so close to his skull that she had to constantly fight the urge to reach up, brush her hand over the bristles. Like those on his jaw.

What would that jaw feel like rubbing against skin she bared only in the privacy of her bedroom?

Groaning, she took another drink of water. It didn't do much good. The adrenaline continued to pump hard and urgent through her veins until it felt as if her skin was going to burst from the sheer frantic energy ricocheting within her body, her wolf as dazed as the human side of herself. So when she heard someone else enter the access corridor, her brain seized on the distraction. And when she scented Vivienne a second before the tall, slender woman appeared around the corner, she wanted to sob with joy.

Ice-cold beauty, that's the initial impression Grace had had of her fellow engineer, with her ruler-straight black hair pulled back into a sleek ponytail, and her almond-shaped eyes of brown, cool against flawless white skin. Then Vivienne had smiled with infectious warmth, revealing the joyous reality of her spirit, as she did now. "Hey, boss. I'm on my way to begin the rehaul of the comm system in this grid. The issue with the 7B comm line was nothing but a slight glitch."

Grace touched the space beside her. "Have a break." Critically for both their working relationship and friendship, while Vivienne was a dominant—albeit on the lower end of the power scale—she had no problem taking orders from a submissive supervisor. The level of such flexibility possessed by each individual, no matter his or her place in the hierarchy, was a fact the "civilian" chiefs in the pack had to keep constantly in mind when they created work teams.

Because when it came down to it, they weren't human; they were changeling, wolf.

"Was Coop here? I love the depth of his scent." It was a cheerful comment as Vivienne took the seat Grace had offered. "It's so quintessentially male, you know? If my wolf wasn't half-terrified of him, I'd be tempted to serve myself up to him on a platter." She sighed. "That scar of his should detract from his looks, but it only adds to his sex appeal. God, can you imagine what he'd be like in bed?"

Grace opened her mouth, and the words just fell out, sounding as surreal as the first time she'd heard them. "He says he's going to court me."

Vivienne's head snapped toward her. "I *knew* it!" Rampant glee. "I told Todd not to flirt with you, but would my dumbass twin listen? No! Hah! I can't wait to see the look on his face when I tell him he was attempting to make time with the lieutenant's woman."

Grace blinked at the unexpected response. "You did not know. And I'm not his woman." It sounded so strange to say those words, to even consider the idea outside of her fantasies.

Vivienne waved away the qualification. "Okay, fine, I didn't *know* know, but I suspected. I grew up in this den, was seventeen when Coop took over, and let me tell you, the man might've kept his distance since you arrived, but he's never looked at a woman the way he looks at you. All intense and protective and ravenous"—a shiver—"like he's waiting to take a bite."

The idea of Cooper's mouth on her skin made Grace squeeze her thighs together, even as another part of her yelled that she'd lost her mind. She did not have the tools to handle a man like that—strong, raw, demanding—in bed. "You're not helping."

"I'm sorry." Voice solicitous, Vivienne patted her thigh. "It's just that he's so hot, I lost my marbles for a second."

Grace snorted a surprised laugh and it was a needed release. "You're an idiot."

Vivienne winked, and asked, "You don't like him?"

"*Like*'s not the word I'd use," Grace said, her voice husky with remembered emotion. "I . . . He *is* hot. Extremely." The kind of hot that could ruin her for other men even as it burned her to a cinder. "But he's a lieutenant."

"Is he using his position to pressure you?" A frown. "I can't see Coop—"

"No! No, he'd never do that." He might be rough around the edges, bad in a way her sensible side warned her put him way out of her sexual league, and definitely dangerous, but he was also honorable to the core.

"If you want me to stop anytime, anywhere, the only word you ever need to use is 'no'."

Vivienne nudged her shoulder, one long leg bent at the knee, the foot of the other pressing against the opposite wall. "Then what?"

"I'm a submissive." An obvious, unalterable fact. "Always have been—and I'm happy with my place in the hierarchy." She was needed, her role in SnowDancer no less important than any other. For one, the pups were utterly unafraid of her. In an emergency, she could grab any child and run, knowing that child would cling to her rather than fight.

On a day-to-day basis, and without throwing the dynamite of passion into the mix, Grace and those like her helped their stronger brethren maintain control of their aggressive natures by inciting an intense and often unconscious protectiveness.

Though, from the submissive end, the effect wasn't always by chance.

More than once, Grace had asked an angry and frustrated dominant to assist her in some task she could just as well do herself, aware that the influence of her wolf would calm theirs. Such things were part of the rhythm of a healthy pack. Those packs that lost their natural complement of submissives—whether through accidents or a lack of care and respect—and didn't redress the imbalance eventually splintered, the energy in the den turning violent.

"Always remember"—a warm hand stroking over her hair—*"as we need their strength to make us feel safe deep inside, the soldiers and other dominants need us to retain their humanity. That is why SnowDancer is such a powerful pack. Because one is not considered more or less than the other."*

"But," Grace continued, heart clenching at the echo of her lost father's gentle voice, "wolves like me don't date pack-mates as strong as Cooper." Desire altered the rules on a fundamental level, changed the effect her wolf had on his, his on hers, until she could no longer predict how either one of them might react in any given situation.

Vivienne's next words were solemn. "He makes you uncomfortable, doesn't he?"

On the most basic female level. "He's just so overwhelming." So masculine, so primal, so harshly beautiful. Just . . . *so*.

"I get that. Coop's not a man who'd ever be an easy kind of a lover."

Grace's throat went dry again at the thought of calling Cooper her lover. "It's not only that," she rasped, having to take a sip of water before she could continue. "You remember what I told you? About how part of the reason I accepted the promotion and moved here was because of how overprotective my family was being?" Until wolf and woman both knew it wasn't good for her.

Though she loved her adoptive parents and siblings with all her heart, and knew she was cherished in turn, at times such as this she missed her long gone "papa" and "mama" so much it hurt. Her father had been a submissive, had understood her on a fundamental level, her mother a dominant soldier who'd mated and loved a submissive long enough to have gained an inherent understanding of what her daughter needed to flourish. They'd both recognized that Grace's need to feel safe, secure, didn't equal a rigid wall of protection.

"I see your point." Vivienne's voice penetrated the bittersweet memories of the happy, content child she'd been before the pack was drenched bloodred. "As a lieutenant, Coop's pretty much built to protect." Twisting her body, she faced Grace. "If you tell him to back off, he will. I guess everything else aside, the question is—is that what you want?"

"No." An instant and categorical repudiation. Grace couldn't bear the thought of never again feeling the abrasive warmth of Cooper's touch, hearing that caressing note of promise in his voice.

Vivienne's lips curved in a wicked smile. "Then you'd better find a way to deal with the big, bad wolf who wants to have you for his own *very* personal snack."

A thousand butterflies took flight in Grace's stomach.

HE'D scared her.

The soldier in front of Cooper paled under the tanned gold of his skin. "Sir?"

And now he was scaring everyone else. Rubbing a hand

over his face in an attempt to dislodge his scowl, his thumb brushing over the jagged scar along his left cheek, he said, "The perimeter incursion; you're certain it was just a couple of human kids necking?" Wolf territory was clearly marked, but juveniles the world over had a mysterious ability to see only what they wanted to see.

Daniel nodded, his sandy hair sliding over his forehead. "I caught them myself. Made sure they knew they were trespassing on SnowDancer land, and told them it was the single warning they'd get before we took action." A flash of teeth. "They couldn't get out fast enough."

"Good." Cooper didn't enjoy putting fear in the eyes of teenagers with more hormones than brains, but it had to be done.

SnowDancer's vicious reputation was its first line of defense.

The pack hadn't always been so outwardly aggressive. However, their discipline and focus on family had made their enemies believe SnowDancer weak; the ensuing bloodshed had devastated the pack. So many had been lost in the carnage—including Grace's parents.

Never again, thought Cooper.

"Keep an eye out for them," he said to Daniel. "Sometimes kids like to play chicken." Youthful stupidity knew no boundaries, regardless of whether the young were changeling or human.

"I'll alert the other sentries. What should we do if one of us catches them again?"

"Disable their vehicle and call me." SnowDancer had sole jurisdiction on their land. Maybe Enforcement would've challenged that claim once upon a time, but not anymore, not with the world shuddering under the violent weight of a change that was redefining power itself. "I'll walk them out personally."

If the human pups were old enough to neck, they were old enough to know better than to dare a predatory changeling pack. Cooper intended to give the two misbehaving teens the same dressing-down he'd give one of the juveniles under his command should they pull a stupid stunt. "No one's ever come back a third time."

Daniel grinned.

Shoving his hands over the bristling roughness of his
scalp after the soldier left, Cooper stared moodily at the
view outside his window. While the majority of the den was
underground, his office was located on the highest level,
tucked into a natural curve of the mountain. The glass was
treated so as not to reflect, but it afforded him a good view
of the main path up to the den. Bathed in sunshine today,
the land beyond was verdant with trees, until you'd never
know the Mojave Desert sprawled just beyond the distant
ridgeline.

He liked being able to keep an eye on things from here,
but the lack of windows in the main den didn't bother his
wolves—they loved coming home to a snug den, a place
where their pups were always protected. Added to that, the
tunnels were wide and bathed in simulated daylight and
moonlight depending on the time of day, the air filtration and
temperature control mechanisms fine-tuned to create an
effortless transition between the outside and inside.

SnowDancer's scientific arm had been responsible for the
original development of the technology, but it was the highly
trained systems engineers who maintained and calibrated the
interconnected systems on a day-to-day basis. Each could
handle most of the minor issues that cropped up from time
to time, but they all had their specialties. Grace's expertise
was in the simulated natural light so important to the pack's
well-being.

His hand fisted, his scowl returning at the reminder of
how she'd trembled under his touch. Yes, he could be scary—
hell, it was an asset when it came to protecting the pack—but
he didn't want to scare Grace. He wanted to pet her, hold her,
learn the intricacies of the smart, sexy woman who handled
her high-tech tools with the care and elegance of a surgeon . . .
and made him wonder how she'd use those same hands on
him. Because he most definitely wanted to coax her to strip
off the workmanlike coveralls that drove him wild, and
breathe his fill of her scent as he explored those incredible,
dangerous, feminine curves with his body, his mouth.

A curl of wood falling to the floor . . .

He realized his claws had shot out, carved grooves into

the wood of his desk. "Great," he muttered, retracting them into his skin. "If you're trying not to scare a woman, learn to keep your fucking claws in, Cooper." Shoving back from his desk, he strode out of his office, taking the steps that led down into the main core of the den two at a time.

NALINI SINGH

Kiss of Snow

A Psy-Changeling Novel

Since the moment of her defection from the PsyNet and into the SnowDancer wolf pack, Sienna Lauren has had one weakness. *Hawke*. Alpha and dangerous, he compels her to madness.

Hawke is used to walking alone, having lost the woman who would've been his mate long ago. But Sienna fascinates the primal heart of him, even as he tells himself she is far too young to handle the wild fury of the wolf.

Then Sienna changes the rules, and suddenly, there is no more distance, only the most intimate of battles between two people who were never meant to meet. Yet as they strip away each other's secrets in a storm of raw emotion, they must also ready themselves for a far more vicious fight . . .

A deadly enemy is out to destroy SnowDancer, striking at everything the pack holds dear, but it is Sienna's darkest secret that may yet savage the pack that is her home . . . and the alpha who is its heartbeat.

penguin.com

*An angel finds passion and danger in the arms
of an unexpected lover...*

FROM *NEW YORK TIMES* BESTSELLING AUTHOR
NALINI SINGH

ANGELS' DANCE
A Guild Hunter Special Novella

A gentle teacher and historian, Jessamy is respected
and admired by everyone who knows her. Yet, unable
to fly, she has spent thousands of years trapped in the
mountain stronghold of the Refuge, her heart encased
in painful loneliness . . . until the arrival of Galen, warrior angel from a martial court.

Rough-edged and blunt, Galen is a weapons-master at
home with violence, a stranger to sweet words—but he is
also a man determined to claim Jessamy for his own . . .
even if their exhilarating passion proves as dangerous as
the landscape of war and unrest that lies before them.

nalinisingh.com
facebook.com/AuthorNaliniSingh
facebook.com/ProjectParanormalBooks
penguin.com

M1190T0912

The PSY-CHANGELING SERIES FROM
New York Times BESTSELLING AUTHOR

Nalini Singh

SLAVE TO SENSATION
VISIONS OF HEAT
CARESSED BY ICE
MINE TO POSSESS
HOSTAGE TO PLEASURE
BRANDED BY FIRE
BLAZE OF MEMORY
BONDS OF JUSTICE
PLAY OF PASSION
KISS OF SNOW
TANGLE OF NEED

"Nalini Singh is a major new talent."

—Christine Feehan,
#1 *New York Times* bestselling author

"I wished I lived in the world
Singh has created."

—Gena Showalter,
New York Times bestselling author

penguin.com

M351AS0712

Photo by Deborah Hillman

Nalini Singh is passionate about writing. Though she's traveled as far afield as the deserts of China, the Highlands of Scotland, and the temples of Japan, it is the journey of the imagination that fascinates her most. She's beyond delighted to be able to follow her dream as a writer.

Nalini lives and works in beautiful New Zealand. Visit the author online at www.nalinisingh.com, facebook .com/AuthorNaliniSingh, and twitter.com/NaliniSingh.

ISBN 978-0-425-25109-6

Adria, wolf changeling and resilient soldier, has made a break with her
past to face a devastating new challenge: Riaz, a SnowDancer lieutenant
already sworn to another. For Riaz, the primal attraction he feels for Adria
is a staggering betrayal. For Adria, his lone-wolf appeal is beyond sexual.
It consumes her. It terrifies her. It threatens to undermine everything she
has built of her new life. But fighting their wild compulsion is a losing
battle.

Their coming together is an inferno...and a melding of two wounded
souls who promise each other no commitment, no ties, no bonds. Only
pleasure. Too late, they realize that they have more to lose than they ever
imagined. Drawn into a cataclysmic Psy war that may alter the fate of the
world itself, they must make a decision that might just break them both.

Praise for Nalini Singh's Psy-Changeling Novels

"A MUST-READ FOR ALL OF MY FANS."
—Christine Feehan, #1 *New York Times* bestselling author

"Paranormal romance at its best."—*Publishers Weekly*

"A completely unique and utterly mesmerizing series."
—*Simply Romance Reviews*

www.nalinisingh.com
www.penguin.com

ISBN 978-0-425-25109-6

$7.99 U.S.
$8.99 CAN